PRAISE ALAN HRUSK

Pardon the Ravens (Alec Brno #1)

"An erudite legal thriller." — *Library Journal*

"With the backdrop of *Mad Men*–era New York, *Pardon the
Ravens* never fears to get dirty with style. Alan Hruska brings it
all—sounds, smells, tastes, and attitude—to life with passion."
— CARA BLACK,
author of the *New York Times*–bestselling Aimée Leduc series

"Vividly real and quite compelling... Hruska really knows how
to write. Fans of legal-thriller stars like John Grisham, John
Lescroart, William Lashner, and especially Scott Turow will
want to add this fine novel to their must-read lists."
— *Booklist*

"The plot rockets along."
— *Kirkus Reviews*

"Grabs readers and leaves them hanging on for dear life...
excellent dialogue and nonstop action."
— *Suspense Magazine*

It Happened at Two in the Morning

"With Alan Hruska you're guaranteed a nonstop pace, witty
dialogue, and characters you care about. *It Happened at Two in
the Morning* was my must-read thriller this year and—wow!—
he delivered."
— PETER LOVESEY,
award-winning author of the Peter Diamond series

"The mishaps and amusing bickering of this mismatched duo bring to mind such 1930s romantic film comedies as *It Happened One Night*. But the mood darkens as the plot thickens… Mr. Hruska—himself a former lawyer—is at his thriller-writing best once Tom sinks his teeth into the investigation of, and subsequent legal negotiations with, these various blackguards."
— *The Wall Street Journal*

Wrong Man Running

"Beautifully written and beautifully imagined, this dark, spiraling, Kafkaesque nightmare might be the best psychological suspense you'll read this year—or this decade."
— LEE CHILD,
author of the *New York Times*–bestselling Jack Reacher novels

"As good as the best offerings of Turow, Grisham, and other legal-thriller hitmakers."
— *Booklist*

"It's like some excellent Hitchcock—*39 Steps, North by Northwest*."
— *Kirkus Reviews*

THE INGLORIOUS ARTS

BY ALAN HRUSKA

PROSPECT
·PARK·
BOOKS

Published by Prospect Park Books
2359 Lincoln Ave.
Altadena, CA 91001
www.prospectparkbooks.com

Distributed by Consortium Book Sales & Distribution
www.cbsd.com

Library of Congress Cataloging in Publication Data
Names: Hruska, Alan, author.
Title: The inglorious arts : an Alec Brno novel / Alan Hruska.
Description: Altadena, California : Prospect Park Books, [2019]
Identifiers: LCCN 2018043425 (print) | LCCN 2018046611 (ebook) |
ISBN 9781945551413 (ebook) | ISBN 9781945551406 (pbk.)
Subjects: | GSAFD: Legal stories. | Suspense fiction.
Classification: LCC PS3558.R87 (ebook) | LCC PS3558.R87 I54 2019
(print) | DDC 813/.54--dc23
LC record available at https://lccn.loc.gov/2018043425

Cover design by Howard Grossman
Book design and layout by Amy Inouye, Future Studio

So restless Cromwell could not cease
In the inglorious arts of peace,
But thorough advent'rous war
Urged his active star.

Andrew Marvell
An Horatian Ode upon Cromwell's Return from Ireland

ONE

January 1973. Yale Law School auditorium. Alec Brno looks out from the stage into a sea of expectant faces. "Five more minutes," the dean whispers as they watch another inflow of students find seats. Not so long ago, Alec would have been one of them. Now he's the "attraction." Happens. Win a few cases; make partner; kill a man. The last item is not listed on the program, although, Alec suspects, it's why most everyone is here.

Breck Schlumberger, a bear-size man who is dean of the school, finally lumbers to his feet, quiets the crowd, recites Alec's credentials for the advertised topic, "Winning High-Profile Litigation." Alec rises with a different agenda in mind. "Trials in civil cases are like wars," he says, without preamble, hearing his voice bound through the hall. "There's no excuse for them. They don't get fought unless someone's being stupid. Or unreasonable, which is the same thing."

And not, he realizes, what anyone came to hear. But no longer is he, in any way, like any one of them. Too many scars. He has yet to lose a case, but in the dozen years since graduation, he's lost the music, most films, all theater—his wife. The coroner reported, as the cause of death: heart failure from an overdose of heroin. Alec's aware of a more telling explanation. He wasn't there. Not there to stop her at the last needle, or the first. For months, he was in another city, at another long trial.

He stands momentarily without speaking. Something he does. What the students see is a rawboned man in an off-the-rack suit who is too tall for the lectern and looks older than he is. His smile, which he gives now, seems a bit sad. Some there have the impulse to feed him or, at least, take him to a barber. No denying the energy, though, no matter how downcast his tone. It's as if he were saying, *Stand with me—walk with me—down the long corridor of my discontent.*

"You probably thought," he says, "when you read the poster for this event, here's another self-promoter who wants to come back and tell us how important he is. How he's conquered the courts and crushed his opponents. And how *we,* if only we'd listen, might be as fabulous as he. Sorry. Not me. Nothing fabulous. What I know, and can talk about, is, if you're trying a case at all, someone screwed up, probably you."

Alec strays off, downstage, taking the hand mic with him. "Who is this hypocrite?" he says, pointing back to the lectern. "He lucks out winning some cases, and he wants to talk about getting to yes?" Alec scoffs at the notion. "Settlements are for wimps! We all know that. We were born to be heroes. To smash our opponents in the mouth. To grind them into the mud. Settle cases? No payoffs there. No glory. Not for the lawyer." He looks upward. "But whatta you know!" he says, as if finding words on the ceiling. "For everyone else—including the client, whom you're supposed to be representing—it's likely to be the best damn way out of the mess he's in. If you can figure out how to do it. And trust me, for this is the little I've learned. There are damn few cases where you can't."

Afterward, when Alec finishes what he came there to say, and answers the questions, and the last of the students stop milling about, Dean Schlumberger, who was once Alec's classmate, ushers him to his car. "Was there any of that spiel you meant?"

"All of it," Alec says.

Schlumberger adds a skeptical squint to his bearded demeanor. "I know what it means to settle one of those monster cases you do. Win-win? Bullshit. Blood on the floor is what I see. Because you're dealing with bloodthirsty people."

"You know them?"

"They're my donors," the dean says. "Atoning for their sins."

Alec laughs and opens the back door of the limo.

"It's strange, don't you think?" says the dean, detaining Alec a bit longer. "The way we turned out. You, the idealist, now cavorting with demons; me, the cynic, now preaching ideals. To children! Before they march off to your hell."

"Someone's got to do it," Alec says.

"Preaching, you mean."

"The hell part. Preaching's just fun."

"Okay," Schlumberger says, "so how 'bout you joining me?"

"The law school faculty?" Alec treats this as a joke.

"You'd be good at it. Not great, necessarily, but good."

"You might have had me with great," Alec says with a smile.

"How 'bout you seriously thinking about it?" Schlumberger says.

"Sure." Alec taps the man's shoulder—as if to say, *Thanks for an offer you know I've no intention of accepting.*

"Like when will you consider it?" the dean asks.

"When I have time."

"So that's a never."

"Probably right," Alec says.

They're standing on Wall Street—in New Haven, of course, not New York—and the wind slaps in, because the winter here is wetter and worse. "I was so sorry to hear about Carrie," Breck Schlumberger says.

Alec drops into the backseat of the limo. "Thank you." It's all he ever says to condolences, though he's gotten a lot of practice saying that.

"About the other thing," Breck says through the open car window. "I don't believe in never. One of these days you'll say yes."

"No doubt. When I'm as wise as you."

The car pulls out, taking Alec through the streets of New Haven and to the highway back to Manhattan. His firm insists on laying on the limousines. At the rate billed for one hour of Alec's time, it's a profit-making investment. Which implies that Alec is expected to work when traveling, and record time for it. Normally he would. Of necessity. Tonight, he has too many other things on his mind.

Like his fifteen-year-old daughter, Sarah Brno. He changed her last name to his when he adopted her. Which he did when he married her mother. Which happened after he plunged a samurai sword through the gut of her father, Phil Anwar, in a marsh in Maine, when Phil came there with four made men to kidnap his wife and kill Alec. Seems now like a Japanese opera. But it was real enough then.

Sarah deals well with the problems of adolescence. Less well with her nightmares. When angry, she knows how to hurt. She hurts herself by lashing out with self-denigrating remarks, especially in earshot of anyone, like Alec, who loves her. As in, "What do you expect? With my bloodlines? Daughter of a junkie and a sadistic killer!" As often, she simply engages in self-wounding behavior. Obvious stuff, like getting great grades for a while, then bailing and crashing. Or finding gang boys to party with. She's smoked some pot, and they've fought fiercely over that. But he loves her deeply and thinks she loves him. She doesn't blame him for her mother's death. She blames herself, even though she was eleven years old when it happened.

"You have a daughter, Schlomo?" Alec asks his driver.

"What?" says Schlomo. "So now you're talking?"

"I don't talk?"

"Not so anyone would notice."

"I'm usually working, it's true," Alec acknowledges.

"But now you want to talk about your daughter, so you ask about mine." The driver twists to fix on Alec a long, condemnatory Old Testament frown before returning his eyes to the road. "Well, I have three daughters, as it happens."

"A blessing, right?"

"Sometimes," Schlomo says mordantly.

"Ages?"

"All are marriageable, except the youngest."

"Ah," Alec says.

"Ah? What's this 'ah'? You think you know something about my situation?"

"It's the way you said it."

"Like what? Like I'm some Tevya? Like this is *Fiddler on the Roof*?"

Alec laughs, seeing his old friend's large face in the mirror. "Sorry I mentioned it."

"Why should you be sorry? We're just talking. Two fathers. It's a long drive."

"Getting longer," Alec says.

"You wanna hurt my feelings?"

"Last thing I want."

"Look," Schlomo says. "I know your daughter. Sarah, right? I pick her up from school sometimes. She's great. Smart, beautiful. What more could you want?"

"You're right." Alec stretches out in the backseat.

"So, what? You're going to sleep now? This is the end of our conversation?"

The roads are icy. Makes no difference to Schlomo. "This is nothing," he always says about road conditions of any sort. "I come from Siberia."

On the still-amazing superhighway I-95, the trip is a mere eighty-five minutes. Alec remembers being limited to the Merritt and Wilbur Cross parkways, which added a good forty-five minutes to the drive. They pull off the FDR onto Ninety-Seventh Street by 10:30. Alec's building is on the corner of Fifth Avenue. He occupies the former apartment of Grantland Rice, the great sportswriter, who died several years earlier. When Alec first saw it, Rice's papers still littered his writing room, which enjoyed a striking view of Central Park, the reservoir, and the surrounding swirl of paths and roads. Alec bought the apartment for that view. The track circling the reservoir is where Carrie had said to him, "Don't be slow, Alec"—which was her way of announcing what she already knew about them, and he didn't, that they were already in love. She never saw the apartment. She died before Rice did.

Upstairs, Sarah's bedroom door, tightly closed, features its customary sign: "Mafia Princess—Beware." But he hears the music and knocks.

"Who is it?" Her voice, not inviting.

"Who do you think?"

"You… okay," she says.

He enters. She's splayed on the bed doing homework and doesn't look up.

"*You* okay?" he asks.

"Why wouldn't I be?" Eyes still on the books.

"Overload of homework, for one thing."

"Nothing new there." Finally she smiles, which he takes as permission to sit on the bed.

"How long tonight? Best guess?"

"The usual." She sits up in her PJs, a twig of a girl with a Roman nose and unruly brown curls. Her fingers are ink-stained. "Two, maybe 2:30."

"It's too much."

"Yeah, well, you're on the board, Alec. Do something about it."

"I'm trying."

"Try harder."

He laughs. "Look… about your Aunt Jesse."

"What about her?"

"She's picking you up tomorrow."

"Which is entirely unnecessary and about the fiftieth time you've told me."

"You'll recognize her?"

"Jesus, Alec! Whatta you think? I'm going to go marching off with some strange woman? To be sold off as a sex slave in the Middle East? I'll recognize her. We met at the funeral."

"That was four years ago."

Sarah stares him in the eyes. "She looks like Mom."

"You remember that?"

"Yes," she says. "That I remember."

"Good."

"Night, Alec."

"Meaning get the hell out of your room?"

"I wouldn't have said 'hell.' It's not ladylike."

Alec laughs, kisses her forehead, and does as he's been directed to do.

TWO

No matter how early Alec arrives at the firm, the presiding partner, Ben Braddock, and the head of litigation, Frank Macalister, get in before he does. This morning they're waiting in Alec's office. Which is a twist, since he once worked for both of them. And not a good signal. They mean to pile on more work, though Alec is already overextended.

Braddock is sitting in Alec's own chair in his black suit and vest, red and navy rep tie. It would be shocking to see him in any other apparel, even at the annual firm outing at Piping Rock. Macalister is in shirtsleeves; suit jackets never last long on Frank.

Alec's office is one of the large ones, with sweeping views of Manhattan, the East River, and much of Brooklyn. Braddock's own office is larger, occupying a corner of the same suite. It has its own conference room as well, though he and Alec generally share it.

As Alec hangs up his coat, Braddock rises in his black raiment like the "ol' preacher man," his sparse gray hairs straying over a worried brow, his garments sagging on his diminishing frame. He takes a seat on the radiator shelf, which is never that warm, and peers out at the view, the January sun dying in the gristle of his complexion. "You know the company Allis-Benoit Electric?" Braddock says. "They make the full range of electrical appliances— from lightbulbs to refrigerators—and heavy electrical equipment, from circuit breakers to turbine generators."

"I know what they make," Alec says, not enjoying the condescension.

"They're our oldest client. And very dear." He pronounces the "dear" in a high-pitched tone of self-mimicry.

"I've never met any of their people."

"Makes you perfect," Mac snaps, rocking his chair back precariously.

"For what? Not that case Harry Hanrahan's been dicking around with."

"Harry's retiring," Mac says.

Alec, still standing, looks from one man to the other, finding no refuge in either face. "It's a sleeping giant, that case."

"The giant has awakened," Mac says, thrusting forward with a thud of his chair.

"It's not getting me," Alec says.

"Little history lesson," Braddock says, turning his attention at last from the window. "Human beings selling heavy electrical equipment—turbine generators and the like—will, it seems, conspire with their competitors to fix prices."

"Always?" says Alec skeptically.

"Always," Braddock repeats. "Invariably and inevitably. The problem is, not only do the damn things cost millions to make, the plants to make 'em in cost billions to build and maintain. The risks scare the shit outta these people. So to reduce the risks, they rig the market. And then get caught. Mac here," Ben says, inclining his head toward Macalister, "represented Allis-Benoit years ago, when half the top management went to prison. Apart from those criminal cases, our client and their co-conspirators got sued by the buyers of these machines—which means every public utility in the country. The utilities won every case and walked away with more than a billion dollars in damages."

"I remember," Alec says.

"How the hell'd you remember?" Mac says. "You were ten years old."

"I was in law school," says Alec. "Kind of thing people took notice of, CEOs, VPs being manacled in their offices and hauled off in chains."

"We'll have none of that here," Mac says. "In your case. No one talked to anyone, let alone conspired in hotel rooms. They did it—"

"In the newspapers!" Braddock laughs, and heaves himself to his feet. As he makes to leave, Alec restrains him.

"Judge, stay," Alec says. Braddock is so addressed, since he sat for years on the United States Court of Appeals in New York.

"Mac will explain it," says Braddock.

"I'm not taking on another case," Alec says. "I'm too god-damn busy."

"Aren't we all," Braddock says airily.

"Then maybe we should turn this one down," Alec says.

Braddock lets out another laugh, shakes his head as if at an absurdity, and shuffles out of the room.

Mac says, "We'll redistribute some of your smaller stuff."

"I'm already not attending to my smaller stuff. You know what my hours were last year?"

"There's no one else, Alec. Not for this." Mac waves off Alec's questioning glance. "Here's the situation. Allis-Benoit's already in deep shit. Getting sued for reneging on a multibillion-dollar coal-supply contract. Different case. We're not representing them on that."

"Why not?" Alec says. "I thought they'd been our client for a hundred years."

"Yeah, well. We advised them not to renege."

"We?"

"Me," Mac says, with a note of belligerence.

Alec now remembers the story. "Which is why you're not do-ing the new one."

"Right."

Alec finally sits in his desk chair, thinking about his early years working for Macalister. At the time Mac was the rising star, han-dling most of the important cases in the office. A larger-than-life Texan, he had the personality John Wayne enacted in movies and was about the same size and build. His intellect was a lot sharper than one might have expected from such an appearance, and he was famous for his audacity and "gut" judgment. He always knew what was bothering a judge and, more importantly, how to fix it. And he read every juror like a shrink. What dimmed his star, and nerve, was an unquenchable thirst for Jack Daniels. When Mac drove his car into the big oak off his country club driveway, Alec, then still an associate, took over the trial that propelled him to partnership. Recovery has salvaged Mac's wits, but leaving those huge hard cases for others has left him feeling, despite the bravado, taken down and depressed. Now Alec, the major beneficiary of Mac's frustration, sits wondering what else he might give up in his life to spend a little time with his daughter.

Macalister goes to the window. For this large man, with his prodigious head, coat-hanger shoulders, and still bright-eyed smile, talking while standing is much more his thing. "After the prison sentences, and the treble-damages cases brought by the public utilities, which, as Ben said, were bloodbaths, almost all the manufacturers went belly-up. That left only two American companies still making turbine generators: our client and the dominant company, Edison Electric. It must have occurred to them, or at least to Edison: with only two competitors, no need to meet, no need to talk—about anything. So one fine day, Edison issued an announcement. In the press, letters to customers— however they could disseminate the word. We're publishing a new price book, said Edison. And henceforth, the prices set forth in that book will be the prices at which we will actually sell. You want a turbine generator from us, you will buy it at the published price. No discounts, no free goods, no under-the-table anything, no special deals. And our sales books are open to anyone. Send in your accountants, we'll be happy to open those books. You spot any deviation from our published prices—any discount whatever to any customer—then you and every other customer in the world will also get the benefit of that discount."

"All of which," Alec says, "is perfectly lawful."

"To be sure. And everyone waited to see how Allis-Benoit would respond. The wait wasn't long, and the result not surprising. Five days later, Allis-Benoit announced exactly the same price policy on exactly the same prices."

"Tricky."

"Signaling," Mac says. "At least that's the theory. No need to meet in hotel rooms. Do it publicly. As good as an explicit agreement."

"The same effect, maybe, but different legally."

"Which is our defense," Mac says.

"Uphill to make a jury believe it."

"Which was apparently the thought of Mid-Atlantic Power & Light—largest public utility in the world and the largest buyer of turbine generators. The case we're talking about is the one they brought. They're suing Edison and Allis-Benoit for price fixing and conspiracy to monopolize. And they're asking for treble damages in the hundreds of millions. Their lawyer is the inimitable Frederick Musselman, the Harvard law professor who made a fortune representing public utilities in the last go-around. You know him?"

"A friend of mine took his course. Thought his name was *I. Frederick Musselman*. Because that's how he started every sentence in class."

Mac laughs and says, "Freddy's a problem. Mid-Atlantic's a problem. But there are much bigger ones hanging over us. Just like in the last war. Besides Mid-Atlantic, there are 125 public utilities in the United States. Like Mid-Atlantic, they've all bought turbine generators from both Edison and Allis-Benoit. If the manufacturers conspired to fix prices, not only does Mid-Atlantic have a claim, they've all got claims—125 potential additional cases under the Clayton Act, which, as you well know, rewards successful claimants with three times their actual damages. Total actual damages would be astronomical. Trebled, they'd bankrupt our client."

"Why haven't those 125 other utilities already sued? The stat-ute of limitations is only four years."

"Hanrahan negotiated a tolling and standstill agreement. The utilities organized themselves into a committee and retained your old friend, Marius Shilling. He agreed to stand still—i.e., not to sue until the Mid-Atlantic case was terminated—in exchange for our agreement to toll the running of the statute of limitations until thirty days after the end of that case."

"Brilliant."

"Except there's a catch. And that's the second Damocles sword. The government—the Antitrust Division of the U.S. De-partment of Justice—is considering suing as well. They've just sent us a demand for documents. If they do sue, the 125 utilities are then freed up to sue as well; it's the one loophole in that bril-liant deal."

"Why's the giant awakening now?"

"New judge assigned. Mark Porter. Also formerly Harvard faculty. Smartest judge in the system."

"And for this case," says Alec, "the worst."

"You know him?"

"Oh, yes. And Mac," Alec says. "Many thanks. You've just fucked up my life. I'd guess for at least five or six years."

Jesse Madigan is out of place, and feels it, waiting with the moth-ers in the cold on East Ninety-First Street, right off Fifth Avenue. Apart from being merely an aunt, she sees herself as a tourist in this city, her home city, having lived in Ireland for the past ten years.

She'd dropped her bag off in Alec's apartment. Before leaving for work, Alec had instructed the doormen to "just let her up." The rooms, of course, were full of him. As she entered and closed the door behind her, she felt something intangible, the air stiff with warning. She should not have come back. She had stayed a long time in Ireland for good reason, and she should have stayed longer.

Her first meeting with Alec was so casual. Like Carrie herself, for whom everything spelled fun. Jesse had returned briefly to New York soon after her graduation from college. "This is my sister," Carrie had said. "She's the smart one, I've told you."

"And beautiful," Alec had said. Offhand, but he made her feel beautiful, which was not what she normally felt. They were lunching at the Manhattan Ocean Club, a midtown restaurant of white walls and oak tables that Alec liked. It was two months after the gun fight in Maine and days before her sister's wedding. Alec and Carrie were trying to move on. Five-year-old Sarah was in therapy. Jesse was not supposed to talk about the incident, although of course she knew; everyone knew. She can't remember what she said, only what she thought: that she would never get the image of him out of her head. She hardly spoke to him at the wedding. It was not for her—or, indeed, any of the few guests in attendance—a truly joyous affair.

A face-biting wind comes in off the park, and she huddles in her parka. *Should have worn a hat*, she thinks. *And a scarf.* It was warmer in Dublin, though much farther north.

Sarah's out early and recognizes Jesse at once. "I don't really need picking up, you know. For all practical purposes, I'm already sixteen."

"I know," Jesse says, "but I thought you might show me a bit of the neighborhood, maybe have tea or coffee somewhere."

"The Soup Burg's good. It's on Madison, right down the block."

They walk and talk, Sarah dutifully inquiring about Jesse's flight, Jesse thinking, *She's learned this, asking polite questions.*

They find a table at the window and both order tea.

"So where you staying?" Sarah asks.

"Ah," Jesse says. "The big question. Somewhere cheap. I still have friends on Staten Island. I think one will take me in. I was hoping to catch on as an au pair in Manhattan."

"You've got a degree from Trinity College, Dublin. In fine arts, for Christ's sake. You'll get a job in five minutes. Have you registered?"

"With an agency, yes. You seem to know about this."

"I was raised by au pairs. A constant stream of them. It was a troubled childhood."

"Yours? I hadn't heard."

"You would've been the last to," Sarah says.

"But you've turned out magnificently!"

"The package looks okay. Inside is a mess."

"If that were true, you wouldn't be saying it."

Sarah's too cool to laugh unaffectedly, but that remark does amuse her. "Talk to the shrinks," she says. "I've had a procession of those too."

"On that you've got company," Jesse says.

"Really. I thought we'd have something in common, other than blood. So you'll do just fine. I'll talk to Alec."

"About what?"

"About hiring you, of course."

"Tenth grade, and you need an au pair?" Jesse gives her a re-monstrative look.

"You can do my homework for me," Sarah says.

"I've no intention of doing your homework!"

"Sure you will. We'll call it something else… like helping me do my homework. You can be my live-in tutor. A lot of my friends have one."

"You're an advanced fifteen."

"Essentially sixteen. *I've said.* And street smart. You'd have to be, in my shoes. That school I go to? Looks elegant as hell, right? It's a snake pit. Kill or be killed. Eat or be eaten. Except for the uniforms, and the family fortunes, it's not that much different from P.S. whatever. And I hang mainly with the public-school kids, anyway."

"So did I," Jesse says. "Back in the day."

"Where'd you go to school then?"

"Catholic school. With your mom."

Sarah pauses with a measuring look. "You of course knew my birth father."

"I never met him, no."

"Really?" Sarah says. "He paid for your school, I thought, in Ireland."

"He set up a fund for me, yes. But he had no real interest in me. He did that for your mom, when they got married. I'd already gone over there. I was living with my aunt."

"Well, that's perfect. You're my aunt, and now you can live with me."

"I don't think that's a great idea," Jesse says.

"You don't like me?"

"I like you fine, Sarah. And I'm sure I will love you. But you may be misjudging me. And Alec's taste for this idea."

"Alec's never been a problem for me," Sarah says with a smile. "And you?" Her smile broadens considerably. "You're a pushover. I love you already."

"Harry, got a minute?" Alec says, intruding on his partner's notorious preference for privacy. Harry Hanrahan is known to be one who closes his door to keep out not only the random sounds of an office, but any person he hasn't summoned there, including other partners.

"Alec!" Hanrahan says, rising in full-suited regalia from behind his Regency desk. "Come in, come in, glad to see you!"

He probably means it, Alec thinks. *Ten minutes with me, and he's officially dumped the worst case in the office.*

Alec steps in, taking the chair where he once did time as Harry's senior associate.

Hanrahan smiles, a smile that always seems to be wan, if not totally bleak. His favorite color is gray, medium shade: suit, tie, shirt, socks, and Alec's betting on even the underwear, though the man's skin tends toward a greenish-gray, which makes the pink of his mouth almost shocking. "Ben tells me," says Hanrahan, reseating his long, pear-shaped frame, "you've volunteered for the Allis-Benoit litigation."

"'Volunteered,' he said?" Alec's laugh is that of a man reacting ruefully to his own hanging.

"Yes, well," Hanrahan says, "I didn't think you'd be that happy taking it on. I'm not happy saddling you with it. I've tried to end it, but the case can't be settled. Donald Strand, the Mid-Atlantic CEO, is a belligerent bully. And I seriously doubt it can be won."

"There was actually an agreement?"

"To fix prices? Nice question. They never met; they never talked. But…."

"Right," Alec says. " 'Agreement' is a meeting of the minds. Offer and acceptance. Doesn't need speech; can be arrived at by signals. Edison's announcement of a new price policy was the offer. Allis-Benoit's announcement of the same policy a week later, the acceptance."

"That's Musselman's theory," Hanrahan says. "And likely to work. Novel situations give judges leeway. What this looks like to them? Just another in a line of cases in which two giant corporations figured out a new way to screw the poor consumer. Here, the rate-payer."

The door opens, then vacillates between open and shut. A stooped young man in well-pressed tweeds and horn-rimmed glasses musters himself in and says, "Sorry."

"Come here, Grosvenor." Hanrahan's impatience is regal. "I believe it was you who told me the AT&T contract had been signed on September 15."

"Ye-es," Grosvenor says, voice wavering on the second sylla-
ble, the associate sensing his likely mistake.

"I now learn it was the seventeenth. You know from whom I
learned this? Our client. I had to be corrected on the point by our
client!"

"The seventeenth," the young man repeats, as if receiving a
great truth.

"I must say, Grosvenor, you are a veritable fountain of misin-
formation."

Grosvenor's eyes blink twice, then descend on his future.
Alec's own experiences in this office unreel in his brain, like a film
flickering on a sheet on a summer camp wall.

Hanrahan dispatches the associate with: "That's all. You may
leave."

Grosvenor about-faces, without speaking, and shambles off.

Alec says, when he's left, "I'm not sure he'll recover from
that."

"We'll see," Hanrahan says. "And then we'll know. About
him."

Alec breathes in on that comment and lets it lie. "You referred
to a *bunch* of cases?" he says.

"Inevitably there will be," Hanrahan says. "The government
will sue. The other utilities will then have to sue." He leans back
expansively. "We are, my young friend, standing at the floodgates. And they are about to burst. Within the year, we'll have
more than a hundred new lawsuits."

"That all?" says Alec, with distaste.

"And all in your lap, sorry. Judge Porter's the ticking bomb.
He's just been assigned and can't wait to explode. He's never seen
a large company he doesn't hate. The fact that this one gives
work to sixty thousand people means nothing to Mark Porter.
He'll rule against us on everything, slant the jury instructions
Mid-Atlantic's way, and the verdict will be binding on us in all

subsequent cases."

"Sounds great."

"They didn't tell you, Ben and Mac?"

"Not quite all of it," Alec says.

Harry's head wags in commiseration.

"Look," Alec says. "On this case—I just got here. But some things do occur to me. In the first place, what Allis-Benoit did, it had to do, acting absolutely independently. Edison Electric is the dominant company. They put out a price book; Allis has no choice but to match those prices. If Allis had tried to lower prices, Edison would have matched those, and Allis would have ended up with only the same slice of a smaller pie."

"That's probably true," Harry says.

"And Allis-Benoit got some business, right?"

"You mean, did they sell some turbine generators? Of course. And circuit breakers and the rest of it."

"So at least on big sales, they cut the price," Alec says. "Probably in a disguised way to prevent Edison from finding out about it—free goods or services, or something like that, maybe better credit terms—but definite price cuts. Has to be true. Because why else would anyone buy from Allis-Benoit? These are huge machines. Very expensive. The customer needs to believe the manufacturer will be around forever to service them. Edison gives rise to that belief. With Allis-Benoit—well, now there's got to be some question."

"It seems you've done your research," Harry says.

"Research? Harry, I just said. I know nothing about this market and haven't had time to think about this case until I walked in here. But—regarding the identical price books—if Allis did what it would have done without any agreement, and—regarding actual sales—if Allis cut prices, then there wasn't a meeting of the minds. Which means no conspiracy."

"Hmm," Hanrahan says, steepling his fingers and puckering his thin, pinkish-gray lips. "I've pursued both lines of inquiry, although"—and he gives another wan smile—"it took me a good deal longer than two seconds to arrive at either idea. But our salespeople aren't being helpful. They vehemently deny giving any price cuts, disguised or otherwise."

"I doubt that's true."

"Maybe, but if they're covering it up—and they might be, since they're under strict instructions from top management not to give discounts—it would be awfully hard for us to dig any such hanky-panky out of the files. These transactions are incredibly complicated. It's never as simple as the sale of one machine. There are many optional parts, many auxiliary devices, and many different types of service arrangements and warranties. You'd need teams of lawyers, businessmen, and accountants working day and night on these files."

Alec sits back. "This case is a nightmare."

"It needs a young man," Harry says.

To turn into an old one, Alec thinks. But he says, "You and Mac did the cases years ago, when they fixed prices in hotel rooms."

"That we did. Nearly put me in the grave. Nothing so depressing and demanding as the unwinnable case. So Alec—if you take this on, clear your decks. Of everything. Professional and personal. You're not going to have room for anything else in your life."

THREE

There are boys his age who live for basketball. Tino Angiapello isn't one of them—he can take it or leave it—but he almost never misses a shot. At six feet, two inches, he's a bit short for college play at his position, which is "small" forward. However, he's not that interested in college sports either. At Trinity School in Manhattan, where he averages more than twenty points in a thirty-two-minute game, his star quality suffices for what he *is* interested in: the girls of his set.

Tino has been admitted to Cornell on a basketball scholarship—another thing he'd rather pass up. His preference would be to start working immediately for his Uncle Sal. Even at eighteen, Tino knows a good thing. *Our thing,* as he and his family still think of it. Cosa Nostra, as it's called now, even by civilians.

Tino was born into the family, but not as an Angiapello. Both his parents were killed in an auto riddled by bullets when Tino was five. He was adopted by Sal's brother and sister-in-law but lost his adoptive father in a gang war. Since then, his male influence has been Sal. And for Sal, who has never had children of his own, Tino is favored, despite the lack of a blood tie, though there are still many tests to be passed.

Uncle Sal's in the stands today. Tino, who loves showing off, always plays better when the don is there. And today, Tino is "unconscious," as they're now saying in the schoolyards; in a definite "zone." Trinity is up, 23 to 8, and Tino has sixteen of his team's total. Near halftime, the game is a complete rout, and the coach sits him down. Though he starts the second half, he gets yanked almost immediately, as penance for five quick points, and rides the bench unhappily until the final whistle.

Postgame, their ritual when Sal attends Tino's games is early dinner at a family-owned *ristorante* on the Upper West Side. After ordering, Tino apologizes for his uncle's having to watch other players.

"No problem," Sal says. "Your coach didn't want to embarrass an overmatched team. I understand." Sal's speech is formal in cadence and tone, which Tino has unconsciously adopted.

"He should have realized you were there," Tino says.

Sal laughs. "This is not my world, Tino. The parent body of your school consists of bankers and lawyers."

"But it will be your world! Right? I know. I hear talk."

"What do you hear?"

Tino gets excited. "I want to work for you, Uncle. Now. Whatever the business, the old-line stuff, the new, the banking, real estate."

"You go to college, first; law school, maybe business school, then we'll see."

"I don't need all these schools, Uncle."

Sal frowns, which in the family is a serious matter. "Are you willing to listen to me? To take my advice?"

"Of course," Tino says.

"You will go where I tell you to go."

"Yes, Uncle."

"I know what's best."

"I understand."

"Good boy." He pats his nephew's cheek. "From time to time, maybe I'll have jobs for you."

"Anything," Tino says eagerly.

"Good. Because I have one now, actually. A job no one else in our *famiglia* is capable of doing. Only you."

"Only me?"

"Yes. Because it involves someone of your age." Sal reconsiders. "Close to your age."

"Just tell me, Uncle. It's as good as done."

"You have a second cousin. Did you know that?"

"No, Uncle. Who is he?"

"It's a girl. She lives in Manhattan. Goes to a fancy school like yours. You probably haven't run across her, since she is a *bit* younger than you. Her father was my cousin, first cousin. Changed his name from ours to Anwar. Phil Anwar. He ran everything in Manhattan, most of Brooklyn, and parts of New Jersey."

"Like you," Tino says. "Only you have parts of Queens and the Bronx too. The best parts."

"I took over his territories and expanded. When I came down from Bridgeport."

"But you knew him?"

"Oh, yes. We did business. But he got careless and got killed. Man who killed him married his wife and adopted his daughter. And all of Phil's money—a lot of money—went to her, the daughter. This was money earned in family businesses. You see what I'm saying?"

"The money should stay in the family."

"You're a bright boy."

Tino considers his new station. A job for the family that only he can do. A heaven-sent opportunity. Except it's not all that clear how it might ultimately be done. "So," he says cautiously, "the first step is to meet her. See where her mind is with respect to the family."

Sal, giving a nod acknowledging his nephew's perception, hands the young man an envelope. "Photograph, contact information, her schedule, which, apart from school, is erratic, friends, also erratic, places she hangs out. It shouldn't be too difficult for you to meet her."

"You said she was younger…"

"She'll be sixteen next month. She's two years, a few months younger than you."

Tino rubs his mouth, as if regretting his enthusiasm for this task. "That makes it harder."

"She's very pretty," his uncle says. "And precocious."

"You know her?"

"I knew her when she was a child. And I've kept my eye on her."

"She knows the history?" Tino says. "And the name? She will suspect me?"

"Yes. She will. She will suspect anyone with our name. Which is why I've chosen you. You are the only one bearing the name who can gain her trust. And who I trust."

"Thank you, Uncle."

"There's a lot at stake here. You understand? More than $300 million. All clean, because her father died."

The amount surprises Tino. It sounds to him like unlimited riches.

"There are, of course," Sal says offhandedly, "other ways of handling the matter. But let's see how this works. How you do. Yes?"

"Yes, Uncle, certainly," Tino says, feeling progressively *uncertain* about what, exactly, he is being called upon to do.

His uncle looks at him sternly. "I have let you close, Tino. Closer than anyone. And there is no male in my bloodline. I believe you know what that means. For the future. Your future. *Capisce?*"

That Tino understands fully.

Alec gets home close to nine. Early for him, but past Sarah's dinner, which a housekeeper provides. An unfamiliar suitcase languishes in the hallway. The hall light is on, and sounds drift down the corridor from Sarah's room.

Alec goes there and knocks.

"Come!" Sarah has learned this from the old James Mason English movies that she occasionally watches on TV. The variations in her taste never cease to amaze him.

She and Jesse seem surprised to see Alec, as if he'd caught them conspiring. Alec's surprised to see his sister-in-law still there, let alone curled up on the end of the bed.

Jesse springs up to greet him. "Alec!" Maybe an inch shorter than Carrie, and even thinner. Hair auburn and thick, as if to compensate. Her bones are delicate but a bit sharp, like that slight jut at the bridge of her nose, which stretches her fine skin. Her eyes are expressive and green, but she looks worn with travel, which, he realizes, she must be.

"So you made it," Alec says.

"All in one piece."

"Not much baggage."

"Oh, I've lots of baggage," Jesse says. "Not the kind checkable at airports, however."

"Where are you staying?"

"Staten Island. With friends."

"Really?" Alec says. "How're you planning on getting there?"

"Subway, ferry. Usual ways. Those things are still running, right?"

Alec looks at his watch. "You should stay here for the night."

"I have a better idea," Sarah says. "Jesse moves in. My au pair."

Alec smiles, humoring this barely.

"It's a great idea, Alec."

"You're a sophomore in high school," he says lightly. "You need an au pair?"

"Tutor, then. I could certainly use that."

Jesse, reacting to Alec's reserve, says, "I've already turned down Sarah's very kind offer. But I will accept yours. For the night. Equally kind."

"Wait a minute!" says Sarah. "I haven't been heard yet. We have a perfectly good bedroom here, totally empty, never used.

It's ridiculous you're going off to live with some other family. We're your family. And au pairing is not what you want to do. Stay here until you hook on with some film thing in New York. In fact, there's no reason you should leave, then."

"Sarah," says Jesse, "we just talked about this."

"Yes, we talked, but—"

"I'm sorry, but no."

"Why not?" Sarah insists, on the edge of anger. "*That* you really haven't told me."

"Okay," Jesse says, if not angry, at least out of patience. "Why not? Because. This lovely man here, your father, of whom we shall now speak as if he weren't in the room, is unattached, as far as I know, and mourns his wife, who looked just like me. And I am also unattached, thank goodness, since that was not always the case. And if I were to move in, how cozy. And awkward. And unendurable. Are you beginning to get it, Sarah?"

Sarah's lips press together. "Yes. Honesty, finally. Thanks."

"You can stay as long as you like," he says, almost meaning it.

Jesse laughs. "Tonight would be great. I should be settled elsewhere tomorrow."

Alec hands her a folded sheet of paper he had in his pocket. "These are the two best agencies in the city. I'm told you can trust them. And they get paid by the family, not you. I'm also told, with your credentials, you'll have your choice tomorrow of ten good jobs."

"Thanks," Jesse says, scanning the paper.

"You can do better," he says. "I represent a media company."

"Oh? Do they make films?"

"Not yet. Print media. Radio, TV, but probably have more openings abroad than here."

"Let me know when they make films."

"Right," Alec says and turns to his daughter. "Jesse's been traveling all day. For her, it's two in the morning. I'll get her settled in the spare bedroom; you finish your homework."

"And then," Sarah says, "what will you do? Watch silly television and relax?"

Alec laughs.

"It's what he always does," Sarah says to her aunt, throwing herself into a familiar comedy routine. "I can't get the man to do any work. Any day now, it's going to be starvation, eviction, out on the street."

"I can see you're hurting," Jesse says.

"Yeah, well, that's what we do, keep up appearances."

Alec leads Jesse down the hall, stopping at the linen closet for blankets and sheets.

"Look," Jesse says, lifting her suitcase onto the bed. "Forget what I said. I sometimes give in to these emotional bursts. Especially when jet-lagged."

"I think you're right."

"About what I said?"

"About the fact that you're very much like her."

"That," she says, "I can't help."

Alec smiles and starts to leave. "Oh, listen. If there's anything you need, I'll be in that small room next to the living room."

"Your study," she says.

"Yes."

"Working all night?"

"A good part of it."

"Sarah was wrong," Jesse says.

"Oh, yes?" Alec says. "About what?"

"That she's the one who needs looking after."

Saying goodnight to his sister-in-law, closing the door to her room, traversing the hall—Alec feels as if he's walking out of his body. The sensation stays with him as he sits at his desk. It's an unaccustomed feeling of lightness. A friend of his, a shrink, said to him recently, "Four years of mourning is not a world record, but it's not that common. And it's certainly not healthy." *But neither*, he muses, *is starting a relationship with my dead wife's sister.*

He opens a brief he was working on. It scarcely dents the new stream of his thoughts. He has the instinct to cool it. He's heard her objection; he knows his own: looks like a crude trade-off. Put one in the grave; take the next-best thing. He drops the brief altogether. *What I'm good at,* he thinks, *is self-laceration. I'm overthinking the goddamn thing, and so is she.*

A further thought arrives—and overrides. Her sleeping in this apartment is tremendously upsetting, but not in a bad way.

FOUR

Ten years ago, in 1963, Alec had served as secretary to the judiciary committee of the Association of the Bar of the City of New York, more popularly known as the City Bar. Ben Braddock, who himself eschewed any bar association committee, had pushed Alec to take the post. One of the committee members, Hiram Starke, was the senior partner of a very small, but respected, midtown firm. Drinking one night in the executive secretary's office, Starke confided to Alec that he had misgivings over the fact that his most junior partner, Cadigan Breen, had "wild" ambitions to build a firm to the unheard-of size of 500 lawyers. Took Breen only ten years to do it—the turning point being his spiriting away his now-major client, Edison Electric, from a "white shoe" firm even older than Kendall, Blake.

Being driven uptown for his first meeting with Breen, Alec sorts out what he's been told about the man by Harry Hanrahan and Frank Macalister. But his driver, Schlomo, it turns out, is a more informed source.

"That address I'm taking you to," Schlomo says as he pulls into the fast lane on the FDR Drive. "That's the fanciest office building in the city."

"So I gather."

"The most expensive too. And you know, the firm that just took over the top floors—the head of that firm, I drive him all the time. As much as I drive you. Maybe more."

"I'm about to meet with him."

"Yeah. I thought so. That's why I'm telling you."

"We're talking about Caddy Breen?"

"Well, I call him Mister Breen," Schlomo says. "You understand. It's the nature of our relative positions in life."

"You don't call me mister."

"You're younger. Although, to think of it, your soul may be older."

"What the hell does that mean, Schlomo?"

"It's an expression."

"Meaning what?"

Alec can see the big shoulders shrug. "You understand Yiddish?" Schlomo asks.

"You know I don't."

"Okay. So I'll try. This man, Mr. Breen, it's like there's joy in him, bubbling up like a spring. All the time. I've seen him angry, but it doesn't last long. Right away, back with the smiles."

"And I'm not like that?"

"No, but you'll like him. Everyone does."

"Everyone?"

"I hear talk. About you too. They like you also. But no one would ever accuse you of having a spring of joy inside."

Upstairs, at reception, Alec is simply directed to the corner office down the hall. No fuss, no imperious "take a seat, please, and he'll be with you shortly," no secretary or assistant offering an escort to the inner chambers of the great man.

Caddy Breen, rising to shake hands, is shorter than Alec, as most people are, and maybe fifteen years older, but there is something about him that's unmistakably boyish. His gray hair springs in ringlets all over his head. His complexion is smooth and on the red side of pink. And he's bouncy: *literally*, Alec thinks, *as if popping out of a box.*

"Sit down, sit down!" This said by Breen exuberantly. "I've heard so much about you from the many good friends we have in common. And I'm agog to hear of your first impressions." Big laugh. "Not of me, of course. Of the case."

"*You* come highly credentialed," Alec says. "We share a driver."

"Schlomo? He drives you too?"

"Pretty often. And just now, as it happens."

"I'll have to pump him," Breen says.

"He thinks I'm an old soul. He just told me."

"Are you?"

"Probably," Alec says. "Whatever that means. According to Schlomo, you have to speak Yiddish to know."

"I'll find out for you. I'm fluent."

"In *Yiddish*?"

"What do you think I'm doing here, Alec? I'm building a firm. You want moneyed clients, you speak their language. You should hear my Arabic. And my Japanese."

Alec smiles. "I've got a lot to learn."

"Me too. From you. So," Breen says. "About the case."

"We have to get rid of Mark Porter," Alec says.

"Oh yes? Do you plan to shoot him? He's a federal judge. He's appointed for life."

"Not to our case."

"You think he's disqualified?" Breen says. "On what grounds?"

"Bias."

Breen gives Alec a look of amused tolerance. "Obviously, he's biased. You think any judge isn't? But my dear fellow. Disqualification motions are sent to another judge of the same court. None will grant this motion. And if you try to mandamus to the Court of Appeals, they will ream you out. And they will never let you forget it. Or the rest of the bar."

"I agree," Alec says.

"Then why make the motion?"

"I have no intention of making the motion."

"Then what are we talking about?"

"Talking to him," Alec says. "To Porter. Telling him what we think. In private. In chambers. With the other side there."

"Okay," Breen says slowly, giving this thought. "I assume you appreciate how such a meeting might blow up in our faces. So what do you know you're not telling me?"

"For one thing, the guy himself. Mark Porter. He was a visiting professor at Yale when I was there, and we worked on an article together for the *Yale Law Journal*. Great guy, very smart, obviously, and very proud. Including pride in his objectivity."

"The latter surprises me," Breen says. "We run a book on judges. In every case Porter sits on, he makes his mind up the first thirty seconds. And he never changes it. It's like a trap door snapping shut. You'd think he knew himself well enough to know what he was doing."

"He thinks that's his brilliance," Alec says. "Not his emotions."

"What else?"

"First case I worked on was a price-fixing case in the pharmaceutical industry."

"Pharmex, I know it," Breen says. "You represented Biogen and won."

"But afterward, Estes Kefauver conducted a Senate subcommittee investigation of the same facts. Got headlines every day. Screaming 'Identical Prices, Huge Gross Profits.' Put enough pressure on the feds to convene a criminal grand jury. We had already won, but ours was a civil case, so there was no double jeopardy. The feds were free to move and felt compelled to do so. The defendants were convicted; the judge was Mark Porter; and the verdict was overturned by the Court of Appeals."

"I remember this too. The Court of Appeals slapped him down."

"Big time. Public scolding. For railroading the defendants, effectively depriving them of a jury trial."

"It was a different case, Alec."

"Not that different. Big companies charging identical prices. Absolutely no evidence that anyone met or talked or communicated in any way about prices, much less conspired to fix them. Also volumes of evidence showing that net profits were a small fraction of the gross, and prices were the same for the simple reason it was entirely self-defeating for any company to cut them. Not a reason for which anyone sheds tears, but not a conspiracy either. None of that meant anything to our friend, Mark Porter. His mind was shut. He wasn't 'going to let the bastards get away with it.' Our case? This judge? We're already dead in the water."

"So what do you tell him?" Breen says. "You were biased in that case, so you're necessarily biased in this one? He won't buy that. Your case involved little fungible products: pills of the identical chemical substance. Any seller who cut the price would get all the business, so no other seller could let him do that. Which meant any price cut would be matched; would therefore be self-defeating; would therefore not be anything any sensible seller would do. Turbine generators are a bit larger than pills. And they sure as hell aren't fungible products."

"But there are only two companies in this country that make them. Neither of which could allow the other to cut prices without matching the new lower price."

"I don't know, Alec. You make this pitch to Mark Porter, you think he politely recuses himself?"

"Yeah. I think he might."

"His pride, you're saying. And we take him by surprise. Remind him of the scolding without even mentioning it."

"That's the plan," Alec says.

Breen blows out a big sigh of indecision. "You said you wouldn't move to disqualify. Do you plan to threaten him with a motion and try to bluff him?"

"No. Wouldn't do that."

"Just straight, here's what we think, and see how he takes it?"

"That's right," Alec says.

"If he doesn't recuse, we're totally screwed."

"You think we aren't screwed anyway? If we let Mark Porter try this case?"

"There's nothing to lose, you're saying?"

"Maybe something to be gained," Alec says. "Even with him."

"If we tell him we know he's biased, he'll lean over backward to avoid it?"

"Something like that, yeah."

"Okay," Breen says, though not totally convinced.

"So you're good with this?"

"Sure. Why not? It'll be fun. I mean, working together."

"No doubt," Alec says, meaning it. "Now let's sell it to our clients."

"Mine's risk-averse," Breen says.

"You know any who aren't?"

"Yeah," Breen says with a laugh. "This'll be fun."

Sarah is having tea at the Soup Burg with her friend Cissy Madden, a transplant from the UK. Two boys she's never seen before walk in. One of them is muscular and pimply; the other, good-looking and very tall. She says to Cissy, "Left shoulder, one o'clock."

Cissy swivels around in the booth and turns back. "Yeah, the tall one," she says.

"I saw him first."

"Yeah," Cissy says, "but I know who he is." Cissy, raised in London and living in New York for only two years, seems to know everyone.

"Oh?"

"He's a bit old for you, Sarah. He's a senior."

"Where?"

"My brother's school, Trinity. He's a big jock there."

"What the hell's he doing here?" Sarah whispers.

"Maybe he lives here. Lot of Upper East Siders go to Trinity."

"We've never seen him *here* before."

"I dunno, Sarah. Maybe he's got a game."

"Then he wouldn't be eating at the Soup Burg."

"Jeez," Cissy says. "If you're so interested, go ask him."

"Right. Like I would."

"Then I will!" Cissy declares, her wide face brimming with determination.

But looming over them suddenly is the subject of their curiosity. "So you two talking about me?" he says.

"You?" Sarah shrugs, though her red face gives her away. "Your friend. Cissy here thinks she knows him."

"Oh, yeah?" He drags the other boy over. "This is Mortimer. He hates the name, but it fits him, so it sticks. Looks like a Mortimer, dontcha think?"

"Dunno," Sarah says. "Not familiar with the species."

"You never been to the zoo?"

The boy called Mortimer responds to that remark with a smirk, which he casts down on the girls. "We staying in this place or what?"

"Yeah," Tino says. "Let's sit here. With your friends. We've been invited."

"These kids? They're sophomores. That's Neeko's sister. A Brit."

Tino, uninterested in Neeko or his sister, pushes his way in next to Sarah. "Hi,' he says. "I'm Tino."

"Sarah," she says, as if bored with the courtesy of giving her name.

"Don't mind Mort. Poor man's got no couth."

"And you do?"

"Oh, yeah. I'm loaded with it."

"We were just leaving," Sarah says. "So, if you don't mind…."

"Leaving? Your teacup's half full."

"I see," she says, as if learning something important. "You're an optimist."

"Always," he says.

"Your friend wants to leave," she says, looking at Mort, who's still standing.

"We going or what?" Mort says.

Tino smiles at Sarah. "Once that man's got an idea in his head, he's like a dog with a bone."

Mort isn't amused. "What the hell we doing here, man?"

"Sit down, be cool."

"Shit," Mort says and heads for the door.

Cissy says, "Big decision, Tino. Robbing the cradle means losing your friend."

Tino wags his head with regret while sliding out of the booth. "That guy's too sensitive." He starts to leave, then comes back. "As for you," he says, looking at Sarah. "I don't see any cradle. Do you see a cradle?"

"No," she says. "I lost it. A very long time ago."

"So I'll see you around."

"I could say, not if I see you first."

"But you wouldn't mean that, would you?"

She says nothing, but he holds her look.

"Good," he says, and leaves.

After a moment, Cissy says, "What are you doing, Sarah?"

All innocence. "I'm just sitting here."

"That guy's notorious. He's slept with every halfway-decent-looking girl his age in Manhattan, so now he's trawling for younger? And you're falling for it?"

"What's his name?" Sarah says. "Last name?"

Cissy sighs. "I knew, but I forgot. He's Italian."

"Ask your brother, okay?"

"Boy!" Cissy says disapprovingly.

A little past ten at night. Alec's alone in his office. Papers encircle him, on the desk, on the floor. The phone rings. He picks up reluctantly.

"'Lo."

"Alec? It's Jesse."

"Hey. How are you?"

"Fine."

Didn't sound it. "What's wrong?"

"Nothing. I just interviewed for a job. You got a minute?"

"Where are you?"

"In a phone booth," she says. "William and something."

"William and anywhere, you're a few blocks away. I'm on Water Street. Come on up."

"You probably want to go home," she says.

"In which case I wouldn't have invited you to my office. Let me tell you how to get here."

"I know Water Street, Alec. Just give me a number."

He meets her in the elevator hall upstairs.

"Pretty fancy," she says, whistling at a sea of marble, dark green and amber.

He laughs. "You, what? Called the apartment?"

"Sarah's fine." She hands him her parka. "She's apparently used to your hours."

"Right." A sore point.

Through glass doors, into reception, where he hangs up her coat, she stands transfixed. It's a two-story gallery, now a darkened interior. And in the high windows looms a glittering Manhattan, as if seen from an incoming plane.

"This is breathtaking, Alec!"

"Yeah, is," he says, leading her down the hall. "You wouldn't believe we were bribed to move in here."

"I can see that," she says. "Giving the place class, like you do. Lawyers in waistcoats and braces."

"Our uniform," Alec says with a grin. "I'm in here."

He opens the door for her. She glances at his upriver view, then down to the circle of papers. "What's this?"

"New case," he says. "And new client, at least for me. I'm in Cleveland tomorrow. Something to drink?"

"Thanks, I'm good." She plunks down on the sofa, spreads

her arms out to be admired in her high-collared white cotton blouse and Irish linen skirt. "*My* uniform. For interviewing."

"So how'd that go?" he says, settling on the front edge of his desk. "Ten offers?"

"I might have had. But I met with only four people. The last was down here. A guy I think you may know. He at least knows you. Or who you are, anyway. Karol Stash."

Alec says, "He was Stashinsky in law school."

"You do know him?"

"Barely. He was in some classes I usually cut. Talked a lot."

"He still does," she says.

"Well, he litigates for the dark side."

"He said you'd say something like that."

"He tell you why?" Alec asks.

"He said he represents large classes of shareholders injured by your big clients and too poor to bring cases on their own."

"That's one way of looking at it."

"What's the other way?"

"It's complicated, and it's late," Alec says. "Stashinsky's made an offer you're considering? That's what you want to talk about?"

"Yeah," she says. "He has. Way more than the other offers."

"Oh? Why?"

"Apparently, he has a problem kid. Ten-year-old boy who's already been expelled from two schools. Karol says he was being bullied and fought back, but admits the kid is a bit weird and has a short fuse."

"Karol?" says Alec.

"He said to call him Karol."

"This a live-in job?"

"Wow," she says.

"I'm just asking."

"There's only one question here. Would taking this job be awkward? For you? Since you litigate against this guy, I gather. And I was your sister-in-law."

"You're still my sister-in-law," Alec says.

"Okay. So maybe it's worse."

Alec shoves to his feet, goes to the swivel chair behind his desk. "Why would you want to work for this guy? He's a creep."

"Really? Tall, good-looking. Dresses well. Vest and suspenders, just like you guys."

She's baiting him, and he knows it, but says nothing. Looking at Jesse, arms spread on the top of his sofa, thin fabrics on her slender frame, he thinks mainly about how it would feel carrying her—maybe into an idyllic forest, or on a beach, or possibly over the threshold to his bedroom.

Her expressive face shows impatience. "And it's like I said. He's almost double the other offers."

"What's his wife like?" Alec asks.

"He's divorced."

"That a fact."

Silence.

"So about what I asked you," Jesse starts to say, "about whether taking this job—"

"Sarah just blurted this out," Alec says, interrupting, "but I've since thought about it, and… I think you should move in with us. Look after her. I'm never home, you're witnessing why. And she's at school half the day. You'd have the time to look for a job you want."

Jesse gives a short sad laugh. "Thanks. You're kind."

"Not at all. It's good for all of us."

Smile and a head shake.

"You won't do it?" he says, not surprised.

"No."

"Reason? Real reason?"

She presses her lips together, which highlights their rim.

"Which you don't wish to tell me," he says.

"I have told you."

"Everything?"

"Enough."

"Leaving me to imagine the rest."

"I can't stop you from imagining."

"You're hot for Stashinsky."

Jesse bursts out with a laugh and rises from the sofa. "So," she says. "Where was it you *stashed* my coat?"

"You won't want to stay there, Jess."

"All I need to know—is there some conflict, moral, ethical, that I'm not seeing? Or some conduct you *know* about—*know,* not imagined—that should put me off?"

"No."

"Okay, then. And if I don't want to stay there, I'll leave."

"May not be that easy," he says. "A troubled kid? You'll be good for him, he'll depend on you, your leaving will do him damage."

"I'll deal with it."

"With Sarah and me, there'll be no downside to leaving."

"Ha!" she says.

"You're suggesting we'd resent it?"

"I'm suggesting I'd rather not talk about it."

Why can't I let this go? he thinks, at the same time getting up to confront her. "This has something to do with Carrie?"

"It has *everything* to do with Carrie," she says. "Dammit, Alec, we've already talked about it. More than I wanted to."

"And less than there is."

With a vehement look, she brings her small freckled face up to his. "You loved her, right? Totally. Blissfully. To the exclusion of all others."

"You know I did."

"Yes. I saw it. Which makes you and me the worst possible combination. I look like her. I am like her. But I'll never be her. So, for you, I'll always *be* less. And a goddamn constant reminder. Of loss!"

"Whoa," he says, reeling back. "If any of that were true—"

"It's all true!"

"Pretty bleak picture. Especially for me."

"Oh, someone good for you will want you. And will never know, as I do, how much you feel you're missing."

He shakes his head, and she moves toward the hall. He says, "This is miles ahead of where we should be right now, don't you think?"

She stops and turns. "Which is another reason I didn't want to talk about it."

Following her to the reception area, retrieving her coat, Alec says, "You're misreading me."

Her look suggests otherwise.

"In any event, you *are* my sister-in-law, and you're Sarah's aunt—we'll be seeing something of you, I hope."

"Yes."

Jesse accepts help putting on her coat, and they walk to the elevators.

Alec says, "Carrie had warmer coats than yours. They'd fit you with a little tailoring. And they're still in the closet."

"See!" Jesse says, stamping her foot, green eyes glaring.

"Oh for Christ's sake, Jesse! I am not trying to dress you up like Carrie. I'm simply trying to give you some warm coats."

"Go to Goodwill, Alec. They'll be happy to have them. You should have given them away years ago."

The elevator arrives, and she gets in.

"Have fun in Cleveland," she says, her tone mollifying.

"It's five below there."

She looks at him sympathetically. "I'm not misreading you, Alec. Or myself."

FIVE

Larry Rilesman looks like a wrestler gone to seed. It's the thick glasses, thick waist, and jacket buttoned to hide it. Though still bristling with a grappler's propensity to pounce, he appears to have lost the capacity.

Or so thinks Alec Brno, seated in the man's office, glancing away now toward views of Lake Erie and the river of slime that runs into it. "Isn't that—"

"The Cuyahoga, yes," says Rilesman. "Don't go near it with a match."

"There was a *Time* magazine article—"

" 'The river that oozes, rather than flows,' they said. Three years ago, when it burst into flame."

"You're not from Cleveland," Alec says.

"I'm from Akron. From the largest firm there, in fact, though it's small by your standards. I've been here less than a year." Rilesman kicks back from his desk. "I've got a surprise. There's a board meeting in session. My predecessor—did you know him?"

"No."

"He regularly attended. Not me."

"What's the surprise?" Alec asks, already uneasy, having predicted the man's response.

"We're on the agenda." Rilesman consults his watch. "Oops. In one minute."

"You might have said."

"Well, it just happened this morning. While you were flying in. But you guys are good at this, right? Wall Street litigators! Wake you up at four in the morning, you can lecture the Supreme

Court?" Rilesman, smiling apologetically, launches to his feet. "Sorry. We're late. You can prepare on the walk down the hall."

Alec thinks, *Great, ten seconds of prep for a presentation on a case I barely know. Before a board that thinks I had all day to work on it. Another asshole creating a test. Wants me to look ridiculous. Why? Maneuvering for his Akron firm? A simple ego play? Well, fuck him!*

The door opens on a meeting of directors: fourteen men, prominent and powerful, vested and tanned. And, of course, seated, few bothering to look up. The Allis-Benoit CEO, Robert Curtis, rises cordially: an actual person, roundheaded, topped and bearded in sandy hair, who only happens to look like a puma. "You all know Larry Rilesman, our general counsel. This is Alec Brno, a young partner of Kendall, Blake, Steele & Braddock. The firm has chosen him to lead us. Out of darkness, one hopes, into the promised land."

Alec smiles, takes the indicated seat alongside Rilesman at one end of the table, and waits for the inquest to begin.

Curtis says, "We've been tutored repeatedly on the nature of the case, so no need to repeat all that, Alec. What we'd like to know is how you're going to win it."

Alec looks at each man, one by one. Takes a few seconds, but that doubles his time to think. He then says, "I would hope to win it by never having to try it."

There's a murmur of incomprehension.

"You don't like trials?" says a stately man at the other end of the table, with a shiny, freckled bald pate.

"On the contrary," Alec says. "Trials are great fun. For the lawyer. Not, however, for the client who goes bankrupt as a result."

"You're saying we'd lose?" says the bald man.

"The case, no. I know how to win the case. What I can't do is stop the facts from emerging. That a trial would make public. Which I don't think your company would survive."

Alec has their attention, because no one has a clue as to the meaning of what he's said.

Rilesman, smoothing the flat top of his crew cut, says, "You had better explain."

Alec gives the man a look of disdain. He doesn't like being trapped into a meeting he wasn't prepared for, but he knows that's Rilesman's fault, not the directors'. "Has anyone computed the damages if you lose?" He looks around again, this time at interested faces. "I see not. Well, damages are $6 billion. Not payable alone to Mid-Atlantic Power & Light. But to them plus the 125 other public utilities who will also sue. Two billion straight up; $6 billion trebled. Add to that sum your prospective damages in the coal contracts case, you have an exposure of $8 billion. That's more than three times the net worth of your company. I was able to do that arithmetic in ten minutes, because, as your lawyer, I have the numbers that make it easy. When those numbers come out at trial, how long will it take the financial press to do the same math? And your customers to look elsewhere for their heavy electrical equipment?"

After a moment of silence, made awkward since no one had previously presented these facts, Curtis says, "Even if we ultimately win?"

"Ultimately, right." Alec smiles. "By the time we win—trial and appeals—there may not be much left of the company."

"If anything," Curtis says.

"Which is why I think our primary goal is to prevent a trial."

Curtis again recognizes the bald man with the questions. "Stanton?" And Alec realizes it's Stanton Ellis, the retired CEO of U.S. Steel.

"Do you know Donald Strand?" Ellis asks.

"Haven't met him, no," Alec says.

"Well, if you think you're going to get him to settle this case without a full payment of damages, you're dreaming, young man."

"Not my intention to settle, Stanton. The goal is to make him drop the case."

"Donald? Drop the case? Just give it up?"

"That's the plan, yes. May not work. But it'd better. Because no other option will save you. If you pay him damages in settlement, then every other utility in the country must be paid a proportionate amount under the most-favored-nations provision of the standstill agreement. Donald Strand must be made to publicly abandon the lawsuit."

Ellis laughs, not with humor but derision. "And how will you pull off that feat of magic, Houdini?"

"Only one way," Alec says. "By making it evident he's likely to lose more by trying the case than by voluntarily dismissing it."

"Brilliant. And that trick?"

"Two parts. First, the obvious: We show him before the trial starts that he'll lose if he goes on with it. Since he doesn't have any evidence of an actual agreement to fix prices, he relies on a theory of implied agreement. Can't hold up if we were, in fact, cutting prices. And we will gather such proof. Make it stand out in pretrial discovery. Rub their noses in it."

"What's the second part?" asks Curtis, now intrigued.

"We sue them. Counterclaim for an attempt to monopolize. Gives them something to lose—and therefore us something to trade."

"Do we have such a claim?"

"Probably."

"They're a public utility, Alec. They're a legal monopoly."

"In the market in which they sell. Not, however, in the market in which they buy. Technically it's called monopsony, and the attempt to monopsonize is the attempt to control the prices of the things you buy. It's just as illegal under the antitrust laws as classic monopolization, which is controlling the prices of the products you sell."

"And we have the proof to support such a claim?" asks Ellis.

"Not yet, no."

Curtis says, "Can you even file a counterclaim without

proof?"

"No." Alec again surveys the table, every face looking hostile and confused. "I'd hope to get it on my deposition of Donald Strand."

Stanton Ellis is not amused. "You expect Donald Strand to admit it?"

"Expect?" Alec mulls over the odds. "I'd say I had a shot at it."

"You do realize that Strand has sued so many companies, he's virtually a professional witness."

"Look, gentlemen," Alec says. "You know I've been on the case two days. I haven't had time to do much more than read the pleadings and some financial reports. But Mid-Atlantic Power & Light is the biggest and most profitable public utility in the country. They didn't get that way without acquisitions or without squeezing suppliers. If we're susceptible to a claim of price-fixing, they're susceptible to a claim of attempting to monopsonize. We'll get the proof."

Bob Curtis breaks the silence brought about by Alec's response. "I got a call this morning, Alec. I'd planned to mention it later, but I think perhaps better to share it now. The call was from your senior partner, Ben Braddock. Most here know Ben, or at least know who he is. Know he's quite probably the greatest trial lawyer of this century. He certainly is for large, complicated litigation. The purpose of his call was to tell me about you. That I will not share while you're here, but will, with the board, later. There is a point, however, Ben and I also discussed, which I do wish to emphasize now, because I believe this will be the first case you've handled for us. It's what going out of business truly means. We're a large institution. Heavy electrical equipment is our core business, but by no means our only business. We employ more than 60,000 people. Almost all of them support not only their own families but, in combination, the families of everyone with a business or professional connection to these workers. Shopkeepers, tradesmen of all sorts, medical people, housekeepers, etc., etc.

Closing the doors of our company would have sad and drastic consequences to literally hundreds of thousands of people, workers and children alike. Putting all those people out of work— that's a lot of human misery. And there is no 'white knight' in the wings to bail us out. We have a great history but, by the usual market standards, no longer a great business. Our ROI is relatively low. Our manufacturing plants need tremendous overhauls and modernization. For that we need not only what's left of our capital, but the ability to borrow far more. I'm impressed with your quick understanding of our problem, but I want you to know there is no solution to it, other than the one that we hope you can bring us. If you can bring us any at all."

"I do understand this," Alec says.

"Good," says Bob Curtis. "Then we'll let you get on with it and wish you well."

SIX

Sarah has prevailed upon Cissy to accompany her to a Saturday afternoon basketball game at Collegiate, where Trinity is the visiting team. Neither girl is that fond of basketball. Nor, as Cissy points out, has any apparent reason for being there, except to gawk at Tino Angiapello, which he will know and use. Sarah just shrugs. "He can't use it if I don't let him."

"A guy like that," Cissy says, "it's like an announcement you're ready to sleep with him."

"Oh, that? That might be interesting."

Cissy looks at her friend as if she's suddenly gone dim-witted.

Sarah says, "Well, you've got to start somewhere."

"True," Cissy says. "But one shouldn't be quite so obvious about it."

At which point both teams come out for their warm-ups. For Trinity, it's a gaggle of ganglies, splendid in blue and white, boys who go into their layup routine as if they were the NBA champion Lakers. Tino's the flashiest, and the one not merely a boy. His passes and dunks rouse the audience of parents and students. They jam the stands: four rows of benches, sectioned by aisles. Tino, now jump shooting, scans the crowd between baskets. Then spots Sarah.

It's like breaking the fourth wall, his coming into the stands, sitting beside her.

Sarah, not liking all the attention, says, "Shouldn't you be practicing, or something?"

"It's called warm-ups."

"Whatever, you should be doing it."

"Hey," he says, "you come to see me or not?"

"Obviously," she says, with a tone of belligerence.

"Good. Because I don't have your phone number."

"Okay," she says.

"So, wait for me after the game?"

"Where?"

"Here's good."

"Okay," she says again, and watches him sprint back onto the court.

She turns to Cissy, who gives her a double-take with wide eyes. "You okay?"

Sarah says, "I think I'm dizzy."

She calms a bit when the game actually starts. Tino is too busy to look at her, so she has plenty of time to observe him. She's never done this before, focused on one boy this long, this intently. He moves with the grace of a cheetah. He also bends all space on the court, since the other team always rushes to cover him, and he either passes to the teammate left open or scores with a move of his own. Her reaction to all this mastery is novel, at least for her, and definitely surprising. She sees him as vulnerable. She wants to protect him. Which produces in her the need to exhibit all the opposite affects.

At halftime, Sarah notices that Cissy is no longer there. If she had said anything during the game about leaving, Sarah has no conscious memory of it. By the middle of the second half, the game has already turned into a rout, and Tino has thirty-one points. She knows this because it's actually announced when the coach substitutes him out and the Trinity fans rise in ovation.

Once on the bench, Tino's attention goes to Sarah's place in the stands. She averts her eyes quickly, and he smiles. He has the look of a young man comfortable in another conquest.

The bleachers clear out within minutes after the game, although some kids with a basketball fool around on the court. Tino comes out promptly, still a bit wet from his shower. Sarah waits in splendid isolation on an otherwise empty top bench. Grinning, he takes two steps at a time and plunks down beside her.

"What's so funny?" she says.

"You and me. We've just met, and we're already hot."

"Then you'd better cool down."

"You waited for me," he points out.

"I have something to ask you."

"Oh?"

"How come you didn't mention that your last name is the same as my birth name?"

"Ah," he says, as if registering a new set of facts.

"But you knew that!"

"Yes," he says sheepishly.

"Are we related?"

"Not by blood. I was adopted."

"But you're an Angiapello! A member of *that* family!"

"Right. Legally. So, on that basis, we're second cousins," he notes carefully. "I thought you'd figure it out."

"What I figured out—you came looking for me at the Soup Burg… that was no accident."

He hesitates only a moment. "Right, yeah."

"You followed me… or learned about me—"

"I did."

"Why the fuck, Tino?"

"You're angry."

"Spotted that, did you?"

"I'm sorry," he says. "I should have told you."

"Told me what?"

"About our uncle," he says.

"*Our* uncle?"

"Well, mine," he says, "legally. He was your dad's cousin. Older cousin. He thought we should know each other. And he knew where you went to school."

"And hung out afterward?"

"Yeah."

"Wow." The more she thinks about this, the creepier it becomes. "What does he want with me?"

"I don't really know."

"But whatever it is, you're his guy, is that it?"

"No," Tino says, offended. "Not if it means harm to you."

"You know this already?"

"Yes," he says.

She gets to her feet. "Good."

"Where we going?" he asks, rising too.

"I'm going home."

"I'm not invited?"

She studies his face, as if it were lacking what she might hope to find there. "You got a lot to prove to me, man."

SEVEN

Most judges' desks and walls bristle with snapshots and memorabilia: news clips of past glories, smiling grandkids, handshakes with powerful men. Judge Porter's chambers on Foley Square exhibit nothing more personal than his suit jacket hanging in the closet. A room this barren makes you feel that its occupant would rather be elsewhere. *Which, with this judge*, Alec thinks, *is probably true.* Mark Porter likes trying cases, not gabbing about them in chambers. But he's allowed this pretrial conference. Alec was his student during his one semester teaching at Yale; Caddy Breen is his friend; Freddy Musselman was his colleague on the Harvard faculty. When any one of them asks for a meeting, the judge assumes a meeting is required.

Alec had a more difficult time convincing his own client. Rilesman's last words were, "I don't like it—too risky—but I'll make this one your call."

Alec said, "Larry, everything regarding the handling of this case is my call. I will keep you informed, as I'm doing now. I will listen to your advice. And if I don't take it, you can fire me whenever you want. But until you do, I run the litigation."

Judge Porter—a slim, beakish man with a receding hairline and the fierce stare of an egret—looks right at him. "Your meeting, Alec."

"Sensitive matter, Judge."

"You think I'm biased and should recuse myself."

Alec smiles cautiously. "Well, that clears the air."

"You guys think I haven't thought about this issue? After that raking I got in your *Biogen* case, Brno, I think I'm pretty sensitive to any such appearance. But that's the point. Any judge on any issue has baggage. The trick is to recognize it and deal with it. Make sure it doesn't get in the way. Maybe I let it get in the way in *Biogen*. I won't here."

He glances around the room. "Does that satisfy you guys?"

Frederick Musselman sits back and gathers himself as if he's about to propound ancient wisdom. "Certainly. This meeting was not my idea, Judge. I want that made clear."

"Thank you, Freddy. Yes, I appreciate that." The judge shifts his eyes once more to the meeting's obvious initiator. "Alec?"

"No, Judge, sorry."

"You're not satisfied," the judge says, as if already extremely tired of this conversation.

"Sorry, no."

"And you feel you must tell me why."

"Two things you said indicate why. You said 'maybe' you let your bias get in the way in the *Biogen* case. The fact is every single judge on the Court of Appeals failed to see any 'maybe'; they thought it a very clear case. And it wasn't the normal three-judge panel. The case was heard by the Court of Appeals *en banc*. Fourteen judges considered the question, and there were no dissents. The second thing you said was that the issue was one of appearance—and, of course, that's absolutely right. And as difficult as it is for anyone to detect his own bias, it's almost impossible to detect whether there will be an appearance of bias to others. *Biogen* shows that. But, of course, the point is obvious."

The judge glances at the long-legged man seated to Musselman's right. "Is it to you, Karol?"

Karol Stash, who has just filed an appearance as co-counsel for plaintiff, says, "What's obvious to me, Your Honor, is that this is a motion made without notice, without papers, and without proof of any sort. If there were any proof, we would have seen it in an affidavit. As it is, it's baseless and presumptuous, not worth a minute more of anyone's time."

"It's not a motion," Alec points out. "Because what would waste everyone's time is the filing of papers. At this stage, Judge—before any rulings have been made in the case—only you can know whether you can deal with it without actual bias. And as for the appearance issue—no reason you shouldn't take counsel on the subject. Not, however, from the parties or their lawyers."

"So what are you suggesting?"

"That you talk to someone. Another judge."

"And you have someone in mind?"

"Yes. Judge Weinfeld."

Judge Porter laughs. "Eddie Weinfeld. The holy man of this court."

"And we keep the matter informal. No motion for recusal. No papers at all. Judge Weinfeld blesses this, we'll shut up."

"Quite a package."

"Meant to be fair," Alec says.

"Freddy?"

"I think this whole thing's ridiculous. You've already thought it through; nothing more need be done."

"Caddy?"

"I agree with Alec, Judge. No one can go wrong taking counsel from Eddy Weinfeld."

The only sound in the room is the exhalation of breath from the jurist.

"All right," he says finally. "I'll sleep on it and let you know soon."

As they file into the corridor, Caddy Breen asks Karol Stash, "What the hell're you doing showing up in this case?"

"Helping Freddy, obviously."

"Really!" Breen says, and turns to Musselman. "I thought you considered this case to be open and shut."

"I do indeed," Musselman says. "But there's the next one to consider."

"Oh, yes? Which one is that?"

"I seriously doubt, Cadigan, that you've forgotten about the 125 other public utilities standing in the wings."

"Oh, those fellows," Breen says, and turns to Alec. "We're not worried about those fellows, are we?"

"Shouldn't think so, no."

They ride down together in a crowded elevator and part with nods in the lobby, Alec and Caddy heading downtown. On the street, they walk together. Breen says, "So you think he'll take your bait, talk to Weinfeld?"

"I think any judge on that court would be happy to have a reason to confer with Eddie Weinfeld."

"And Weinfeld will tell him to recuse?"

"Like a shot," Alec says.

"No other judge on that court would."

"I know."

Breen stops at the corner of Water Street. "You're what? Fifteen, eighteen years younger than me? How the hell do you know these judges so well?"

Alec smiles and looks toward the entrance to his building. "That's me, Caddy, 60 Water. If you hear first, let me know."

Upstairs, in Alec's office, Ben Braddock and Frank Macalister lie in wait.

"So how'd that go?" Braddock asks from Alec's chair.

"He didn't hold us in contempt."

"He'll talk to Weinfeld?"

"I think so."

"Then you got him," Mac says, circling to the doorway, possibly to block Alec's retreat. "See, Ben? I told you about this kid. He eats with the judges. You want to predict how they'll react, talk to Alec."

"What the hell you mean," says Braddock, " 'eats with the judges'?"

"Judges' lunchroom," Alec says. "Federal courthouse, Foley Square. Awful food. I think you're familiar with it."

"What the fuck you doing in the judges' lunchroom?"

"I'm invited there. Once a week, usually. By the chief judge, Rivington Kane. We consult."

"You do *what?*" Braddock says.

"You remember," Mac says, "that job you pushed him to take? When was it? Ten years ago. Secretary to the Judiciary Committee, City Bar. Well, two years later he was secretary of the whole damn bar association. That put him on the Planning and Program Committee of the Second Circuit Judicial Conference, and now he's the chairman. So the chief judge, who actually cares about how that conference is run, pulls him into his lunchroom once a week to talk about it—and, as it happens, to witness all the interesting things that go on there."

Alec hangs up his suit coat in his closet and sits facing Braddock, who still occupies Alec's desk chair. "Whether or not Mark Porter steps down," Alec says, "we have a case to deal with, and there's only one way to do that."

"You want some facts," Braddock says.

"Right. Facts. On about a hundred transactions. Gathered and analyzed by a large team of lawyers and businessmen. Which should show that, no matter what our client was signaling in the press, it was doing the opposite—cutting the hell out of the price. For any sale it wanted to make."

"Nice theory," Braddock says.

"Which is why we need facts," Alec says.

"What you're talking about," says Mac, now seated on the radiator shelf, "is what we call an elephant fuck."

"Correct," Alec says.

"Bad timing," says Mac.

"I know everyone's strapped."

"Strapped!" Macalister says with a laugh. "You know what happened while you were in Porter's chambers this afternoon? You remember we asked the Court of Appeals for a writ of mandamus against Judge Ettinger in the government antitrust case against U.S. Computer Corp.?"

Braddock chimes in with his singsong voice. "The *extraordinary* writ of mandamus. Highly disfavored, never granted—unless the trial judge is behaving like a total ass."

"Well, they just granted it here," says Macalister. They told Ettinger, in effect, to stop fucking around. That trial will now move with a vengeance."

Braddock rises. "My signal to leave. You can have your chair back."

As Braddock ambles out of the office, Mac watches while Alec regains his seat.

Mac says, "You'd better talk to Jack."

"Jack Stamper?"

"Yeah. You want half the office to work day and night on Allis-Benoit? He wants two-thirds for U.S. Computer Corp."

"We need a firm meeting," Alec says.

"Department heads, anyway. Ben just went off to schedule it. Saturday morning. Not here. Basement of his co-op building. Get your speech ready."

"I need a speech?"

"You want to take associates from forty partners who consider themselves overworked—and most actually are!—you need a speech. And it'd better be damn convincing."

Jesse, still feeling very much not at home, opens the door to admit the owner of the apartment.

Karol Stash says, "Did you lock the door?"

"You don't?" Jesse says.

"Not usually," he says, dropping his attaché case in the hallway and stripping off his jacket. "There's no one else on this landing."

They look at each other awkwardly for a moment. "Have you had dinner?" he says.

"A couple of hours ago."

"All good?"

"Lizzie, your housekeeper, did all the work. Kenny's been asleep for an hour."

"Any coffee left?"

"There's a pot of tea, still warm."

"Would you join me? I'd like to hear about the day."

"Sure," Jesse says.

The apartment occupies the top floor of a new condo building with views from the living room across the Hudson River and out to New York Bay. More interesting, however, is the northern view from the kitchen: up the Hudson River coasts to the dim lights of New Jersey and the bright lights of New York.

They settle at the kitchen table with two cups of tea. "So tell me," Stash says, "how'd it go, how'd the boy do?"

"For our first day together, I thought it went fine."

"Fine?"

"Well, I picked him up from school. We went out to lunch to a burger place he said he liked, but he didn't eat much. Ordered a burger, then just stared at it. He had a couple of the fries. I think something happened at school that he didn't want to talk about. So I didn't push hard. Early days, right? The rest of the day went okay. I found a book I thought he might like and read to him."

"Really? He stood still for that?"

"For almost an hour, yeah."

"Hey, that's terrific."

Stash stirs his tea unnecessarily, which makes Jesse feel her own discomfort. This man is uncomfortable—in his own apartment, in his own skin. And there's rather an abundance of that, which he carries about on a dominating, thickish frame.

"I spent some time with your brother-in-law," he says.

"Alec?" Involuntarily she puts her hand to her face.

"Do you have any others?"

She tries to smile, despite the unpleasant expression she finds on the long, fleshy cheeks of his face. "No, he's the one."

"Tricky guy."

"Oh?"

"Yeah, something that happened in court. He doesn't like our judge, so he's trying to get rid of him."

"How?" she says. "I thought once a judge is assigned to a case—"

"Alec asked him to recuse himself. To declare himself biased and step down."

"Is he biased?"

Stash shrugs. "All judges are biased."

"It would be a matter of degree, wouldn't it?"

"Sure."

"So what's tricky about asking him to admit it?" she says, keeping her tone level. "Seems rather straightforward."

He laughs. "You wouldn't understand. But Alec was always like this, even in law school. Bit more surface than substance."

"Really?" Jesse says. "I thought he was editor in chief of the *Law Journal.*"

"Exactly. That's the equivalent of being head of the Politburo."

"Wow," she says. "You really dislike him."

"No," he says, patting her hand. "Not at all. I wouldn't do some of the things he does, but he's a very effective lawyer. We get along fine."

She gets up. "It's been a long day."

He rises too. "I see I've upset you. Sorry. I hadn't realized you were so attached to him."

"I am not attached to him," she says in a steady voice.

"Good," he says. "Go to sleep. I'll clean up." He flashes a smile. "My penance."

❖

"So we gonna talk about it, or not?" Cissy says to Sarah.

"Talk about what?" Sarah says from the guest bed in Cissy's room.

"The subject you've been dodging, girl. Like ever since that dumb basketball game you dragged me to."

Both girls are in pajamas. No one else is at home, except for the austere Jamaican woman who's already asleep in a maid's room on the first floor. It's an ideal night for the girls' sleepover, since Cissy's parents left for London, taking her brother with them. The apartment is a swanky duplex on Park Avenue. As is customary, the daughter has the better room, Cissy's facing front, with two windows on the avenue; the brother's, a cave on the courtyard.

"You mean to torture me about Tino," Sarah says.

"Well, I think it's very interesting, actually."

"Oh, yes, to you?" Sarah says sarcastically.

"Yeah," Cissy says. "The school I went to in London—you'd never meet a guy like that. Or someone with *your* background, for that matter. In fact, in that school, *I* was an outcast for *months*. My dad's filthy rich, of course. God knows what he gave that school to get me in. But my granddad started as a mere—you'd say a clerk—we spell it the same way and say *clark*, since we're so goddamn British and posh, don't you know. But our people way back? No one talks about what *they* were. Probably horse thieves. Here, people don't seem to care that much. I mean, everyone's nosy as hell, but it doesn't trash how they treat you."

"That's what you think."

"And you don't?" Cissy says. "Not your experience?"

"Forget it."

"Sarah?"

"Just tell me," Sarah says. "What do you think you know about Tino… and me?"

"Well, you know."

"I don't," Sarah says. "You had us investigated?"

"No. I just asked my dad. He knows about everyone. He's a banker. He has to."

"And? What the hell did he tell you?"

"He knew about your birth father," Cissy says. "And about the Angiapellos. I always thought the sign on your bedroom door was just you being clever. Now I think it's a scream. And he knows who your adoptive father is. Big-deal lawyer, right?"

"I wouldn't know. He doesn't talk about it."

"You like him?" Cissy asks nonchalantly.

"Alec? He's the best. How about your father?"

"Simon… well… I can't say I really know him that well."

"Your own father?"

"My family… they're more into sons. I get the nice room, and Simon III, who you know as Neeko, gets the time. But there are obvious advantages besides the room. Freedom. Spending money."

Sarah's not fooled but overlooks the apparent hurt and says, "So what'd you learn about Tino?"

"More about his family. Which, I guess, is still your family. Christ, he's your cousin."

"He's adopted."

"No, really?" Cissy says. "You're both adopted? Now that's *really* interesting. No wonder you've got a thing for him."

"Who said I had a thing for him?"

"Sarah, Jesus! You practically fall over at the sight of him. At the game I thought you'd gone into a trance."

"I hardly know him."

"What do you need to know? He's a little too sure of himself, but he's gorgeous. And he can't be so dumb, he's at Trinity, for

Christ's sake. The problem is, girl, I don't want to see you end up as a victim."

"I'm not even sure I want to see him again."

"So you did talk to him after the game?"

"Yes."

"Well, *that's* interesting too," Cissy says. "Tell me more."

"It gets complicated."

"I'm all ears!"

"I really don't think I want to talk about this boy."

"Why on earth not?"

"Because, if you must know," Sarah says, "I'm getting really fucked up thinking about him."

EIGHT

Larry Rilesman, gazing out of Alec's office window, says, "It's great to see a river actually flowing, compared to that sludge pit I get to look at all day."

"So move in," Alec says. "You're going to have to be here often enough. Now that we have a new judge, the case should start moving again."

"The folks in Cleveland are amazed, Alec. I'm amazed. And you called it. How the hell did you know? I mean, two days after you ask, he steps down!"

"He's an honest guy."

"Well, it's gonna help us get approval for the transaction file project, I can tell you that."

"There was opposition?"

"Opposition," Rilesman says and laughs. "It's gonna cost money. Big bucks. We're businessmen, Alec. We do what is known as a cost-benefit analysis."

"Great," Alec says. "So analyze this: losing the case will cost you $6 billion. Even more importantly, trying it will cost you the company, and your jobs. Consequently, you'll want to prevent such a trial. And this is the way. The only way. That enough benefit?"

Rilesman muses the point for a bit and nods reluctantly. "Okay. I see that. Maybe I can sell it."

"You want me out there to pitch it?"

"Maybe. Maybe yeah."

"Just let me know," Alec says.

"Will do." Rilesman sits thinking again. "One more thing.

The counterclaim against Mid-Atlantic Power & Light for monopsonization."

"I'll have a draft for you tomorrow."

"Actually, I was thinking... that's really a sideshow. And given how busy you guys are, maybe we should let Stevens, McKay & Rilesman handle that one."

"Your old firm in Akron," Alec notes.

"That's right."

"Larry, let me say this. I'm probably too busy to find evidence to support a counterclaim. Probably too busy to prosecute one, even assuming we get the evidence to bring it. I'm probably too busy to handle your defense. But if you want me to handle your defense, it's a mistake—potentially, a really bad mistake—to let another firm deal with the counterclaim. No matter how good they are, and I'm sure they're fine."

"They'd take direction from you," Rilesman says. "They'd argue nothing you hadn't approved in advance."

"And how's that supposed to work? Say, in the middle of an oral argument? Or even in the questioning of a witness? Look," Alec says, "in litigation you want one voice. One captain and one voice. Otherwise, not only does it get confusing, it gets inconsistent. Particularly in a case like this. Mid-Atlantic is charging us with having monopolized the market in which we sell. Conspiring with Edison to do it, but still monopolization. We're charging Mid-Atlantic with having monopsonized the market in which they buy. Or, in the alternative, attempting to monopsonize. There is, therefore, a terrific opportunity for what we say, especially on the law, to get mired in contradictions. Because a party alleging monopolization normally wants to argue a much different view of the law than does a party defending against a monopolization charge. You understand?"

It's apparent he doesn't. "Listen," Rilesman says, "*you* get the evidence, *you* draft the counterclaim. Just let them do the work on it. Probably it will be only drudge work, until we get to a trial, and then we'll see. Actually, the plan is to never get to a trial, right?"

"That's the hope. But another lawyer talking in court? That will make it a pipe dream."

Rapid thought twitches across Rilesman's face. "Don't fight me on this, Alec. I am the client."

"No, Larry, you're not," Alec says. "The company is the client. Which ultimately means the stockholders, as represented by the board of directors."

"That's philosophy. In reality—your reality—I'm the client, unless Bob Curtis, our CEO, intercedes."

"Tell you what," Alec says, as if placating a child. "At the moment, the counterclaim is still an academic issue. Let's talk about it again when we know we can file."

"Whatta you mean? I thought it was a slam dunk."

"Should work," Alec says.

"*Should work?*" says Rilesman, now getting excited. "I've taken a position with my board about this."

"Really?" Alec says with a laugh. "That was brave of you."

"You're saying it's questionable?"

"Calm down, Larry. It just hasn't happened yet."

"But you'll get the proof we need? For the counterclaim?"

"Probably," Alec says.

"*Probably?*"

"Those are good odds."

"How will you get it?"

"Like I said. From Donald Strand. Horse's mouth. If we're lucky."

"*Lucky?*" Rilesman says, pitch rising. "And isn't it too early to be taking the deposition of their CEO?"

"Not necessarily. The papers will be served tomorrow."

"They'll allow this? The Mid-Atlantic lawyers?"

"I seriously doubt it," Alec says. "They'll probably move for a protective order to stop it."

"We could lose that motion! Everyone will know we're fishing for a counterclaim."

"We won't lose," Alec says.

"*That* you know?"

"I do."

"Mind telling me how?"

"The new judge assigned," Alec says. "Just happened. I got word five minutes before you walked in."

"And now you tell me?" Rilesman says. "Who is it?"

"Hal Richardson. He was a partner at the Dewey firm."

"Friend of yours?"

"Hardly," Alec says. "We tried a case together years ago. I nearly got him disbarred. Long story."

"But now he's going to rule in our favor?"

"He doesn't like me very much, Larry, but he's a hardwired guy."

"Like Porter, but the other way?"

"Even more so, the other way."

"So that's what we want, isn't it?"

Alec considers how to explain this. "Friend of mine, man named Bill Piel, terrific trial lawyer, terrific guy, once said to me, 'You know, sometimes it's as dangerous to have a trial judge biased in your favor as it is having one biased against you. What you want, especially if you've got a good case, is what I call a judgey judge. Down the middle. Not a flaming ideologue. One who calls it like it is.' "

"You think we have a good case?" Rilesman asks in a voice that implies the opposite.

"Don't know yet, Larry. Let's do the transaction file project and find out."

Leaving school for the day, Sarah finds Tino waiting outside. "We hadn't finished," he says.

Cissy, alongside her, starts shaking her hand, as if it were burning. "Wow, Tino! You here? Waiting for Sarah? Quite a statement! I'll just be off, I will."

Sarah, carrying her bag from the prior night's sleepover, watches her leave, then turns to Tino. Standing on the pavement, they part a river of girls. "So you have something to say?"

His look is intent. "Elsewhere I do."

"I'm good here."

"Okay," he says. "It's simply this. Whatever my uncle wants from you, I'm on your side, not his."

She gazes up at him for a moment, girls still streaming by. Then hands him the bag and says, "I live a few blocks from here."

Maid's day off. Sarah wonders, going up the elevator in her building, whether Tino knew that. The doormen said nothing. They're under no instructions from Alec. She wants a boy in her apartment, that's her business, unless her father directs otherwise. And he probably would, if he knew, Sarah realizes. Tino may be family, but it's not a family she or Alec admires, although she, at least, is intrigued: by the family and the boy. And the risk of being alone with him is part of the fascination.

Entering, looking around, Tino says, "Nice pad."

"This way," she says, heading to her room.

It's a bedroom converted from two maids' rooms in the rear of the apartment. She has never shown it before to any boy, and her allowing him entry is exhilarating.

Tino says, "I saw a big bedroom in the front with a great view of the park."

"That's Alec's room," she says, disappointed in his reaction.

"You don't call him Dad?"

"He was introduced to me as Alec."

"When you were what? Five?"

"Close," Sarah says.

"But he is your dad, he adopted you?"

"That's right."

"I was also adopted," he says offhandedly.

"Yes, you did happen to mention that, Tino. And by whom. But that information, as I recall, was a little belated."

"My dad," he says, ignoring her jibe, "who worked for the Angiapellos, was killed. Then my adoptive father, Uncle Sal's brother, was also killed."

"I'm sorry," she says.

"Ancient history. But, you see, we've got a lot in common."

"A bloody family," she says grimly. "A stupid family."

"Hey," he says lightly, as if they were still talking about the apartment, "I love your room. But where's you? No stuffed animals, no art, no posters?" He goes to her night table, picks up a photo in a frame. "Is this your mom?"

She takes the picture from his hands carefully and returns it to its place on the night table. "You want something to drink?"

"You have some booze?"

"I'm not giving you booze."

"Easy," he says. "I'm kidding. I don't drink. I'm an athlete."

"There's soda and juice. I think."

"I'm good. Let's not break the mood."

"We have a mood?" she says.

"I'm kidding again. Sorry. Can we sit down? On the bed?"

"Are you nervous?" she asks bluntly.

"Why do you think I'm nervous?"

"Because you're acting like a jerk."

"What?" he says, offended.

"It's okay. I'm nervous too, but we're not sitting on the bed." She plunks down on the rug, her back to the bed, and points to the space next to her.

He says, "You're not ready to sit on a bed with me?"

She points again.

"If you patted the space, it might be more tempting."

She whacks it with the flat of her hand. "Tino!"

He joins her, laughing. "At least it's a good-quality Persian," he says. "Soft."

"So now you're an expert on rugs?"

He tries to engage her in a smile. "Let's stop, Sarah. The kidding around. I'm serious about you. I want us to be friends."

"Serious?" she says, pulling down on her school-uniform skirt. "We've met twice, and you're serious?"

"Yes," he says flatly.

"Okay," she says. "Then open up."

"I just did."

"Not that. Tell me about this creepy uncle of yours."

"We should talk about us," he says.

"There is no 'us' yet, Tino."

"Yet?" he says, as if that prospect were hopeful.

"*Yet*," she repeats, as if such a hope were unfounded. "Your uncle, your adoptive uncle, whatever. Tell me about him."

Tino turns one hand in a gesture of impatience. "Uncle Sal. He's a boss. A capo. Like your birth father was, only more powerful, because he's taken over Phil's territory in New York and Jersey as well as his own in Connecticut."

"What's his interest in me?"

"I told you."

"Tino! What did he say? The words!"

The implications of honestly answering that question furrow Tino's young brow. "He said you inherited a lot of money from your father."

"And?"

"And he thought the money should stay in the family."

"Ah," she says. "It's that simple."

"Not to me. I'm not sure exactly what he meant."

"Oh, really? You may be dim, Tino, but not that dim."

He makes a hurt face, which turns into another smile. "You think I'm dim?"

"Honestly, I don't know what you are. Aside from vain. You're like that Carly Simon song."

"I hate that song!"

"Because you probably think that song is about you!" she sings, delighted with the fit.

"One thing I'm not," he says, with all the gravity he can muster, "is someone willing to take advantage of you. No matter what my uncle said or meant."

"That's great," she says. "So how am I supposed to trust that?"

"You want proof of trust?"

"Yes," she says. "That's what I want."

He leans over to kiss her, but she pulls away. "You're going to prove I can trust you by making out with me?"

"No, I'm going to make out with you because I want to. And so do you. And because there's too much ice in this room. It's very hard to get trust with all this ice in the way."

"Okay, Tino," she says, getting to her feet. "Enough bullshit."

He shoots upward to face her. "Every word was sincere."

"Now you're making it worse."

He rubs his face. "I know we started out bad," he says. "And I know that was my fault. And that I can act like a wiseass. But I'm really not a bad person. And I really like you. A lot. I don't even know why. You're very beautiful—which I'm sure you know—but it's more than that."

She gives him a smirk.

He says, "How old did you say you were?"

"I think we're done here."

"Easy," he says. "I'm just learning who *you* are."

She starts moving down the hall.

"Look," he says, following. "Whatever my uncle has in mind, he'll tell me."

"You know this?"

"Yes, because he sees me as the guy who will carry out his plan."

"And then you'll tell me, you're saying?"

"Yes."

She stops in the front hallway. "That's a pretty good test," she says.

"Not honoring my uncle? Yeah." He lets out a sad laugh. "You couldn't know."

"And you'll do it?"

"Yes."

"Why?" she says, looking right at him.

"Because," he says, returning her stare, "hurting you is not anything I could ever do."

"Okay," she says and turns away with a faint smile. "I've decided to trust you, but we'll see." She opens the front door.

"You're still throwing me out?"

"Only out of my apartment, Tino. Not out of my life. *Yet.*"

NINE

Jack Stamper was a law school classmate of Alec's, although he's five years older, having served in Korea as a Marine captain right after graduation from college. In mufti, he's still a Marine—from the rod up his spine to the clip in his speech, and the manner in which he pulverizes opponents. The term "scorched earth" was coined to describe Jack Stamper's style of conducting litigation.

This morning, Saturday, he stands before the heads of the various departments of Kendall, Blake, Steele & Braddock. They're in the basement of Ben Braddock's co-op on Park Avenue, where a conference table has been jerry-rigged to accommodate them. Jack is giving a tutorial on the government monopolization case against U.S. Computer Corp. A small bull of a man nearing forty, square headed, small eyed, and pale skinned, he has the drained look of someone having worked too many weekends of his life. Nonetheless, he generates an energy that commands attention.

"The case was filed," he says, "on the last day of the Johnson administration. It was an old complaint that had been kicking around the Justice Department without support for several years. The attorney general then was Ramsey Clark, who knew little about the antitrust laws and less about the facts. He didn't have to. Antitrust was not the purpose of the pleading he signed. It was meant to embarrass the Nixon administration with the most enormous and spectacular civil action ever brought—one that had to be prosecuted but couldn't be won. Right now it's a tar baby for both sides. But what's helping the government and hounding us is that the judge trying it, Eustace Ettinger, is a lunatic."

Jack pauses to look around the table, his glance lingering on Alec, who nods. He knows the charge to have ample license. He had another case before that judge.

He and Jack were moot court opponents first year of law school. They hammered each other and emerged as friends. Alec, who had already accepted Kendall, Blake, recruited Jack to join him. Had Jack returned to St. Louis, his hometown, he'd probably already be governor of Missouri on his way to a bid for the White House.

When the two of them became partners, Ben Braddock invited both to lunch. During the main course, Braddock casually announced, "Jack, you're to take over U.S. Computer Corp.; Alec, your job is U.S. Safety Vault & Maritime, all our banking clients, and Telemarch News." "Okay," Alec said; Jack just smiled; and both went on with the meal. As if nothing important had happened. In fact, what had happened was that Ben Braddock had just divided his empire. Even then, senior partners did not relinquish huge clients, unless their next breaths were certifiably their last—the certification having been issued by a medical board. But to Ben Braddock, it was simply the obvious next step in the firm's best interests: splitting up the work of the office and "bringing young partners along."

Jack flourished at U.S. Computer. They ran the company much like the Marine Corps, and he fit right in. He squashed the opponent in every case, until the government antitrust suit began. Almost fifty motions were made; the government won every one of them. Which severely damaged Computer Corp.'s ability to mount a defense. Which was Judge Ettinger's obvious agenda.

The judge knew he was despised by the bar and most members of his own court. But the government suit against Computer Corp. presented him with a unique opportunity: to go down in history as the jurist who broke up the most successful computer company in the world. This, he believed, would redeem his reputation. One built, it should be noted, on failing the bar exam three times, mangling virtually every case ever assigned to him, and leaving most lawyers who practiced before him questioning a system that could put this man in robes rather than an asylum.

Once the trial started, stranger things occurred. The government offered in evidence portions of the pretrial depositions that they designated as relevant, and Jack offered his counter-designations. This is the normal practice in a bench trial. Only in a jury trial are the designated passages read aloud, which is done, obviously, so that the jury might hear them. Judge Ettinger, however, ruled that any deposition testimony that either side wished to use must be read into the trial record. There then ensued one of the most bizarre procedures in the history of American jurisprudence. Lawyers for both sides sat in court and read deposition testimony aloud to one other and, of course, to a court reporter. In effect, one transcript was being read, and typed, into another. For months. It wasn't done for the judge's edification. He decided being present would be a total waste of his time.

"It didn't take long to figure out the reason for this madness," Jack says. "The judiciary receives a monthly report showing the number of trial days for each judge. So for months and months lawyers droned on to court reporters in a vast, otherwise empty, ceremonial courtroom so that Judge Eustace Ettinger could get credit for work he wasn't doing—and, ironically, everyone knew he wasn't doing, because this ridiculous charade soon became the talk of bench and bar—yet no one could put a stop to it."

Alec says, "But you did."

"Finally," Jack says. "What happened was so extreme, it gave us grounds for mandamus. Obviously, mandamus is a disfavored writ. Almost never granted. It requires the Court of Appeals to make a public spectacle, as it were, of a lower-court jurist. Call him out for outrageous behavior. We filed such a petition, and the Court of Appeals granted it. The Court's opinion excoriated Eustace Ettinger and made him stop the absurd practice, but otherwise you'd never know he even read it. Same sort of outlandish conduct goes on, except now he's actually attending the trial, and it's beginning to move. While the travesty was happening, we'd slimmed down the team. Now it's got to be ramped up. Big time. And immediately."

Alec says, "Which brings us to the reason for this meeting." He stands as Stamper takes a seat.

Braddock says, "You need more help too?"

"You know I do, Judge."

"Yeah, I know, but these people don't. Make it good. It's not a friendly audience."

It wasn't. They knew what was coming. Litigation partners and associates were already working hundreds of hours more per year than other lawyers in the firm. To put additional manpower on the jobs that had to be done would result in a raid on the associates of the other departments—corporate, trusts and estates, and tax—and maybe even on the partners themselves. Alec's transaction file project, for example, could be done by a team of corporate associates, headed up by a corporate partner. Projects in the computer case could also be done by corporate lawyers, or even trusts and estates or tax lawyers. No lawyer in any such field would want such an assignment. It would sidetrack his own career. And who the hell wants to work that hard anyway?

Alec lays out the situation in the Allis-Benoit litigation: the Mid-Atlantic Power & Light case already being prosecuted, the threatened government criminal action, and the almost certain suits by 125 public utilities waiting in the wings under the aegis of a standstill agreement that would end, either if the Mid-Atlantic case did or the government brought one of its own. "We have one hope to stave off massive losses and bankruptcy for this client," he says. "We have to find out what actually went on in more than a hundred extremely complicated heavy-electrical-equipment sales transactions—which means a lot more than merely analyzing the documents. Price cuts on these deals were under the table. They had to be, because part of the announced price policy was to open the company's books to all customers. So we have to talk to the salespeople involved. And while they'll be instructed by management to open up to us, they won't want to. They probably lied plenty to sales managers and customers about what other customers got, and among the last people they'll want to tell otherwise is us."

Randall Conn, head of the corporate group, says, "I know Donald Strand, the Mid-Atlantic CEO. I play golf with him. Has anyone approached him about settlement?"

"Two problems," Alec says. "One, I hear he's impossible to deal with."

"He's tough. He's the head of a power company. But he's also damn smart."

"Doesn't help us now, because of the second problem. He thinks he can't lose. There's only one way to show him otherwise."

"Your transaction file project."

"'Fraid so."

Ben Braddock says, "Tell them about the new judge you got."

"Hal Richardson," Alec says. "Some of you may know Mark Porter. He recused himself, and Hal was appointed."

"I know Mark," says Ted Wright, head of Trusts and Estates. "Classmate of mine at Harvard. "Why'd he step down?"

"Honest guy," Alec says. "Predisposed against us, and admitted it."

"Just like that?"

Frank Macalister breaks in. "Nothing in litigation is just like that. Our young friend here led him carefully into the light. The lesson was brilliant and painless. But now we have a judge in Hal Richardson who will be open to our defense. If we can prove it. Which means, if this project Alec's proposing gets done."

"We know Hal Richardson pretty well," Alec says. "He represented Pharmex in that case we won years ago for our client, Biogen. Price-fixing case with issues very similar to those in the Allis-Benoit case. Hal'd be moved by the facts we think this project can establish."

No one says anything for almost a minute. Finally, Ted Wright raises his hand. "I doubt that I'm qualified to help much on your project, Alec, but if Jack can find some financial or market analysis I can do on the weekends, you've got my Saturdays and Sundays. And, of course, nights when needed."

Not exactly the start of a bandwagon, but others then volunteer, no one happily—how could they be? "You understand," says Randall Conn, looking at both Alec and Jack. "We all have a choice coming out of law school: go for litigation or lead the less exciting, less glamorous life of a corporate lawyer. Many of us chose the latter, precisely because we don't want the crazy hours you people put in. And we each head large practices. Now you're asking us not only to work as hard as you—to do something we aren't even trained for—but to work, in effect, as your senior associates. It's not a job brimming with rewards."

"What about saving the firm?" Braddock snaps. "Because if we lose these two cases, there's not going to be much left of your cushy lives."

The assemblage chooses to treat that with quiet laughter and as a signal the meeting has been adjourned. As they file out, Braddock holds Alec's arm and leads him to the other end of the room. "You just bet the firm," he says. "I hope you realize that."

"*I* bet the firm?" Alec says.

"You will get what you want, Alec. Because everyone here will do what they have to do, and do it damn well. But there'll be a price. My guess—most of those guys are sick of hearing about how much harder you're working. And I doubt they'll forgive you for dragooning them into your wars."

"You see an alternative?"

"No," Braddock says. "But I don't think even you know how bad it is. You talk about 125 claimants waiting in the wings. Jack's got ten times that. We let his crazy judge issue a decision, we'll get a thousand new cases coming down on our heads. Every customer of U.S. Computer. Every competitor, domestic and foreign. And they won't just go away if we win the government case on appeal."

"And in my case," Alec says, "it's not just the utilities. It's—"

Braddock breaks in impatiently. "We can't let Jack's case go to judgment. We can't let your case even go to trial."

Alec laughs. "Yeah, what I've been saying."

"Okay," Braddock says, slumping into a chair. "No pressure. No pressure on you at all. You simply have to figure out a way to make both cases disappear, stop the other thousand or so claimants from suing, keep both clients alive, save the jobs of several hundred thousand people and your own law firm. And make all that happen almost immediately. You can do that?"

"You say both cases?"

"Yeah," Braddock says. "Jack's great. You need smash-mouth litigation, Jack's your man."

"He's in charge of that case."

"And will stay in charge."

"But I'm somehow supposed to make it go away."

"I just said."

"Right."

"So you up to that?"

"Piece of cake," Alec says, wishing he meant it.

"Let me tell you something," Braddock says, then takes a moment to reflect. "You think I've just handed you an impossible job. There's no such thing. Not for a partner of this firm. Because you walk into a room—any room, anywhere—courtroom, statehouse, White House—you are already credentialed. The test here is the highest in the world. Everyone knows it. And when you pass it, you have access to anyone you need. No exceptions. Anyone. So you have, for all practical purposes, unlimited credit. To do what *others* would regard as impossible. All you've got to do is perform." He looks at Alec for another moment, as if to make sure his point has sunk in, then gets up and leaves him standing alone in the basement.

TEN

Sunday morning. Alec and Sarah go running on the reservoir track in Central Park. As a family of two, they observe few rituals, but they practice this one religiously every Sunday Alec is in New York.

When Sarah was four, Alec and her mom, Carrie Madigan, fell in love. This, according to the books Sarah was then fond of, would have been an event, not a process. "So where did it happen?" she wanted to know. Which turned out to be easy for Carrie to answer. She trotted her daughter out to one of the bridges over the bridle path that ringed the reservoir track. "It was here," she told Sarah. Which was absolutely true, although, at the time it happened, Carrie was the only one who knew it.

When Carrie met Alec, she was estranged from her husband, Phil Anwar. Sarah has of Phil only the little she can remember and the great deal she's been told. Although he was not unkind when, rarely, he had time for her, Sarah's memories are mixed. She knows Phil went to Maine to kill Alec, because she was dragged along as bait to draw her mom away from the fight. She heard the gunfire while hiding under a bed. She knows Phil beat her mother, because she heard the cries and saw the wounds. And she knew Alec, from the first moment until the present day, as the kindest man in her life, one who loved her mother and Sarah too, and would protect either of them with his own life. As he already had.

And will think he has to do again, she knows, once she tells him of the Angiapellos. If there's a problem with Alec, it's his presumption that only he is capable of solving *her* problems, that she can't cope for herself. *It might have been true ten years ago*, she concedes to herself, *but not now. The sooner he realizes that the better.*

Their routine is to enter the park at Ninety-Seventh Street, jog on the paths leading up to the track, then sprint to the first bridge and stop at the benches there for a few moments before jogging the rest of the lap. They go out just before seven in the morning, in good weather and bad. For a teenager, getting up that early on a Sunday morning takes an unusual sort of devotion to ritual. Sarah doesn't think of it that way, however; rather, as something she likes doing with someone with whom she likes doing it.

That morning, as Alec gets up from the bench to resume their jog, Sarah says, "I've met someone." She stays put on the bench and stares firmly at the ground in front of her.

"Oh?" He settles back down. "A boy?"

"He's a basketball player," she says, and still looks away. "You used to be an athlete, right?"

"Track team."

"No wonder you run so fast."

"I was a high jumper," Alec says. "Who is this boy?"

"A boy," she says, as if they're all interchangeable.

"So, having raised the subject, why are you now trying to change it?"

"I'm not!" she says.

"Is he someone your age?"

"A little older."

"A year?"

"He's a senior."

"That's two years, Sarah."

"Yeah."

They're both dressed in woolen sweats, caps, and gloves. The temperature is no more than thirty degrees, but a rising sun warms through it. She says, "I'll tell you his name, but I don't want you to freak out, okay?"

"Then you'd better tell it to me quickly."

"Tino Angiapello." She looks at him now.

"Ah," he says.

"He's adopted," she says quickly. "He's not really a cousin."

"Okay." It's a tentative statement, not approving.

"But his adoptive uncle is Sal Angiapello."

"The man who took over… your father's… businesses."

"You're my father," she says.

"You know what I mean."

"Yes," she says. "And you know what I mean."

"Yes." For him, too, it's a statement of love.

Neither now shows any sign of leaving.

Alec says, "Your meeting this boy…."

"He found me. Tino did. He came looking for me, actually."

"He told you this?"

"Yes."

"He tell you why?"

"I think he told me as much as he knows."

"Which is?" Alec asks.

"His uncle asked him to do it."

"Right," Alec says, with a grim snap to the word. "Okay, I'm glad you told me."

"Nothing's happened."

"It will," Alec says. "Sal Angiapello wants your money."

"Yes. That's what Tino says. It seems he feels entitled to it."

Now Alec does get up, and Sarah follows. "Let's get back," he says.

"We haven't finished our run," she says. "And it's Sunday morning. What can you do? No one's up but us."

"I have friends in the district attorney's office. And I have their home numbers. They're probably building a case against Sal Angiapello now."

"He hasn't done anything yet. To me."

"They can pull him in," Alec says. "Talk to him. Scare him.

And he has done something. He's tracked you down. Sent one of his henchmen to see you."

"Tino's at Trinity," Sarah points out.

"Doesn't mean he's not loyal to his uncle."

"Actually, on this, I think Tino's on my side."

"And what?" Alec says. "We should just wait for this young man to tell us what Sal Angiapello is thinking?"

"He's our best source!"

Alec puts his hands on her shoulders. "Look, my love. When it comes to your happiness, your health, and your safety, I'm not willing to take risks. Any risks."

"For God's sake," she says, "what could they do to me? I'm one of them. I'm blood."

"I don't even want to think about what they could do to you. And I'm certainly not willing to trust you to an incipient mafioso who's a teenager." Alec lowers his hands. "How long have you known this kid?"

"I just met him. A couple of weeks ago."

"And you've spent how much time with him?"

"Are you grilling me?" she demands to know.

"Sarah!"

"Not much," she relents. "I dunno. A couple of hours."

"And you're willing to believe that, out of loyalty to you, he's ready to defy his uncle, the most powerful, most vicious mobster probably in the country?"

"I'm not sure of it, Alec!" she says, suddenly raising her voice. "No, how could I be? But I know if you get the cops involved in this, I'll never find out."

Somehow, in that outburst, he sees so clearly her mother. Which makes him see himself with Carrie on another weekend morning on the other side of this track.

"Okay," Alec says, going to the railing on the bridge. "You see what you're doing? You like this boy, I can understand that. But you're fifteen."

"Sixteen," she says, ambling over to get in his face.

"At any age, much less at yours—you don't put yourself in jeopardy for a boy you hardly know."

"You should meet him," she says. "And you will. I've invited him to my birthday party."

"We're having a birthday party?"

"A dinner. You, me, Jesse, and Tino."

"Oh, yes? You've made the reservations too?"

"We don't need reservations. We're staying home. Jesse and I will do the cooking. It'll be much easier to talk."

"You've thought all this out?"

"Just now." Sarah turns back to the track. "Come on, Alec."

"Home?"

"No," she says. "To the other side of the reservoir."

"Home's closer."

"There's better. I've got a bridge for you there. One that will put you into the right frame of mind for this conversation."

In his office, Alec calls Harvey Grand. He dials the call himself, a private number, and Harvey picks up. "Alec?"

Harvey is the private investigator for Kendall, Blake. He's a lawyer and has a practice but devotes himself predominantly to unearthing otherwise unobtainable facts for the firm's partners—principally Alec. How he does this, no one at the firm is anxious to learn. Alec has a good general idea, although he's never asked for particulars. Harvey is uniquely and extraordinarily plugged in to almost every government agency, state and federal, including the FBI and the IRS, and many other offices and departments, public and private, here and abroad, having useful files on every POPI (person of possible interest) on the planet.

Alec says, "Sal Angiapello."

Harvey says, "Stay away from him."

"Wish I could."

"His cousin wasn't enough for you?" Harvey says. "Look, this guy may be emotional about his family—even emotionally sentimental—but anyone outside? Christ, he'd step on you as casually as an ant."

"Sal has an interest in Sarah. Or, at least, her money."

"Ah," Harvey says.

"You saw this coming?"

"It's a lot of money."

Harvey is on his speaker box. Alec can tell from the slight echo.

"What can you tell me about him," Alec says, "that I haven't read somewhere?"

"How the hell do I know what you've read?"

"The latest was the piece in *LOOK* magazine."

"You mean the mobster going legit? Now a real estate genius? Which is, of course, PR bullshit."

"Why you think I'm calling you, Harvey?"

In the momentary silence, Alec pictures the large man in his finery, striding about his office, collecting his thoughts. Then Harvey's voice on the box, "Phil, as we know, was a brutal and sadistic monster. Sal is all that plus weird."

"Like how?" Alec asks.

"Like, for one thing, he owns an island off Sicily."

"Not weird."

"It's what he does on the island," Harvey says. "Sal and Phil were cousins, but they're from different branches of the family—and different worlds. Phil's branch came from Palermo. City people. Catholics. Sal's branch is of and from that island. They're not Catholics."

"So what are they?"

"Throwbacks. Primitives. They believe in gods, plural. Of which Sal, self-styled, is one."

"He thinks he's a god?" Alec says.

"I've no idea what he thinks. But he acts like a god. Especially on that island. Where he's also worshipped as one. Maintaining a small army probably helps this."

"Is he deranged, or just indulging a fantasy to keep troops in line?"

"I can't be sure. Probably a combination of both."

"How many men?"

"The numbers shift," Harvey says. "On the island itself, typically around fifty. Well trained. Employed, supposedly, in his business, but schooled more in savagery than mortgages. If there's a difference."

"His real business is what, drugs?"

"A sideline at most now. Old-fashioned. Like gambling, sex slavery, all the old rackets he controls here. And Sal does buy and sell buildings. Mainly, though, he deals in things that kill people fast. Like tanks and small missiles. Like poisonous gas. For which there is, not surprisingly, a huge market."

"The feds know this, I assume. And are trying to prove it?"

"They may never prove it."

"He must be worth billions," Alec says.

"Multibillions."

"Yet he's fixated on Sarah's inheritance."

"That's his sentimental side," Harvey notes dryly.

"I'd like you to keep an eye on him for me."

"Physically?"

"Paper record, Harvey. I'd rather not get you killed."

"Oh, good," Harvey says. "That's where I thought this was going."

ELEVEN

A nother meeting at the courthouse is about to begin—this one also requested by Alec. And now there's a new judge, Hal Richardson, greeting the lawyers one at a time: Professor Frederick Musselman, lead counsel for the plaintiff, Mid-Atlantic Power & Light; Karol Stash, second chair; Cadigan Breen, counsel for Edison; and Alec Brno, counsel for Allis-Benoit. All are wearing suits, as is appropriate for court; but the judge, disdaining judicial robes out of fellow feelings for his former compatriots, sports a bespoke shirt and an Hermès tie.

Normally, the longer a judge has been in office, the more fully furnished his chambers are. This has not been true, however, in the case of either judge associated with the heavy-electrical-equipment litigation: the recently recused Mark Porter and the newly assigned Hal Richardson. Porter's space was devoid of any decoration whatsoever. He took the chambers first given him five years before and continued to use what was there without embellishment. Richardson, on the other hand, in office only two months, has assembled furnishings more suitable to a stately home. His desk, chairs, photographs, and art were carted over from his offices on Wall Street. The Oriental carpet is new—or at least newly purchased—and the judge, eyes darting downward every other moment, seems to expect praise, or at least some comment, for its acquisition.

Musselman gives him what he wants, and Richardson turns beamish. He knows all the lawyers at this meeting and welcomes them by name. First name. A slender man of medium height, his handshake is firm, his skin a bit weathered, as from a robust outdoor life, and his wavy gray hair groomed by an excellent barber. Yet as the judge returns to his Queen Anne desk and the lawyers sit around it, Alec notices a tremor in Hal's hand that belies the firmness of that shake and suggests a more spirituous cause of his ruddy complexion.

"Thank you, Your Honor," Alec says, "for the opportunity to discuss this motion in chambers."

"Well," the judge says expansively, "when I looked at the names on these papers, I thought, 'Whatta you know! I've tried cases with every single one of you guys.' Sometimes on the same side, sometimes opposing. And, of course, sometimes it was hard to tell." He gives a loud bark of a laugh, inviting everyone to join in, which they politely do. "Your first trial, Alec. Remember that? I wanted to get my man, J.J. Tierney, off the stand. You insisted on cross-examining. Tierney was the damn CEO. If you and I hadn't won that case, that son of a bitch would have fired me."

"I remember, Judge."

"And now you're doing the same thing, more or less. You want to depose Donald Strand, the CEO of Mid-Atlantic Power & Light."

"I do, Judge, yes."

"It's hard to understand why, Alec. He's charging your client with price fixing. So the case isn't about what his company did; it's about what your client did—if anything—with Edison Electric. What in the world do you need Strand for?"

"Several reasons, actually. As you say, Your Honor, he's charging us with fixing prices. We could sit back and say, you've got the burden, try to prove it; we don't even need to put on a defense. But if Donald Strand knows for a fact we weren't fixing prices, we have a right to find that out now. Before trial. Before wasting many thousands of hours of everyone's time, including Your Honor's."

"You think he's going to tell you that?" the judge asks with a wink at the opposition.

"Probably not in those words, but in substance—why not? It's the truth."

"He authorized a complaint claiming the opposite."

"That's a legal conclusion," Alec says. "And it would obviously buttress our defense if he admits he has absolutely no evidence of price fixing."

The judge smiles. "Freddy?" he says, calling on the portly, sleek Harvard professor Musselman.

"It's a fishing expedition, Judge. And at this stage of the case, an obvious attempt to harass and annoy a very busy man."

"Caddy?"

"I agree with Alec, Judge."

"Yes, of course. Karol?"

"I'm with Freddy. Defendants are on a fishing expedition. It shouldn't be allowed."

Alec says, "I think both the professor and Your Honor have known me long enough to believe I wouldn't be asking for this deposition if I thought we'd come up empty."

"What's he fishing for, Freddy?" the judge asks.

"The usual in a case like this. He knows he can't win on the main claim, so he's looking for a counterclaim. Something to bargain with in the hopes we'll settle. But let me tell you this, Your Honor. There will be no settlement here. We want to bring this case to judgment. We want to bring these defendants to justice. Prison sentences didn't stop them in the last go-around. We aim to stop them now. Bring an end to price-fixing in this industry. There's a public purpose to this case, Your Honor. Not only for the customers of these manufacturers, but for our ratepayers."

"Fine speech," Alec says. "But I wonder whether Professor Musselman is willing to stipulate that Mr. Strand will never testify as a witness in this case?"

"Of course not," Musselman exclaims. "I can't possibly predict the future so early into this case."

Alec shrugs. "That's really all I need."

The judge says, "I'm afraid that may be true, Freddy."

"He hasn't answered *my* question, judge," says Musselman. "The federal rules do not allow pretrial discovery for the purpose of fishing for a claim or counterclaim. You either have the basis for pleading such a claim or you don't. You can't go fishing."

"Actually," Alec says, "if my deposition of Mr. Strand turns up evidence giving rise to a counterclaim, I'll have a perfect right to file one and will certainly consider doing so. But all we need to know today is that there's a chance—no doubt a good one—that Mr. Strand will be called by Mid-Atlantic as a witness at this trial. That, without more, gives me a right to depose him. And I don't have to sit here and give his counsel a tutorial on what my questions might be."

"I need no such instruction," Professor Musselman says with disdain.

"Good," Alec says, and looks to the judge.

After a momentary silence, Judge Richardson says, "Yes." Then again, more profoundly, "Yes." He cups his left hand over one eye, as if preventing distractions. "I do see both sides. But I'm afraid, Freddy, I must rule in favor of allowing this deposition."

"Not necessarily, Judge," Musselman says soothingly. "At least not now. What might be done is to defer the issue until we file our witness list for trial. If Mr. Strand is on it, then allow the deposition. If it's not the defendants' purpose to fish for a counterclaim, they should have no objection. And Judge, Mr. Strand is an *extremely* busy man, devoting his time to the job of furnishing energy to this country. His time should not be wasted on a wish-and-a-prayer deposition such as the one our learned friend is planning."

"Oh, my," says Judge Richardson. "'*Our learned friend?*' Freddy, you've seen too many English movies." He laughs at his own joke and invites Musselman to join him, which is greeted with a facial contortion resembling a sneer. Treating it as bonhomie, Richardson goes on. "So what about that, Alec?"

"I suggest we get real, Your Honor. The opposition here has nothing to do with sparing anyone time. Donald Strand is the most litigious man in America. He is constantly testifying all over the country—in the depositions and trials of cases, like this one, that *he* brought. He is also a well-known micromanager. He admits it. He even boasts about it to the press. I have in my briefcase more than twenty media profiles of this man in which he's quoted as saying exactly that. No one in his company dares to buy as much as a pencil without his approval. I have little chance of learning what this plaintiff is really about, and what its vision of the market is, without deposing Donald Strand. Doing it now could end this case or at least shape my defense of it. Denying the deposition—or even postponing it to the eve of trial, when everyone is consumed with other trial preparation—would be highly prejudicial; even, possibly, reversible error."

Judge Richardson sits back. It's plainly decision time, which induces in the jurist pressed lips, thoughtful nods, and a jutting jaw. "Okay," he says. "Here's my ruling. You can have two days, Alec. If at the end of two days, Freddy, you think it's going nowhere, a waste of time, you can move for a protective order to stop it."

"But I always have that right, Your Honor," Musselman protests.

"Quite so," says the judge, rising.

It's a command for counsel to do the same, and to leave—one side confused, Alec and Caddy smiling. They hold back, letting the others take the first elevator so they can talk in the hall.

Caddy says, "Porter would never have let you take that deposition. Not now, at least."

"I know."

"He likes whole schedules agreed to first, or hammered out before a magistrate."

"That he does," Alec agrees.

Caddy Breen spends a moment studying the younger man's

face. "So whatta you got going, Alec? Monopsonization claim?"

"Yeah," Alec says. "Like to join? You're more than welcome."

"We've been thinking about it."

"And?"

"It's a hundred-to-one shot. At best. And trying to prove it out of Donald Strand's mouth—you could look pretty foolish. The man eats lawyers for breakfast. Crunchy food."

Alec smiles. "So I guess you've no problem with my leading off."

"Problem? Ha! I keep saying—this is gonna be fun."

TWELVE

It's a bit awkward at Alec's front door.

Tino arrives first—jamming the door frame with his six-foot, two-inch frame.

Sarah says, "Dad, this is Tino; Tino, my dad"—surprising Alec, who's not used to hearing her address him as such, and Tino, who hadn't before seen her so tight.

Tino says, "Thank you, sir, for inviting me."

Alec winces at "sir."

The elevator door opens immediately on Jesse's fair smile, making another embarrassment clear: Tino must have been hovering over the doorbell before ringing it, because the elevator could not otherwise have returned so quickly with Jesse.

"You must be Tino. I'm Jesse, Sarah's aunt."

"I know," Tino says. "Pleased to meet you."

And they all stand there a moment, wondering what else they might possibly say.

Alec then says, "Why don't we all go into the living room?"

So they troupe down the hall as directed, where Sarah has laid out on the coffee table a bottle of white wine, presumably for Alec and Jesse, and some soda bottles for Tino and herself. As Alec pours wine for Jesse, he says to Sarah, "Listen. Maybe you and Jess should start on the dinner. I'd like to have a minute with Tino."

"Sure," Jesse responds, taking her glass and leading a reluctant Sarah toward the kitchen.

Tino settles on the sofa with a bottle of soda, Alec to the right of him on an upholstered chair. The younger man wears a sport jacket, which he unbuttons.

"We don't know each other," Alec begins. "I gather you and Sarah hardly know each other. But—"

"I think we do, actually," Tino says, interrupting.

"Oh, yes? You and Sarah?"

"I know what you're thinking," Tino says.

"Do you?" Alec says. "Perhaps you should tell me, then."

Tino responds with a firm chin and a nod, ignoring the irony. "This guy—me," he says, pointing to himself, "I'm still in high school, so how can I know anything? Sarah? She's the same, maybe worse, 'cause she's even younger. And we've only just met, really. So how did this get so serious so fast?"

"Is it serious?"

"Yeah," Tino says. "In part because of my uncle. When Uncle Sal has an interest, it's serious."

"What's the other part?"

"Just Sarah and me. We met; we know."

Alec gives him a questioning look. "What, exactly?"

"That we like each other," Tino says, obviously meaning more. Then adds, "A lot."

"Sarah has said this?"

"Not in so many words," Tino admits.

"What's your uncle's interest?" Alec asks.

"I told Sarah. I'm sure she told you."

"You tell me."

"Okay," Tino says. His eyes slit with the effort of finding the words. "You have to know Uncle Sal."

"Haven't had the pleasure."

"It *is* a pleasure. For me. He's been like my father. I doubt you'd like it that much, though. I mean, meeting him."

"Not a genial man," Alec says.

Tino laughs. "He's not what you'd call genial, that's for sure."

"So what's his interest?"

"I'm sure he has no reason to hurt her."

"That's a relief," Alec says sarcastically. "Because otherwise he would?"

"I think it's like—" Tino stammers, "what he has in mind… you know, an arranged marriage."

"Sarah and you?"

"I know," Tino says, trying to make light of it. "It sounds ridiculous. Marriage? At our age? No matter how we feel about each other? But Uncle Sal—he's still old country. Marriages were arranged for kids there all the time."

"And he'd like Sarah's inheritance to be in the family."

"Yes. That's his… motivation. But not mine."

"Okay," Alec says. "What's yours?"

"Me? I'm eighteen. What were your motivations at eighteen?"

"I was a Depression baby, Tino. My motivations were probably a bit different from kids' now. But you're saying, at this stage you'd just like to have fun."

"That sounds frivolous?"

"No. Sounds fine. Honest. Stay with that plan."

Tino nods, finally opens his soda, and sips from the bottle.

Alec says, "Sarah tells me that, if Uncle Sal asks you to do anything specific with regard to her, you will tell her, even if Sal has instructed you not to. Is that right?"

Tino nods again, even more deliberately. "Yes."

"You'd be loyal to Sarah and not to your uncle?"

"Yes." His response is immediate.

"Would you mind telling me why?"

"Because Uncle Sal cannot understand. I wouldn't really be disloyal to him. Not if he could understand."

"Understand what?"

"Who Sarah is. Who I am. How things are done here… by people like us. Who like each other."

"I see."

"I mean it."

"Yes. I believe you do. Now."

"I won't change about this," Tino says.

"I'm sure you mean that too. But Tino, now you're under no pressure, except to say what you just said. Later you may be under considerable pressure—you may be under a threat—to do what your uncle wants and to keep silent."

"He'd never threaten me like that. Not a life threat."

Alec gives a look of dubiety.

"If you knew him—"

"I knew Phil," Alec says.

"Yes, I've heard," Tino says solemnly.

"He wasn't very genial either."

"But Mr. Brno—"

"Call me Alec. Sarah does normally."

"It wouldn't matter—threats wouldn't. Not where Sarah's concerned."

"Look," Alec says. "As a practical matter, I can't stop Sarah from seeing you, if that's what she wants. But I can hold you responsible. Fully responsible to prevent *any* harm to her. You understand?"

"Yes."

"Do you, Tino?"

"Yes. I understand that *you* have made a threat. I understand why. And I respect it. I also know that you are the man who end-ed Phil Anwar's life."

"So," Alec says with a smile he tries to *make* genial, "shall we see what the young women are getting up to in the kitchen?"

"It's risotto."

Alec gives him a questioning look.

"I saw the package," Tino says. "Jesse's. When she came out of the elevator."

"Observant," Alec says with approval. "And smart. If you're also honest, Tino, we'll get along great."

❖

Walking briskly down Madison Avenue later that night, Sarah asks, "Aren't you freezing?"

Tino huddles in his sport jacket, regretting not wearing an overcoat. "Why, you wanna keep me warm?"

Sarah stops short, making Tino pull up to face her.

"What's wrong?" he says.

"Don't talk like that," she says. "Not to me."

"Hey. Just a joke."

"Right. Smarmy joke. The kind said by nervous boys. To girls they want to make out with."

"You keep telling me I'm nervous!"

"Because you are! So am I. But it's not going to happen yet. I told you."

She resumes walking and he follows. "It was that dinner," he says.

"It made you smarmy?"

"Nervous, anyway. You too; I saw."

She nods, and says, "Yeah," and they walk two blocks in chilly silence. Until they come to Ninety-Fourth Street, across the street from the façade of the Madison Avenue Armory.

"What the hell's that?" Tino says. "They ripped that old armory out? I used to go to drills there when I was a kid."

"No!" she says. "You were in the Knickerbocker Greys?"

"So you know about that?"

"How the hell'd you land there?"

He shrugs. "Uncle Sal."

"It's meant for Upper East Side ninnies."

"Hey," he says. "I was ten. I went where they sent me."

"Yeah," she says. "I know about that."

"But what about this façade?"

"Huge neighborhood hoo-ha," she says. "Some people wanted to keep the whole building. Some wanted to tear it all down. This wall is the stupid compromise. Now all the druggies hang out behind it."

"So we're gonna cross," he says, leading her to the other side of Madison, walking fast.

"So where we going?" she says, maintaining the pace.

"Dunno," he says. "Nothing much up here. Except the Soup Burg."

"No way."

"I'd invite you to my apartment, but my mom's there."

"And what?" she says. "You don't want me to meet your mom?"

"I do, but now? Spring you on her? She'd kill me."

Sarah laughs. "We could go to the Carlyle. Listen to George Feyer. Have you ever been?"

"It's a pretty fancy place."

"I've got some money," she says.

"I've got plenty of money," he says.

"Uncle Sal? Seduction money?"

He laughs. "Well, we might as well use it."

It's still early, so there's no trouble getting a table. The maître d' gives a bit of a look, but he's used to Upper East Side rich kids playing grown-up and seats them not unfavorably near the piano.

George Feyer has just started a set, and his delicate chords dissolve in the blue light and low chatter of the room. Tino orders a Coke, and Sarah, more sophisticatedly, an iced tea.

Tino says, looking around, "We're kind of underdressed here." All the men are wearing ties; the women, evening dresses.

"Perfect," she says. "It shows how important we are."

"Are we?" Tino says with a laugh.

"Absolutely. We're young, got everything to look forward to. We just survived an inquisition. In fact, Alec kind of likes you, I think."

"He said?"

"I could tell."

"You're pretty close, you and Alec."

"Very."

"Do you remember your—"

"Phil? Yes."

"You know what happened… how Phil…?"

"I was there."

"Oh, wow."

"I didn't see anything. I was five years old and under the bed. But I heard it. And you want to know how I can be so close with the man who killed my natural father."

"No, Sarah. I wasn't going to ask that."

"You're just thinking it."

He says nothing.

"Did you ever meet him?" she says. "Phil?"

"I did, actually."

"And what was your impression?"

"I was six. My memory of him? It's really just a shadow."

"He beat my mom. He did it often. I saw what she looked like afterward. No one gets a pass for that."

"I agree."

Their drinks arrive. Sarah puts sugar in her tea. Tino sips his Coke. They listen to the music.

Sarah says, "Do you have that in you, Tino?"

"What?" he says, quickly lowering his glass and splashing soda on the table. "Beating up a woman? How can you even ask me that?"

She shrugs. "I mean that kind of violence."

"He was *your* father," Tino says.

"Maybe we're equally prone." Her eyes widen and catch a glint of the beam meant for Feyer. "*Being children of mobsters!*" she says, her voice rising. "In the blood, right? So together? Pretty explosive potential."

Alec and Jesse stand at adjoining sinks, rinsing dishes and racking them in the dishwasher. Alec squirts in some detergent, closes the door, starts the machine, and looks at her.

"What?" she says.

"Nothing. Want a drink? Some more coffee?"

"What was that look, Alec?"

"Absolutely nothing. Brandy? I could make stingers. I have crème de menthe."

"I ought to be going," she says.

"Ought to be? He's waiting up, is he? Stashinsky?"

"Okay, Alec, stop that."

He squares his stance. "You have a better job waiting for you here, Jess. You were looking at it, tonight."

"So you *do* want me to spy on your daughter," she says.

"No," he says. "I don't. I want you to make sure she doesn't take dangerous risks."

"Isn't that your job?"

"Yes. And I'm not very good at it. I need help."

"I'll spend more time with her," she says and turns to leave.

Alec follows her to the main hallway, but not happily. "One drink," he says. "Won't kill you."

"You see why I shouldn't be living here."

"If you were living here, I wouldn't worry every five minutes that you'd fly off."

She heaves a sigh. "Brandy."

Alec leads the way into the living room, where he finds a bottle and two snifters in the liquor cabinet and pours their drinks. They sit on side chairs at opposing ends of the sofa.

Alec raises his glass, Jesse hers; no toast, they drink.

"Why do you think she's in danger?" Jesse asks, swinging her legs up under her on the chair. "I know you told me that Tino is the nephew of Sal Angiapello and was sent by him to befriend her. But that doesn't necessarily mean a threat. She is a member of their family."

"It's hardly a normal family, Jess."

"No, it's not normal. But it's not as abnormal as it was. Isn't that right?"

Alec gives a sour expression. "You never knew Phil."

"I was told what he did to Carrie. And tried to do to you."

"Sal's worse. More powerful. More destructive. More sick."

"How do you know this?" she says, not entirely believing it.

"He's an infamous arms dealer, drug dealer, real estate magnate—which, given his business methods, is also a murderous occupation."

"So why isn't he in prison?" she asks, her feet coming down to the floor.

"He probably will be. Eventually. There must be hundreds of people working to put him there."

She looks perplexed. "Tino seems… okay, really. Another kid."

"And if he is what he seems," Alec says, "he could be a very good friend to us all. If not…."

Her face pinches. "Sarah, I think, really likes him."

"Pretty obvious, isn't it?"

"Very," she says.

"As it is," he says, smiling, "with you… and me."

She puts her drink down. "As is the reason I should leave right now."

"This disturbs you? Our sitting here? Just talking?"

"It's the subject."

"So change it," he says.

"Okay," she says boldly. "The Paris Peace Accords were signed last month. Do you approve?" She fixes him with a fierce look, which only draws his smile.

"Absolutely," he says. "It was a horrendous war that caused unforgivable suffering."

"How come you weren't in it?"

"I was too old. They didn't draft me and wouldn't have wanted me."

"Would you have wanted them?"

"Wanted?" he says. "Well, that's a harder question. But if I had been drafted, I'd probably still be in the stockades."

"Because you don't like taking orders?"

He laughs. "Is that why you chose this subject?" he says. "To make that point?"

"Hardly," she says. "You just fell into it. But I'm not averse to finding out more about you."

He spreads his hands in a show of openness.

"You don't fool me," she says. "I'm sure you'd rather be cross-examining people than answering questions yourself."

"Depends on who's asking the questions and why."

"You think I have an ulterior motive?"

"I don't know," he says. "Do you?"

"You *do* suspect me!"

"Of what?" he asks, as if totally blameless of any such charge.

"You think I'm looking for more reasons not to move in here? I already have enough reasons."

"Yes. I know that's what you think. Ask your questions."

"Very well," she says. "What do you like doing? Besides cross-examining people."

"Lots of things," he says.

"Yeah, like what? You like movies?"

"Good ones, sure. Love 'em."

"Have you seen *Last Tango in Paris*?"

"Not yet."

"But you plan to?"

"If you'll come with me," he says.

"You're afraid of going alone?"

He can't help laughing again. "I'd just like your company."

"The film," she says, "is about a depressed middle-aged American man who seduces a young French woman into having anal sex. They do it with butter."

"And you're asking me whether I find that plotline appealing?"

"Yes," she says with a straight face.

"I'd have to see the woman," he says.

She laughs out loud, and he moves to the sofa. "You should stay on the chair," she says.

"You're actually afraid of me?"

"Yes," she says.

"You could simply trust me," he says. They're almost touching knees.

"To do what?" she says, moving away. "Make me fall in love with you?"

"Might turn out well."

She gets to her feet. "Okay, Alec!"

"I want us to know *each other*," he says, not moving.

"Biblically," she says.

"Not tonight," he says.

"What's wrong with tonight?" she says ironically.

"That might be rushing things," he says, rising to face her.

She blows out her cheeks and heads toward the front hallway. "We wouldn't want to do that!"

"You think I *am* rushing things?"

"Ha!" she says, and yanks her coat out of the hall closet.

Helping her with it, Alec says, "You'll think about this?"

"I will try very hard not to," she says, and goes into the elevator hall.

"Great." In a down tone.

She punches the elevator button too hard and hurts her thumb. "What's so great about it?"

"The ridiculousness of our situation."

"What's ridiculous," she says, "is your standing there watching me wait for an elevator."

"Goodnight, Jess," he says, shutting the door between them.

"Oh, you don't have to do that!" she says with exasperation.

He opens it. They exchange helpless looks. The elevator arrives, and she gets on with a departing grimace in his direction.

THIRTEEN

The large conference room at Kendall Blake is narrow and long, with one table dominating the length of the room. Windows on the long wall offer a northern view of three boroughs. Depositions of men such as Donald Strand are normally conducted here, more for the number of chairs than the prominence of the deponent. CEOs at his level do not arrive without entourage.

Alec is called when the court reporter, Manny Seifert, checks in at reception. Alec brings the man to the conference room and helps set him up at one end of the table. Manny is an old pro, bearded, bespectacled, chubby, and fussy, with fat little hands that flash over keys with the finger dexterity of a concert pianist. He's employed by the reporting service of the United States District Court for the Southern District of New York, which is the federal trial court in Manhattan. Alec and he have been through many depositions together and several trials. This morning's experience they expect to be different.

Donald Strand is known for using the court as a weapon. If he had his way, the nation's legal system would be bent more specifically to his needs. Opposing litigants fear him; lawyers fear him, even those on his side. Mid-Atlantic Power & Light has not won every case it has brought, but the ranks of the most prestigious associations of lawyers are littered with those who have fallen on his sword.

Cadigan Breen arrives early with his team of young lawyers, who start unpacking their files on the opposite end of the table. Caddy pulls Alec toward the windows. "Let's review this for a minute."

"Sure."

"You told the judge you weren't fishing for a counterclaim."

"What I said," Alec notes, "is that I *would* file a counterclaim if Strand were so kind to provide the grounds."

"Fair enough," Breen says, "but let me ask you this. Is there any realistic possibility of getting Strand to admit the elements of such a claim, attempt to monopolize?"

"What are the elements," Alec says, "according to the most famous judge in the history of our federal Court of Appeals?"

"Learned Hand," Breen says. "In *Alcoa*." He puts the flat of his hand against the window. "Attempt consists of the intent to monopolize, while coming 'dangerously close' by acts that are 'not honestly industrial.' "

"And to know if someone's come dangerously close to monopolizing, you have to know what a monopoly is. So what is it?"

"Power over price."

"Right," Alec says. "So how do you know when Donald Strand has such power?"

"When he can buy anything he wants at the lowest possible figure."

"Which is zero?"

"No. Of course not." Breen sits on the window ledge. "It's the lowest price at which the manufacturer can sell and still, barely, stay in business."

"His subsistence level, right. And how does Strand squeeze his suppliers that much?"

"Obviously, by exerting the buying power that he continually tries to increase."

"By means that are not honestly industrial," says Alec. "Such as acquisitions of other utilities. With the intent ultimately to dictate the price at which he buys anything—especially anything that can be sold only to utilities. Such as heavy electrical equipment."

"Our counterclaim," Breen says without conviction. "Which, as I said, is almost impossible to win."

"We don't have to win it, Caddy. At least not now. We just have to develop the basis for pleading it." Alec glances over the room to see the younger lawyers of both teams still setting up, studiously ignoring them. "Tell me this. If your client had to comply with Mid-Atlantic's discovery demands as written, what's the burden?"

"Fifty depositions and about 10 million documents."

"We're facing about the same," Alec says. "They get even half of what they've asked for, it's a license to inflict pain. Which is the real purpose of their discovery demands. And as matters now stand, in defense of a price-fixing charge—"

"We have little basis for any discovery of them, except on damages."

"So this morning," Alec says, "we ask Donald Strand to hand us the basis for serving on him a set of discovery demands that match the hurt he's putting on us."

"Discovery in support of our counterclaim. Once we get leave to plead it. Great," Breen says. "Something to trade with. Reduce the pain. Get down to essentials. Okay, what else do you have up that sleeve of yours?"

"Whatever he's willing to give us, Caddy."

"Terrific. So let's get back to reality. This witness. Who's probably the most experienced fucking witness in the country. How the hell you going to get him to say anything we need?"

Alec shrugs. "He's also a notorious hot-tempered bully. So let's piss him off first, and see what happens."

On cue, at the appointed hour, Strand arrives with his subordinates and lawyers, including Musselman and Stash. A white-haired, pink-faced man of little more than medium height, Strand strides in with a thrust in a Saville Row suit, ignoring Caddy, greeting Alec curtly, and taking his seat across from him and catty-corner to Manny's machine. Without further words, he signals his readiness to be sworn in. Alec waits for Frederick Musselman, Karol Stash, and their staffs to be seated, then signals

Manny to administer the oath.

Set piece: Lawyers snap to attention. Makes Alec think of his first deposition. Ben Braddock was conducting. As the swearing-in ended, Alec felt a poke in his side and heard a rasp in his ear: "You don't look away, Brno, you don't shuffle papers. You watch! Get it?"

"It's the God part," Alec said later.

"You're a heathen," said Braddock. "Great. Shows you're smart enough to know it's symbolic. So when a witness gets sworn, where're your eyes?"

"On the Bible."

"Fucking right," Braddock said.

Now Alec's own associates are rapt. It's a good team. To Alec's left, his second chair, Trevor Joffrey from Harvard: dark, sleek, soothingly smart; next to him, Stanley Woolscraft from Yale: an oh-golly-gee giant who's brilliant; and then Rick Smollet from Columbia: a mop-haired quirk who can be made to focus just often enough. They know the drill. They watch the oath. And when it's over, Alec moves in.

"Please state your full name and position for the record."

"Donald Ulysses Strand," says the witness in a reedy voice, curiously at odds with his rank. "I'm president, chairman of the board, and chief executive officer of the Mid-Atlantic Power & Light Company."

"Isn't there a conflict in those positions?" Alec asks.

"A *what?*" says Strand, mouth open in an expression less of wonder than contempt.

"As president and CEO, you're head of management. The function of the board is to keep a check on management activities. As chairman, it's like you're keeping an eye on yourself."

"Perhaps, Mr. Brno, you're unaware of the fact that, in many companies throughout the world—mature companies—such trust is reposed in a single leader."

"So basically you run the company?"

"Yes." Strand straightens up, with a jerk to his head. "That's what I do."

"And what exactly does that job consist of?"

"I beg your pardon?" Strand says, as if Alec had now lost his mind.

"You don't understand," Alec says sympathetically, as if indulging an uninformed man. "Let me put it this way. What are your duties?"

Strand looks with disgust, first at Alec, then at his own lawyer. Musselman, hunched over, gives dark looks to his pad, but none back to his client. "To serve the stockholders," Strand says. "And, of course, the ratepayers."

"And how do you do that?"

"Is this a joke?" Strand looks around, expecting to find an audience laughing.

Musselman smacks the table, but then controls his voice. "It is. A very bad one. To which I object. Mr. Strand is not here, Mr. Brno, to give lessons on corporate management."

"I'm sure that would be worth listening to," Alec says, "but not in response to this question. I'm interested in specifics, and to achieve that, I'm happy to break it down. So, let's start with the pricing of your product, Mr. Strand. In a broad sense your most important product is electrical power, is that right?"

"Yes."

"And since your company is a public utility, the pricing of that product is done by public utility commissions, right?"

"Correct."

"So you don't even have the job of setting your own prices, correct?"

"You think the PUCs pick these prices out of the air?" Strand says, his voice mocking and shrill.

"Of course not. Your company makes presentations, argues for specific price increases. But you, as CEO, don't personally get involved in that sort of nitty-gritty, do you?"

Musselman, visibly constrained: "I object to the form of the question. Also, to its relevancy."

Alec adopts the posture of a man relaxing in his own home. "Are you directing the witness not to answer?"

"Up to now, counsel, you've been given a very long leash. You've just about reached the end of it."

"So, Mr. Strand, your attorney is allowing you to answer the question. Please do."

"There is nothing 'nitty,' Mr. Brno, about the rate increases of a public utility—either to us or to our ratepayers."

"So you're involved?"

"As is true of any major part of our operation, it is done under my direction and control."

"As is, therefore, the buying of products?"

"Significant purchases, yes."

"Such as the purchase of a turbine generator?"

"That would be a significant purchase, yes."

Alec pulls a sheet of paper from the stack before him on the table and hands it to Manny. "I ask the reporter to mark this one-page document as Allis-Benoit's Exhibit 1 for identification."

Manny, after entering the request, sticks a label on the document, prestamped "A-BX1 for id."

Alec says, "Can you identify this document, Mr. Strand?"

The witness studies the paper for several minutes. "Looks like a list of the acquisitions we've made during my tenure as CEO."

"Acquisitions you've made of other utility companies."

"Correct."

"Is it an accurate list?"

"As far as it goes, yes."

"There may be additional acquisitions you've made not included on the list?"

"I'd have to study it further against my own records."

"You've made so many acquisitions, you can't remember them off the top of your head?"

Musselman erupts. "Stop it, Alec."

"We'll let that pass," Alec says with a smile and returns his attention to the witness, "A-BX1 lists fourteen acquisitions made by your company since 1951. Is the number at least that large?"

"It is at least fourteen. I wouldn't characterize the number further."

"You object to the word *large?*" Alec asks.

"Are we here to debate semantics, counsel?"

"Well, you are aware of the fact, aren't you, that it is more than triple the number of acquisitions made by any other public utility in the United States during the same period?"

"If you say so."

"You're indifferent to the fact?" Alec pulls another document from the top of his stack and reads it to himself.

"What do you have there?" Strand asks. "Show me the document."

"Just answer the question, please."

"I may have asked someone to compile this information."

"And you know it to be the fact? Three times the number?"

"Yes," Strand says belligerently.

"So, in 1951, you took over a relatively small public utility in Virginia, and set upon an acquisition program that's broadened your reach into five states and transformed your company into the largest public utility in the United States, correct?"

"To shorten this," Strand says, altering his tone to smooth insincerity, "let me simply say we have consolidated with a sufficient number of like-minded companies to expand our ability to serve the ratepayers of five states, and yes, I believe we are the largest domestic public utility."

"In terms of what?"

"Well, ratepayers served."

"And gross revenues?"

"Yes."

"But not net profits?"

After a pause, "Not yet."

"Inefficiencies drag you down, do they?"

"Certainly not. We're extremely efficient. We're still paying for the acquisitions, but as soon as we complete that program—"

"You mean pay off your debts?"

"Yes," Strand says. "Then we should see a large improvement in net revenues as well."

"Since you can't raise your prices without PUC approval, how will you achieve that? The PUCs won't allow you to raise prices just because you've paid off your acquisition debts."

"Of course not."

"Nor will they allow you to raise rates because you've gotten bigger by swallowing up fourteen other utilities, true?"

Apparently riled once more, Strand laughs to cover it. "We don't swallow companies, Mr. Brno, but otherwise the answer is yes."

"You've gone to a lot of trouble and expense to enlarge the size of your company. If it's not going to help you raise your rates, what was it for? Personal power?"

Musselman slams the table with both hands. "That's enough. Don't answer that."

"You're directing the witness not to answer?"

"I am. The question is irrelevant and insulting."

"It's pretty obvious that being CEO of the largest American public utility is a more powerful and prestigious position than managing the relatively tiny firm Mr. Strand started with."

"You'd better go on, counsel," Musselman says, "to something having a bearing on this case. Or we're simply going to ask the court for an order ending this deposition."

"So, Mr. Strand, if you didn't buy fourteen companies simply to enhance your personal standing, and you didn't expect those acquisitions to enable you to increase your rates, why did you go to the trouble and expense?"

"Asked and answered," Musselman says.

Alec, ignoring the professor, says to the witness, "There's no direction. You may answer."

"As he said, I already have."

"You said, 'to serve the ratepayers.' I doubt that answer was complete. Surely you wished to serve your shareholders as well."

"That's obvious."

"How did you expect the fourteen acquisitions to do that?"

"In the time-honored way. By increasing share values and dividends."

"You increase dividends by increasing net profits, right?"

"Obviously."

"But how do you make more money if you can't increase your prices?"

"Economics 101, Mr. Brno. You reduce your costs. I've already told you, when we pay off our loans, we will eliminate the interest costs of the money we borrowed to make our acquisitions."

"Is that your only way of reducing costs?"

"There are many ways of reducing costs, Mr. Brno."

"And being the size of fourteen companies rather than one helps you do that?"

"You've never heard of buying power?"

"I have, yes," Alec says, as if reminded of a forgotten concept. "So when you're buying, say, ten turbine generators, you expect to get a lower price per machine than if you were buying one?"

"That would normally follow." Strand's mouth sets in smug repose.

"And the more you buy, the lower should be the price?"

"Up to a point."

"The point being the manufacturer's ability to sell at those prices and still stay in business?"

"Yes."

"Economics 101," Alec says.

"Quite."

Alec sees Musselman scowl. "In your purchases of heavy

electrical equipment," Alec says, "have you been able to get prices that low, down to the manufacturers' subsistence level?"

"Of course not. That's why we brought this lawsuit."

"I see. So if you win, you'll expect to achieve that, subsistence pricing?"

"I didn't say that."

"You'd need some more acquisitions?" Alec says, as if stating a self-evident proposition.

"I'd need," Strand says, hackles again rising, "manufacturers who are willing to compete with each other for my business. Not price-fixers, which is what I'm confronted with now."

"Really?" Alec says. "Let's focus, then, on your purchases of other types of equipment—things not made by the defendants in this action. Has your increased buying power helped you reduce the prices at which you buy any of those products?"

"No doubt."

"As far as those prices can go and still let those manufacturers stay in business?"

"I think not."

"So you have a ways to go?"

"No doubt we can do better."

"Which is your aim."

"To do better? Naturally."

"In that respect?"

"In all respects."

"Including that one. Reducing your costs by reducing the prices at which you buy?"

"As I said."

"A simple yes will do nicely."

Strand looks at his lawyer, who registers the usual objection, "Asked and answered."

"You may answer," Alec says.

"Yes," Strand says, as if now bored with the whole affair.

"And you have the same objective with regard to your

purchases of turbine generators?"

"Of course."

"To use the increased buying power gained by your acquisitions to lower prices on turbine generators?"

"Yes."

"As low as those prices can be driven?"

"Yes."

"Right down to the lowest price at which they can sell, and still stay in business?"

Strand looks at his lawyer, who shrugs. "Yes," he says uncertainly.

"Are you considering further acquisitions?"

Musselman says, "That's confidential."

"Okay," Alec says. "So we'll mark this portion of the deposition confidential and place it in camera, until we can obtain a ruling as to whether your claim of confidentiality can be upheld. Mr. Strand, there's a question pending."

The witness looks at his lawyer, who reluctantly nods. "Are we considering?" Strand says, repeating the question. "We're always considering."

"Specific companies?" Alec asks. "As acquisition targets?"

"Yes."

"Public utilities?"

"Yes."

"So as better to serve your ratepayers and stockholders?"

"Of course."

"By lowering your costs?"

"Yes."

"By lowering the prices at which you buy as far as your bargaining power will let you?"

"Yes."

"To the subsistence level of your suppliers?"

"Yes!" It's both an explosion of annoyance and a war cry of pride.

"And are you close to achieving that?"

Strand's face hardens with anger. "Only your client's conspiracy stands in the way."

For the first time during the deposition, Alec glances at Caddy Breen, who simply lowers his eyes. Alec says, "I have no further questions of this witness at this time."

"I think you got it," Caddy Breen says in Alec's office, after Strand & Co. have left. "As we said, monopoly is power over price, meaning, on the supply side, the ability to drive your suppliers down to their subsistence. Strand clearly admitted that's his end game. That he's ramped to do it, not by moves that are honestly industrial, but by acquisitions. And that he's gotten 'dangerously close,' to use Learned Hand's test. You've practically proven the case."

"Maybe," Alec says. "At least we've got enough to file." He's seated at his desk, sorting out the documents he bought into the deposition, mostly for show.

Breen is pacing excitedly. "Exactly," he says. "To get the rest is why we need discovery. Lots of discovery. Even more than they've asked from us!"

"Actually," Alec says, switching the tone, "for us to win on the counterclaim, they'd have to *make* some more acquisitions."

Breen considers that. "Which Strand won't do," he says, reality now dawning, "so long as the counterclaim hangs over his head."

Alec smiles.

"You knew this going in," Breen says. "The very filing of a counterclaim will make it impossible for us to win it."

"Is that your objective?" Alec says.

Breen plunks down on the sofa. "Your other point," he says.

"The important one," Alec says. "We're talking about Donald Strand. A man unmatched in rapacity for buying public utilities.

He's already laid out a program for doing a lot more of that. However, there's suddenly an obstacle. The case he himself brought. Getting to trial in a case this large, with a huge claim and now an even bigger counterclaim—then actually trying both claims, taking the case up on appeal—could last ten, maybe fifteen years."

"He won't like that," says Breen excitedly. "Being shut out of acquisitions for that long."

"He's got a quick way to change it," Alec says.

"That's *our* end game."

"I've been saying it from the outset, Caddy. This is not a case that ought to be tried."

FOURTEEN

In the twin-towered condominium on Central Park West, it's the southern tower that's preferred—for obvious reasons. The downtown view of Manhattan is spectacular. And the southern tower, by having that view, blocks the northern side from enjoying it. Sal Angiapello, who deprives many people of many things, appropriately lives on the top floor of the southern tower. It's one of three apartments he uses in the city. In the others, he lodges his two mistresses. They are luxuriously provided for, but not welcome in the CPW establishment. There he once lived with his wife, who died at an early age. Possibly of grief over Sal's succession of other women, although the diagnosis was cancer. His living alone on CPW might be out of respect for their marriage or avoidance of warfare between two other women. No one would have the temerity to ask. But it is the place where he most often sleeps, and the sanctuary he fortifies for his convenience and safety. In New York City, at least.

In general, he prefers his own island off the east coast of Sicily. To travel there easily, Sal maintains two Lear jets at the Westchester Airport. And to reach that location at maximum speed, he has established a heliport on the roof of his tower, accommodating a brand-new Sikorsky chopper. The tower is, in fact, his, since he has recently completed a buying program to acquire all the apartments in it and many throughout the rest of the building. As a result, he controls the board and hires the building staff, who are quite willing to serve his interests. All in all, he feels better protected than he would in a townhouse, and comfortable in surroundings of splendor. So it is also the place where he meets or dines with favored associates.

Such as his nephew, Tino, with whom he is now having dinner, being served by an excellent staff in a room offering that spectacular view. For the young man, this apartment is the exemplar of good taste. Sal knew better than to apply his own. He hired a famous decorator. After all, it was meant to impress. Sal himself is indifferent to furnishings and has no time to spend on them. Actually, since it isn't his kind of talent, he rather deprecates the skill and those who possess it.

"So you've met her," Sal says, "and you've become friends."

"She invited me to her birthday party."

"Yes. You said. Small party. Family and you. Very nice. And"—he nods gently in his nephew's direction—"she's in love with you now?"

"It's a bit early for that, Uncle."

"Oh, yes? Young people like you? In my time, we fell in love—and out of it—in a flash. Like lightning."

"This is different."

"Ah," Sal says. "So you've fallen for her."

"I think we're both at the same stage."

"Oh? And where is that?

"We think we may have something remarkable."

Sal laughs, which sounds like the rumble of a large animal's stomach. "No offense, my dear nephew. But throughout the history of the world, every couple who thought themselves in love also thought, at the beginning, it was remarkable. Only later to learn it was not."

"I'm sure you're right, Uncle."

"While all the time you're thinking, no, no, we're quite different."

"I wouldn't contradict you, Uncle, even in my thoughts."

Sal laughs again, this time slapping the table. "Good boy. You really are. So tell me, have you been intimate with her? Sexually intimate?"

"No, Uncle."

"She won't know she's in love with you, Tino, until she makes love with you."

"It's a bit early for that too."

"No, really, my boy, it's not. She's of a marriageable age. She could have babies."

A married couple—the man tall and gaunt, the woman squat and beefy—arrive to clear the table, which gives Tino time before answering. "Uncle, with the greatest respect," he says, when the couple depart. "This could work very well—very naturally and very well—if not rushed."

Sal looks displeased by this. "Do you understand what that means in this situation? For us? 'Work well'?"

"I think so. That her money stays in the family."

"*Stays?*" says Sal. "Not quite the right word here. The money she came by *left* the family. At present, it *stays* with her. To become the family's money once again, it must be *returned*. And for that to happen most gracefully, *she* must be returned to the family."

"Which would happen if eventually we were married," Tino says.

Sal puckers his lips into a round, musing position. "You say 'eventually.' I had in mind a more abbreviated schedule. The longer the delay, the greater the risk. While we are being patient, the fortune might be spent, given away, invested unwisely… or appropriated by someone else."

"It's likely her adoptive father would look after her… and her money."

"You say *her* money."

"The family money," Tino says, correcting himself quickly.

"Yes. And this adoptive father. The one who killed my cousin. You're prepared to trust him?"

"He wouldn't steal from her."

"You know this already?" Sal says. "You've met him once, and you're sure?"

"Hasty judgment, Uncle. Sorry."

"I can't afford to make such judgments." Sal rises. He's not a tall man, but somehow imposing at full height. "I'm sorry, my boy. Your head's not in the right place on this. In some ways, you are my natural heir. And yes, I know, you want to become a member of this family. A real member. But you're not thinking like one. You're thinking this old man—me—already has so much money! Why does he need this girl's money? But what you should be thinking is *famiglia*. Pride of *famiglia!* You've been raised as an Angiapello, now think like one! People not admitted to our family should not be allowed to keep what's ours! Amount is not the point. The point is affront! Her possession of this amount is an affront! To the *famiglia!* You understand that?"

"Yes," Tino says, having trouble articulating this simple word.

"Do you?" Sal's voice sounds sad, not believing.

"I do, Uncle, yes. So tell me. What's best?"

Sal waves off the couple about to arrive with dessert. "What's best, Tino, I've already said. Not to wait. No need for waiting. Act now, my boy!"

"We're too young to be married, Uncle. I think it may even be against the law."

"Oh, yes? Whose law?"

"The law of this country!"

"Then go somewhere else."

Tino looks mystified, then troubled.

Sal laughs. Adopts a total alteration of demeanor. Becomes an uncle who's only been fooling with his young nephew. "Look, Tino, you're doing fine. You should just continue. And of course keep me informed. We'll work this out, you and I. One step at a time. Okay?"

Tino, while uttering the sounds and words of agreement, knows it's very far from being okay—knows he's been slapped in the face. The night, for him, has lost its good nature and promise.

❖

Jesse, reading in bed, decides to call it a night, when she hears a knock on her door.

"Saw the light on. Can we talk?" The voice behind the door, a bit thick, is still recognizable as Karol Stash's.

"I was just turning in," she calls out.

"It won't take long. Something important."

"Can't it wait 'til the morning?"

"This conversation through the door," he says deprecatingly, "is getting…."

"All right, all right." She looks for her bathrobe.

"I'll come in," he says, and does so, barging.

"Whoa!" she says, caught getting into her robe.

As she scampers back under the covers, Stash, still in his suit, still carrying his attaché case as if he might need it for this meeting, slumps down on the one chair in the room and lets out a sound of mixed mirth and exhaustion. "Never fear. I'm quite civilized."

In a voice of undisguised scorn, Jesse says, "Were that true, Mr. Stash, you'd not be on this side of that door."

"It's been a long day, Jess. Can we drop the formality?"

"Just… say what you have to say that's so urgent."

"It's not urgent," he concedes. "But morning's not a great time for this subject."

"And this is not a great time—or place—for any subject."

"Okay," he says. "You're tired and pissed off at me. Sorry. But you know I'm a good guy, so listen. And I do mean listen. You might have a negative reaction at first, but then sleep on it. I hope you will see that what I suggest makes sense. Makes sense for both of us, maybe even more for—"

"Can this preamble come to an end, please?"

"Yes," he says. "Quite right. End of preamble. The thought I had was this: we're both young people. You're a bit younger than

I, but probably equal on the curve, if you get my meaning."

"You have a meaning?" she says, not hiding her scorn.

"Well, let me put it this way. We are both unattached, yet live here in a state of propinquity. The curve I made reference to was the curve of very natural, very healthy desires. Sexual desires. At our time of life. So I wanted to say, there need not be a door between us. I am available to you. I realize what I'm proposing is unconventional, but that's me. An unconventional kind of guy. Obviously, I wouldn't have said anything if I weren't attracted to you. Or if I didn't think the attraction might be reciprocated." He gives her a contented smile and says, "I'm right, aren't I?"

She says, "Are you finished talking?"

"I have said what I wanted to say."

"Good," she says, holding the covers to her neck. "I'm finished listening, and would like you to leave this room."

"You've no reaction to what I said?"

"Apart from revulsion?"

"You don't mean that."

"You're right," she says. "I mean a great deal more."

"So you will think about it?"

"Oh, yes."

He rises unsteadily, his face showing the strain of a search for something clever to say. "In the morning," he begins.

"Everything," she interjects, "will be made clear to you in the morning."

"So glad," he says, apparently satisfied with that as his exit line.

At 2 a.m., Alec's wrenched out of sleep by the blare of the intercom. The damn thing sounds rhythmic, as from jabbing fatigue. Alec yanks up the receiver. The doorman bleats his apology: "I would never have dreamed of disturbing you, sir—"

A loud scratch of static, as if someone has ripped the instrument from the man's hand. "Alec, it's me, Jesse. This kind man wouldn't let me up—that's understandable—but was prevailed upon to call. I would not be here, unless—"

"Jess, just put him back on, okay?"

Alec directs the doorman to send Jesse up, then proceeds to the bathroom where he splashes water on his face before opening the front door.

"You're in your underwear," Jesse says.

"You noticed."

"Would you like to put on your bathrobe?"

"I don't own one," he says.

"Of course. Why would you."

"Are you offended?"

"Not in the least," she says. "Alec—"

"Why don't you come in? Take the room down the hall, next to Sarah's. Whatever it is that drove you here in the middle of the night, we can talk about in the morning. Or at least when I get back. I'm on an eight o'clock to Cleveland. In any event, you're more than welcome to stay as long as you like."

"Thank you, Alec."

"You're welcome, Jesse, and goodnight."

FIFTEEN

Larry Rilesman, getting up from his desk, says, "The counterclaim's great, Alec; shouldn't have dragged you out here. There's only one thing."

Alec glances around Rilesman's office. "Morning, Larry. Any chance for some coffee?"

"Coffee, of course, sorry." Rilesman picks up his phone, puts in the order.

"So what's the one thing?" Alec asks, pulling up a chair that looks comfortable.

"You've put only your firm's name on it."

"Yes, I did that," Alec says, without a change in expression, "because it will be my firm that will be prosecuting the claim."

"You say 'prosecuting.' "

"It being a claim," Alec says, "it requires prosecution."

"Yes, but we talked about this. You could be listed as lead counsel, but let another firm do the work."

"Meaning your old Akron firm, Stevens, McKay. And I've considered that, but—"

"Stevens, McKay & Rilesman."

"Yes, of course. No doubt it's a fine, reputable firm."

"But not up to your level."

"I've no idea of its level," Alec says. "Nor is that relevant."

"Really? Firm from Akron. You put that down. Big New York lawyer like you."

"Jesus Christ, Larry," Alec says, rising. "I've told you. I don't know the firm; I've never worked with it. And that's not what matters here."

"You've worked with me," Rilesman says, getting up too.

"Look," Alec says, trying to make the man understand reason. "We're in a lawsuit. It's a battle. You can't have two generals leading your army. You want Stevens, McKay... and Rilesman to take over the case, that's your prerogative. I will bring them up to speed, and the case is theirs. No hard feelings. My firm is overworked. I'm overworked. If your Akron group is good, and they have the time for this, you may be improving your situation."

"You're threatening me?" Rilesman blusters. "I bring another firm in, and you quit?"

"I'm advising you. For the good of our mutual client. You need a couple of days to think it over, consult with your CEO, Bob Curtis, talk to your board—that's fine, just let me know as soon as you can."

"Bob wanted to join us for lunch."

"All right. Let's thrash this out with Bob, then. You tell him why you think having two firms in the case is a good idea, and I'll tell him why it's suicidal."

Rilesman reflects for but a second. "I'll let you know my decision in a couple of days."

His secretary—a plain-looking middle-aged woman—arrives holding out a cup of coffee like the offering of a plant.

"I'll take that," Rilesman says.

Alec grins at the woman and leaves, but not before receiving a surprisingly wry look from her in return.

Outside her school, Sarah spots Tino. As do most of her class, who part around the couple with backward looks, mainly smirky. Sarah waits until the last girl has passed.

"You can't keep doing this, Tino." She stands, looking up to him, in her camel hair coat open to her white collared blouse and short plaid pleated skirt, which is her school uniform.

"Destroying your reputation?" he says with a laugh.

"You think you're not?" She starts walking to Fifth Avenue, he following, she allowing him to do so.

"I wanted to see you."

"You could call," she says. "Make a date."

"I don't want your dad picking up."

"You afraid of my dad?"

"Maybe."

"Well, he's never home. You've no need to worry."

"We should have telephones we could carry around," he says. "Like Dick Tracy."

She stops walking and faces him. "You want to see me, Tino? Then call."

"Okay." He brings his face down to hers so that their fogged breaths mingle. "You want to see me?"

She looks away, then back at him. "Yes," she says.

"Good." He stands up tall, hands in pockets, and she can see he's cold in his Trinity basketball team jacket.

"Okay," she says, as they resume walking up Fifth Avenue. "Let's get you someplace warm."

"My place?" he suggests brightly.

"Your place? You mean your apartment?"

"Right."

"I'm to meet your mother at last?"

"She's out," he says. "Working."

"Oh, yeah. What's she do?"

"She's a bookkeeper."

"You going to tell me for whom?"

"She works for Uncle Sal."

"Ah," she says.

"Yes, true, the family business. But Mom just keeps the books."

After a couple more blocks, Sarah says, "You will be good, Tino; I can trust you?"

"Sarah," he says, getting all serious, "your person is sacred to me."

"Sacred?" she says. "Where'd you get that?"

"I go to church," he says, a bit hurt.

"Well, calm down, choirboy. I'll take regular gentlemanly behavior."

They see a crosstown bus on Ninety-Seventh Street and make a run for it.

Tino lives in an apartment on West Ninety-First Street between Broadway and West End Avenue. It's two bedrooms facing the courtyard, small living room on the side street, kitchen with a corner table for two. Sarah utters the first thought in her head. "Two places."

"I told you. My dad's not living."

"I know. I'm sorry. You did say."

"I don't remember him. Either of them. They died when I was too young."

"It's just so awful."

"I guess you'd know."

"Yeah, great," she says. "I do. We come from a really great family."

They're standing in the kitchen, an array of old-fashioned appliances and wooden furniture, which his mom has left spotless. "Want a soda?" he says.

"Whatcha got?

He opens the refrigerator. "One Coke, one Dr. Pepper."

"You choose," she says.

"No, absolutely not. You're the guest."

"I don't really care, Tino."

"Okay," he says. "I'll take the Coke."

"That's what I wanted," she says.

He looks at her, sees she's kidding, and they laugh. She then yanks the Dr. Pepper from the fridge and starts walking to his room. He follows with the Coke and opener.

"Nice records," she says, leafing through his collection. Then, "Omigod! You've got the new Beach Boys album! Can we play it?"

"It's too fast," he says.

"Too fast," she says. "I see. Not the right mood for seduction."

He bounces down on his bed, a narrow affair of quilt and maple, which he's already outgrown. "Join me?"

"So what happened to sacred?"

"I want you with me in this bed," he says. "You want to be with me in this bed. Why are we even talking about it?"

"You're right, Tino. We shouldn't have to talk about it. You already know." She sits next to him. "Because if I lie down with you, our bodies will rub together, and we'll get crazy, and then I'll make us stop. And then you'll be angry at me for good reason. Because I will have let us start."

He sits up. "How can you know so much?"

"I read a lot."

"You know you'll get crazy?"

"Yes."

"Even though you've had no experience—"

"I think about it, Tino. Just like you."

"You think about our being naked together?"

"I'm not answering that question."

"So that's a yes."

"It's not going to happen, Tino, so talking about it just makes it worse."

He laughs, jumps out of bed, and pulls her up with him. "I agree," he says, takes her by the shoulders, and kisses her on the mouth.

She looks as if she might change her mind about the whole lying-down-together thing, when he says, "So let's drink our sodas, listen to the Beach Boys, and watch each other being good."

❖

Alec arrives home late from Cleveland. He missed his scheduled return flight. As he was leaving the Allis-Benoit building, Rilesman caught up with him, reality having dawned. Whatever their differences, lunch with Curtis was not a date either of them could blow off. Hours later, bad weather over LaGuardia kept his plane in the air for an extra hour before forcing a landing in Philadelphia. Alec then spent almost two hours getting to and sitting in the railroad terminal, before boarding a train to New York. It's close to midnight when he opens the door to his apartment. Nonetheless, Jesse is waiting up.

"You shouldn't have," he says, by way of greeting.

"We didn't have a chance to talk last night."

"Nor will we now, Jess. I'm pretty wiped."

"Just a word," she says.

He drops into the wing chair in the living room, loosening his tie. She takes the sofa, tightening the sash to her bathrobe. He looks at her with resignation. There's actually no one he'd rather be talking to, if he must talk. And he already knows that. As tired as he is. *And it's not, dammit, because you look like your sister.* But she's plainly keyed up to talk about something else.

She says, "I had to leave that job. I had no place else to go but here. I'll move out as soon as I can."

"What did he do, Stashinsky? Proposition you?" Her expression confirms it, and Alec's laugh is dry. "Little early, even for him."

"I know you warned me."

"Which makes it worse, sorry."

"He apparently considers himself irresistible," she says.

"What he is—"

"I know what he is," she says with a twist to her mouth. "And no doubt should have seen it coming."

"All right," he says. "You're here now with absolutely no pressure to move out. Stay until you find something you really want.

Independent film is ready to get hot in New York. You'll land someplace."

"There are lots of jobs. They pay nothing."

"So take one anyway," he says. "Learn the scene, meet the people. Stay on here a little longer. And I know why you're thinking no, but the fact is—you see how I work. I'm almost never home. What time I have is devoted to Sarah, and she needs me less and less. She probably needs you now more than me."

"Thank you, Alec, but—"

"Just think about it, Jess." He starts to get up.

"Why *do* you work so hard?" she says.

"What?"

"You're working seventy, eighty hours a week. No one does that. Why you?"

He relapses into the chair. "Lots of people do that."

"Constantly? All year long? Maybe lawyers and cab drivers. The cabbies don't love it. Do you?"

"It's awful late for this, Jesse."

"Okay," she says. "Some other time."

He doesn't move. "To do what I like doing as well as I like doing it, I have to work harder than I—or most anyone—would care to work."

"So… just do fewer cases. Lawyers in Dublin—even London—don't work this hard."

"The good ones do. It's the nature of the practice. You either have too many cases or too few."

"So choose the latter."

He laughs and shakes his head sadly.

"Why the hell not?" she says.

"Takes your name off the playbill. Very bad. And, if you're a member of a firm, you have responsibilities to your partners. So can we now go to bed?"

It's slight, her reaction, but a perceptible flinch.

"No worries," he says. "I'm not Stashinsky. I've many faults, but an illusion of irresistibility is not one of them."

"Because you don't think it's an illusion," she says with a faint smile.

"Oh, really?" he says. "While you're standing proof of the opposite fact?"

She closes her eyes for a moment, with a small shake of her head, which he can't quite interpret. Or ask about, much less use to end the conversation. "How do you know about lawyers in Dublin?" he asks instead.

"I lived with one," she says. "For almost a year. It didn't last. It couldn't."

"That was your baggage?"

Her double take is a question.

"First night, when you arrived. You said you had baggage."

"Hmm," she says. "Yeah, that was it. My boyfriend lawyer in Dublin."

"Nice guy?"

"Yeah. He was. Is. I'm sure you'd like him."

"Did you talk about marriage?"

"He did."

"You didn't want to."

"Correct. I did not wish to be married."

"You knew that beforehand?"

"I've known that for… well… never mind." She rises from the chair. "Much too late for this."

"To be continued," he says, also rising.

"No, actually," she says, "this for me is dangerous waters."

'Ah," he says. "Then we won't swim in them. At least, not tonight."

"Good for you," she says, kisses him on the cheek, and leaves the room.

SIXTEEN

Something happened in Cleveland you ought to know about," Alec says to Ben Braddock at eight in the morning.

Braddock puts down his copy of the *New York Law Journal*, which he reads every morning at this time, but leaves his legs propped on the corner of his desk. "What makes you think I ought to know about it?" Braddock says.

"It's your client. They originally came here for you."

"No, they came here for Chauncey Kendall, a hundred years ago. And we don't own clients here. What the hell kind of firm you think this is?"

"Well, you're the head of it," Alec says. "And Allis-Benoit is not likely to be anyone's client here much longer. So you want to know what happened in Cleveland?"

"I already know. Your friend *Larry*"—Braddock pronounces it as if relishing some absurdity—"that's his name, *Larry?*"

"He called?"

"He did," Braddock says. "Very upset. Seems you don't value his judgment."

"That's accurate."

"And you laid down an ultimatum, he tells me."

"I don't think we should be defending a monopolization claim while another firm prosecutes our monopolization counterclaim in the same lawsuit."

"That right?" Braddock says. "We really have a counterclaim?"

"We do. Might even be winnable, if we could afford to go to trial."

"Isn't it a bit late to be filing a new pleading in this case?"

"Newly discovered evidence."

"I see," Braddock says, bringing his feet back down to the

floor. "You're talking about your deposition of Strand."

"Have you read it?"

Braddock grunts. "Of course I read it."

"So you know?"

"I know you've got half a leg to stand on."

Not easy following the twists and turns of the older man's mind. "What about Larry Rilesman?" Alec says.

"What about him?"

"I assume he told you he wants his old firm to handle the claim."

Braddock scoffs. "You think I'd let that twerp bring another firm into this case?"

"Which is what you told him," Alec says, now understanding how that conversation was affecting this one.

"In words you and I would recognize as having that meaning, yes I told him."

"And he's backed down?"

"Of course he's backed down." Braddock swoops up his *Journal,* repositions his legs on the desk, and recommences his morning read. "Jesus Christ, Alec. Whatta you got, jet lag? From Cleveland?"

When Jesse awakes, at 8:30, she feels like a layabout. Alec's already downtown; Sarah's already at school. It propels her to action. *Or was it that conversation last night?* she thinks in the shower. Toweling herself in front of a full-length bathroom mirror, she thinks, *Look what he's missing.* Then at breakfast reflects, *Who am I kidding?* and *Who's missing what?* She's beginning to talk to herself. Aloud, but in short sentences. *Stupid sentences!*

Then, popping bread in the toaster, she declares, as if reciting a monologue, *Being alone in an empty apartment is not a good thing! Especially* his *apartment!*

She butters her toast, spreads jam on it thinly, takes a bite, drinks her coffee, and calls her agent. *I have an agent!*—an exhilarating thought, except when one remembers the agent is a nobody who'd tacked her number to a billboard at the Thalia movie house on West Ninety-Seventh Street. *As desperate as me!* When Jesse first called in response, she got, "I am, in fact, Peggy Goldsmith. Used to be Goldschmitters, but I figured, why not go for the spiffier version?" To date, Peggy's "representation" has been unrewarding. She did put an ad in *The Village Voice* that listed clients, including Jesse, but that supreme effort, thus far, has yielded nothing, which is hardly surprising.

Peggy remains cheerfully optimistic, however, even after not remembering Jesse's name at the outset of this morning's call. "I do have something, a possible assistant director job," she says. "There's a man who worked for Cassavetes on *Minnie and Moskowitz*. Can't recall off the top of my head what he did for *John*"—she pauses for emphasis on her implied acquaintance with the noted director—"but he's starting his own project and might need an AD."

"So you haven't actually talked to him?" Jesse says.

"Not actually, no."

"You what—read about this in *Variety*?"

"Not *Variety*, no. Not quite that established a publication. But he must have some money for the project. He has an office in the Brill Building."

After collecting the man's name and address, Jesse is there within the half hour. The famous Brill Building on Broadway. With its splendid ebony and gold art deco front and lobby. From the 1930s through the 1960s, piano sounds erupted from every room, since Tin Pan Alley, at least in spirit, had moved into its halls. In 1973, it still houses music publishers, but with a fringe invasion by producers of films. Including Justin Jankowski, who occupies a cubbyhole on the seventh floor, with a desk, a phone, and a wary expression, the latter worn on a pale and weary face, which is also unshaven. "Who are you?" he asks, his expression unchanged, as Jesse peeks through the door.

"My name is Jesse Madigan, Mr. Jankowski." She boldly steps in. "I'm an assistant director, recently with the Ardmore Studios, which is the largest film producer in Ireland. My agent said you're starting a new project, and I've come to see whether you might be interested in someone of my credentials." All rehearsed in the subway, and Jesse is pleased the way it came out, but Jankowski's reaction is not encouraging.

"You a bill collector?"

"No, I just said—"

"They're very clever now. Sending a beautiful young woman like yourself would be entirely the sort of thing they would do."

"I can assure you—"

"You just did. And I believe you. And I don't know you from Adam, but I'm prepared to give you some advice. Would you like some advice?"

"About the film business?" she says. "From you? Very much, please."

"Then, sit down."

There's one chair, and she takes it. He's a worn-down-looking man in his late fifties, with cheeks sunken beneath the overgrowth of beard. "You've hit me at an excellent time," he says. "Not for a job—I don't have one to offer. But for wisdom. Are you open to wisdom?"

"Always," she says.

"I'm inclined to impart it, because I'm bitter, and I like an audience for my bile. More fresh-faced the better—and yours, my dear, looks quintessentially naive."

"That's probably an accurate reflection," she says.

"No compliment intended."

"None received."

"I have no job to offer you, or anyone," he says. "Indeed, I'm firing those I previously overzealously hired, because my

project—insidious term in this business, *project*; insidious because it implies a venture capable of taking on life—my *project*
has gone down the toilet. Which is a crude term, but apt. Let
me assure you, *apt!* Especially for this *business*." He throws his
hands up. "I keep using that word, business. There is no business.
Not in New York. There are bands of desperate people prowling
the streets. They have no money, and no one will give them any
to make their films. Their precious film *projects*. So, like drug
addicts, they drain their relatives. Or take shitty jobs and hoard
their pennies. Then steal locations and shoot on the cheap in
sixteen millimeter, even eight millimeter, natural lighting or floor
lamps, camera sound or no sound. And they don't want you. Ireland means nothing here. They want people who can give them
money, or the *name* actor—which is the holy grail. Which will
get the great *New York Times* to condescend to recognize the quality of a film and put tushies in the seats if, by some miracle, you
get a theater to take it. Or take your money to four-wall it."

"People do succeed at this," she says.

"Here?" He laughs at the notion, then turns on her a serious
face. "What's your dream? You want to be an AD all your life?"

"Of course not."

"Of course not," he repeats. "You want to be an *auteur!*" He
gives the word a flurry of fingers.

"I'd like to make films of my own, yes."

"Okay." Now businesslike. "So here are the ways to do that.
The easiest, of course, is to have your own money. Like Cassave-
tes, who made a lot as an actor, then poured it all into *Minnie*.
You got any money?"

"I'm afraid not."

"Didn't think so. Do you have any friends who are rich or
famous?"

Slight hesitation. "No."

"You had to think about that?"

"No," she says. "There's no one."

"And you have no friends in the business, or you wouldn't be here."

"Correct."

"There's a group now… out of film school, NYU… tight little community. They're pooling their talents, resources; low-cost films with fresh 'method' actors. You know any of these people? They're near your age or just a bit younger than you."

"No."

"Right," he says. "You were in Ireland. But I'm sure one of them would take you on as a lover. Or trade a job for a night in his bed. Get you a PA gig, or maybe a second-second. For which you will be paid exactly nothing."

"I'm a damn good first assistant director," Jesse says evenly. "I've already been a PA. And a second-second."

"Not here. And so what? You don't know people here. People who matter. They're having a tough enough time. Why would they let you in? What do you have to offer? There are hundreds like you. Who also didn't go to the right film school with the right people. Who also didn't already do five films here for no pay and suck up to everyone on the set." He reflects. "Or are too old to work for nothing, because they cannot any longer sleep on other people's sofas."

"Like you?" she asks.

"Right. Like me."

"So what will you do?"

"Go west," he says, "of course. What you, with your wonderful fresh face, would probably call selling out."

"I wouldn't actually," she says. "A real job? I'd applaud you."

"And you? How will you cope?"

"I'll hook on somewhere."

"Hook?"

She stands abruptly. "I won't be selling my ass, Mr. Jankowski." He laughs. "Good girl. I wish the best for you."

"Thank you," she says.

"I did mean to frighten you."

"I know."

"Didn't succeed, though, did I?"

"I was born frightened, Mr. Jankowski."

"Best state to be in," he says. "Especially for this *business.*"

It's 4:30 in the afternoon. Sarah is on the carpet, unloading her book bag; Cissy is lounging on Sarah's bed. They're talking about sex—Cissy's favorite subject.

"So you two do it yet?" Cissy asks.

"No-o," Sarah says, her voice rising in umbrage at the question.

"You were alone in his apartment and you didn't score?"

"No, Cissy. Neither one of us *scored.*"

"So what did you do? You let him touch your boobs?"

"Jesus, Cissy!"

"Hand jobs?"

"We didn't have sex, all right? What is it with you? You talk as if you're the Lolita of the Upper East Side. You're not even experienced."

"That's what you think."

"I think it," Sarah says, "because if you'd done it, you would've told me. You couldn't have waited to tell me."

"I didn't think you were ready," Cissy says.

"To what? Hear about how you let Fergy Campbell put his hand on your ass under your panties?"

"Did I tell you that?"

"You know damn well you did."

"Well, that was nothing. I've known Fergy since I was six. He actually lived across the street from me in London."

"So what are you saying?" Sarah says. "You're no longer a virgin?"

"No. Technically I am."

"Technically?"

"There were these two guys I met at a party last week."

"*Two* guys?"

"From Princeton, yeah. Beautiful guys. We were, you know, drinking, smoking—"

"You're smoking now too?"

"Everyone smokes at these parties."

"What… were you smoking?"

"You know."

"No," Sarah says firmly. "I don't."

"A little pot."

"Oh, Cissy."

"Well, you've done that! You told me!"

"Twice," Sarah says. "Made me weird. And I told you so you wouldn't."

"Anyway," Cissy says, brushing that aside, "we were, you know, just talking, listening to records, off in some bedroom in this huge apartment. There was a wonderful mood—dreamy, sexy—which made me realize that I really wanted to fool around. Also, I had the power, these guys were so turned on. So I'm lying on the bed, and I kind of squish down a bit and let my skirt ride up a bit. Then I watch them watching me. Two guys, mouths open, gaping at my legs." Cissy laughs. "You dig this?"

"They might have raped you."

"I know," Cissy says. "They might have. That was definitely part of the thrill. And I was playing that too. Staying ahead of them. I mean, God, we were *all* so fucking hot! I said, 'I see you guys looking. Tell you what—you get up, and you strip. I'll watch. Then I'll let you watch me.' It was like someone else was saying those things. I couldn't believe it was me."

"And they did what you said?"

"Like a shot."

"And you did too?"

"Every stitch."

"And then you let them have sex with you?"

"I did stuff to them. They did stuff to me. They started putting on rubbers, I finally got scared, so I grabbed my clothes, found a bathroom, got dressed, and got out of there. The funniest thing was how the elevator operator looked at me as if nothing had happened. And you know, it really hadn't. It was fun. We were just playing around. It didn't mean a thing."

Sarah says nothing. She considers whether Cissy has just made up the whole story, and then thinks, *The way she told that story: If she hasn't done it, she wants to and will.*

Cissy says, "So you've done nothing like that with Tino?"

"No." Flatly.

"But you will?"

"Not like that, no," Sarah says.

"Like what? When?"

"When it means something. And it's not just play."

Sarah, still in her school uniform, is eating alone at the kitchen island when Jesse walks in. "Mind if I join you?" Jess says.

"Great." Sarah pushes her Caesar salad and chair over a bit to make room.

Jesse unwraps her own salad from a Madison Avenue emporium. "Good day?" she asks as she settles in next to her niece.

"You know," Sarah says, "you don't have to do that."

"Do what?"

"Pay a fortune for some takeout at a local hold-up shop. We have plenty of food here. Amelia, the maid, does all the shopping. Just tell her what you like."

"That's a bit awkward, Sarah."

"You think Alec cares about food money?"

"You're his daughter."

"And what?" Sarah says. "You're no relation? You should know, Alec is the most generous man alive. He'd be terribly offended if he learned you were buying your own food."

Jesse puts down her plastic fork. "So we won't tell him, right?"

"Jesus!" Sarah says, staring at her aunt's plate. "You won't even use our silverware. That's ridiculous, Jess."

Jesse groans. "I've got to move out of here."

"Move out?" Sarah exclaims.

"I really have to."

"What did I say?"

"It's the situation, Sarah."

"What situation?" Sarah cries out, clattering her own knife and fork to the tiles of the counter.

They stare at each other, equally bewildered by the outburst, until Sarah, embarrassed, lowers her eyes. "What about me?" she says.

"You'll be wonderful. As always."

"No, I won't," Sarah says, and her eyes, involuntarily, start tearing.

"Omigod," Jesse says, and wraps her arms around her niece.

Sarah pulls away, rubbing at her eyes. "I don't know where that came from."

"No?" Jesse says. "You're home alone here every night. I come along, and I'm company. Then I talk about leaving."

"You're more than company."

"Yes, that's true. I love you. But I can do that from another apartment."

"We could take one together," Sarah says.

"Oh, Alec would thank me for that."

"So you know the easy solution."

"Yes," Jesse says. "I do. We all do. The one that's easy, obvious, and not good."

"I know you like him," Sarah says.

"Of course I like him."

"And he likes you. That's obvious too."

"Yes." Jesse frowns. "Even to me."

"So I know what you think is the problem, and I think it's ridiculous, but I'll shut up."

"Good idea."

"Not," Sarah says emphatically.

Jesse kisses her on the cheek and goes for a silver fork in the kitchen drawer. "But I won't move out tomorrow. How's that?"

"It's better," Sarah says, "than your opening position."

"You sound like a lawyer."

"Wonder where that comes from?"

"Okay, then," Jesse says, returning to her salad. "Let's talk about you."

"We've done that."

"Insufficiently."

"It's a dreary subject," Sarah says.

"And why's that?"

"Usual teenage angst. Sex, no sex, that sort of thing."

"You're being pressured?" Jesse asks.

"Not by Tino. Of course he wants to. So do I. But if you remember, it's not so simple at my age. And he's a goddamn saint. Doesn't make it any easier."

Jesse stops eating. "I'm hardly the one to give advice on this subject, but what I know—think I know—is this. Pretty much everyone wants to have sex with the right person. But there are actually only two kinds of right people. There's the kind it's just fun to have sex with and who gives you no grief about it. And there's the kind you love so much, you can't bear not to. It's a necessary deepening of that love. At your age, I don't think the first kind is a good idea, and I'm not sure you can be ready for the second kind."

Sarah says sharply, "So, you're saying, basically, my only option is no."

"Sarah…" Jesse puts her hand to her mouth. "I hope I don't

sound like I'm preaching. Just follow your heart."

"Unlike you," Sarah says.

And Jesse laughs. "Yes, maybe."

SEVENTEEN

It starts midmorning with a call from Cadigan Breen. "Alec. Can you drop everything, get up here right now?"

"What the hell's happening?"

"It's bad. Client's in my office. Just get here."

Flagging a cab on the street, Alec lands at their meeting in twenty-five minutes. Walking in on a session of gloom. Until then in Alec's experience, Caddy Breen, quick with an impish smile, had always borne the look of an engaging adolescent. He was also a lawyer who treated good news and bad with infectious humor and charmed every client in sight. But gone from his face now is any trace of bonhomie. And absent is any charmed client. Instead, prominently seated in Breen's office and equally glum is a spindly older man with a pinched face and combed thin hair. Breen introduces him as Edison Electric's general counsel, Standish Moore, and rattles off the names of Moore's two associates. Serious men dealing with a nasty turn of events, and they look it.

Alec says, "So let's hear it."

"Well," Moore says, "I'm about to retire. And though it's not a very well-known fact, somehow word of it reached your judge, Hal Richardson."

Sensing where this is going, Alec lowers himself into a comfortable chair, as if he expects to be there a while.

"Last night, he called me at home," Moore continues. "No idea how he got the number. I've never met the fellow. It took him a while to get to the point, but what he wanted was for me to give my job to a friend of his, the assistant general counsel of Pharmex."

"His old client," Alec says. "And yes, I remember the guy—pleasant, capable enough, but, at the moment, that's not particularly relevant."

"No," Moore says. "It's not."

"And what did you tell him?" Alec asks.

"That my successor had already been chosen."

"And was that the end of the conversation?"

"Not quite," Moore says. "Richardson took the news badly, but it was obvious he was drunk."

"Doesn't help," Alec says. "If Richardson had no connection whatever to Edison Electric, that call would have been improper. It would look like a federal judge using the influence of the court to extract a favor for a friend. Since he's actually sitting on your biggest case, the ethical violation was so stupidly flagrant that only drunkenness might explain it—but obviously not excuse it."

"Right," Breen pronounces. "That's what I said before you got here. So the question is, do we have to inform Freddy Musselman of the call?"

Alec gives Caddy a sour smile.

Moore says, "No one is likely ever to hear of this. I'm sure Richardson regrets what he did. And when he's sober, he's an excellent judge."

"He's biased, Stan," Breen says. "Happens to be biased our way, which, I grant you, is a unique experience for us—but he hasn't left us with any choice. You agree, Alec?"

"Sorry, Stan," Alec says. "Caddy's right, and it's not a close question. We violate our own ethical rules if we sit on it."

Breen nods and presses his intercom. "Get me Musselman on the phone." He stares at his client, who says nothing.

Alec says, "Stop the call."

Hesitating only briefly, Breen does just that. Then looks at Alec for an explanation.

"Let's call chambers instead. Set up a conference for later today or tomorrow. Then tell Freddy."

"Okay," Caddy says, "but what's the point?"

"You care who we call first?"

"It's the same difference to me."

"Then trust me," Alec says.

After school, Sarah and Tino lie in her bedroom, amidst soft coverings but few girlish things. They wear their school clothes, which Tino evidently finds uncomfortable.

"No," she says, placing her hand on his.

He ceases the unbuttoning and pushes away from her in the small bed.

"Now you're angry," she says. "Classic."

"I'm not angry," he says. "You're not ready. You've warned me. I should have known."

She sits up. "Jesse will be back."

He gets up on one elbow. "That's the reason?"

She says nothing.

"And what?" he says. "She'll just barge into your room?"

"No, she's cool."

"Then… what?"

"Then… nothing. You're right. I'm not ready."

He takes a moment, then says, "I will never force you, or push you, or make you do anything you'll regret."

"Good."

"So maybe I should leave."

She blows out her cheeks. "I don't want you to leave."

"Okay," he says with resignation, and lies back. He doesn't wish to leave either.

It's an old building, and they listen to the radiators lisp.

"So," she says, "you've done this with lots of girls?"

"I haven't done *this* with anyone."

"All the other girls just let you do anything you wanted?"

"That's not what I meant," he says, and hoists up again. "The sex thing doesn't really matter for us. It will come."

"Oh, yes?"

"Definitely," he says. "In time. Naturally."

"You know this, of course, from your worlds of experience."

"It hasn't been *worlds*."

"But you've had sex," she says. "The actual doing of the thing."

"Yes."

She lies back. "How many girls?"

He holds up a fist, then unfurls three fingers.

She says in a rising voice, "Three girls?"

He raises his pinky belatedly.

"Four!" she exclaims.

"It was just sex. And before I met you."

"But multiple times with each one?"

"More than once," he says. "With three."

She elbows up too, so they are now face-to-face. "The problem as I see it," she says, "is this inequality of experience. Maybe I should have sex with four guys, and then you and I could get started."

"Not funny."

"Of course, you could teach me," she says in a derisive tone. "You'd like that, wouldn't you?"

"You're making fun of something I'm not sure you understand."

She says, "The fact that I haven't done it before doesn't mean I don't know how it's done."

"I'm not talking about the… mechanics of the thing."

"Oh, I see," she says. "You mean the spiritual adventure of letting a boy shove his erect penis into me."

He lifts himself from the bed. "I'm going."

She watches him hunt for his shoes, find them, sit back on the bed to put them on.

She says, "I was right, after all. The problem is you're experienced, and I'm not. I've never even let a boy see me without my clothes on."

"Bodies are bodies," he says.

"That's not true! I've seen lots of other girls naked, and, believe me, there's tons of differences. I'm sure it's the same for boys."

"You'd be shocked to learn, probably, how little that means after the first time."

"Really?" she says with a show of innocent surprise.

"Yes. Really."

"Okay," she says. "So I have a possible solution."

He has his coat in his hand but stands waiting. Sarah lying on the bed, with her school skirt rucked up, still, obviously, affects him.

"What's the plan, Sarah?"

"See, you're entirely more comfortable with this thing than I am, so to even it out...." She looks at him expectantly.

"Yes?" he says with growing impatience.

"You take all your clothes off. Right there. And I'll watch."

"Just like that?"

"Just like that."

"And then you'll take your clothes off?"

"Maybe."

"*Maybe?* You think that's fair?"

"Fair?" she says. "Hmm. Good thought. One should be fair. So this is a test! Does he trust her to be fair, or doesn't he?"

More radiator music.

He tosses his coat on a chair, kicks off his shoes, and lifts his T-shirt over his head.

Her impulse, when he gets to his jeans, is to stop him. But the jeans come down with a thrust, dragging the boxer shorts with them, get stepped out of and kicked to one side. This boy's body in her room, naked and exclamatory, is a miracle.

She's far from being in a trance but rises as if she were. She places her hand on his chest and her lips on his mouth. Then says, "So you did trust me."

"Yes."

Squirming to get free, she squeals, "Shouldn't have!"

Her problem is his arms encircling her waist. Then his fingers undoing her blouse, her bra, her skirt.

She kisses him and clings. She thinks her body is ordinary, compared to his. "Should we stop here?"

"Is that what you want?" he says.

"Ah, want."

"So, I've got a better idea," he says.

"I bet you do."

"But I could stop," he says.

"*Stop?*"

"I don't *have* to."

"Are you prepared?" It sounded breathless, even to her.

"I'm always prepared."

"Yeah," she says. "I thought you might be." She leads him to her bed and sits to observe him fish out the small package and go through his "preparations."

He gives her a self-conscious look, as if to say, *Do you really have to watch this?*

She says, "It's my first time, Tino. I don't want to miss anything."

Sal Angiapello takes a turn around the rink. He's still capable of some flourishes and enjoys exhibiting his skill. One of his lieutenants, Lou DiBrazzi, watches from behind the dasher board. DiBrazzi, a protégé of Sal's, is just forty, but now on the rise. Thus far he's been loyal, as well as ruthless and smart, although he sometimes seems more sadistic than brutal, and possibly too independent. So Sal has a test in mind. It would give Lou the opportunity to prove he recognizes the line—and has the sense to stay clear of it.

Sal picks up speed on the ice. He makes a bracket turn that resolves into a waltz jump, swishing up to DiBrazzi at the barrier. *Not bad for an old man,* Sal thinks, *even if a bit cheated.* "Walk with me," Sal says as he clumps off on his skates to the locker room.

He won't shower; he's barely raised a sweat. Quickly, he changes into his street clothes and slips on his custom-made shoes as Lou scouts the room.

"No one's here, Sal."

Sal nods toward the door. "It's okay, we're leaving."

On the street, Sal says, "Don't trust that place."

"The Skating Club of New York?" says DiBrazzi, showing surprise.

"Wired up the gazoo. At least since I became a member."

They walk a while, Sal's car and driver following. With skates, Sal was DiBrazzi's height; now considerably shorter. But Sal is used to commanding men of greater physical stature. In his world, no one has greater stature than Sal.

"I have a job for you," Sal says. "To do it discreetly, quietly, will require great skill."

"Then I am honored," Lou says.

Sal further appraises the man as they walk. He's always doing this. With everyone. What he sees in DiBrazzi is a strong six-footer, with rough features, who has learned to hide his muscular frame in Italian tailored suits and pay more than $100 a week to a master barber for the maintenance of his thick black hair. He has also patterned himself after Sal in speech and manner. A definite mark in his favor.

"Did you know Phil Anwar?" Sal asks.

"Of him, sure. We never met."

"I want you to meet his daughter."

DiBrazzi says nothing, waiting for the more to come.

Sal signals the driver to pull to the curb. With his hand on the door handle, he says, "She's sixteen. You'll take her on a trip. I think to the island. You'll stay with her. Obedience training, but no scars."

"And then?"

"Then we'll see. But I think we'll put her in trade. A rental, however, not a sale."

"You know, I've run some figures on that."

"Really," Sal says, getting in the car and gesturing for DiBrazzi to follow. "Office," he says to the driver and closes the glass partition between them. Turning to Lou as they speed off, "And yes, the figures?"

"A well-negotiated sale to the right buyer for a girl's first entry into trade brings a higher return than a long string of rentals."

"I've no doubt. In the ordinary case."

"This will not be ordinary, of course," DiBrazzi says, musingly. "Anwar's daughter."

"Right."

"So the first rental?"

"Also no scars."

"*That*," says DiBrazzi, "drastically limits the market."

"The market, Lou, is quite incidental to our purposes here."

"I understand. You just want her broken."

"Not in pieces," Sal says. "Merely compliant."

"I see." DiBrazzi rubs his cheek. "Yes. I may have just the right man."

Sal looks at his suddenly eager subordinate, who beams back at him.

Sal shakes his head, no.

"I can do this," DiBrazzi says.

"Some other girl. Not this one."

EIGHTEEN

Frederick Musselman pushes a distinguished old man in a wheelchair into Judge Richardson's outer office. Alec recognizes this personage; so does Cadigan Breen. Karol Stash walks in Musselman's train, preening like a cat with a mouse in its paws. It's Stanley Fuld they're now brandishing, former chief judge of the highest court in the state system, the New York Court of Appeals. Judge Fuld nods to those waiting—he knows them both—and Judge Richardson's secretary announces that all have arrived.

They are ushered into chambers at once, word evidently having been communicated to Judge Richardson beforehand that the celebrated jurist would be joining them. Richardson is up immediately to greet him. Fuld says, "You'll excuse my not rising. It's the gout. Freddy has been good enough to push me about, and into your chambers."

The meeting commences without further exchange. Everyone knows why they've been assembled. Caddy states the facts simply. Richardson acknowledges the call he made to the Edison Electric general counsel. "I was simply trying to do a friend a favor," he says, and then shocks everyone by beginning to weep. "Of course I will recuse myself"—barely heard through the sobs.

It's over almost before it begins.

The visitors make their way out of chambers, Frederick Musselman suppressing a smile, Alec and Caddy genuinely somber. Fuld hadn't uttered a word on the merits. He didn't have to. He'd done his job: Moses flashing the tablets. The plaintiff's team goes off to celebrate. Alec and Caddy are left standing on the courthouse steps.

"You wanted this," Breen says.

"I did."

"And you thought that Freddy, with more time to think about it, would let Richardson off the hook."

"Might have. You said it yourself. Freddy is smart, but not quick."

"And maybe I'm the same," Breen says. "Why is this good for us? Hal Richardson would have handed us the case."

Alec's in a rush, but he allows a Checker cab to drop passengers and leave. "After a trial, sure," he says. "Temporarily. With an opinion full of holes, easily reversible. But I keep saying it, Caddy. We really don't want to try this case. And we can't settle it without paying off every other public utility. We want Donald Strand to drop it, walk away. And for that we probably need not only the counterclaim, but a good judge. One that Strand respects. Who's willing to tell him not only that his main case sucks, but that he's in trouble on the claim against him."

"What're the odds?" Breen says. "Getting a judge like that? Coming off the wheel? One in thirty?"

"We're not on the wheel, Caddy. Two straight recusals in a conspicuous case like this? Looks bad. For the institution."

"So we're getting who? Eddie Weinfeld?"

"Too obvious," Alec says.

"That we're off the wheel."

"Right."

"So who?"

"Charlie Metzner. Most underrated judge on the court. No flamboyance. No reaching for headlines. Indifferent to limelight. Arrives every day, does his job, and basically does it better than most anyone."

Breen searches Alec's face. "You know something?"

"Same facts you do."

"Then this is crazy, Alec. You're reaching for a fucking inside straight."

"Yeah. Right. That's what we're doing. Because"—and Alec opts to return it with Breen's emphasis—"we have no *fucking* alternative."

"So by now she loves you?" Sal asks.

"We love each other," Tino says.

"That's nice," Sal responds, as if soothing someone of diminished capacity. "So when's the wedding?"

Tino takes a seat on the sofa. He feels the colors in his uncle's living room: variations of blue with highlights of pale gray. Cool, like Tino's mood, the boy having been confronted after practice, and driven here, by a lurking hood named Lou DiBrazzi.

Tino forces a laugh. "We're a few years away from that."

"Yes?" Sal says. "How many years?"

It has the tone of a serious question, chilling Tino even more. "I have no doubt we will marry, Uncle. Probably when she graduates from college."

"That's what? Six years from now?"

"Should be, yes. Unless she goes to graduate school."

"Graduate school! Wonderful! So much schooling. You need your wife to be so educated?"

"It's not a question of what *I* need, Uncle. Women today—"

"Yes, yes." Sal laughs good-naturedly. It's all been a fine joke. "I know, dear boy, I know. Times have changed. I'm hopelessly old-fashioned. We'll just deal with it."

Will we? thinks Tino, who already resents the way he was brought here. And that condescending tone! For years, Tino realizes, while trying to please his uncle, he has felt like a swimmer enmeshed in weeds. And now, suddenly, he is streaming free. What has happened to him and, he thinks, to Sarah, is that they have thrown off the traces of childhood. Also, for the first time in his life, he has someone to protect. It's a fierce sensation. And the man whom he once regarded as his surrogate father is mocking him. Is becoming his enemy. His worst and most fearful enemy. Because Sal's evil is now pointed at Sarah. "Deal with what?" Tino says in a controlled voice.

"We'll be patient," Sal says. "It is, after all, no less than I expected. The long game. We'll play the long game. Best for everyone, eh?"

"You're referring to—"

"The restoring of her fortune to the family, yes," Sal says.

"I've told you, Uncle, we are very much in love. What you want will happen naturally."

"As I said. Let the natural come to pass. And now, dear boy, I've others to see. Lou will drive you home."

"I'd rather walk, Uncle, but thank you."

"As you wish, but take care of yourself. You are very important to me."

Downstairs, blown by a sudden wind he barely notices, Tino lurches out of that building and struggles into the night. He needs to warm himself against the chilling implied threat of that meeting. He will say nothing of it to Sarah. But he will track down Alec as soon as he can.

Jesse is in Alec's kitchen with the ingredients for an omelet spread out before her on the countertop next to the stove. She is not thinking about the omelet; she is thinking about Sarah and her surprising outburst the evening before last; she's thinking about allowing herself, still, to be in this apartment; she's thinking about Alec, which, for her, is like thinking about gravity. *Which is close to insane! And all the more reason I should not allow myself to be in this apartment.*

As she finally starts cooking the omelet, Alec walks in.

"You're early," she sings out.

"Eight thirty? I guess, yeah. Smells good."

"Take it," she says, pointing him to a seat at the kitchen island. "There are plenty of eggs. And there's toast." She shoves the place setting to him, lowers the plated omelet on it, and breaks another two eggs in the bowl.

"This is excellent," he says. "What's in it?"

"Herbs, a very good cheddar, and parsley. Simple."

She flips her omelet in the pan, gives it a few seconds, scoops it onto her own plate, and sits across from him at the island. They eat silently for a moment.

"Some wine?" she says.

"Sure."

She retrieves from the fridge an uncorked bottle of sauvignon blanc and pours out two glasses.

"So," she says, "tell me about your day."

He laughs. "Our domestic routine."

"No, I'd really like to know about your day. Why coming home at this hour is early. Why you hadn't the time to eat dinner. Why you have no idea where your daughter is. Why—"

"Where is she?"

"Out with Tino."

"He called my office," Alec says.

"Oh, yes?"

"He wants to see me. I told him—at least my secretary did; I was on another call—to come by tomorrow."

"Alec," she says, with some impatience, "your daughter's boyfriend calls you at the office. That's very unusual. You couldn't find a minute to see what he wanted?"

"He was told I would, if it were urgent. He said it could wait."

"Okay."

He stops eating and looks at her. "You're building a case?"

"No," she says. "Really, no. I'd like to understand. I want to know what you do all day. Why it's so pressured. Like today."

"I think I know why Tino is calling. Nothing for you to worry about."

"Then I won't."

He puts down his fork. "What I do," he says. "Today is typical. Planned one way, went another."

"So tell me."

"You know who's the biggest computer company in the world?"

"U.S. Computer Corp.?"

"So you know the government is suing to break them up?"

"I didn't know that, no."

"Well, they are. One of my partners is handling the case. This morning he grabs me and tells me what's going on. He needs me to help him. I don't really have time. Then I run off to court. Judge on my case—another big antitrust case—recuses himself."

"Why?" she asks. "What did he do?"

"Something stupid. Anyway, I get back, tell the client what happened. That plus the court conference eats up most of the morning. I try to get to some of the other fourteen cases I'm supposed to be handling when the phone rings, changes everything. You've heard of Telemarch News?"

"Of course."

"But you probably didn't know they own a book publishing company."

"Do they?" she says, trying to show interest

"Or that that company published *The French Connection*— the book on which the movie was based."

She shakes her head.

"Anyway, the call was from the general counsel. He says they're being sued for libel by a guy named Henry Lowenberg. I say, 'Who's that?' He says, 'A criminal lawyer in town, and he'll call you in ten minutes.' Next thing I know, a copy of the complaint is delivered to my desk along with a copy of the book. I see that the author, Robin Moore, has written that Henry Lowenberg, during the course of a criminal trial, feigned a nervous breakdown to get a mistrial for his client. If that's false, it's defamatory. It accuses a lawyer of an unethical act. Damages could be substantial. Then the phone rings. It's Lowenberg. He says, 'I'm having my medical records sent to you from New York Presbyterian. Then we'll talk.' Medical records arrive. Seems that Lowenberg is an epileptic. And on the day in question—when, according to Robin Moore, he feigned a nervous breakdown—Lowenberg had a seizure and was taken from court to the hospital. So then I called Robin Moore. Said, 'Where the hell did you get this story?' He said, 'From my researcher, who said he got it from the judge on the case in Brooklyn, Samuel Leibowitz.' Who was once the most famous criminal defense lawyer in New York and is now a state Supreme Court judge. So I called Judge Leibowitz. He said he never met or talked to Robin Moore's researcher, and that Henry Lowenberg was one of the finest lawyers of his acquaintance. 'In fact,' he added, 'I know about his libel suit, and I plan to testify on Lowenberg's behalf.' So now it's serious. I call my researcher, Harvey Grand, whom you'd probably call an investigator. He calls back end of day. 'Lowenberg's clean,' he says. 'I could dig deeper.' I say, 'Hold off.' "

"So what will you do?"

"Don't know yet. I'm having lunch with Lowenberg tomorrow. Anyway, after all that—"

"It's okay," Jesse says. "I get it. You're crazy busy."

"Pays the rent."

"I'm sure," she says, and starts clearing dishes. "Let's clean up and do something fun. Like watch television."

"I have a television set?"

"Yes, Alec, you have a television set. It's in the living room in a cabinet with doors, so you might not have noticed it."

"I'm kidding, of course. I watch it almost every election night."

"Meaning every four years?"

"Well, I've missed one or two."

"Ed Sullivan?"

"Who's he?"

"You represent a television network, and you don't know who Ed Sullivan is?"

He shrugs.

She says, "You're kidding again."

"Yes. I am. And his show has been off the air for a year and a half. But tonight there's a play on. *Harvey.* With Jimmy Stewart."

"You know this?"

"I came home to see it. Hopefully with you."

"You *are* human," she says.

"Sometimes."

NINETEEN

Alec calls in his team. When a small group of people meet often in the same room, they generally arrange themselves in the same places. Three chairs face Alec's desk. Trevor Joffrey, the senior associate, camps in the middle. Next senior, Stanley Woolscraft, flanks to his right; and the junior, Rick Smollet, drapes himself in the third chair, pulled back a bit from the arc.

Alec says, "We need an economics expert."

"Now?" It's Stanley Woolscraft, who tends to be cautious.

"I assume you don't mean as a witness," Trevor Joffrey says. "Assuming we still have the plan to try to end the case before it goes to trial."

"Still the plan," Alec says. "And this is in aid of it. *If* we find an economist who can help."

"You mean to worry them—Musselman and Strand?"

"Why not?" Alec says. "And there's one economist I know of who can do that. George Stigler. Nobel Prize winner. From your school, University of Chicago."

Rick Smollet chimes in. "I know Stigler. He was visiting at Princeton when I was there. He hates litigation. Makes a point of avoiding it. Absolutely refuses to participate."

"A well-known fact, yes. Up to now. Which is why he'd worry Musselman if he signed on with us, and additionally why we should want him. You say you know him, Rick?"

"Sorry. Know of him."

Trevor says, "I took his class. Not sure he'd remember me."

"Seminar?

"It was, yes."

"He'll remember you." Alec picks up the phone. Says to his secretary, "George Stigler, professor of economics, University of Chicago."

While they're waiting, Trevor says, "You've given her the number?"

"She'll find it."

"He'll take your call?"

"We're about to find out," Alec says.

In another two minutes, his secretary's voice on the box, "Professor Stigler on one."

Alec pushes that button. "Professor Stigler, this is Alec Brno from a law firm in New York called Kendall, Blake, Steele & Braddock. I'm sitting here with a former student of yours, Trevor Joffrey, who thinks you won't remember him."

"I remember him," Stigler says. "I'm not entirely addled... yet. Besides, I gave him an A."

"You remember your A students?"

"Naturally."

Trevor says, "Hi, professor. Good to hear your voice."

"Hi to you, Trevor. I even remember voices. So what can I do for you?"

Alec says, "Trevor and I are representing Allis-Benoit in an antitrust case brought against them by Mid-Atlantic Power & Light."

"I know the case, yes. You want me to testify. Answer's no, sorry."

"Sounds like I'm not the first one to have called you."

"And I gave them the same answer."

Alec says, "I'm actually sorry you did. You are the authority on the issues we're litigating."

"So you're simply a seeker of truth?"

"Truth, in this case, will end it. Before there's even a trial."

"Sorry, boys. Good luck to you."

"May we come out to see you, professor? I'd be grateful for

ten minutes. For the chance to explain why you would want to state your opinion in this case."

"You'd like to make me a rich man."

"I'm not talking about the fee. The fee will be what you say it is. I'm talking about the preservation of more than 60,000 jobs. I'm talking about the national interests involved in not limiting this country to a single domestic manufacturer of heavy electrical equipment. And I'm talking about stopping this case with an affidavit that will say nothing more than you've already written in two of your more famous papers."

After a pause, Stigler says, "You'll be wasting your time, but I have an opening this Friday at 2:30. My office at the university."

"Thank you," Alec says. "We'll be there." Hanging up, he turns to Rick Smollet. "Whatta you think?"

"He won't do it," Rick says.

"Stanley?"

The young man grimaces. "I'm not sure."

"Trevor?"

"I think you got him."

"He said we'll be wasting our time," Alec notes.

"He said a lot of things. What matters is he's letting us come to his office. Freddy Musselman—I'll bet anything—never got close."

"Yeah," Alec says with a laugh. "That's how I see it. But Rick may be the only hard head in the room."

The Wall Street Club was once an exclusive and all-male association, limited to those of fortune and social rank. As a result, through the years its membership dwindled to an unsustainable level. Its demise became imminent at about the same time Chase Manhattan Bank began planning the erection of One Chase Manhattan Plaza, a few blocks uptown. So the club moved to the

Plaza, took on new members liberally, including women, and, like several other downtown establishments, no longer operated on the street for which it was named.

Alec invited Henry Lowenberg to join him there for lunch. He thought Henry might appreciate the view, which, from the fifty-ninth floor of One Chase, is like a picture map of Manhattan. Emerging from the elevator, Henry turns out to be a jovial man of large frame and features—especially his ears—and silver hair with a ridged-ladder pompadour. Yet he's vigorous in his gestures, firm in his handshake, and unreservedly proud that he looks younger than he is. Almost the first thing he says to Alec is, "You know, I'm seventy-six."

They take a corner table, from which the view is particularly grand, and Alec suggests that Henry order the oysters and Dover sole, which is the daily special. They are served fairly rapidly, but Henry is not to be rushed. He seems to be enjoying the surroundings and the opportunity. Alec is, after all, a captive audience, and Henry has an unending supply of what trial lawyers call "war stories"—revisionist histories of trials they have won. After the eighth or ninth such epic, Alec says, "Henry, even these brief accounts of your victories give me a brilliant idea. You've had a fabulous career. People should know about it. And at your age, prosecuting a libel suit? Waste of time! You should write a book! And I happen to know a company that will publish that book. In fact, I know someone who will help you write it."

It took but a moment for Henry's eyes to gleam. "You could make that happen?"

"Not, of course, with a libel suit hanging over our heads."

"Of course." Henry spreads his hands magnanimously.

"So what do you say?" Alec asks.

"I have a title. Just thought of it. *Until Proven Guilty!*"

"Sounds great."

"Published by your client?"

"That's the thought I had, yes."

"As told to Robin Moore?"

"The very man I had in mind," Alec says. "We have a deal?"

"How many copies?"

"Well, for a first printing—"

"I represent the pipefitters' union," Henry interjects. "Every member will be required to buy a copy of the book. And there are 10,000 members."

"In that case—"

"A minimum of 12,000 copies," Henry insists.

"Which I'll take to my clients with a strong recommendation."

"It's win-win for you guys."

"Henry," says Alec. "I'll even arrange for you to throw your book party right here."

On his way home that night, at barely past eight, Alec realizes, after a few minutes of unaccustomed silence, that Schlomo, apparently deep in thought, is totally ignoring him. *I really don't know this man,* Alec thinks. *But, of course, how well do I know anyone, including myself?* Which makes him realize he can't even track his own thoughts. The person he's actually thinking about is Jesse—subliminally, because he wants to see her. Another person for whom he cares—and knows so little about.

From the scraps of information Carrie revealed, she and her sister were locked, from early childhood, in a sibling rivalry that left wounds, mainly on Jesse. Carrie was better looking, taller, more popular, far more skilled at dance and sports. The victim now, however, is Alec—at least that's what he thinks. He'd like to say, *We are no longer children. And Carrie is dead. There is no "best" at anything now, between her and you. I certainly don't make such comparisons. What I think about now is wanting to be with you. It's not a small feeling. And it's not secondary to anything.* He believes, in fact, he has said almost that. And it's not getting them where they need to be.

When Alec finally arrives home, Sarah is still doing homework, but Jesse is waiting with a hot pan and eggs. "Not much variety," she says.

"You know you don't have to do this at all," Alec says.

"I want to hear about Tino. What did he say?"

"Couldn't come in. Game day."

"So when will you talk to him?"

"Tomorrow. On my way to the airport. I've got a nine o'clock flight to Chicago."

"You're going to drag him out to JFK?"

"LaGuardia," he says. "And Schlomo will pick him up and return him to school."

"Schlomo?"

"A car service guy who usually takes me."

"You mean your driver."

"Well, he drives a lot of people, not just me."

She breaks two eggs in a bowl.

Alec says, "You building a case again?"

"No," she says quickly. "How'd your lunch go with Henry Lowenberg?"

So he tells her, whole story: buildup, Alec's offer; Lowenberg's demand for a large print run.

"And did Telemarch buy that?"

"In ten seconds," he says.

"What took them so long?"

"Their general counsel is a very deliberate man."

"What about Robin Moore?"

"He wasn't so easy to sell. Which is understandable. Burden falls on him. He'll have to write the book. Probably from scratch."

"But you got him to agree?" she asks.

"I asked him how long it would take him. He said two weeks. I told him he'd spend twice that at depositions and trial, but this way avoid the stigma. For a writer of nonfiction, just to be sued for libel on grounds of falsity—not great for the reputation."

"So he agreed to do it—to write Henry's book?"

"You're calling him Henry already."

"I'm on his side!" Jesse says. "He's a seventy-six-year-old epileptic, for God's sake."

Alec laughs. "Robin starts tomorrow."

She whips the eggs in the bowl, then looks at him. "You're not so bad at this, lawyering. Maybe you should stick to it after all."

"Thank you," Alec says. "But what you should know? If I can't end the Allis-Benoit case soon and help get rid of the case against U.S. Computer Corp., the next ten years will be a living hell—for me, and anyone close."

"How close?" she says, beating the eggs more vigorously.

"Small group. Only two people."

"Your daughter and father."

"Sam?" Alec laughs. "He gave me up years ago."

"Then, Alec," she says. "Your group seems to be smaller than you think."

She tosses the eggs in the pan, and they both listen to them sizzle. In less than a minute, she flips the omelet onto a plate and hands it to him. "Thanks," he says.

"Don't mention it." She cracks another two eggs in the bowl, starts whipping them.

"This is great," he says.

"Yeah," she says, splashing her own eggs into the pan.

"So how'd you spend your day?"

"Oh, the usual," she says. "Cleaned myself up in the hopes of impressing somebody. Studied the trades in the hopes of finding someone to impress."

"The 'trades' meaning the trade papers in the film industry?"

"Yep. Those."

"And did you? Find anyone?"

"Well, y'know," she says, "you get to the point where you'll try anything. Anything that looks even halfway promising."

"You knock on doors?"

"Yes, you do."

"And find? Anyone interested in your manifest talent?"

"My talent? No." She plates her omelet and starts eating. "Not for filmmaking, anyway."

Alec watches her stab at her egg. He says, "You will succeed at this, Jess."

"Oh, yes?" she says. "Maybe one of these days."

"I know what an assistant director, an AD does," he says. "You basically run the crew, the set, even the actors, getting ready for every take. Whatever has to happen before the director says 'Action,' you make happen. As well as schedule the whole shoot. I know you, Jess, better than you think. And I know you've got everything it takes to be damn good at this."

"Oh, yeah? How come—in the infinitesimal time we've had together—you know me so well?"

"Because we *are* close, Jess. Maybe—one of these days—you'll admit that."

TWENTY

Tino is already in the backseat when Alec piles in. "Thanks, Schlomo," Alec says. "Now close the glass."

It shuts; no back talk. Schlomo is used to this; he has the only sedan in the fleet with a closable partition. But Tino looks doubtful about its effect.

"Believe me," Alec says. "It's okay. He hears nothing, and doesn't care. It's part of his business."

They're already turning onto Ninety-Sixth Street, heading for the FDR Drive.

Tino gives a lip press and a nod. "I don't have anything for sure to tell you. But I promised, if I saw anything, I'd let you know. So that's what I'm doing."

"Okay, Tino, what did you see?"

"He said all the right things, like 'We'll wait, be patient,' but the way he said them…."

"You're talking about your uncle, and you suspect he meant the opposite?"

"I don't know!" Tino says. "But yes, I suspect it. It's not like him to wait."

"So what's his move?" Alec asks. "What are the possibilities?"

Tino's face loses all color. He's definitely not comfortable with this conversation. "He might grab her. Have one of his men do it."

"Names?"

"There was a guy there that night. Lou DiBrazzi."

"You have other names?"

"Not in my head. I can get them."

"Any other reason to think it might be DiBrazzi? Other than the fact he was there that night?"

"He's the scariest."

"I see." Alec looks out the window. They're speeding over the Triboro Bridge, and the morning sun shimmers on the river below. "If they were to kidnap her, where would they be likely to take her?"

Tino shakes his head. "I don't know. The island, maybe."

"Your uncle's island?"

"Yes."

"And then what?"

"Marry her to someone he can trust."

"And after that?"

Tino looks sick.

"Right. At that stage, no reason to keep her alive."

"Can you do something?" The boy now is desperate.

"Yes," Alec says. "I will do something."

"Should we tell her?"

"Not yet. Do you have any sense about how fast this might happen?"

"It won't happen this month," Tino says.

"You know this?"

"It's a holy month."

"For whom?"

"Do you know about my uncle's religion?"

"Yes, I've heard. He takes that seriously?"

Tino laughs. "They all do."

"But not you?"

"Right now, there's only one thing I take seriously. Protecting Sarah."

"Good, Tino," Alec says. "Because her life is now dependent on you."

❖

Alec meets his senior associate, Trevor Joffrey, at the American Airlines gate. It's sunny as they take off, but O'Hare, on landing, is cloudy and bleak. Their cab driver knows a shortcut through blighted streets and soon deposits them at their destination. The University of Chicago campus sits like a pile of gray stones under a grim sky in a desolate neighborhood.

They make their way directly to George Stigler's office. Trevor, Stigler's former student, had been there often.

Stigler pours them cups of bitter coffee, then repeats the admonition he delivered on the phone. "You're wasting your time, coming out here."

"Give us the few minutes we asked for," Alec says. "Then it won't be a waste."

Stigler frowns, taking a seat behind a cluttered oak desk. It's as if he had said, *A few minutes is all I agreed to.*

"Okay, first fact." Alec sits on the edge of a table supporting large stacks of papers. "Mid-Atlantic Power has retained Mason Scott."

"He's an idiot," Stigler says.

"No doubt. But he is a professor emeritus at Harvard. And he writes that Edison's publication of its price book was a deliberate offer of a price fix and would have been so understood by Allis-Benoit. Because, he says, it's widely understood that price competition cannot occur in an oligopolistic market, unless prices are kept utterly secret. Of course, the heavy-electrical-equipment market is not simply oligopolistic; it's a duopoly, occupied as it is by only two sellers. In that situation, Scott says, price secrecy is even more important as a means of generating price competition."

"The opposite is true," Stigler says. "In the first place, price secrecy is a myth. No way customers don't blab. In the second place, disclosure of prices is what promotes competition, not what suppresses it. One seller learns of the other guy's price, and he shaves it if he wants the business. He might cut it outright or, more likely, try to keep the cut secret by offering better terms under the table, free goods, delayed payment at low interest, or zero interest, whatever it takes. And he *tells* the buyer to keep it secret. At which the buyer laughs. Not in his interest. What is in his interest is to go back to the first seller, tell him of the better offer he just got, and try to get terms even lower. So competition gets more intense. That's reality."

"As you will therefore expect," Alec says, "that's also our view of reality, that's how Allis-Benoit acted, and that's our defense. Problem is, the jury's not likely to believe it, unless it's fed to them by an expert who can trump Mason Scott. In which case, this country will be left with one manufacturer of heavy electrical equipment, and many thousands of unemployed workers. That's not my imagination. Without an expert of your stature in this case, that's the highly predictable result of this litigation. And the fact is, there is no expert of your stature for this case other than yourself."

Stigler drinks his own coffee, apparently with pleasure. "You can find ten other professors emeritus at very good schools. They're a dime a dozen."

"Problem there," Alec says, "they've already taken the dime. So has Scott, to be sure, but there's only one economist in this country more highly regarded than Scott and has also, as a matter of principle, never testified before."

Stigler does not look persuaded.

Alec says, "I have bound galleys here from the Harvard University Press. Will be published in two months." Trevor Joffrey pulls the volume out of his attaché case. A colorful bookmark sticks out from its middle pages.

Stigler looks interested despite himself. "Scott's new tome, you're saying?"

"Yes."

"How'd you get that?" Stigler asks.

"Guy I know. Business writer for Telemarch News."

"And?"

"I'll leave it with you," Alec says. "I have another copy."

"Just show me the goddamn page you've got marked there."

Trevor lays the book on Stigler's desk. The professor scans the highlighted paragraphs and looks up. "What do you think, Trevor? You haven't said anything."

Trevor, seated in the one comfortable chair in the room, makes a show of considering the question. "I think you've already decided to do it, Professor. Scott's theory—which Mid-Atlantic relies on in this case—makes a mockery of everything you've written on the subject. Allowing the courts to adopt it and put all those people out of work? I don't really see you letting that happen. Especially since he names you as the principal author of the opposing point of view."

Stigler laughs, then says to Alec, "You ought to make this man partner."

"We're both hoping, Professor, there's a law firm left after this case that he can become a partner in."

"All right, all right," Stigler says. "Get out of here, both of you. You've used up your 'few minutes.' "

Trevor says, "We'll just leave these court papers for you to read in your spare time."

"Ha!" Stigler says. "I had none of that before you walked in here. What do you think I've got now?"

Alec arrives home to a dark apartment. In the hallway to the bedrooms, he hears Sarah breathing, then Jesse, both asleep.

He closes the door to the kitchen and calls his researcher, Harvey Grand.

"Yes?" says a deep voice, as if impersonating someone who might be genuinely interested. It's the way Harvey answers the phone at two in the morning.

"You were awake?"

"I sleep alternate nights now. What's up?"

"There's a risk, I think serious, that Sal Angiapello is planning to kidnap my daughter."

After a pause, Harvey says, "Here we go again."

"This might be worse than last time."

"You got leverage?" Harvey asks. "Something to scare him with—or someone inside?"

"The latter. Sal's nephew. He's fond of Sarah, and the source for what I know. But he's not likely to learn anything more beforehand."

"No leverage," says Harvey unhappily.

"Nothing that would work. Not on this guy."

"Then we need a tail," Harvey says. "On her."

"She'd spot it."

"Then tell her."

"She'd scream."

"Then I'll tail her myself. She won't spot me."

"You're kidding," Alec says. "She'd spot *you* in a stadium. From the other side of the field."

Jesse comes into the kitchen: tousled hair, dark blue PJs, bare feet. Harvey is talking, but Alec is not now listening. She says, rubbing her eyes, "Who you talking to?"

Harvey says, "Is someone there, Alec?"

"Harvey…" Alec says into the phone, "Let me sleep on this."

"You do that. Me? I'm just gonna sit here all night pondering who you might be doing that with."

"Whom," Alec says reflexively, hanging up, paying attention to Jesse. "Where'd you come in?"

"On Sarah," Jess says. "Or maybe just the sound of your voice, I don't know."

"Light sleeper."

"Yeah," she says. "Sometimes. What the hell's happening?"

Alec goes to the refrigerator, looks in. "Want something?"

"Information."

He shuts the refrigerator door, leans against it. "If I tell you, you're in danger. If I don't, you're pissed off."

"I'm already pissed off," she says. "What's going on? Something Tino told you, right? The evil uncle? He's threatening Sarah? She's rich, is that it? The uncle wants her money? So… what's his—" Her next thought comes with a muffled scream. *"He's going to kidnap her?"*

"That didn't take long."

"That's it?" she says. "That's what Tino said?"

"He suspects it. With good reason. Sal asked him to do pretty much the equivalent, and he refused."

"Jesus!" she says, thrusting spread fingers into her hair. "What kind of world…?"

"Can get primitive, the one Sarah was born into."

"Tino told you this plan, good for him. But now he's at risk too." She pulls out one of the kitchen stools and plunks down on it. "So you'll call the police? The district attorney?"

"Wouldn't stop Sal Angiapello. Might even help him. Would certainly prevent Tino from helping us."

Jesse's stare seems to go right through him. "Okay," she says. "You want a tail? Now I'll take the job you've been offering. But she has to be told."

Alec shakes his head, more in resignation than denial. "This is so damn unfair to her."

"Otherwise it's impossible, Alec. If she's not aware of the danger—"

"I get it, and agree," Alec says with distaste. "And we *have* to bring in Tino. She can't be allowed to go wandering off with him."

Jesse is still plotting. "There's another solution. She could give away all her money. To some causes a lot better than the Mafia."

"Someday," Alec says. "Maybe that's what she'll want. Not now."

"What's wrong with now?"

"It's too much money."

"Like… tens of millions?" Jesse says, as if a figure that high would be preposterous.

"Ten times that," Alec says. "When she's your age, she can decide what to do with it. She's too young to know enough now."

"*Hundreds* of millions?"

"And growing."

"I really think you should go to the police," Jesse says. "They'll give her protection. Or go to court. You're a lawyer. Get some sort of order against this creep."

Alec gives a sad laugh. "Believe me, I've been through this. When Phil Anwar was hounding your sister and me, I remember the advice I got. 'Sure, go get an order. When he violates it, they'll protect you. Of course, by then you won't need protection; you'll be dead.' "

Jesse looks up in disbelief.

Alec says, "We need protection, we provide it ourselves."

"So you want my help?"

"Of course. I *need* your help. But the risk to you is not small. If Sal wants to snatch, he could snatch both of you. So I'm bringing Harvey in."

"He was with you and Carrie in Maine. Fighting the bad guys."

"And got shot, yeah."

"Right," Jesse says. "*That's* the kind of world this is, where ordinary people get shot."

"Nothing ordinary about Harvey Grand," Alec says.

"Carrie liked him."

"They were good friends, yes." Alec takes off his jacket. "So, after all, you're here for a while more."

"I guess I am."

"We'll speak to Sarah in the morning."

"Good," she says.

They stand for a very awkward few moments without speaking.

"Night, Jess."

"Night, Alec."

"Those pajamas…."

"You don't have to say it."

"It's just—"

"I know what it is," she says. "I have a bathrobe. Next time I'll put it on."

TWENTY-ONE

The Honorable Charles B. Metzner. A real judge in real chambers, who is known to do serious work there. The man is not physically imposing, with his thin shoulders and slightly stooped posture. He also looks a bit older than his sixty-one years, with his gray-streaked hair, lined face, pale blue eyes. And his intellect is not in your face. *He just knows what the hell he's doing*, thinks Alec, listening to Judge Metzner take charge of the case.

"All right," the judge says, "you've got two weeks to work out a discovery schedule. I suggest you not waste time in a case like this with interrogatories. Document production comes first, then depositions. Final witness lists and trial briefs to follow. If you can't agree on a schedule or resolve objections to document requests, take your differences before Magistrate Koulas. I'll hear appeals from his decisions—but let me tell you, your arguments better be good. I'm giving you six months to get it all done. Trial immediately thereafter. It's a complex case—I understand that— I'm allowing four weeks. No adjournments, no extensions. That's the program. We're all going to have to live with it."

Dead silence.

The judge smiles. "Freddy? You represent the plaintiff. You have anything to say?"

"Sounds good, Judge."

"Caddy? Alec?"

They look at each other. Caddy speaks. "They can do it, we can do it."

The judge looks to Alec, who nods.

"Okay," says Judge Metzner. "Freddy, you draft the order,

send it around. No objections, it'll be signed. Good to see you fellows. Looking forward to this."

Out on the street, Cadigan Breen signals Alec toward a bench in Foley Square Park. Thumping down on it, Alec says, "We need a way to derail this train."

"Yeah, well," Breen says, "bigger train's coming."

"The 125 other utilities are tired of waiting? They're going to sue too?"

"That disaster will inevitably follow," Caddy says, still standing.

"So you're saying what? The Department of Justice, Antitrust Division?"

Breen grimaces. "Them's the ones, yeah."

"They're going to sue us now?"

"Any day," Breen says.

"Criminal case or civil?"

"That appears to be their question. Unfortunately, their only question. I got the call as I was leaving for court."

"Call from whom?" Alec asks.

"A friend. Inside. It's better you don't know who."

"Can he get us a meeting?"

"Doubt it. He's too low."

Alec's thinking fast. "The head of the Antitrust Division— Eric Stapleton—you know him?"

"No."

"He's from Chicago," Alec says. "Stigler would know him."

Breen looks shocked. "You've got George Stigler?"

"Just happened. Sorry. Was going to tell you today."

"No, it's great. Stigler! He could win the case for us."

"You know… beating the government… not really the issue right now. What we've got to do is to stop them from suing."

"Any ideas?" Breen asks.

"You mean, apart from telling them what a lousy case they have?"

"Be nice if that could work."

"Be nice if that were true," Alec says.

"I thought you were a believer."

"Still in the hope phase, Caddy. Be nice if I'd had time to learn the actual facts."

Ben Braddock sits back with a caustic expression. "You know, until now, we had some time to save our client. The public utilities knew that if Mid-Atlantic won, they all would get the benefit of it. Under the law, we'd be stopped from protesting our innocence again, and the only issue in the other utilities' cases would be how much we owed them. So they were content to sit and wait for the Mid-Atlantic case to end. Now, if the government sues, up go the floodgates. Especially if the DOJ files a criminal complaint. Damn public utilities will stream into court. PUCs won't let them hold back. And Allis-Benoit will float dead in the water. Belly-up before any suit goes to trial." Nothing new in that prediction, but Braddock, with his heels rammed against the top edge of his desk, his legs tented in black flannel, delivers it like a pronouncement of doom.

Alec had come into Ben's office upon returning from court. Frank Macalister, who has joined them, says, "You or Caddy going to call Stapleton?"

"I'll call," Alec says. "I think he'll take it. And give us the meeting."

"He may be too pissed," Braddock says. "That you even know about it."

"Yeah, he's likely to be pissed. That's one of the reasons he's likely to see me."

"Because he thinks you'll give up your source," Ben notes.

"Yeah, maybe."

"And since I've no idea who the source is, it's a good reason for me to go down there, not Caddy."

"Caddy won't like that," Mac says.

"I think he trusts me, and he should. Both our clients want the government to stand down. And Allis-Benoit has the better arguments."

"So what else you got?" Braddock asks. "To get through the door?"

"Stapleton is new," says Alec. "Got there less than a month ago. This thing has been bouncing around the Antitrust Division for more than a year. Someone there jumped him. Talked him into it. Why wouldn't he want a free look at the other side before taking the plunge? Starting a fight with two of the largest companies in the world? The only two domestic suppliers of turbine generators? When the only people egging you on have already been turned down by the prior head of the division?" Alec looks from Mac to Ben. "I think he'll see me."

"You'll bring Stigler?" Mac asks.

"No," Alec says. "At this stage, it's more useful to use his name than to have him there. And I don't think he'd be happy being there."

"You going alone?"

"I'll bring Bob Curtis."

"The CEO of the fucking company?" Mac says. "Whatta you going to do? Have him cry on Stapleton's desk?"

"Pretty much," Alec says.

Crossing the suite to his own office, Alec tells his secretary, "Get Caddy Breen." She's a large young woman, blond, who looks like she's from Minnesota, and is. Her name is Sweeta Gottsen. She's saving to go to law school. Alec has been blessed with wonderful secretaries, and she's the best of them.

Breen is on in two minutes, and Alec lays out the plan. Breen says, "Not sure I like this, you going alone."

"Going first is all it is. And Caddy, this is the Antitrust Division. For what we both want, Allis, the weaker company, has the stronger position."

"Of course. But why not go together?"

"Because they're charging us with a conspiracy, Caddy. We can act together when we're talking about how to litigate. Not necessarily when the subject is a possible deal for their not bringing the case."

"You're going down there to deal?" Breen says, now getting aroused.

"In a manner of speaking, of course," Alec says. "But I'm going to say things you don't want to hear, okay?"

"Really? Maybe I should hear them now."

"You should not hear them," Alec says firmly. "Ever. But listen to me. There's no way I can undermine your position, even if I wanted to. And I don't."

"You could take a plea to a criminal indictment."

"I won't do that."

"I have your word on that?"

"Absolutely," Alec says. "They want to go criminal, there's no deal at all."

Long silence before Breen speaks. "It's a big ask."

"Not if you trust me." Alec says.

Another long silence. "Okay," Breen says. "But you call me first thing. Before you even get to the airport."

Alec's next call is to Larry Rilesman, who had been waiting impatiently.

"It must've been some meeting," he says.

"With Metzner? No. Scheduling. Took five minutes. What delayed my getting back to you was the news coming out of the DOJ." Alec briefly summarizes the morning's discussions and plan.

"I'm in total agreement," Rilesman says. "We should get down there as quickly as possible. You and me, right? I expect to be part of this."

"Sure," Alec says.

"Do you know Eric Stapleton?"

"Never met him, no."

"But you think he'll see us?"

"Yeah," Alec says. "When he knows who we're bringing."

"Bringing?" Rilesman says after a pause. "Who are we bringing?"

"Bob Curtis."

"*What?*" Rilesman says. "You outta your fucking mind? CEOs do not go to Washington, hat in hand, to see the head of one division of the Department of Justice."

"Vale of tears is what I had in mind, but hat in hand will do."

"Would you be fucking serious?" Rilesman is now almost screaming. "On top of everything else, Bob Curtis will not be good at this."

"Then it'll be my job to make him better."

"*Your* job? No one prepares the CEO of this company but me."

"Okay," Alec says.

"Not 'okay.' I just told you. He's not going."

"You want to keep your job, Larry?"

"You threatening me?"

"Not at all. I'm advising you. General counsel of nothing is not a job. And if Bob's not in Stapleton's office with us, nothing is what your company will be."

Eric Stapleton seems to have been waiting for Alec's call.

"You know who I am?" Alec says.

"I know who you are, who you represent, and why you're calling."

"Then you must know I was tipped."

Stapleton laughs. "Since I was the one who tipped you, yes. Or I at least in effect tipped Caddy Breen. A former associate of his works here. And I told him not to tell anyone, especially his ex-boss. The fact he did tells *me* two useful things. I can't trust this young man, which, of course, is what I suspected when I told him. But Caddy trusts you, which means maybe I can as well."

"I'd like to come down to see you," Alec says. "With Bob Curtis. We have things to say you'll want to hear now rather than later."

"You mean before we sue?"

"Yes."

"The complaint is already prepared, Alec. And signed. By me."

"That complaint was prepared more than a year ago."

Stapleton laughs. "Actually, there are two complaints."

"One civil, one criminal?" Alec asks

"Correct. And what I'm still considering is whether to file one or both."

"I think you have other issues," Alec says.

"Which you'd like to tell me about. So. How's day after to-morrow, 10 a.m.?"

"We'll be there."

"Good. I was holding the time for you. Or, of course, Caddy. That it's you tells me a third thing."

"I won't disappoint you. Or him."

When Alec arrives home, Harvey Grand is perched like a Buddha on a kitchen stool while his keen eye keeps tabs on Jesse at the stove, stirring what appears to be a pot of stew.

"I thought we were going to order something," Alec says.

"So I did," Jesse says. "And then I cooked it."

Alec leans over the pot. "Is that lamb stew?"

"I thought with three men, they'd probably want to eat meat."

Harvey uncoils and joins the inspection. He's a tall, square, coffee-skinned man—square in the way offensive linemen are square. His features are heavy and thick, but Harvey dresses in fine clothes and moves with grace. And nothing fazes him. He deals in catastrophes—with a job description that includes calming everyone down. "I wasn't planning on dinner, but this?" he says, peering into the pot, "Irresistible! You wouldn't also, by any chance, have dropped in some potatoes?"

"Stew without potatoes?" Jesse exclaims. "What do you think this is? Low-grade cuisine?"

Alec says, "Glad you two have gotten so convivial."

"You're twenty minutes late," Harvey says. "What did you expect? We'd wait for introductions?"

"You're even beginning to sound alike," Alec says. Then to Jesse, "You've talked to Sarah?"

"Most of the afternoon," Jesse says. "While we cooked up this brew. She and Tino are in her room."

"She okay?"

"You'd better talk to her."

"Right," Alec says. "Let's do this in the living room."

Jesse rounds up Sarah and Tino, and the assemblage, including Harvey, seat themselves in the room and look to Alec to start.

"For what we know, we can thank Tino," Alec says, and gives a nod in his direction. "He was alarmed by his meeting with Sal, which means we ought to be. You understand that, Sarah?"

"Of course," she says. "But that doesn't mean we have to call up the National Guard."

"National Guard," Alec says. "Good thought. Since Sal Angiapello is a man with an army. But for what this man wants from you, my love, he doesn't need more than a couple of men. Which is why Harvey is here. He doesn't have an army. But he has the people we need."

"You're going to have me watched, aren't you?"

"You have a better idea?"

"Yeah," Sarah says. "Let me take care of myself. Anyone comes near me I don't like, I start running and screaming."

Harvey gives a grunt. "Okay," he says, "let's play that out. Best-case scenario. You're on Madison Avenue. Lots of people. A van pulls up. Three guys jump out. Two lift you into the van, while the other one treats you to a nose full of chloroform. This being New York, we have a reasonable chance everyone keeps walking, no one even calls 911. But if they do, by the time the cop cars arrive, you're in another vehicle, maybe already in a box, halfway to some private airport, where Sal's jet will fly you to his island in the Ionian Sea. Where he can do anything to you he wants."

"He's a blood relative, for God's sake."

Harvey jerks his large head side to side. "And how do you think that cuts with this man, Sarah? Where money is concerned."

"So what follows?" Sarah says, shaken, but trying hard not to show it. "Are you planning on having someone following me to school every day? Standing guard in the street? Trailing me wherever I go? Protecting this building at night? Watching every building I'm in? Sitting next to me in the movies? I mean, this is ridiculous." She turns to Tino on the sofa. "Don't you agree?"

He obviously doesn't. "What Harvey just said—it's horrible, but it's true. It could happen."

Harvey says grimly, "It *has* happened. More than once. We'd like to see it doesn't happen to you, Sarah."

"So how long will this go on?" Sarah asks.

Everyone again looks to Alec.

"I don't know," he says. "The alternative is to meet with the man. Give him reason to back off. But I doubt that would work. Now. For Sal, this is likely a game. Sick, scary, but not to him. It's what he does, and probably enjoys. He'll regard our putting a watch on you as a move in the game. Let's see how he reacts before we make another move."

Sarah looks too depressed to say anything.

Tino says, "How do you know my uncle so well?"

"I don't. I'm guessing. But that's based on someone who was probably very much like him."

"You mean Phil," Sarah says.

"Yes," he says softly, and it quiets the room. He stands and puts on a smile. "So let's all go and eat that stew."

"As if one could eat anything," Sarah says as everyone else rises.

"Sarah!" Alec snaps. "Listen to me!" Everyone does, and he softens his tone. "I will not let Sal Angiapello hurt you."

TWENTY-TWO

Alec lands at Cleveland Hopkins International Airport at 3:27 p.m. He had offered to arrive in the morning. "Trust me, Larry," he said to Rilesman on the phone. "There's nothing on Bob Curtis's plate more important than getting ready for this meeting." Rilesman said, "All necessary preparation will be done by the Allis-Benoit Law Department. Come at four, if you'd like, but not earlier."

The flight is smooth; there's little traffic to the corporate head-quarters downtown. Alec is shown to Rilesman's empty office by his secretary, the same middle-aged woman Alec previously met, although he now notices her dyed brown hair and dark-framed glasses and is a bit surprised by her stern look. She asks, "Is there anything you need while you wait?"

"He's still in with Mr. Curtis?" Alec asks.

"He is," she says, "and he suggests you'll be comfortable here." If there's irony in her tone, she shows nothing in her expression.

Alec says, "Might you tell me where Mr. Curtis's office is?"

"Certainly," she says. "Down the corridor behind you, turn right, and go to the end." Not a blink.

"Thank you," Alec says and heads toward it.

As he walks into the CEO suite, two secretaries rise to protest. He opens the inner door anyway. Larry Rilesman and two young men, presumably his assistant counsel, stand before an obviously irate chief executive, who is in the process of flinging sheets of paper into the air. "Goddamn worthless hogwash!" he says, fine vellum still fluttering to the floor. "I asked for a white paper to read. I can't read this." He picks up the stack he hasn't yet thrown.

"It's sixty-five goddamn pages. It's not simply unpersuasive. It's unintelligible. It's gobbledygook. I'd look like an idiot trying to read it, because an idiot plainly wrote it." He then hurls the stack directly at Rilesman, and the pages cascade to his cordovans.

Bob Curtis is known as a man of great dignity who is normally kind, almost avuncular. He had risen through the ranks of his company with grace and ease. At this moment, however, he is literally shaking with rage.

"Perhaps I've come at a bad time," Alec says.

"Why weren't you here three hours ago?" Curtis says. "I leave in ten minutes. We're opening the opera tonight, my wife is the chairperson, and we're hosting a dinner. I simply do not have the time to rewrite this crap."

"Nor do you have to. If you have a secretary here who can take dictation, and a driver, I will have your white paper waiting for you at home when you return from the opera tonight."

Curtis says, "Larry, I think your secretary fits that bill."

"But I'll need her," Rilesman says. "To produce a shorter version of my draft—so you can see an alternative—or riders on Alec's."

Curtis makes a face of derision. "Go home, Larry. Change for the opera as we planned. I think we can trust Alec to know what's required."

Alec says, "I'll need several minutes of your time, Bob. There's something I need you to say tomorrow that we haven't had a chance to discuss."

"Let's talk about it in the plane tomorrow morning."

"It's too big. You'll want to sleep on it. Maybe talk to others on your board."

Curtis gives him a long hard look of appraisal. "All right, you come with me now. We'll talk in the car."

Rilesman says, "Be ready in a sec."

"You stay, Larry. Arrange for the secretarial help and driver." Curtis goes for his coat and beckons Alec to follow him. Leaving,

Alec casts Rilesman an apologetic glance and receives back a look of pure hatred.

On the morning flight to Washington on the company jet, Curtis says to Alec, "You're absolutely certain we have to take this extreme position?"

"See it from Stapleton's eyes," Alec says. "He's new to the job. His staff wants blood. He needs to make a splash, and this looks easy. In effect, the Antitrust Division is being upstaged by Mid-Atlantic's private lawsuit. Big upside if Stapleton sues—politically, and in the media; bad downside if he doesn't."

"He could lose the case."

"Years later. By which time someone else will be head of the division."

Curtis turns to face Larry Rilesman.

"I think it's insane," Rilesman says.

Curtis turns back to Alec, who says, "We have no other leverage, Bob. This is the one thing that will scare them."

Bob smiles. "At least you've whittled my speech down to one page."

Heads of government departments are given offices designed to impress. The assistant attorney general in charge of the Antitrust Division operates from such an office. It's about fifty feet long, twenty feet wide, and reeks of history. Many famous occupants have wielded power here, from Thurman Arnold on down—smashing monopolies, blocking mergers, punishing conspirators—and the furniture, which is plain, bears the scars.

Alec and his small band are ushered into seats in front of an eight-foot-long desk, behind which sits Eric Stapleton, large nosed, balding, professorial in dress and manner. As he rises slightly in greeting, lowering the papers he'd been reading, Alec notices more particularly his receding chin, covered with a small goatee. Stapleton is flanked on either side by rows of younger staffers.

Introductions are brief. Pleasantries are dispensed with. It's a working room meant for the conduct of momentous business, and Alec is invited to get on with it.

"We have basically three things to tell you," Alec begins. "First, if you sue us, you will lose, for reasons you don't know, because your staff"—Alec rivets each row of suits with a stare—"hasn't bothered to find the facts from the documents we've given you. The second is, if you sue us, we will shut down our plants, discharge our workers, and stop manufacturing and selling heavy electrical equipment. In other words, we will go out of the business, leaving Edison Electric with a domestic monopoly."

If it's possible for silence to become quieter, that's what happens in that room. Bedlam would have been less startling. Stapleton says quietly, "That's a bombshell decision. You ask me to believe your client has already made it?"

"When we finish here this morning, you will not only believe that decision's been made, you will understand why there is no choice but to carry it out. So... third point, which is one you might actually like. If you were to sue us and win, all you'd get, in addition to an injunctive decree, would be a judgment collaterally estopping us from defending ourselves against others on the price-fixing charge. Obviously, if you sue, everyone sues—every public utility in the United States. And if we're collaterally estopped from defending ourselves—that would put us in bankruptcy. If we're already out of the business, you probably wouldn't care, but I can't see why you'd affirmatively want that. So we will give you the only thing you really do want. The decree. We will sign any decree you write. We don't even have to read it. On only one condition: you get Edison Electric to sign the same decree."

Stapleton laughs. "The decree that we hand you? You'll sign, sight unseen?"

"Whatever it says. Your economists believe they know better than we how this industry should be run. Fine. Let them make the new rules; we'll follow them. Because now we're number two in the market, and far behind. Can't do much worse. With your rules, maybe we'll do a bit better. Although," Alec says, and pauses a moment, "on that, we could offer you the assistance of our economics expert witness, George Stigler."

"You have Stigler?" Stapleton says, not even trying to hide his surprise.

"Yes. Recently joined us. I know he's never testified before. But he believes your case is so antagonistic to the public interest; he feels obligated to help defeat it."

Stapleton touches his goatee reflexively, as if launching a thought. "You say you don't want us to file a complaint. To get a consent decree 'so ordered' by a court, we need a case pending in court, which we don't get unless we file a complaint."

"You have a consent decree we signed during the troubles of '62—when there actually was a price-fixing conspiracy. All we need to do now is to amend that decree."

One of Stapleton's young staffers speaks up. Ralph Woodson. Already known to the antitrust bar as a near-fanatical enforcer. "What's your supposedly exonerating evidence? The facts we allegedly missed?"

"I didn't say you missed them," Alec reminds him. "They're sitting in your office. I said you never took the trouble to read them. The transaction files—hundreds of them. Has anyone in this room but me ever studied those files?" Big smile. "Let's see it, shall we? Show of hands." Alec looks around. "No one? What I thought. And yet the whole case is in there. Absolute and irrefutable proof we never conspired to fix prices with anyone. Because they show that we cut prices on virtually every deal we made—that's how we got whatever business we got—and offered price cuts on many deals we lost. And the reason I know you guys haven't read these documents is because, had you read them, we wouldn't be sitting here. You wouldn't be so damn eager to sue us."

Stapleton looks like a man who would smoke a pipe. And now he pulls one out of a desk drawer, along with a pouch and other implements. "I'd like to hear from Mr. Curtis on this"—he stuffs his pipe, lights it, and draws—"I guess you'd call it a 'threat' to leave the turbine generator business."

"Not a threat," Curtis says. "The inevitable consequence of your filing a complaint. And let me tell you why." He unfolds a slip of paper, rests it on Stapleton's desk, and starts reading what Alec had written.

"Heavy electrical equipment is not a wonderful business. The risks and capital expenditures are extraordinarily high, profits low and un-certain. In the last ten years, we didn't lose money, but we would have made a great deal more investing in municipal bonds. We have stayed in business because it's in the national interest, especially during the current energy crisis, and because putting tens of thousands of people out of work would be a human tragedy.

"If we are to continue in business, and re-main competitive, we must invest, short-term, nearly half a billion dollars in R&D, and more than that in plant and equipment. We also face a potential liability of several billions in the coal-requirements contract litigation that I'm sure you know about. So this is what would happen if, on top of those problems, you added the filing of a government complaint.

"Mid-Atlantic Power & Light has been prose-cuting the same claim against us, but the finan-cial industry has not taken it that seriously, apparently regarding it—accurately—as a power play by Donald Strand. Were you to sue, those charges would be taken very seriously indeed, and produce these immediate effects.

"First, it would render us utterly and completely unfinanceable. We've already been advised by our investment bankers that we are teetering on that edge. Your complaint would push us over it. Without access to the capital market, we could not exist.

"Second would be the impact on sales and on the cash flow of the progress payments we receive when we make sales. Turbine generators are enormously expensive and require extensive servicing through the years. No one will buy them if they fear that the manufacturer will be out of business when those machines need service and replacement parts. The publicity given our problems by the filing of a government action would substantiate precisely that fear, drying up or totally eliminating our sales volume.

"Third, your complaint would trigger suits by the entire public utility industry. Right now they are waiting in the wings, shielded from the statute of limitations by a tolling and standstill agreement. You sue, they'll be free to sue, and every one of them will. All the problems I've mentioned will be compounded exponentially.

"So if you sue, we're going out of business. I've made that decision and will recommend it to my board. I've already talked to key members of my board, and they will support me on this. In fact, as I've said, we'd have no choice. The devastation of massive unemployment—to the city of Cleveland, the state of Ohio, and other regions—will be a fact."

Curtis folds up his paper and returns it to the breast pocket of his jacket. There are literally tears in his eyes.

Alec says, "Questions?"

Stapleton says, "We'll think about what you've said."

TWENTY-THREE

At Kendal, Blake, incoming calls are directed to secretaries who, when their principals are unavailable, record messages on pink slips. Waiting for Alec on his return from Washington is a sheaf of such slips, with the one on top marked conspicuously, "URGENT." It's from the chief judge of the United States Court of Appeals for the Second Circuit, Rivington Kane. It reads, "Come to my chambers at once."

Alec drops his bags, calls Caddy Breen to report quickly on the Stapleton meeting, and heads downstairs to the cab line. He arrives at Foley Square in ten minutes. The chief judge had already eaten his lunch, so a meal in the judges' lunchroom is not in the offing. But he greets Alec by rising from behind his desk, directing Alec to his customary seat at the conference table, and beginning immediately to pace.

"Your firm represents U.S. Computer Corp. in the government monopolization case, am I right?"

"That's right, Judge. It's being tried by my partner Jack Stamper."

"Right, right, that's what I thought." Then, still pacing, "I've had an idea," Kane says, obviously bursting with it. He's a diminutive man with a small round head and boundless energy, barely contained. He wears his dark gray vest buttoned up and his black hair cut short. "A plan, really," he continues, "and rather novel, but before revealing it, I should tell you there's no other lawyer in this circuit to whom I would entrust it." Turning on Alec a rapturous smile, his face wrinkles into a maze. "How would your people like it if I were to take the U.S. Computer case away from

Eustace Ettinger?"

Alec knows, as does most everyone in the federal bar, that in the U.S. Computer Corp. trial, Judge Ettinger is running amok. He grants every government motion and upholds every government objection, while denying every motion and objection made by the defense. He penalizes every attempt by the defense to call a witness by allowing, months past the discovery deadline, the government's outrageous new discovery demands. He interrupts every examination by the defense of its own witnesses, and invariably takes over the questioning himself. And he screams tirades daily at anyone connected to the defendant. The reprieve comes after the lunch break, when Judge Ettinger falls asleep. It's no surprise that the chief judge of the circuit is distressed about the light in which these antics place the judiciary. But while Chief Judge Kane can admonish another judge, he does not have the power independently to remove him.

So Alec wonders what the hell the man is talking about. "Take the case away?" he says.

"Yes," Kane says, "remove him from it by removing it from him." The judge blinks with satisfaction, then nestles into the chair next to Alec's. "The thing could be brought about, you know, but I need your help. You're friendly with the attorney general?"

Alec says, "He was once my local counsel in New Orleans on Telemarch News libel cases."

"Ah," Kane says. "Then this could work."

"Sorry, Judge, what? What could work?"

"Arbitration!" Kane says, as if pulling a rabbit out of a hat.

"Arbitration?"

"Yes! *You* get the AG to agree to allow the case to go to arbitration; then I give you—voilà! Walter Mansfield, a great Court of Appeals judge, as the arbitrator! Perfect, right? An expert in the antitrust laws, a highly distinguished jurist, and a brilliant and fair man."

"All of the foregoing," Alec agrees, "but Judge—"

"You're thinking it's never been done. A federal case ended, so it can be decided by another federal judge sitting as an arbitrator. Well, I had it researched," Kane says. "It's not been done before, as far as we could see, but there are no rules against it. None, legal or ethical. And no reason I can think of that should prohibit it. Of course, the parties must consent to it."

"And the AG won't unless Stapleton signs off."

"Probably right," Kane says, relapsing a bit in his chair. "So that's where you come in again. You must also talk that man into it!"

"Tough sell, Judge. Stapleton can't lose before Ettinger."

"Which means only he can't lose this round."

"I see."

"Do you?" Kane says, leaning into Alec's face. "Do you understand fully what I mean when I say *this round*?"

"Of course."

"You can't say I said it, but you can nonetheless stress the point, because it's the conclusion any reasonably astute person would come to."

"Yes," Alec says.

"And you should understand why I'm doing this. Eustace Ettinger is a disgrace to the court. He is a disgrace to our system of justice. The judges in this courthouse agree. We want it to end."

"So do we all."

"So now it's on you, Alec. I've given you the means. Make it happen!"

The door to Ben Braddock's office is always open, and Alec strides in. "We need a meeting. You, me, and Jack, with Lee on the phone."

Braddock looks up slowly from the pages he was apparently

editing. "You going to tell me how it went in Washington?" Without waiting for a response, he directs his secretary on the speaker box to ask Jack Stamper to join them.

"Reasonably well. Stapleton will let us know."

"And then you dashed off to see our chief judge."

"You been leafing through my telephone messages?"

"Don't have to," Braddock says. "Your secretary, Miss Gottsen, keeps mine informed. And I assume—since you wish to bring in Stamper and Lee Norris—that Rivvy Kane wants to know something about the Computer Corp. case."

"He already knows more than he likes. He wants to take it away from Ettinger."

"Reassign it? Ha! He doesn't have the power."

"He wants it arbitrated," Alec says. "Before Walter Mansfield."

"*What?*" Braddock lets out a yelp of a laugh. "And he wants you to talk the government into it?"

"That's the plan."

"Oh, my! Now I truly have heard everything." Wiping his eyes, Braddock tells his secretary to get Lee Norris on the phone. Then, to Alec, "You knew Norris, right? Before he became attorney general?"

"He was my constitutional law professor at Yale."

"But you haven't worked with him since he became Computer Corp.'s general counsel?"

"No."

Jack Stamper walks in. "Whatever this is," he says, "I've got a room full of people."

"You're in recess, right?" Braddock says.

"For a few days. The government's been given the right to depose our next witness—again—before we put him on the stand."

Braddock holds his hand to his head in a mock gesture of suffering. "Still going on, is it? Depositions in the middle of a trial? Ettinger ended the deposition schedule almost a year ago."

"For us," Stamper says. "Not for the government, apparently."

"Well this is certainly the day for odd shit," says Braddock.

They fill in Stamper on what they've already started to call "the Kane initiative." "Great for us," Jack says, "but Stapleton will never buy it."

"Probably right," Alec says. "But there's no downside to making the offer."

"Time," Stamper says. "I don't have a day to waste on a fool's errand."

Alec looks at Ben Braddock. "I don't think we have a choice."

"Why?" Stamper says. "You feel we've got to do this just because the chief judge proposed it?"

"Don't you?"

Stamper laughs. "Maybe. Yeah. But what the fuck do you need me for? Do it yourself. Take Lee."

"Okay," Alec says.

"Knowing you, you've got something else going in Washington, anyway."

"We'd be telling the entire Antitrust Division that the Court of Appeals has already decided to throw out whatever opinion Ettinger writes. Can't help their morale."

"That's it?" Jack says dubiously.

"Of course not."

"You want another shot at him on Allis-Benoit."

"Wouldn't you?"

"Alone, without the circus, yeah." Then Stamper says, "Today didn't go so well?"

"Hard to tell. Stapleton is thinking about it."

"Then push him, Alec. End that damn case. I need your help."

Back in his office, Alec finds Lee Norris on his line. "What's going on?" Norris says. "I call Ben, get transferred to you."

Alec relates his meeting with Kane.

"Weirdest goddamn thing I ever heard of," Norris says.

"And?"

"No reason not to go for it," Norris says. "No legal or ethical problem. And Walter Mansfield, if he had the case, would throw it out in ten minutes. I don't see Stapleton agreeing to it, however. He might not even give us the meeting."

"He will if I say you're in on it."

"Oh, I don't think so," Norris says.

"You have a history?"

"We do."

"Should I know about it?" Alec asks.

"No need. Just call him. See what he says."

"I have another reason to see him."

"Your Allis-Benoit case?"

"Yes."

"Not a problem," Norris says. "Of course I assume"—and he laughs—"you're not planning some trade-off."

"Correct assumption."

"Okay, then. Just let me know when. If he gives us a date, I can move anything."

When they hang up, Alec takes a moment. He has met only two truly great men. Not Tom Dewey, whom Alec had once taken to dinner, then offered up to a City Bar roast. Certainly not Richard Nixon, against whom Alec had litigated. And not even, surprisingly, Harry Truman, as much as Alec enjoyed the man's company the night he spoke at the *Law Journal* banquet. But Thurgood Marshall—no question, he had all the attributes of greatness. Thurgood judged the law school moot court finals, when Alec, then third-year, also sat on the panel. A friendship formed that night lasted through the years. And then there was Lee Norris, another hero of the civil rights movement. A powerful man with a towering intellect and an immense capacity for humor and love, he moved everyone with a soft voice, and, in government office, achieved astounding victories with honor intact. If Eric Stapleton couldn't recognize Lee's greatness, had to be something wrong with Stapleton.

Alec's secretary buzzes. None other than Stapleton is on the line.

"I just received a very strange call," Stapleton says. "Supposedly from the chambers of the chief judge of the Second Circuit Court of Appeals. I was told to expect your call, Alec. I was told you'd ask for a meeting. And I was *instructed*—by a fucking clerk—to grant that request. Was that a joke?"

"No joke. Your call anticipated mine by a few seconds."

"Really?" he says. "You're on intimate terms with the chief judge?"

"Simply a messenger. But it's a message to be delivered in person."

Stapleton could be heard flipping pages, presumably of his calendar. "I have an opening for 3 p.m. tomorrow."

"I'd like to bring Lee Norris."

"Norris. You don't say. So this is a Computer Corp. thing?"

"It is."

"You're on that case now too?"

"Peripherally."

"And in collusion with the Court of Appeals?"

"Hardly."

"Ha!" Stapleton says. "That was a joke."

"I understood it as such."

"Tell me this, Alec. This Kane initiative—"

"Funny, that's what we're calling it."

"Does it have anything to do with Judge Ettinger?"

"Yes."

"And?"

Silence on Alec's end.

"That's all you'll tell me?" Stapleton says.

"Until tomorrow."

"I can hardly wait."

No sun this afternoon on St. Mark's Place. Jesse sits on a bench in front of a church as streaked and bleak as the sky, which looks like emulsions of pewter and ash. Pigeons flock to her feet as if she had something to offer. *Like me,* she thinks, traveling to three different film sites, tracking three indie producers. All men, of course. And no job as a result of it. She's simply not willing to work for no pay. Much less to come into their "honey wagons" to talk about it.

Her original plan was the basic fantasy, but one that others had achieved. Take a paying job doing most anything, save some money, write a film script, make it herself, get it into a festival, catch a wave. Events intervened. Sarah intervened. Sarah and Alec. *Yes, right, mostly him.*

She can't talk to Alec about money. She obviously needs some, and he obviously knows that. She found a checkbook in her handbag, with a note that said, "Let me know when this runs out." The bank teller informed her that the "this" was $1,000. So she imagined the conversation she needed to have. "If I'm to stay here, doing whatever for Sarah and you, I have to be earning something. It needn't be large, since you're covering my room and board, but we should have a formal arrangement. We should...."

It's too cold to be sitting here. The last guy she interviewed was the one with the "honey wagon" trailer. Unimaginable luxury for an indie film. "Let's get warm," he said. "Get to know each other better." Hitting on her with those stupid code words. *My situation,* she thinks, *is ridiculous. I'm actually living with the man I want and can't have him.* It's a line of thought she's traveled down repeatedly, and is tired of. She says aloud, "I have to move out or in!" *Fortunately,* she thinks, *no one hears me. Here or there.*

Alec arrives home dead tired. Sarah is in her room doing home-work. Jesse is waiting up. "If this is a pattern," he says, "I could get used to it."

He's standing at the doorway to the kitchen, still in his suit. Jesse, in her bathrobe, is seated at the island with a novel. She looks at him distractedly, seemingly deep in thought about some-thing else.

"What are you reading?" he says.

"Nothing. Nothing important." She gets up and takes his hand.

"You want to talk?" he says, a bit off-balance.

"Yes," she says. "I have something to say to you." Not letting go of his hand, she leads him out of the kitchen and to his bed-room, where she closes the door and sits on his bed. Now totally mystified, but certainly interested, Alec tosses his jacket and tie on a chair and joins her on the bed's edge.

"So this is what I want to tell you," she says, looking down to the bedspread. It's as if she'd summoned the courage to tell him her feelings but not to look him in the eye.

He says, "Jess, whatever it is—"

She bursts out in a rush, as if afraid he will take her off course. "This will seem to you like a total reversal… but it's not. Not of my feelings. Not of my own state of mind." She has to stop to gulp air. It's not going as she rehearsed it. It's already going too fast. "I know you want to make love to me," she says.

"Of course I do. How could I not?"

"Easily, but don't interrupt me."

"Sorry."

"I want it too," she says, face burning, forcing her gaze to return to the pattern on the bedspread. "To be brutally honest, which is what I'm trying to do here, I've wanted it since we met. I also think you want us to be a couple."

"Yes. That too."

"Right," she says, taking another hard breath. "I stayed in

Ireland, even after Carrie died, because—though I didn't know your situation—I thought, if I came back, I'd be drawn to you and eventually we might… happen. And be happy for a while," she says with a strain in her voice. "And then… crash." She raises her eyes. "For the reasons I've already told you."

"You know my feelings about that," he says.

"Yes. I do. But my thoughts haven't changed, my rational thoughts, to the extent I still have them. Yet my feelings have… grown stronger."

"Jesse," he says, gathering her hands. "I'm in love with you. I have been from the moment I saw you back here last month, even though it might have taken me a half a day to realize it."

"Yes." She wraps her fingers with his. "I know you believe that. Me too with you. And I think I should stop putting you off. And we should become lovers. But—"

He kisses her, and they stay like that for a languorous moment, lips pressed, hands entangled. Until he says, "There are no buts."

"Okay, one," Jesse whispers. "We should go slowly."

"Even more slowly than we've been going?" he says with a grin.

"No, but more slowly than you probably want."

He pulls back. "Why is that?"

"I think it's better. Slow is better, don't you think?" Her look scarcely conveys great confidence in the proposition. "Tonight I'll sleep in your bed, and you'll just hold me."

"Okay," he says hesitantly, getting to his feet.

"You think I'm being ridiculous," she says.

"Well… quaint."

She feels happy and laughs. "Yes, I'm sure that's true. But go wash up and come to bed."

"What *were* you reading tonight when I came in?"

"Nothing serious. Nancy Mitford."

"Loving and light," he says.

"Yes."

"Which is how you want to keep us?"

"No, Alec. Not light. I really don't. I'm just trying—"

He lifts her from the bed and holds her. Wraps his arms around her and feels hers close tightly around him. They stay like that lengthily, until she steps back. "Okay," she says, breathless.

"Okay what?"

"Maybe slow's not so clever."

"So what do we do?" he says, smiling.

She unsashes her bathrobe, and lets it fall to the floor. She's wearing a nightgown, which she raises over her head and lets fall on top of the bathrobe. The shock of the real—her slim-hipped, small-breasted bare body—reduces his usable vocabulary to two exclamatory words. "You're extraordinary," he says.

"I wish I could be that," she says. "But I've never felt it."

"Then it will be my job to see that you do."

TWENTY-FOUR

At the Westchester Airport, Lee Norris stands waiting, his bulk curled over a cane. He hates to sit, he says to Alec, because it's too hard to get up. Then he gives that shy look of his, which is also mischievous. It's never only about that moment or statement. It's as if he's found some broader absurdity—in himself, or others, or the world—and wants you to share the discovery. When he was attorney general, and then secretary of state, that look became famous. But Alec remembers it from a much earlier time—from law school, when Norris, behind a steaming jug of coffee, at 8 a.m., reacted to all labored efforts, including his own, to make sense of constitutional law.

They take off in a Computer Corp. jet. Once in the air, Alec asks, "What's between you and Stapleton?"

Norris smiles. "We both clerked for Felix Frankfurter. We didn't see eye to eye. And didn't much like each other, either. But we didn't actually hate each other, like Ettinger and Kane. They once worked for the same senator, the one who got them both appointed to the bench. What flared up then smolders to this day. And it's the reason we're now on this plane."

"Kane wants only to humiliate Ettinger?"

"No, I think he also wants to put an end to a situation that's humiliating the court. But sinking a spear into his old enemy would be an attractive bonus. And he's come up with a unique solution to a bad problem. Trouble is, Rivvy Kane doesn't know Eric Stapleton."

"Who has an aversion to originality."

"A deep fear," Norris says. "Eric has risen to his current post by avoiding anything that might smack of originality. Which is why his current post is the highest to which he will rise."

After several minutes of silence, Norris says, "Oh, by the way, I have some news that might interest you. Ever heard of Hannah Valley Light and Gas?"

"A public utility?"

"In West Virginia, yeah. I happen to be on the board there. For some years, it's been the thorn up the ass of your friend Donald Strand."

"Oh, really?"

"Turns out," Norris says, his big face gleaming, "he's been stalking them for years, but the good folks of Hannah Valley did not wish to be engulfed by the rapacious Donald. Now they're interested. I can't tell you why, and there's no need for you to know. But, strangely, Strand now seems a bit wary about making a deal. It might be a bargaining tactic. It might be something real standing in his way. Like, maybe, an antitrust problem? Would you know anything about that?"

"I might, yes," Alec says. "Especially if Hannah Valley is a large utility."

"It's quite sizable. In fact, it's the largest utility within a 500-mile radius that Mid-Atlantic has not already acquired. Which, for Donald Strand, is like owning Broadway and most everything on the board, but not Park Place."

"Then maybe I can help."

"Good," Norris says. "I thought I might have come to the right place on this."

When they land at National Airport, a company car awaits on the tarmac to drive them into town. No matter how many times he's been to Washington, Alec, an outsider to the Beltway scene, cannot ride unimpressed past the nation's great monuments and buildings. Norris appears not to notice. Entering the Department of Justice, however, which he ruled for nearly two years, he says under his breath, "This is too fucking nostalgic," with that shy smile turned briefly to Alec.

They are ushered into the big office immediately. Stapleton has no mind to play games with Lee Norris. But the meeting goes as predicted. Alec unfurls Judge Kane's plan. Stapleton, suspecting something unusual, is nonetheless flabbergasted, bursts out with a boisterous laugh, and even proclaims, "Ingenious!"

"Paperwork couldn't be simpler," Alec adds. "All that's required is an agreement to submit the issues of the litigation to arbitration by Judge Mansfield. One sentence. One page. In fact, I have it right here," he says, laying the proposed stipulation on Stapleton's desk. "You sign it; we move to dismiss the court case on the grounds that the parties have agreed to arbitrate; Mansfield reads all the evidence put in so far plus anything further either side wants to introduce; and he renders a decision which is not appealable. That's it. A clean and final disposition of the largest, most ridiculous circus in the history of the federal courts."

Stapleton picks the paper up carefully. Glances at it for a moment. "Of course, I will have to think about this."

Alec says, "Let me add this to your thoughts. Everyone knows you will win before Ettinger, because they also know that he's biased. He's been mandamused three times by the Court of Appeals. There's no honor to winning before a biased judge. And by this initiative, the chief judge is telling you that Ettinger's decision is dead on arrival. It's an ugly situation for everyone, Eric. Letting an honest judge decide the case will clean it up."

Stapleton lays the paper back on his desk and pushes it away from him. "As I said—"

"Let me also add something," Norris says, interrupting. "I realize you're probably out of here by the time Ettinger's decision gets shredded by the Court of Appeals. But you know what his decision will leave in its wake?"

"Of course. A few hundred private treble-damage actions."

"More like a thousand," Norris says. "Claimants hoping to cash in, even though they would know it was a baseless decision of a biased judge. And you know the cost of that? To everyone? Courts included? No, of course you don't. It's too big to measure. But I'm sure you know what your own case is costing the government. That's got to be well over a hundred mil. Already. By the time we finish, it will be double that. And for that extravagant waste, Eric, the buck stops here."

"You say baseless. My people tell me—"

"Oh, come on, Eric!" Norris says, slamming his fist to the desk. "Your entire case rests on your contention that the market is limited to the United States. And that's palpable nonsense. The market is worldwide, and you're smart enough to know it. Every day we're losing ground to the Japanese. And this case is only accelerating that loss."

"So end it today, Lee. I have a draft of a consent decree in my drawer. Damages are a mere half billion, and we break up U.S. Computer into only three different companies."

Norris struggles to his feet. "You know what you may do with *that* draft," he says quietly.

"I *will* think about this," Stapleton says, pointing to the draft stipulation. And then to Alec: "You tell the chief judge I've taken this under advisement."

"Sure thing," Alec says, not hiding his assessment of the outcome of that process. He and Lee Norris start walking toward the door.

"One moment," says Stapleton. "I have some light reading for your trip home, Alec. Please share it with Caddy Breen."

Alec turns as Norris goes into the hall. "You're willing to amend the old consent decree?"

"Not quite," Stapleton says. "What I'm giving you is a new one."

"Meaning you'll sue us first."

"Civil, Alec. Not criminal. And we won't actually prosecute any case. We'll announce the filing of the complaint and the new decree simultaneously. That will be the end of it. This sort of thing is done all the time." Looking at Alec's face, he adds, "Sorry. Best I could do. But you'll like it. It reduces the risk that the rest of the public utility industry will sue."

"Marginally," Alec says.

"It's a good deal, Alec. You get Caddy to sign it."

In the car to the airport, Norris says, "What was that all about? Your Allis-Benoit thing?"

Alec nods and starts filling him in while reading the two-page decree.

Norris asks, "Is he forcing you to admit liability?"

"The opposite," Alec says, actually surprised. "He's allowing us to deny it."

"That's pretty good. What's the bite?"

"No public announcement of prices by the manufacturers. Confidentiality provision in sales contracts, prohibiting customers from revealing prices and terms."

"That's it?"

"That's it."

"So now you can cut prices with less chance of Edison Electric finding out about it."

"If they sign, yeah."

"Of course they'll sign!" Norris says. "How the hell you pull this off?" He grabs Alec's arm. "No, don't tell me. Stapleton's neither that smart nor that generous. But he is a coward. So you frightened him."

Alec smiles.

"With what?" Norris says. "Hmm. Ah. Obvious. You threatened him with going out of business—and blaming him for putting thousands out of work."

"Wasn't an empty threat," Alec says. "Bob Curtis told him face-to-face he'd already lined up board support."

"You brought Curtis to Stapleton's office?"

Alec relates the story, from the meeting in Cleveland to the session with Stapleton.

"Jesus Christ, Alec. That's fucking out of this world. Do something like that for us here."

Alec's first call from his office is to Larry Rilesman, who's unsure how to take the news. "Sue us, settle the same day, how's that get read? I mean by the public utilities?"

"Should get read for what it means. Stapleton wants a consent decree. So he brings a new suit instead of amending the old decree, because it makes him look more aggressive."

"The utilities may need help understanding that."

"We're here to provide it."

"That lawyer who represents them, what's his name? Marius Shilling? He's a friend of yours, right?"

"We get along. I'll talk to him."

"Better be soon. The standstill agreement is about to run out. Needs extending."

"That it does."

"But as I think about it, this result with the government is really fantastic, Alec. Barely a slap on the wrists for us. I'm sure Bob will be pleased. And I guess the other public utilities will stay in their cage, right? Just sign the extension? I mean from their standpoint, why not simply await the outcome in Mid-Atlantic's case? If Mid-Atlantic wins, they get the benefit of it. We're collaterally estopped from defending ourselves on liability. If Mid-Atlantic loses, why spend money on a losing claim?"

"That's the analysis," Alec says, wondering if Rilesman had just figured it out.

"And the Mid-Atlantic case will go on for years."

"Probably right," Alec says.

"Whatta you mean, 'probably'?"

"What I said."

"It's the way you said it. Something you're not telling me?"

"No, it's fine, Larry. Let me get Caddy on the phone. He's dying to hear, and we need him to agree."

Caddy Breen's reaction is simply, "That's all Stapleton wants?"

"That's it," Alec says.

"And the whole government threat goes away? You must have put on quite a show."

"Seems to have worked."

"Well, I can see how your guys would like this more than mine, but it's still a great deal for both companies. Thank you. Of course a simple amendment to the old decree would've been better, but there's no reason this deal should stop the public utilities from extending the standstill."

"Something else might," Alec notes.

"Oh?"

"Suppose we could get Mid-Atlantic to drop its case right now? In the next few weeks. Before the standstill runs out?"

"By paying them what?" Breen says. "A hundred mil? Two? And then paying out proportionate amounts—billions—to 125 other utilities under the most-favored-nations provision of the standstill agreement? I don't think so, Alec."

"Not an option, no. But I think Mid-Atlantic may be peculiarly open to settlement right now." Alec relates the news about Hannah Valley's change of heart about being engulfed by Donald Strand. "So what do you think? What does Strand want more: a 50-50 chance of collecting treble damages from us, or living his dream of owning every public utility in the six states surrounding him?"

"Which his lawyers tell him he can't do with our counterclaim dangling over his head."

"Good chance they're giving him that advice, yes," Alec says.

"But he won't drop his claims just because we agree to drop our counterclaims. He'll want more."

"So we give him a bit of a sweetener."

"What sweetener?" Breen asks. "I just said—the most-favored-nations provision kills that. We can't pay Mid-Atlantic *anything* without paying off every other utility in the country."

"Yeah, we can," Alec says. "Reimbursement of counsel fees."

"Ah," Breen says. Then, "Hmm, clever. Might not trigger the MFN. But you think Mid-Atlantic would settle for that? Fees can't be that high a figure. Freddy Musselman is probably doing this case on a contingency arrangement."

"Let's say Freddy were offered a lump sum? Now? Without having to do any more work? And we might also agree to reimburse Mid-Atlantic for their out-of-pocket expenses. The key is *reimbursement*. Of money Mid-Atlantic has already spent, or is committed to spend. What triggers the MFN is a payment settling the damage claims."

"Whatever you call it, Alec, from Strand's standpoint, it's peanuts."

"Worth a try. And it's your play. Or your CEO's. I got Bob Curtis to cry on Stapleton's desk. Now you get your guy slamming on Strand's. Okay?"

"I dunno," Breen says. "Play it out. Let's say we pull off this miracle, get Mid-Atlantic to drop their case for the reimbursement of peanuts. There's nothing left for 125 other utilities to stand still for. Why won't they just sue us? In fact, how the hell would their public utility commissions let them do anything else? And then we're looking at 125 suits instead of one."

"Unless," Alec says, with a greater show of confidence than he feels, "we talk them out of it. Bring all 125 together and show them how unwise such lawsuits would be."

"Oh, yeah?" Breen says with a bit of an edge to it. "How the fuck you plan to pull that off? I mean, even if you could somehow get them all in one room. From their standpoint, every reason says—no, *shouts*—'Sue the bastards!' "

"I'll think of something."

"Great," Breen says. "Because this would be your play."

"Not a problem," Alec says. "With no government case and

no Mid-Atlantic case for them to take a free ride on, they should be open to reason on the subject."

Breen laughs. "Reason, huh? Wow. You, man, are chutzpah incarnate. All right, Alec, let's see what my client thinks about all this."

Alec knows what they'll think. Edison Electric does not have Allis-Benoit's problem. Going to trial with Mid-Atlantic would not put Edison out of business. Moreover, Edison had a better chance of winning that trial than it would, if it settled, convincing 125 utilities not to bring the same suits. In fact, if Edison tried the case and beat Mid-Atlantic—demonstrating the strength of the turbine manufacturers' defense—then, and only then, might there be a decent chance of persuading the other utilities, and their PUCs, to go away.

This whole plan, Alec thinks, *is pretty damn close to hopeless. Yet Caddy has to believe in it enough to even make the argument to his client; they have to believe in it enough even to start negotiations with Mid-Atlantic; Strand must somehow want to get rid of that counterclaim so badly that he'll take peanuts to settle the whole case; and all 125 public utilities must then desist, when every conceivable reason points to their suing the moment Mid-Atlantic drops out.*

Alec's secretary, Sweeta Gottsen, opens his door. "While you were on the phone, chief judge's chambers called. He wants you up there. Now."

TWENTY-FIVE

I didn't want to discuss this on the phone," Judge Kane says, pushing away from his desk. He beckons to the chair in front of it, which Alec takes.

"Understood," Alec says.

"So tell me. You met? You put the proposition?"

"This morning."

"And Stapleton's reaction?"

"Very guarded."

"The nature of the man, so I gather. And what is your assessment of the outcome?"

"He won't go for it," Alec says. "Too novel. Too risky. He's got a sure thing while he's in office—a sure win before Ettinger. After that—let some other assistant AG try to deal with the appeals and nasty aftereffects."

Kane's reaction devolves into a peevish frown. "What about the AG?" he says. "I asked you to call him."

"I know. And I agreed. Then I thought more about it and realized how he'd take the suggestion. He expects his assistant AGs to make that kind of decision. Asking him to do it first would just annoy him."

"And asking him after Stapleton turns this down?"

"I think you know the answer, Judge."

Kane rises with displeasure. Begins his ritual pacing. After some moments of scuffing the carpet, he turns and says, "What about getting Stapleton fired?"

"Great," Alec says. "Can you do it?"

"Hmm," says the jurist. "Probably not."

"Can you get him promoted?" Alec asks. "Say, to deputy AG. There's an opening."

"Really?" Kane seems to like that idea. "You know I might. Might actually be able to do that. You have a candidate for the Antitrust Division?"

"I do, as it happens. But isn't that a bit over the line, my proposing him?"

"What line?" says the judge in a tone scoffing at the notion that any line should stand in the way of something he wanted.

"My firm's got two huge cases pending there, Judge."

"So you do. Very respectable, Alec." Judge Kane issues a barking laugh at what he evidently considers an overly nice, and punctilious, sentiment. "So what are we looking for?"

"Smart. Gutsy. An original thinker."

"Well," says Kane expansively, "those criteria should certainly narrow the field."

"Probably too big a hint on my part."

"No doubt," says the judge. "I can't identify such a person offhand, but with that lead, I'm sure to find him soon enough."

"You might want someone with both trial experience and academic credentials."

"Now," says Kane with another laugh, "you're probably pointing right at him!"

"Not at all," Alec says. "There are at least six or seven people I can think of who fit that profile."

"*And* are original thinkers?"

"Well, that, I agree—that's more difficult to find. Can be done only by someone having the same characteristic."

"Leaves me out, you're saying," Kane says with a smile.

"On the contrary, Judge. Means you're about the only one who can do it."

Kane gives a guffaw. "How the hell do you get away with that stuff, such blatant flattery?"

"It's just knowing your audience, Judge. Like anything else."

❖

Harvey Grand sits waiting in Alec's office. He has carte blanche
to use it. Anything there still confidential has probably been supplied by Harvey himself.

Always good to see Harvey, Alec thinks, though his visit without notice likely means trouble.

"So, what's up?" Alec says, bracing.

"We've seen some of Sal's men near the school." Harvey beckons Alec into the facing chair. "That's the bad news."

"What's the good?" says Alec.

"They're biding their time," Harvey says. "They know we're
watching them. The chances they'll try to snatch are a bit less
when they know we're there."

"Is it time to call in the cops?"

"What're the odds you can do that without Sal finding out
almost immediately?"

"Very low," Alec admits.

"And how long will the cops stay on it if Sal's people don't
appear?"

"Couple of days." It's a rueful comment.

"So we'd gain a little time," Harvey says, "which in this case
means little, and we'd maybe lose some credibility."

"Can you add people?" Alec asks.

"Sure," Harvey says. "But when Sal's ready to move—if that's
his plan—they can outnumber us very easily."

"I ought to get Sarah out of this country."

Harvey breathes deeply with glumness and fatigue. "Where?"

"You're saying, Sal can find her wherever."

"And when he does," Harvey points out, "it'll be easier for
him to grab her."

"So what're you suggesting we do?"

"What we are doing, Alec. I just wanted you to know how
it is."

❖

Alec arrives home, carrying, as usual, a full attaché case. It's battered and old and nearly dilapidated, which is pretty much how he feels.

"Tell me about your day," Jesse says from the kitchen. She looks to him settled in now, standing there in her jeans and T-shirt, perfectly right where she is. Balancing his life. Filling it, despite everything, with an undercurrent of joy.

"My day," he repeats in the doorway while dropping his bag. "Well…." And then he abruptly tells her about Harvey's report.

A plate goes smash on the counter, fallen from her hand. She doesn't move. "So it's started," she says. "How do we deal with this?"

He spells out the depressing alternatives. But then adds, "Sal knows we know. He may go away."

"Or he may just grab her sooner."

Alec says slowly, "We're doing what we can, Jess, to stop that."

"This sucks."

"Yes," he says.

"It must be like what you went through with Phil."

"Very much like."

"But you beat him," she says.

"Yes."

She sits at the island in front of her broken plate. "You want a salad?"

"No thanks," he says, getting a glass of water for himself. "Ate at the office."

"What?" she asks.

"I'm sorry?"

"What did you eat?"

He laughs. "Haven't the slightest memory of it."

She laughs too, but wryly, and gathers the shards of porcelain into a pile. "So tell me. Anything. The rest of your day."

He takes the chair facing her and tells of his trip to Washington, his meeting with the chief judge, and other encounters.

"My god!" she says. "How can you get through a day like that without coming home catatonic?"

"Can't," he says with a smile.

"So no sex tonight?"

That sends a current. "You were hoping we might?"

"My days are not as complicated as yours," she says. "I have the time to think about anything. Which very often means sex, if I'm to be totally candid."

"Candor is definitely best."

"Not always," she says.

His look is pensive, which is not what she expects. "Last night—" he starts.

"Yes. It was wonderful."

"And tonight?"

"Tonight," she says. "Yes… tonight I will sleep in your bed."

"Sounds… provisional."

"No, Alec, it's not. It's…." She touches his arm, shrugs, then gets up for a dishrag with which she sweeps the broken plate into a trash can. She finds another plate for her salad. He's been watching every move, and she looks up from spooning her salad onto the new dish. "You knew my parents, right? Conner and Kate?"

"I knew your mom. Briefly. She came to the wedding. Never met your dad."

"You didn't miss much. She was no prize, but he? A drunk, a hanger-on looking for handouts. A lawyer, if you could believe it, but mainly a bagman for the mob. It's how Carrie met Phil. Conner worshipped Carrie but was so self-seeking, he brought her to meet Phil. Who eventually killed him. You know that story?"

"Yes," he says softly.

"When Conner and Kate produced Carrie, there might have been something left to whatever relationship they once had. But

I was an accident. Or probably worse. It might have been rape. I know Kate hated him. And neither one of them thought much of me. I couldn't leave that house fast enough. When Phil offered to pay my tuition and board in Ireland—no doubt to keep me out of the way—I jumped at it. When I came back, I met this guy, and I had a surprising physical attraction to him." She stops. "No, that's less than I mean. It was surprisingly *overwhelming*. But, of course, Carrie had gotten there first. As always."

"Jesse—"

"It's the answer to your question," she says. "Boiled down from—I don't know—a couple of hundred hours of therapy."

"I didn't ask a question."

"Yes you did. And I'm saying, I'm not your normal put-together-right girl. I can get pretty wacky. Like now. About thoroughly trusting any relationship. I need more than the—what do you lawyers call it?—the standard quantum of proof."

"Where'd you get that expression?" Alec says.

"The guy in Dublin—the one I had a relationship with—he was a barrister. A kind, graceful, very smart man. Like you. Only he wasn't you. So you see? For me you're a double whammy. Can't have other guys, because they're not you. Can't have you, because I'm not my sister."

"You do have me, Jess."

"Why?" she asks straight-faced.

"Why?"

"Yes. Why me?"

"Why do you think? I like wacky girls."

"I thought you liked candor."

"Okay," he says. "Candor. Because you're the sexiest woman alive."

"Alive, right. That's the key."

Alec says, "I think we should stop talking about this, Jess. I love you; I loved your sister; and there is no connection whatever between those two facts. In ten years you will have forgotten you ever thought there was."

"Ha."

"You want proof?" he says. "You will have it. That's a promise."

"A promise?"

"Yes. Absolutely. So finish your dinner so we can go to bed."

After she eats her salad and cleans up, they go to his bedroom, Jesse making no pretense of going anyplace else. But she says, "I'll use the bathroom in the other room and come back."

Alec undresses in his own bathroom and washes up. By the time he emerges and turns off the light, Jesse is already in bed. He slides in and holds her. "You forgot your nightgown," he says.

"Nope. I didn't forget." She turns to kiss him on the mouth, her tongue slipping between his teeth. "I like your toothpaste," she says.

"I know what you're doing," he says, squeezing her bare bottom. "You are de-romanticizing this moment."

"What I am doing," she says, "is exerting the little control I have left, because in another moment I will have lost every bit of it."

TWENTY-SIX

Cadigan Breen calls the next morning. Edison Electric will accept the decree as written. "The other project—your crazy settlement-for-counsel-fees idea—is underway," Breen adds, "although, I'll tell you this, Alec, no one gives it a snowball's chance in hell."

Ten minutes later, Eric Stapleton's on the line. "Regarding the decree, Alec—you have Edison Electric ready to sign?"

"I do."

"Okay. You get your signed copies to me by courier today and we'll put out a release tomorrow. No crowing. Just the facts."

"I'd like to see that, the release. And I'm sure Caddy would. You have one drafted?"

Long pause. "Okay," Stapleton finally says. "It's four sentences. I'll have my secretary dictate it to yours." Shorter pause. "Now on that other matter."

"Computer Corp."

"Yes. I'm afraid I can't do that."

"Mind saying why?"

"Off the record?"

"Yes, okay."

"Well, morale," Stapleton says. "Within the division. Too many people working too long. I can't just change their direction."

"There'd be no change at all," Alec says. "Not in direction. They'd be trying the same case on the same record. Only difference, they'd be doing it before a judge who was sane. And smart. And objective."

Stapleton lets out a weary sigh. "Do I really have to spell this out for you, Alec?"

"No," Alec says. "You just did."

Alec calls George Stigler and fills him in on the turbine generator situation.

"Well, that's typical," Stigler says. "There was one small ember of price competition left burning in this market, and the government decree will now snuff it out. Nice going, Antitrust Division. But I suppose *you* are to be congratulated. Let's hope your victory isn't Pyrrhic."

"But you think otherwise?"

"Look at the facts," Stigler says. "The government has now declared that your guys and Edison Electric have been fixing prices. That's probably not true, but that's what their new complaint will say. Do the PUCs need more? Populated as they are by political animals. Their function, as they see it, is to be popular with the rate-payers. And the ratepayers are happy only if they can get lower rates. This can happen if the utilities collect damages from you. And the only thing stopping the PUCs from forcing the utilities to sue now is that Mid-Atlantic is doing it for them. The question is, how long will they all wait? Any one of them sues, every one of them will follow. I'm told that Philadelphia Electric lawyer—what's his name?"

"Harold Kohn?"

"That's the guy. You know him? I'm told he's the toughest antitrust lawyer in the country."

"Haven't had the pleasure," Alec says, "but I'm aware of him, yeah."

"Well, keep me posted—I always enjoy watching someone trying to perform magic. It's what makes church so much fun."

One more essential call. Alec dials the chief judge's private line. "They're not buying it," he says.

"That's final? You sure?"

"Yes." Alec waits for Rivvy Kane fully to ingest it.

"All right," says the jurist. "I hate to reward this man, Stapleton, for his limitations. But that's the process, isn't it? The Peter Principle. Isn't that what it's called? Promoting everyone to the level of their incompetence? Ha!" And he hangs up without giving a clue as to how he plans to achieve such an elevation.

Days pass. The government complaint is filed; the decree is entered; space is bestowed to both events in all major media, especially the financial press. No word from the utilities lawyer, Marius Shilling, about his clients' reactions to either. Nothing from Caddy Breen about Edison's attempt to rid themselves of the Mid-Atlantic litigation. And not a whisper from the chief judge about the chances of promoting Stapleton from his Antitrust Division job. Finally, however, Harvey Grand calls with good news. "They've gone. No trace of them for two days."

"But you'll stay on it," Alec says.

"Of course."

"And—"

"I know, Alec, I know. I'll call you the second they come back."

"Because they will."

"I know that too," Harvey says.

That night, arriving home even later than usual, Alec finds Jesse reading in bed—their bed—and Sarah still out. "Where is she?" Alec asks.

"At Tino's," she says, putting her book down. "My guess is his mom's out, and they have that apartment to themselves."

"You think they're sleeping together?"

"They're having sex, Alec. I assume they're doing it in bed, the conventional way."

"Hmm," he says, sitting close to her on the edge of their bed.

"Does this news disturb you?" Jesse says. "You think she's too young?"

"I think she's sensible. And I think he's okay."

"So it doesn't disturb you."

"Of course it *disturbs* me," Alec says. "On some primal level, it disturbs the hell out of me."

"Does it surprise you?"

"No."

"Are you happy for her?"

"Mixed feelings, like I said. Very mixed."

"But you'll do nothing about this," Jesse says. "Including not insulting her intelligence by telling her to be careful."

"Right," he says with an evident lack of enthusiasm.

"Good man," she says, reopening her book.

"One more thing." He relates Harvey's news.

"So it's what you expected. They caught you watching them, and they've gone off for a while."

"Yes."

"Okay," she says. "An interregnum. Now go wash up so *we* can have sex."

TWENTY-SEVEN

Marius Shilling invites Alec to lunch.

Lunch with Shilling means 12:30 at the Downtown Association. Neither place nor time need be mentioned; both are assumed. The routine was established in the days leading up to Alec's first major trial—litigation involving a giant fraud financed by mob boss Phil Anwar, Sarah's natural father, and ending with a victory for Alec that brought him into partnership in his firm. Shilling had also been retained by Alec's client, not for the trial but to settle its debts to the banks on a related matter. Alec tried the case because Frank Macalister, who, before getting dry in AA, drove his car into a tree in the driveway of his country club. And Alec was assigned the job of getting along with Marius Shilling because Mac, the sort of character often played by John Wayne, and Shilling, one best depicted by Erich von Stroheim, were born to be at each other's throats.

Arriving at the Downtown Association is like entering another world, one taking place *circa* 1880. Alec thinks of it as shabby genteel, although the gentility is richly displayed in red plush fabrics, worn thin in very few places, red leather chairs, slightly cracked in one or two seats, starched white tablecloths having only an occasional tear, and glinting silver. Porters and waiters are, of course, formally dressed. Members speak only in murmurs.

Shilling is waiting at his usual table and gives his customary half-rise acknowledgement of Alec's arrival. After greeting each other, reminiscing briefly, and ordering their meal—done in a place like this with the member, Shilling, writing it out and handing it to a geriatric waiter—they get to the business at hand.

Shilling says, "You do realize, my dear boy, that our standstill agreement is nearing its termination date?"

"Well aware, yes."

"We'll have to extend that, for a while at least."

" 'A while'?"

"The statute of limitations has already run out—or rather would have had it not been extended by the tolling agreement. So if the agreement terminates, the limitations period snaps shut retroactively to wipe out any claim. If you're not ready to extend the standstill, my clients will have to sue right now."

"That's not what I was asking," Alec says. "We're perfectly willing to extend. But your people had always made clear you would actually *stand still* so long as Mid-Atlantic was still prosecuting the claim. And that will go on for more than *'a while.'*"

"Well, that's the problem—or, at least, part of it."

"Oh?"

"It's not moving very fast, Alec. And now, with the government affirming the validity of the claim...."

"Come on, Marius. You know better. The filing of the government complaint was inter-department politics. And ending that case on the day it was filed, with a consent decree that's essentially meaningless—you think those were the acts of a confident prosecutor? If the government thought they had a winner, they'd have gone for a win, which would have collaterally estopped us from defending ourselves against your clients on the liability issue. They would have handed you a free ticket to damages."

"You should talk to Harold Kohn, Philadelphia Electric's outside counsel."

"Why? Is he going to take over your job?"

"If Philadelphia Electric sues," Shilling says, "he'll probably represent all the utilities."

"Not Freddy Musselman?"

"I'm told he'll give way to Kohn."

"And Kohn wants to sue?" Alec asks.

"Harold always wants to sue."

"So what are you telling me, Marius? What's this about?"

"I think we should talk settlement now," the older lawyer pronounces.

"Of 125 claims that may never get filed?" Alec says.

"It's the best time. Before anyone's spent money on such cases. Before Harold Kohn steps in—because he won't settle. He likes blood. Before you lose to the coal companies and have no money left. And before you lose to Mid-Atlantic, and have no defenses left. When, obviously, the price of settlements will be a great deal higher."

"And before we beat Mid-Atlantic, when the price will be zero, because the other utilities will walk away."

"You've very little chance of that, Alec."

"We'll see."

"So that's a no?" Shilling says. "You're unwilling to talk?"

"On the contrary. Anything you like. Standstill extension— just change the dates on the old agreement, we'll be happy to sign. Settlement? Make an offer. Make 125 offers—happy to pass them on."

"With your approval?"

"Of course not. We're going to win our case against Mid-Atlantic, your clients will go away, and that will be the end of it."

"My dear friend, I don't believe you."

"Then test it. Make your offers and watch them be turned down. Wait out the case and watch us win it."

"You will destroy your client, Alec!"

"Funny," he says. "I think right now staying the course might be the only thing keeping them alive."

From the backseat of Harvey's Cadillac, Sarah complains. "This is ridiculous, Harvey. You're not a driver. If I needed someone to drive me, I'd call Schlomo."

"Not in these circumstances."

"What circumstances?" she says. "They've gone away. You said so."

"And I've told you—"

"Right. They're coming back. So when they do, you can drive me."

The light changes and Harvey heads up Madison Avenue. "Where we going, Sarah? You haven't said."

"Tino's."

"Is he there? Waiting?"

"Maybe. If not, he'll be there soon."

"You have a key?" Harvey asks.

"Yes," Sarah says. "I have a key."

"But until Tino arrives, you'll be there alone?"

"I told you," she says with asperity. "He'll be there soon. Can we return to the subject, please?"

"The subject is your safety. When the threat is removed, you can have Schlomo."

"You think he can't deal with a threat? If it comes, he'll drive away from it. Would you do anything different? And with Schlomo, I get to sit in the front seat."

"Which is part of the problem."

"Huh?"

"If they come shooting," Harvey says, "they won't be aiming at the backseat. And as for the threat, Sarah, who do you think has a better chance of seeing it coming?"

That stifles her for a block.

"You know my… uncle?" she says.

"I know who he is."

"And Phil?" she says. "Did you know him?"

"We never actually met."

"But you were there? That night?"

"You don't remember?"

"Seeing you then? No. But you were there?"

"Yes."

"And you were wounded," she says.

"Yes."

"Phil didn't do that."

"One of his men."

"Who you killed."

"Yes."

"A gunfight," she says, showing sudden anger, "with a five-year-old kid upstairs. Which Phil started. My father, the man who brought me there. But I lived through that, and I can live through this."

"You remember that night?" Harvey says.

"Oh, yeah."

"Well, your uncle is worse," Harvey says. "By reputation—but the stories are real. And he'll be a lot more reckless with your life than Phil was. So until we know this is over—totally over—you want to go somewhere, you drive in my car."

When Tino arrives home from basketball practice, Sarah is in the kitchen fixing dinner. "We're playing house," she announces.

"We're not playing," he says, taking a seat at the small kitchen table. "What are you making? Is that sauce?"

"For our spaghetti."

"You have a recipe?"

"I'm making it up," she says. "It can't be that hard."

"From a can?"

"Lots of cans. Pretty much anything with tomatoes in it. Plus there's meatballs."

"You made meatballs?" Now he's really surprised.

"I thought you'd like them."

"What about you?"

"I'll have one."

Tino laughs. "Can I help?"

"Yeah, you can set the table."

It turns out to be an excellent meal, which surprises them both. She says, twirling her pasta, "The secret is to make the spaghetti al dente. "

"You're speaking Italian now?"

"I am Italian," she says. "Half, anyway."

Tino, soberly, says, "My mother's coming back in a few days."

"I know."

"Can we do this in your apartment?"

"That would be awkward," she says.

"So let's get married."

She laughs. "Make an honest woman of me?"

"Yes." He isn't kidding.

"I'm a sophomore in high school, Tino."

"Yes, and?" he says with a show of emotion. "Can you think of yourself being married to anyone else?"

"No," she says quickly, pushing aside any doubts.

"Me neither. I didn't expect this. I'm sure you didn't. But it's not going to change."

"Okay," she says, slowing her voice, "you're probably right. But I'm sixteen. A very mature sixteen, no question. But big decisions? We should wait a bit on that, don't you think?"

"It would make things a lot easier if we didn't."

"Oh?" she says, suspicious. "You mean with your uncle?"

He says nothing.

She says, "And that's what this is all about?"

"No!" He gives a lopsided smile. "I'm just using all the arguments I can think of."

"That's not a good one."

"Sorry," he says. "You're right, it's not good."

"And he'd be disappointed, Tino. My money's in a trust. I can't get at it. Your uncle is just wasting his time."

Tino reflects on that. "That's not like Uncle Sal. He doesn't waste time. He must know something."

"Like what?" She's almost indignant.

"I dunno. You couldn't get it, even if your life was in danger?"

"And you're suggesting what?" she says, voice now rising. "This is Sal's plan? You know this?"

"Of course I don't *know* it. It's just how he thinks."

"There's nothing like that in my trust."

"Have you read it?"

"I don't have to read it."

"Well, I don't want to talk about your money," Tino says. "I don't want any part of it."

"Then why are we talking about it?"

"Because Sal does. Talk about it, because he wants it. And it worries me sick, Sarah. What he would do to you to get it."

They've stopped eating, and for a long time don't talk. Finally, Sarah says, "How could you have ever thought of working for such a man?"

"I don't know," he says. "I couldn't now."

"But you did. Think of working for him. You planned to do it."

"Yes. It wasn't real. This is real. What we have. It's not playing house. It's not *playing* at anything."

"But it's stopped being fun."

"Sarah," he says, almost pleading.

"This conversation makes it no fun."

"I will talk to him," Tino says, looking at her very hard. "I will tell him, he goes near you again, he loses me."

TWENTY-EIGHT

Midweek, midmorning. Cadigan Breen says on the phone, "Alec, are you sitting down?"

"Sitting, Caddy, what's the news?"

"Well, I'm at the Mid-Atlantic Power & Light building in Richmond, Virginia, where we've just concluded a deal. It's contingent on your client's accepting it. Think you can get them to do that?"

"Might help if I knew the terms."

"Terms, right," Breen says. He's in high comedy. "We drop our counterclaims. You okay with that?"

"Stop jerking around, Caddy. What's the rest of it?"

"What was our wish, our biggest wish, for a settlement with Mid-Atlantic that wouldn't trigger the most-favored-nations provision?"

"That it be limited to counsel fees."

"Bigger wish."

"That it be less than the total counsel fees?"

"Yes!" says Breen, "and that's what we got. Contribution to counsel fees. You hear that word, *contribution!* Turns out ol' Freddy was not doing this on a full contingency, after all. He was billing them right along, and so was Stash, so the bill total was gigantic. What Mid-Atlantic will take from us as a *contribution* to fees is one million bucks. And my client, Edison, is willing to split that very favorably with Allis-Benoit—we do $670,000, you do $330,000. In other words, your guys get out of this mess for less than a third of a million, which, against a more than $300 million exposure, is chump change. Think you can sell *that*, counselor?"

"Yeah, I think I can sell that. Well done, Caddy. Brilliant deal."

"Hell, it was your idea, Alec. The whole fucking thing. Your client should be made aware of that."

"I'll be sure to tell 'em."

Breen laughs, knowing the opposite will likely be true.

"The guy we need now," Alec says, "is Marius Shilling."

"Okay," Breen says with a slight hesitation. "But he represents the utilities only on the standstill agreement."

"Right. And how do we—in a few weeks—persuade 125 utilities not to sue us? Go from office to office? Not feasible. Write letters? Waste of time."

"We need a meeting," Breen says. "With the whole group. One hundred twenty-five companies and their lawyers. In one room. And only Marius can arrange such a meeting."

"I'll call him," Alec says.

"You think he'll go for it?"

"I think he'll love it," Alec says. "The thought of turning all those clients over to Harold Kohn is probably making him sick."

Alec persuades Larry Rilesman's secretary to pull him out of a meeting to come to the phone. When given the report, Rilesman needs a moment to consider the ramifications that really matter. "I suppose credit for this must go to Caddy Breen."

"I guess," Alec says noncommittally.

"But we should get some of it," Rilesman says.

"You and I?"

"Well, yes."

"You mean with management," Alec says.

"Of course."

"I could fly out right now, explain things," Alec says without the slightest trace of taunt in his voice.

"No need, no need," Rilesman says quickly.

"You mean, you can handle it?"

"Absolutely, Alec, no problem. No reason for you to get on a plane."

"Of course I could do it on the phone," Alec cannot resist saying.

"No, no," says Rilesman, as if he were being magnanimous. "Got it covered. Rest easy and thanks for the news."

Hanging up on the man, Alec, in his empty office, gives way to a laugh before considering what's next and does matter, which is how he will put this development to Marius Shilling.

"What is it, Tino?" says Sal Angiapello, coming from behind his desk. "What's so important that I have to clear the room? You can see how busy I am."

What Tino sees are the angry faces of the three men with whom Sal had been meeting. In Lou DiBrazzi, anger is expressed as a contemptuous burr in the back of his throat, which is all the more menacing for being unspoken. As the door closes behind them in Sal's study, Tino says, "It's important to me, Uncle, and I hope it will be to you."

"Let me guess," Sal says. "It's about the girl."

"She has a name, Uncle."

"Oh, yes? What is it? Anwar? That's a made-up name. Phony, means nothing. Brno? That's not her real name. Has nothing to do with her. Angiapello? She spits on that name, as did her father."

"Men have been following her, Uncle."

"I know. They're my men. I take an interest in her. I want to give her a name."

"She will have a new name. Our name."

"Yes? Good."

"You were worried it might take too long, our getting married. But it may be sooner than I had thought."

"And my dear boy, I think you are wrong."

"With all respect, Uncle, this is something I can know better than you."

"That right?" The tone and smile change, and are chilling.

"We've actually discussed it, she and I. If you could have heard our last conversation!"

Sal turns away, seats himself behind his desk. "I did hear it."

"You bugged my apartment?"

"Actually, Tino, it's my apartment. Your poor father worked for me, as does your mother. As such, and as my relative, she is entitled to live in one of my apartments. And all of my apartments are equipped, shall we say, appropriately. Saves time, my knowing what my people think, their needs."

Tino's eyes close involuntarily as he speaks, "If anything were to happen to Sarah—"

"Stop, Tino. You do not want to be threatening me."

"I would not do that."

"You are doing it. With your voice," says the older man, his own now unguarded and dangerous. "It says you would want me dead. Is that what you would want, Tino?"

"No, Uncle. But you would be dead to me."

Alec calls Marius Shilling and is put right through. "I'd like to suggest a change in our routine."

"Our lunch routine?" Shilling says, sounding very uneasy. "You want to meet later?"

"No, 12:30 is good. But not the Downtown. The Wall Street Club, where I can reciprocate for all those lunches you've bought me."

"I'm also a member of the Wall Street."

"I know. But this time, I'll pay."

"Why?

"As I said."

"I heard you, I don't believe it, and I already don't like it."

Alec laughs. "You will."

"I'm hearing rumors, Alec, and I tell you, I don't like them. You will need something very comforting to tell me."

"We're having an adventure, Marius, and it will turn out well. Trust me."

They got the same corner table at which Alec had hosted Henry Lowenberg. Shilling was not nearly as impressed with the corner location, or as expansive in his personality, though in the glare of the sun his blue eyes, and dueling scars, glistened. "What's going on, Alec? Have you settled with Mid-Atlantic Power & Light? Because if that's happened, I should have known about it the second the papers were signed. It's already too late to be telling me this."

"You see, Marius, my respect for you is even greater than that. I give notice to you even before the event. We will be settling. The papers have not been signed. They have not even been drafted."

"Ah," Shilling says, settling down. "So this is why you want to buy me lunch. Sorry, dear friend, you are wasting your money. When you settle with Mid-Atlantic, you will trigger the most-favored-nations provision of the standstill agreement. I'm afraid I will not be representing the utilities on that. Harold Kohn will. Even though it should be a rather cut-and-dried matter. Say you pay Mid-Atlantic 10 mil, which represents 10 percent of its purchases from you. You owe every other utility in the country 10 percent of its purchases. That's what the MFN says. That's how it will be done—by you, or by a court."

"Not in this case," Alec says bluntly.

"What do you mean? You said you were settling."

"Not for damages. They are dropping the case for a fraction of their counsel fees."

"*What?*"

"You heard it."

"Counsel fees?" Shilling expostulates. "You got them to cave for counsel fees?"

"A portion of their counsel fees."

"How much?" Shilling asks, now suspicious.

"For my client, $330,000."

"That's unbelievable."

"It's the fact."

"And Edison Electric?"

"Slightly more than double."

"So for a measly million dollars the two biggest manufacturers in the world of heavy electrical equipment get rid of a suit claiming 300 million? How the hell did you do this, Alec? Was it your counterclaim? Were they actually afraid of that unprovable assertion?"

"You'll have to ask them."

"Oh, yes!" Shilling says. "Ask Donald Strand? Very amusing."

"No doubt they finally realized they were pouring money into a losing case."

"Hmm, hmm," Shilling says, nodding his head while thinking. "It must be the counterclaim. It stood in Strand's way. Now he can continue his plan to engulf and devour. Very clever, Alec. But what do you need from me?"

"A meeting. I want you to bring them all in. Early next week."

"Just like that?"

"Why not? They have something better to do?"

"Alec! We are talking about bringing to New York on short notice 125 utility companies! Executives, house counsel, outside trial lawyers. The logistics alone are staggering."

"And if they all went outside in the rain, what would they do? Put their umbrellas up, right? This is the same thing. Send them all telegrams. Tell them where they have to be, when, and why this is a meeting they'd be fools to miss. They'll come. They'll know they have to."

"And where will you put them? For this meeting?"

"You'll rent a ballroom at one of the big hotels."

"I'll rent?"

"They're your clients, Marius. They'll feel more comfortable in your room."

"And what?" Shilling says. "You hope to talk them all out of suing you? And bring down upon their heads the wrath of their public utility commissions? Are you dreaming?"

"Just get them here, Marius. They will bless you for it, I promise you. And they'll love to have an excuse for coming to New York on the company dime."

"What arguments could you possibly make to them?"

"I'll think of something."

"You'll *what*?"

Alec smiles with the self-assurance he wishes he felt. "Don't worry. The reasons will convince them. You bring them to this meeting, and not one of them will sue. And you and I will not have to watch Harold Kohn bill the utilities industry for the next five to ten years."

"And based on that," Shilling says, "based on your *I'll think of something*,' I should arrange this huge meeting? You realize, if it's a dud, Alec, they will blame me."

"Have I ever failed you, Marius?"

"Ah, we're down to that."

"We are."

Shilling blows out his copious cheeks. "You're asking a lot. And giving very little."

"Lunch?" Alec says.

"That's not funny."

"You will thank me, Marius. I give you my word."

Again the inflated cheeks. "I don't know, Alec, I really don't know."

"Yes, you do. Because time is running out, and this is the only thing to do with it that makes the slightest bit of sense."

Shilling picks up the menu and pretends to study it. "What's good in this place now? I haven't been here for years."

Alec and Jesse are in bed. She has just finished reading *The Bell Jar,* puts it on her night table, and picks up Jane Goodall's *In the Shadow of Man.* He's lying on his back, staring at the ceiling, with *Rabbit Redux* on his stomach.

She lowers Jane and says, "Updike not doing it for you?"

"Not this one, anyway."

"You liked Rabbit when he was running."

"I did. Not as much now."

"So you wanna talk?"

"With you, Jesse, always."

"Updike is a contemporary of yours," she says. "Do you know him?"

"No," he says. "Different schools. He was at Harvard."

"What about Sylvia Plath? She was at Smith when you were at Yale."

"How did you know that?"

"I figured it out," she says. "It wasn't hard."

"You looked at her bio and me and thought, wonder if those two bumped into each other? On one of his reconnaissance missions, maybe, to Northampton?"

"Something like that, yeah."

"In point of fact," Alec says, "she and I once double dated— she with the bad Yalie from *The Bell Jar,* who wasn't actually so bad, and me with another young woman from Smith. We went, as I recall, to a truly awful movie in New Haven. Sylvia was pissed off at this guy and not easy to talk to. What a missed opportunity, right? But she gave no signs that night of being a genius. And of course, then, who knew?"

Jesse thinks about that for a moment and says, "How about you?"

"Never in danger of being mistaken for a genius."

"I'm talking about *being* you, what was that like during all those years before we met?"

He shrugs. "You know what I've been doing the past dozen years. Well, I did a lot of the same sort of thing when I first came to work. Before that, college and law school, and before that, I grew up in Queens. Near the ocean. And you know that too."

"I don't know what it was *like*," she says. "How you felt about it. What was important to you?"

"I was a kid," he says. "Having fun was important."

"And how did you do that?"

"At what age?"

"Nine, ten?"

"You really want to know this?"

"I do," she says.

"All right," he says, scrunching up to a sitting position. "At that age, it was mostly sports. But my big day? Catch a subway into Manhattan with a couple of friends. Take in the early show at the Paramount, the Roxy, or another one of those movie palaces. Great films for a ten-year-old. Plus a stage show. Sinatra, with those screaming bobbysoxers, Martin and Lewis,plenty of dancers, comics. Old vaudevillians like Smith and Dale. Big bands, Tommy Dorsey, Benny Goodman, Harry James. Then lunch at the Horn & Hardart. Or splurge at McGinnis, which was next to the Roxy. Hot roast beef sandwiches on a bun. Wedge of strawberry shortcake ten inches high. Absolute heaven. Then the Seventh Avenue up to the Polo Grounds for a Giants doubleheader, getting home around 9 o'clock."

"Good God," she says. "Just you and a couple of friends? Roaming the city with no adult?"

"In those days, sure. Didn't you?"

"When I was sixteen, maybe. When most of the stuff you're

talking about was gone."

They lay back in silence. After a moment, she says, "You know about me, what I've told you, what Carrie no doubt told you. Generally, I'm not the warmest of persons. To have feelings about people, I have to know them a long time, know things about them, what their values are, how they react to stress, to affection. But you? I knew absolutely nothing about you when we met, and in seconds I was flushed in the face. Do you remember? And it wasn't anything you did or said that was especially clever."

"I don't think I did or said much of anything."

"That's my goddamn point, Alec!" she says, pounding him in the arm. "It was very upsetting."

"Are you still upset?"

She takes a moment before answering. "Not as much," she says with a smile.

He decides to leave that alone, and asks, "So what did you love doing as a kid?"

"I was horse mad. A few blocks away was a livery stable that gave lessons. I worked for them in exchange for two lessons a week."

"Trail riding? Jumping? Dressage?"

"All of it," she says. "I wasn't great, but I loved it."

"Still?"

"Oh, yeah! I rode lots in Ireland."

"So when we're married, maybe we'll buy a horse farm upstate?"

Long silence.

"Jesse?" he says.

"Did you just propose to me?"

"I thought that was a given."

"We've just started," she says.

"And?"

"Y'know, we're doing so well now, just as we are."

"So we should go slowly, as you've said."

"Ye-ah," she says. "In that, at least. Can we?"

"Sure," he says.

"Do you mind? Really? It's been good for us."

"It has."

"You are the love of my life, Alec!"

He kisses her and turns off the light.

"You're not angry?" she says.

"No, my love. Just tired. Big day tomorrow."

"Do you ever have small days?"

He laughs. "God forbid."

TWENTY-NINE

Thursday afternoon. Alec's office. He's on the phone with his local counsel in Chicago. After a hiatus of several months, things are moving in an FTC proceeding against the magazine industry in which Alec represents all but two of the defendants. Sweeta bursts in. "Mr. Shilling's on your other line. He says it's life or death, and you must talk to him immediately."

Alec apologizes to the Chicago lawyer and picks up on his second line. "Marius?"

"It's not working, Alec! I told you it wouldn't. I sent the telegrams out yesterday, right after lunch. First few responses were fine. Any excuse to come to New York, and so on. But then they got mixed, some yes, some no. And now the bulk of them say they're not coming. It's a disaster, and I've already booked the room!" He pauses for breath. "At your expense, of course."

"Well, don't panic," Alec says. "What did you tell them?"

"The facts," Shilling says. "What do you think? That you and Edison are settling with Mid-Atlantic, and you want to tell them why it's in their best interests not to sue you. And, of course, I urged them to come listen."

"That's it?"

"In essence."

"Let me ask you this," Alec says. "Do you want them to sue?"

"I'd rather they didn't, of course."

"Sounds to me, Marius, you may not want it enough."

"What do you mean?"

"You're a well-known trial lawyer. You've tried other antitrust cases. You've built a reputation you don't want impaired."

"Where's this going?"

"Yet suddenly, you are rejected by 125 of your clients. They all dump you conspicuously in favor of Harold Kohn. Frankly, I'm surprised you're not more upset about that."

"Hmm," Shilling says.

"So I think you need to send a follow-up telegram."

"I might have to, yes. Do you have some wording to suggest?"

"I do," Alec says. "Three points. One, that I have assured you I will make them an offer that they will absolutely want to accept. Two, that you personally believe my assurance to be true, based on our long association. And three, that those failing to attend will miss out."

"Miss out on what? The offer won't go to them?"

"Just say 'miss out.' More intriguing."

"For Christ's sake, Alec. You talk about reputation. I'd be putting my entire reputation on the line with that message."

"Yes, but I won't let you down, Marius. I never have, and I won't now."

"All right, then," Shilling says. "No more screwing around. What's the offer you're going to make them?"

"I don't know yet," Alec says.

"You still don't know? You want me to trust the fact my clients will be happy with your offer, and you still don't know what it is?"

"I have the entire weekend to think about it," Alec says.

"Oh, Alec," he says. "This time you're asking too much."

"No I'm not, Marius. Because the alternative—Harold Kohn taking over your clients—is certain, and quite possibly ruinous. With me, you've got a chance."

"That you'll come up with a brilliant offer?"

"That's it," Alec says. "But you know I've done it before and have a powerful motivation to do it again. For both of our benefits. Whereas Kohn can't wait to eat you alive."

After hanging up, Alec sits silently and still for a few minutes.

So much bravado. Born of desperation. He has never before put as much pressure on himself without a single idea of redemption. Then he asks Sweeta to call Cadigan Breen.

When Breen comes on, Alec summarizes his lunch meeting with Shilling and the telephone conversation they've just had. "What kind of offer?" Breen asks. "We just need to tell them why lawsuits against us would be a waste of their time and money."

"That won't get them here, Caddy."

"How the hell can we make any offer? It would bankrupt your client and devastate mine."

"I'm not talking about a money offer."

"So… what, then?" Breen asks. "Magic dust? You've going to sprinkle it over hundreds of hard-bitten lawyers and businessmen and expect their heads to turn soft?"

"Sounds ridiculous, doesn't it."

"Yes, Alec. This time you sound ridiculous. Sorry, but that's the truth."

"Somehow, I think we're missing something. Some way to convince these people."

"I'm old-fashioned. I'm just going to tell 'em why they'd lose. Why we have the better case."

"Okay," Alec says. "Let's hope that works. But I've committed myself to do more."

"Maybe *you* ought to be committed," Breen says.

"I hope that's a joke."

"Yeah," Breen says. "Me too."

Alec calls Larry Rilesman and fills him in on the hoped-for meeting with the 125 utilities. "Great," Rilesman says. "So you'll persuade them not to sue us."

"That's the idea, yeah."

"Will it work?"

"Don't know."

"So what should I tell Bob Curtis?"

"That we're doing our best to keep his company alive."

"Okay, Alec. What the fuck should I tell him? We're at another critical pass. What are the odds on success? Our success, or your failure?"

"Your success isn't really at risk, Larry. My chances of failure are fairly high. I wouldn't put money on a win here. I wouldn't even bet on there being a meeting."

"Jesus Christ, Alec. I can't bring that news to Bob Curtis."

"Want me to call him?"

"Don't you fucking dare!"

Friday afternoon, 4:30. Marius Shilling calls. "Okay, Alec," he says.

"Okay? You mean they're coming?"

"Yes. All but Philadelphia Electric."

"That's Harold Kohn's client," Alec says.

"Correct. And will your offer apply to them, even though they won't be there?"

"Not sure."

"Because you don't even know what it is yet?"

"Correct!" Alec snaps the word off in his best Prussian accent, which is to say, mimicking Shilling's come-to-attention bark.

"You're killing me, Alec."

"Not doing great for me either at the moment—but stay cool, Marius. As I said, I have the weekend."

In reality he doesn't. At the last minute, events conspire to force a meeting in Chicago on the magazine case. The flight there is spent preparing for that meeting. On the flight back, he falls asleep.

Sunday comes and languishes. Alec tries devoting it to thinking about Monday's meeting.

Jesse says, midday, "Can we go to a movie?"

"You go," Alec says.

"You'd think better if you went to a movie. It might clear your head."

"Okay," Alec says, and they take in a show at one of the movie houses on Second Avenue. Doesn't help. No ideas come to him. And ten minutes after the film, he can't even remember the name of it.

By nightfall, with the lights out, neither Alec nor Jesse is sleeping. She twists around to look in his face. "What is it, Alec?"

"I've told you," he says. "The meeting tomorrow. With hundreds of people who don't want to be there. All of them think they must sue. And I know no way to talk them out of it."

"Don't look at me," she says, which at least makes him laugh. "What I do know is that the longer you stare at the ceiling, the less likely you'll know what to say."

"I should simply fall asleep right now is your point."

"Yes," she says. "That's my point. It's obvious, and I think it's your only hope."

"So I'll just do that," he says.

She kisses him lightly. "Night, night, Alec. Close your eyes. Let it happen. It will work."

"It'll be like our trip to the movies," he says.

THIRTY

The meeting is scheduled for 10 a.m. in the grand ballroom of the Sheraton New York. According to Marius Shilling, more than 500 people will attend. It might seem extraordinary that so many will arrive on such short notice, but, then again, who wouldn't be drawn by the extraordinary offer Alec has promised to make them? In fact, Alec's offer must be so extraordinary that, not only must everyone love it so much they'll immediately go home and persuade their boards to accept it, but Breen and his client, Edison, must also join on the spot. Offering the same thing without having heard it before. Because if the utilities need to sue Edison, they won't leave Allis-Benoit out.

So it would be nice if Alec had any idea what that offer might be. At 9:30, Alec gets into Schlomo's car—still with no answer to that question. Because of Shilling's urging, the attendees may be willing to listen. But not to agree. They are, in fact, corporate executives or advisers who can't conceive of being talked out of their position. It's what their boards want, their PUCs want, and what common sense dictates. They have claims the federal government has endorsed. In two weeks, the statute of limitations will run out on those claims if they don't bring them. So why wouldn't they? Alec, though thinking about it intensively, has come up with no argument sufficiently compelling to lead them to do anything else.

He'd told Shilling he would conceive of some offer, and the fact is he hasn't. He discussed the problem with Braddock and Macalister. They had no solution. He'd hoped he might wake up with the answer in his head. It didn't happen. One-on-one, in

a small room, he might have been able to talk these utility people into most anything. Confronting a faceless crowd in a large
auditorium, he had one shot to hit on an idea that would move
everyone at once in the direction he needed them to go. Such an
idea had simply refused to appear in his brain. *And the time for
finding it is about to expire!*

Schlomo says, "So, what's your problem this morning?"

"You think I have a problem?"

"And you think what?" Schlomo says. "You think you're a
poker player? Difficult to read?"

"Not by you, Schlomo. And you're right. I have a problem."

"So maybe you should tell me what it is."

"Because maybe you have a solution?"

"Maybe I do. Or maybe, if you break it down, make it simple—"

"Right," Alec says. "So this is the problem. I have to convince
500 people to do something they think is bad for their companies
and worse for themselves."

"Is it?"

"Not really. But the reasons are complicated."

"Complicated for the companies?"

"Yes."

"And for the—"

"The people themselves, well…." Alec says. And the idea
dawns. Like a radiant light. And it burns even brighter as it un-
ravels in splendid simplicity. Days of pounding against an apparent impossibility, and the solution is there. Right in front of
him. In the back of a car. Clear. Ingenious. Eminently doable.
"Schlomo, you're a genius!"

"I have my moments, it's true."

"You should send me a bill," Alec says.

"A large one?"

"Very large."

"I'd rather just hold it over your head, if you don't mind."

"We'll add it to the list, then."

"Yes, but now every time you get in my car, you say, 'Schlo-mo, you're a genius.' I'll take that."

"You got it," Alec says. And they've arrived. Seventh Avenue and Fifty-Third Street.

He bounds up the stone steps, through the revolving front door, and down the long hall to the back of the building. Marius Shilling is peering from the hall outside the ballroom, making no attempt to look calm. "Almost 600 here, and they're getting restless. They came early. Had their own meeting. They're talking about a class action. Harold Kohn has sent them a memo."

"Is he here?"

"He wouldn't stoop," Shilling says. "Harold doesn't go to other lawyers' meetings. They come to him."

"I'll need a minute with my client."

"One minute," Shilling warns. "That's it. Literally. We have to start, or *they'll* start leaving."

Inside, Alec's entrance causes a stir that heightens as he walks down the center aisle of seats. Hundreds of people, almost all men in suits and ties, occupy nearly thirty rows of hotel folding chairs, in a vast but relatively low-ceilinged ballroom, under many glitzy blue-and-gold fixtures casting dazzling lights. Generally, the men are late middle age or older, resolute in demeanor, and not having a good time. Rilesman, standing at the foot of the stage, signals Alec and tries to talk over the drone of the crowd, which is becoming louder and more restive. "Sorry for the short notice, Alec, but I just got this from Bob Curtis. You can't tell them we've been cutting prices. And you can't tell them we'd go out of business if they sue."

"I wasn't planning to."

"You weren't?" Rilesman says, surprised. "What the hell else is there to say?"

Alec quickly lays out his plan and asks, "Any problems with that?"

"I have time to think about it?" Rilesman says angrily. It's okay for him to toss a last-minute bombshell, but one coming at him is unpardonable. Even worse if it's simple and can't fail.

"If it makes you feel better, Larry, I just thought of it. Three minutes ago. Or I would have filled you in before this."

Alec takes his seat onstage. Shilling is already introducing Cadigan Breen, who gets up beaming and tells a joke. Hundreds laugh. They like him but have little interest in what he has to say.

He tells them his client set its prices independently with absolutely no contact with Allis-Benoit. He says management learned their lesson when the last round of price-fixing cost the company more than a billion dollars and sent many of their key executives to prison. He speaks of the importance in this business of close personal relations between manufacturer and customer, particularly with regard to the servicing of these extremely complicated and expensive machines, and how further litigation would disrupt those relations. His speech is written, and he reads it well. Then it's Alec's turn. When Shilling introduces him, with a lot of nice words about their work together on other cases, Alec gets to his feet and looks out on hundreds of glazed eyes.

"We're here," he says, "Caddy and I, because our clients have a problem. A lot of pressure is being put on every one of you to bring lawsuits against us that will be costly and protracted. Very costly. Very long. For your clients and ours. But, of course, for them, the companies… that's just money. For you guys… well… the problem is personal. Personal to every one of you. Maybe not so easy to see at first, but the fact is… sue, don't sue, *you* lose either way. Maybe your jobs. At minimum, *you will be criticized! Marked down!* Take a hit to your careers. Whichever way you decide to go."

Alec picks out some faces to stare at. "You're not buying that? I'm exaggerating, you think? Being presumptuous? Okay. I understand. It's not that obvious. So let's play out both scenarios. Say you sue. As to the probable outcome, you have before you the judgment of the most litigious man in America, Donald Strand,

and the Antitrust Division of the United States Department of Justice. Both looked at this case a lot longer and harder than you've been able to do and finally saw the light.

"Donald Strand, after spending God knows how many millions, dropped the case for a small contribution to those costs. You think he would have done that if he thought he could win? The United States Justice Department asked us to produce more than a million documents, and we did. Then they walked away for a meaningless decree. So you bring this case and lose—as Mid-Atlantic and the Antitrust Division have already concluded they would—and the blame for that will be catastrophic. On everyone. Everyone sitting in this room."

Alec again scans the room. "Right, that's the obvious part. Here's the part that's not so obvious. Say you win. That's not likely to happen, but say it does. Roses for you, you think. Take another look at reality. Your trial lawyers will not do this on a full contingency. Not this case. Way too iffy for them. Their costs and their time will have to be paid for. And that's a slippery slope, because the costs of this kind of litigation mount every year. Probably exponentially. So every year you will have to explain to your boards and your PUCs why the whole thing is so damn expensive and taking so long. And you'll be trying to explain this while your top executives are being dragged through depositions, their files invaded, and their lives upset with something they really don't want to spend time on. And for what? While you have little or no chance of winning anything on the merits, if you do, damages cannot be that high, because now—as a result of the last round of litigation—neither of these companies makes much money on these machines. Read their financials. And if there were any damages, a huge slice will go to the lawyers, even though they have been billing you handsomely for their time. So, when your bosses, your boards, and your PUCs look back on this, will you be the hero or the scapegoat? Will you even still have a job?

Alec gives them a moment to ingest this. "So the other

scenario is you don't sue at all!" He beams a knowing smile, as if to say what he then puts into words: "How could you possibly justify that? The second-guessers would swarm like bees. So you're damned if you do, and damned if you don't. Between a rock and a hard place. Right?" Alec laughs. "Not right. Because I'm going to offer you a way out. I'm going to lay out a plan by which you can decide not to sue and not be criticized by anyone! Not your bosses, your boards, or your PUCs. An absolutely foolproof, blame-free solution. Anyone interested?" Alec looks down, picks out a friendly face belonging to a portly bald man with a bow tie and vest. "You, sir? You interested?"

"Sure," the man says.

"And you, sir?" Alec asks, pointing to a young man who is taller than anyone in his row.

"I am, yes," says the young man in a voice that suggests he might actually mean it.

"Of course you are!" Alec says in a deep tone of confidence. "I'm offering you a way to save your jobs and your future. A way to leave this room with the awful prospect of vexatious litigation—the damn problem of *sue or don't sue*—lifted from your shoulders and never allowed to haunt you again! But I'd like to know, guys, that *you want to hear it!* So—anybody else?"

It starts, as at a revival meeting, with a smattering of "yeses." Then Alec repeats, "Yes, you there, you want to hear this?" Getting that response, he starts jabbing his finger in all directions, saying in his hyped voice, "You, sir? You? You?"

The "yeses" grow louder.

"I can't hear you!" says Alec, like a cornball coach in a football locker room.

And they're on their feet, laughing and shouting, "Yes!"

Alec laughs with them and says, "Okay. Here's the deal. Couldn't be simpler, and it can't fail." All sit, and the room falls silent. "If no one does anything, in two weeks the statute of limitations will snap shut and wipe out your claims. So we *will* do something. Something big to stop that from happening. No charge. Absolutely free. Tonight we will send you a letter unilaterally extending the tolling of the statute of limitations for one month. In short, we will give you all an additional month to think about it." Alec pauses and looks over the crowd. "Like it so far?"

The roar is spontaneous.

"Good," Alec says. "You'll like the rest even more." Alec glances at Breen, who looks back bemused and suspicious, but Alec goes on. "Our letter tonight will also say this. It will say: From now until the end of that month, if any one public utility brings suit against Allis-Benoit or Edison Electric for alleged price-fixing, every other utility-signatory to the standstill agreement—that means every company represented in this room—will have yet *another thirty days* to think about joining that suit or bringing one of their own." Alec pounds on the lectern. "*Do you like that?*"

Pandemonium shakes the room but then descends into a strange silence. It's like the sudden deflation of a balloon. It's coming at them too fast, and they're trying to work it out. Even Caddy, who's sitting up there looking perplexed. Alec had promised there would be no chance of blame. Where does that fit in?

Alec says, "Think about it. Now there are two different scenarios as a result of that letter we will send you tonight. Scenario one: During that first thirty-day extension we're giving you, if one company sues, everyone else here gets another thirty days to consider what's best for *your* company. If you want to sue, you go right ahead and do it. Given our letter, everyone here will be better off than they are now. Right?" Heads are wagging. Obviously right.

"So, let's take scenario two: The first thirty-day extension period comes and goes, and… no one sues. The claim is extinguished. So you get a call from your most troublesome outside director—or from the most vocal commissioner of your PUC. He says, 'Joe, how come you decided not to sue Allis-Benoit?'

And you say, 'Fred'—or whatever his name is—'not only did the Department of Justice decide not to prosecute such a case, and not only did Mid-Atlantic Power & Light drop such a case after wasting millions of dollars on it, but every other public utility in the United States—124 of them—arrived at exactly the same conclusion—not to bring this lawsuit. Really, Fred, it's a no-brainer!'

"In short," Alec says, "in scenario one, you're totally protected by having another thirty days for decision-making; and in scenario two, you have a gold-plated guaranty against second-guessing. When 125 utilities take a hard look at the same possible course of action and unanimously reject it, not one could rationally criticize you for doing the same thing. You are totally insulated by being in excellent, unanimous, and very populous company."

They get it, they like it, and Shilling gets up and suggests a five-minute break. He had read Caddy Breen's surprise, and correctly decided he and Alec needed to talk. They do so at the dais in whispers, Caddy still looking *dubitante*. Alec says, "You know, I know, and even they know how they will respond to this extension I've granted. Like sheep. During the first thirty days, everyone will wait for someone *else* to bring suit. And no one will. The time will come, it will go, and billions in claims will evaporate. In thirty days, we'll be out of this. If Edison joins. I wish I could have mentioned this idea to you yesterday, but I didn't have this idea yesterday. It didn't occur to me until ten minutes before this meeting. As I was coming to this meeting. In the back of Schlomo's car."

"Ah, Schlomo," Breen says, Alec's report now, somehow, making sense to him. "I have a call to make," he says, rising and leaving the ballroom.

Shilling restarts the meeting when Breen returns. Caddy heads right to the microphone, signaling Shilling to go back to his chair. He says, "I'll be brief. My client, Edison Electric, joins in the handsome offer made here this morning by Allis-Benoit.

Tonight we will send you an identical letter, containing the same unilateral offer that you heard Alec Brno so clearly describe a few minutes ago. Thank you."

Shilling looms up and ushers them from the stage. Away from the microphone, he whispers, "I have further business with these people, but Alec, don't think I missed what you just did here. The most extraordinary thing I've seen in thirty-five years of practice."

Rilesman joins Alec in the back of Schlomo's car. On the way downtown he says, "I have something to tell you."

"I'm listening," Alec says.

"Later." Rilesman jerks his head in Schlomo's direction.

Alec laughs, but waits. Rilesman's face reads, *bombshell.*

Upstairs, while walking into Alec's and Ben Braddock's compound, Rilesman says, "What you did there, at that meeting, very clever, but it may all have been for naught."

"You're saying one of those utilities will sue?"

"PECO. Philadelphia Electric."

Alec drops his coat on the sofa. "Harold Kohn's client."

"Yes, but it's not Kohn who's driving this. I understand he doesn't really think much of the antitrust claim."

"He told you that?" Alec says, sitting behind his desk, leafing quickly through mail.

"Me? No. Harold Kohn doesn't speak to me. A friend who works for another utility. He got Kohn's letter and read between the lines."

"The lines being?"

"His firm will not do the case on a contingency arrangement. He expects to be paid normal hourly rates. With, nonetheless, an as-yet-unspecified premium for winning."

Alec, letter opener suspended in air, regards the man with scorching incredulity. "You sat on this until now?"

"You *said* the same thing to that crowd. It sounded like you knew."

"What I *said*, Larry, I made up. What I might have *said*, had you thought to give me the facts earlier, would have been ten times more effective. For our client. And for you."

"Anyway," Rilesman says, as if oblivious to such rebukes, and still sitting there with his coat on, "that's not the point. The point is what PECO says, which is that we screwed up on the last turbine generator we sold them. Cost them downtime of about 900,000 bucks. They're withholding that amount from their last installment payment. Our guys have threatened to sue, although I gather it's an iffy claim."

Alec slams the letter opener flat on the desk. "Threatened to sue them, have we?"

"Correct."

"And if we were to sue, PECO would want to be able to counterclaim for our alleged price-fixing with Edison Electric. To have something to trade off against our claim for nonpayment."

"I would assume so, yes."

"Problem is," Alec says, with rising ire, "they can't simply wait for us to file a complaint, and then file theirs as a counterclaim, because, even with the extension I just gave PECO, their claim runs out in a month, whereas we have six years to sue them for nonpayment. They need to sue now or watch their antitrust claim die. We can't stop their suing us now by excusing their $900,000 debt in exchange for their releasing the antitrust claim, because that would cost us hundreds of millions under the most-favored-nations provision of the standstill agreement. And once PECO sues, what do you imagine every other utility in this country will do?"

"That's the problem, yeah." Rilesman finally removes his coat.

"Bad problem," Alec says. "For the sake of a less-than-$1-million '*iffy*' claim, '*our guys*' have created a situation that will inevitably make public an $8 billion exposure that will destroy the company before any of these claims go to trial."

"I know," Rilesman says.

"Anything else you'd like to mention that maybe you haven't told me?"

"No, that's it. Except when we delivered the machine, it didn't work, and PECO did experience downtime. Although, the guys who made it say the malfunctioning was PECO's fault."

"And?"

"And what?"

"That's it?" Alec says. "You talk to anyone else? Check that statement for accuracy?"

"The guys I talked to ought to know," Rilesman says, sounding offended.

Alec picks up his phone, says to his secretary, "Harold Kohn, with a K, in Philadelphia."

Rilesman says, "You're calling Kohn this minute?"

"How long would you like to wait? For all we know, he's got a guy driving to the courthouse with a complaint ready to be filed."

They listen for a few moments to the room tone of an office, punctuated randomly by voices and bells. Then Alec's secretary on the box. "Mr. Kohn's on the line."

Alec says, "Harold?"

Kohn's voice, "Alec." Smooth delivery. Neither deep nor thin, but cultured, despite a bit of a rasp.

"We haven't met."

"I know who you are," Kohn says.

"And I you. I have you on the speakerphone, if you don't mind."

"You have a gathering for our conversation?"

"Just Larry Rilesman, Allis-Benoit's general counsel."

"Oh, yes?"

"We'd like to come down to see you."

"Very well," Kohn says. "How 'bout tomorrow?"

"For what I need to do before we meet—need to do on this matter—gonna need a few days. Say, Thursday? By then I can be absolutely sure."

"If we meet then, we must resolve this then. We don't want to let this linger."

"I understand," Alec says.

"And I understand what you're saying." Kohn pauses. "All right. Thursday. We'll meet at the Philadelphia Electric Company. Executive suite. Two p.m."

"We'll be there."

"I'll look forward to it. And Alec. Having just heard of your Houdini stunt at the Sheraton this morning, I should enjoy watching you submerged in the present box. You'll find it a bit tighter, though."

"There's always a way out, Harold."

"Oh, yes?" Kohn says with a laugh, and hangs up.

In stride, Alec asks Sweeta to get Bob Curtis on the phone, which makes Rilesman extremely uneasy. "Is this really necessary?" he asks.

"You listen, Larry, and you be the judge."

In minutes Curtis is on. He knows the result of the Sheraton meeting, congratulates Alec on it, and says he just got off the phone with the head of the Allis-Benoit Heavy Electrical Equipment Division about the PECO job. "It's difficult to tell who's right at this stage. I'm told the machine passed our tests before we delivered it. PECO says it failed their tests on arrival."

"Can we get to the bottom of that in a couple of days?"

"Not possible."

"Then it doesn't matter. You understand what the mere filing of a PECO lawsuit would do to your company?"

"Unfortunately, I do."

"I realize that even an uncertain claim for $900,000 has considerable value. But how would you value it in comparison to the loss of the company?"

"Piddling, obviously."

"So do I have my marching orders?" Alec says. "I'm meeting

with Kohn this Thursday."

"Marching orders? We can't agree to excuse PECO from paying the $900,000 in exchange for not suing us. If we did, we'd owe every other utility a chunk of that money."

"Of course."

"So what will you offer him?" Curtis asks.

"Nothing."

"So how will you stop him from suing?"

"I'll think of something," Alec says. "What I need to be sure of is, *if* they don't sue us, and allow the limitations date to pass, we will in fact not sue them for nonpayment."

"Yes," Curtis says. "You've got that. But you can't offer it."

"Understood."

"Very tricky."

"Yes."

A long silence ensues.

Curtis finally says, "I've no idea how you can get us out of this mess, but good luck. We need one more miracle out of you."

As Curtis hangs up, Braddock and Macalister enter. "So you going to tell us what happened, or what?" Ben asks.

Alec introduces Rilesman and gives them a brief report of the meeting that morning. "Will that work?" Mac asks.

"Thought it might," Alec says, "until Harold Kohn appeared." He lays out the problem with Philadelphia Electric.

Mac says, "You ought to talk to Harry Hanrahan. He knows Kohn better than I do. But I know this: Harold Kohn is ruthless. He has no interest in anything but money and power. He's supersmart and only marginally ethical. He rules the system in Philadelphia. Other lawyers fear him. The judges—federal and state—love him. Hanrahan despises him—with good reason. They battled each other for five years, and Kohn ruined his career."

Rilesman absorbs this with an expression of open-mouth fear. "Hey, Larry," Alec says, "sounds like fun, right?"

THIRTY-ONE

Another night when Alec comes home late and Jesse's in bed reading. "So how'd it go?' she calls out.

In the bedroom, he bends down for her kiss. Real enough, yet tonight it seems urgent. And the covers are pulled up to her neck. He gives her a pared-down version of the morning meeting.

"It sounds so simple," she says.

"It is, which is probably why it took me so long to think of it."

"So now you can take it easy, right?"

"Well—" he starts, cut off by her laugh, and she says, "I know, Alec. Just come to bed. I have news for you too."

"Is Sarah home?" he asks.

"At Tino's. Doing homework."

"Homework?"

"So she said. He'll bring her home."

"This is what?" Alec says. "Every night now?"

"His mom's been away. I've told you about that. She's returning tomorrow."

Alec sits on the edge of the bed. Jesse puts her book down. He says, "Your news?"

"I have a job."

"Hey! Great!"

"It doesn't pay much," she says.

"Not necessarily a stopper," he says. "World of film?"

"Indie. It's a new project. They say they have financing, which is always the question. I'll be assistant director."

"What you've wanted."

"Yeah," she says. "It's a pretty big project, so a start for me here. A good credit. And though, as I say, they pay almost nothing, they'll feed me and put me up."

"Put you up?"

"Yeah. That's the bad part. We're shooting in Italy and Greece. The rest of the crew will be hired there."

"Low-budget indie?" he says. "Shooting abroad?"

"They say that's where the money is, such as it is. And it's where the cast is. Though it's an English-language film." At Alec's skeptical look, Jesse adds quickly, "These people—the producer, director—are known. They've done other films. Festival quality."

"How'd they find you?"

"Through Ardmore. The studio I worked for in Ireland. They had my contact info."

"Why would a production in Italy be looking for crew in Ireland?"

"It's the film business, Alec. It's its own world. People know people all over. There are no borders!"

Still dubious, he holds his tongue. "How long will you be gone?" he asks.

"Yeah, right, more of the bad part. About a month."

"About?" he says.

"Well, a little more than."

"How much more than?"

"Portal to portal… hmm… six and a half weeks?"

He says nothing, starts getting undressed. This conversation is already skidding on ice, yet he lets himself skate toward the crack in it. "Y'know," he says, "thing sounds a bit fishy."

"Fishy?" she says. "There's nothing fishy. I'm known for the work I've done. I got recommended. They found me."

"Okay," he says, not convinced.

"Honestly, Alec… you're kind of raining on my parade here."

"Right, sorry." He goes into the bathroom, then after a while, calls out from inside. "Tell you what," he says. "I'll negotiate your contract for you."

He returns to a look. "Contract?" she says. "As in written contract? I mean, what the fuck, Alec? They don't give me a ticket, I won't go. They don't feed me, I'll leave. I don't think anyone's suing anyone here."

"Okay. What are the names?"

"So you can—" she toggles her head in a mimicry of aggression—"*check* them out? Call some of your important friends?"

"Why not?"

"Because I'm happy about this, Alec. I think it's okay, and I don't want you queering it."

"I'll call Harvey Grand. Tell him no footprints."

"Alec, no!"

"All right," he says, sitting back on the bed. "I'll leave it alone. When do you take off?"

"Day after tomorrow."

"Jesus!"

"Yeah, sorry. Another part of the bad part."

"Okay, look," he says. "I know why you want this. And I want it to be good for you, no matter how long it takes. So I'm not saying anything beyond this: I'd like to know where you are when you get there, and how I can reach you. I'd like you to call me collect at least every other day, even if it's just to say hello. Will you promise me that?"

"Yes."

"Now you can pull the covers off."

"I'm not wearing anything," she says.

"I know you're not wearing anything."

"How did you know?"

"For that I don't need an investigation."

She smiles and throws off the covers. "Investigate as much as you like."

❖

Sarah and Tino, having made love every night since his mother left town, are now, in their own estimation, exceedingly adept at "doing it." Sarah especially is quite pleased with herself, having gone from inexperienced to proficient almost overnight. All those whispered exchanges of hokum and guilty glimpses at books, when it all turns out to have been so simple.

Sarah comes off the bed, no longer shy being looked at or looking. "So Mom's back tomorrow, right?"

"Yes, tomorrow," Tino says, sinking back in the pillows.

"I wonder whether her trip—off working for Sal—had anything to do with Sal calling his men off of me."

"Why would it?"

"I dunno," she says. "Gratitude?"

Tino sits up with a bitter laugh. "My mom is his sister-in-law. He's head of the family. Who else would she work for? He tells you where to go, that's where you go. He tells you what to do, you do it. That's the way he thinks."

"And you?"

"Me? I think anyone who puts women in cages is a hateful person."

"Women in cages?" she exclaims. "Who told you that?"

He shrugs.

"Y'know," Sarah says, "I listen to you, to Harvey. I'm having trouble with this whole thing, believing that this man is so evil. You make him seem like one of those villains in a James Bond movie."

"You've never met him, you wouldn't know."

"You used to like him," she points out.

"Now I'm afraid of him."

"Because he's having me watched?"

"Because I don't want to think of you stashed in a cage somewhere."

She sits hard on the one chair in his room. "You actually

know this?" she says. "He really does this to people?"

He shakes his head, more in distress than denial.

"You do know!" she says. "Actual women he's done this to? How long have you known?"

"A few days."

"Did he tell you about this? Sal?"

"No."

"Your mother?"

"What difference does it make?" Tino says. "I know."

"Your mother told you," she says, wrapping herself in her arms. "She knows this and she still works for the man."

"It's bookkeeping," he says unconvincingly.

"For a man who puts women in cages?"

"She comes from a different time, Sarah. A different place."

"And can shut her eyes to it?"

"She can. I can't. I've woken up, Sarah. You should too. We've both had fathers killed."

Sarah stays silent. Then, "Where does he live, this uncle of ours?"

"Central Park West, why?"

"What's the address?"

"Why would you need his address?" he says slowly. "You thinking of dropping in?"

"Dropping in, yes, that's a good way to put it. I want to introduce myself. And tell him to bugger off."

"That's not funny."

"It's not meant to be," she says. "I want the man out of my life."

Tino twists the blankets around him with a tug. "Sarah, listen to me. Do not go near this man. Ever. He's not like someone you can just talk to."

"He doesn't talk?"

"Yes he talks," Tino says. "And you listen. He's not interested in what you have to say, unless it's 'Yes sir, I will do exactly what you ask.' Do you understand what I'm telling you?"

"Yes, Tino. I understand. I know you're afraid of him. I'm sure for good reason. But if he wants to hurt me, I want him to see who he's doing it to. I want him to know who I am. I want him to know how I feel about it."

"I'm afraid he won't care."

"Then I'll just kick him in the balls and get out of there," she says.

THIRTY-TWO

Sal Angiapello knows peace only on the island that bears his name. Although the island is not large—about eight miles by five—and it's shaped like a centipede, with rocky shores and few beaches, he owns every inch of it, rules it, and uses it as the base of his main businesses. The power to rule comes with the ownership, since the island of Angiapello is, in effect, a sovereign state. This status is less of an anomaly than the phenomena that produced it.

Very early in the island's history, these roughly forty square miles in the Ionian Sea became the site of an enormous hemp plantation. Naturally a factory was built, and through the years it was often renovated, to transform the seed of *Cannabis sativa* into its more popular forms. Greece originally owned the island and called it Cannarouna, but decided ultimately that it wanted neither to destroy this crop nor be associated with it. The problem was solved by allowing the landowner, Sal's ancestor, to continue to farm and manufacture, and ceding to him, at an enormous price, the right to rule. Later, Italy seized the island but eventually recognized the same problem. The Italian government solved it the way the Greeks did, but, being cannier, much closer, and therefore more threatening, they charged the Angiapellos an even higher price.

Nonetheless, the investment proved rewarding for the Angiapello line, especially the current head of the family. With a steady crop and an expanding world population, revenues from the "farming" business annually expanded. Sal added warehouses at the northern and southern tips of the island, where the armaments and munitions are still stored. And that line of business dwarfs everything. The island's sovereignty, useful in the drug trade, is indispensable for arms dealing, which most countries surveil more effectively and punish more severely.

So Sal's sleep is peaceful here, and his roaming among the small populace is quite serene. To them he is a monarch and virtually a god. He does exactly what he wants, without interference or question from anyone. His power elsewhere among his fellows is prodigious; but on Angiapello Island, it is absolute.

His favorite time here is breakfast. He has it alone on the bedroom terrace of his villa, overlooking the harbor from the island's highest elevation. If, the night before, he'd had a woman in his bed, she will have been removed by others before breakfast is served. This morning, he has had his walk and is enjoying his breakfast, but the meal is disturbed by the arrival of a plane attempting to land on the airstrip a mile away. His house manager, Nicoli Gura, appears on the terrace, his leathery face wreathed in a question.

"It's the Englishman," Sal says. "Vivian Kniseley."

"Who was to arrive yesterday," Nicoli says. He has a way of expressing disdain with a twitch in the nostrils of a very large hawk nose.

"So get word to him to stay at the airport. I'll see him there."

Sal's luggage is already packed and waiting for him in the front hall. He checks it quickly, then gives the sign for it to be loaded into the Bentley parked in the driveway. At the airport, he finds the Englishman standing on the apron in front of his twin-jet plane.

Kniseley is a loud, boastful man with a moon face, straggly hair, and a Midland accent that seems deliberately impenetrable. He's younger than Sal, though not by much, and always greets him, as now, with a booming semblance of good cheer, as if he has failed to notice Sal's distaste of him. "So sorry, old man, being tardy to the party, so to speak. Unavoidable delays. But I do have quite a bevy for you." Kniseley points to the plane. "I thought I might bring them to the house, clean them up a bit, do a catwalk in the usual way."

"So sorry," Sal mimics the Englishman's cadence. "I'm due in New York." He glances at his watch. "A quick look here is what I have time for." Sal makes a move toward the steps.

"Not in the plane, surely," says Kniseley.

Sal stops and looks back at him. "You might come another day, then. On schedule."

"You won't be seeing them to their best advantage, Sal."

"Or at all," Sal says. "Your choice."

Kniseley's sweat has darkened his neck silk, and his voice comes out strained. "They're manacled to the seats. The cabin smells of urine."

"Well, next time, then."

"No, no," Kniseley says, unhappily leading the way. The cabin door is open, but the fan turned off. One look is enough for Sal. Four women of different races, barely clothed, barely living, chained to seats. The stench is overwhelming. He turns away and descends the stairs. Kniseley clambers down after him. "As I said, Sal, if I could just—"

Sal interrupts impatiently. "What are you playing at, Kniseley?"

"How do you mean?"

"Are you a child? You're new to this business?"

"You don't like those girls?"

"They're not girls," Sal says with annoyance. "And I don't deal in women of that age. That's a market I don't trade in. For good reason."

"They're at their prime, Sal! If you'd see them cleaned up…."

"I'm leaving. You can pay to refuel at the pumps."

Kniseley grabs Sal's shoulder, and the capo stops abruptly. "With respect, Don Salvatore," says the Englishman, removing his hand as if from a flame. "I've incurred great expense. Collecting these women, bringing them here. Each one of them is worth, wholesale, a half-million pounds sterling at the very least. And they've been promised good situations, under your protection. If you reject them—"

"You think you had the right to make such a promise?"

"No," Kniseley says quickly. "I assumed, shouldn't have. A thousand pardons, Don Salvatore."

Sal brings his hand to his mouth as if he were reconsidering. "Tell you what. You and your people take them up to the house. Rest, stay here maybe a day. I'll be back. I'll think about it."

"Oh, thank you, Sal, thank you. If you see them prettied up, maybe use them, I'm sure—"

"No more. Just do what I said."

"Absolutely, Sal. Thank you again. Thank you so much."

In his own plane, before takeoff, Sal radiophones his house manager. "Nicoli, I'm sending up Kniseley. He'll be with his crew and four women. Please have them disposed of before I return."

"All of them?"

"Well, there's a Japanese woman."

"Hold her until you get back?"

"Yes," Sal says.

"And the plane?"

"Check it out. Put it in the hangar, change the colors. It might be of use."

"Regarding the women, Don Salvatore… before disposing of them…"

"Yes, all right, if you have favors to dispense, you can choose some of the men. Just one night, though."

"But not the Japanese one."

"Correct," Sal says and turns off the phone.

Alec, about to take off for the office, goes back to the bedroom and finds Jesse packing her suitcase. She looks up, surprised. "Didn't you leave ten minutes ago?"

"Came back," he says. "Forgot something on my desk. Then I made a call." He points to her suitcase. "Thought you weren't leaving until tomorrow?"

"I'm leaving the *country* tomorrow," she says, folding a sweater. Her hands jerk unnecessarily at the final fold.

"So we have tonight," he says, pretending not to notice.

She lays the sweater into the suitcase. "I thought, since my flight's very early in the morning…." And she looks at him rather hopelessly.

He says, "So we don't have tonight?"

"I'd just wake you when I left." She pulls some blouses from the dresser. "I thought it better—"

"That you just leave without saying goodbye?"

"I'd planned on writing a letter."

Alec drops his briefcase to the floor. "What's happening, Jess?"

She drops the blouses on the bed. Then sits on it and looks away from him. "What was always going to happen, Alec. It's just happening sooner."

"Like this? Out of the blue?"

"It's not out of the blue. I've said."

"You're back to that?"

"I never left it."

"Fooled me," he says.

"This is better," she says, eyes now on him, trying to engage. "Really. Having to go now, because of that job, it's just better timing."

"Better than what?" He's now raising his voice. "A kick in the stomach?"

"I'm sorry you're angry."

"Angry? That doesn't quite describe it. How do *you* feel?"

"I feel awful," she says, now suddenly crying. "What the fuck do you think?"

"Then why the hell are you doing it?"

She looks away again. "I know what a breakup after a long affair feels like."

"We weren't starting an *affair*," he says, moving to sit next to her on the bed. "I wouldn't have left you. No matter what."

"I know," she says. "But I would have left you."

"Jesse, look at me," he says. "You can't possibly believe that. Not now."

"I've never not believed it."

"Just because I was once in love with your sister?"

"You're still in love with her."

"This is crazy," he says. "Your sister is dead. We both loved her, now we love each other."

"It's not the same," she says. "That's what I *feel*."

"A sibling rivalry with your dead sister?"

She dries her eyes with the heels of her hands and starts packing again. "This is why I didn't want to have this conversation."

He gets to his feet as well. "What we have, Jess…." He stops, his throat tightening. "Carrie and I went through…." He stops again, trying to calm himself. "Very, very bad times. I ended up killing a man. And she was very sick. Which ended up killing her. I did not enjoy any part of that."

"And yet…"

"What?"

"It was a measure of how much you loved her."

"And what are you saying? I went through hell for her and wouldn't for you?"

"You make it sound ridiculous."

"It is ridiculous!"

"No," she says, now almost screaming, "it's not! We don't have that sort of love, Alec. We never will. We can't. You were drained by that love, and by Carrie's death. You are always thinking of Carrie. As you should be. No one recovers from a love that strong. That I'm her sister doesn't make it better for me. It makes it worse. Being a close substitute makes it worse! I'm sorry to be so goddamn melodramatic, but that's the way it is. And it sucks for me. *Do you see that?*"

Alec stands where he's standing for what seems like a long time. "I see what you're seeing," he says. "Maybe someday you'll see us more clearly. But not now. I hope you have a great trip, and a safe one." He picks up his bag and leaves the apartment. Getting on the elevator is like a parachute jump from a dream.

THIRTY-THREE

A very tall building in downtown Philadelphia houses the corporate headquarters of the Philadelphia Electric Company, which supplies power to the southeastern quarter of Pennsylvania. Locally, the company is referred to as PECO, and the building as the Tower of Light. The CEO, a small, plain man named Hewitt, has a corner office on the top floor. Alec and his team meet there with Harold Kohn, Hewitt, and other senior utility management. Masking the intensity of the agenda, their greetings are quite cordial. In contrast, through eight-foot-high windows, an impending storm turns the sky purple with rage.

Alec has brought with him his senior associate, Trevor Joffrey, and the general counsel of his client, Larry Rilesman. Joffrey is there mainly to take notes. Rilesman is there to bear corporate witness to the events, which will determine the viability of Allis-Benoit—and his job.

Kohn turns out to be a silky man of medium height, thickening waist, thinning hair, and easy, confident manner. From a weekend under tropical sun, his balding pate, and the noticeable rest of him, are tanned to walnut or splurged with freckles. He takes a seat at one end of a sofa and invites Alec to sit at the opposite end. Everyone else he ignores, including the executives of his own client, apparently regarding them as nonessential to at least the opening round of these proceedings. Alec—despite everything he's been told about Kohn—likes the man almost immediately.

"Let me net out the problem," says Kohn to Alec. "We both know whom we represent, so for brevity, I'll use personal pronouns. You have a contract claim against me for almost a million dollars. I have an antitrust claim against you for many millions. Trouble is, my claim lapses before yours does, in less than a month, so if I don't bring it within that time, and if you sue me thereafter, I will have been stripped of my best weapon—a potent antitrust counterclaim."

"And I can't *agree* not to bring my suit," Alec says. "For if I were to relinquish my claim to avoid yours, I'd owe many millions to many other utilities."

"So," says Kohn, "in anticipation of the fact that you might sue me at some indeterminate time in the future, I have to sue you in a matter of days. Right?"

"I don't think so, Harold."

Kohn's smile is as warm as the beach he just came from. "Do you have a plan?" he asks.

"Not a plan, no. But I do have a few thoughts."

The storm announces itself with a lightning crack that illumines, then shakes, the city, including the Tower of Light. Given the temperature outside, it should have brought snow, but instead bursts into a rainstorm of torrential proportions.

"Theatrical!" says Kohn admiringly. "Must have cost you a bundle, these pyrotechnics. But we're unimpressed. We *make* electricity. More horsepower than almost any other utility in the country. Admittedly with your machines. But once we file that antitrust claim—" he wafts one hand before him like a seer—"I see a stampede of other utilities galloping to join the herd. We will pound your company into the earth. No longer will it produce anything. No longer will it be your company, or, perhaps, anyone's. I'm sure you have that vision too, or you wouldn't be here. And yet you come down here with just 'a few thoughts'?"

"They are what I have," Alec says with a smile.

"Then they'd better be very powerful thoughts."

"That will be for you to judge."

Kohn gazes out the window. "Well, it's raining outside. The

club course will be closed. I suppose I will listen." He folds his arms and gives Alec a look of calm expectation.

"The first thought," Alec says, "concerns your word *potent*. The claim you have is not that, and it is very far from being that. This is obviously not a case in which competing manufacturers met in hotel rooms and fixed prices. The fact is they didn't meet. They didn't speak. They had no contact with each other whatever. What happened was a weak company matched a strong company's price book—and then proceeded to cut prices below that book on every transaction it wanted to win. That's not a price fix. It's the opposite of a price fix. And you know that happened. In fact, you know as well as I that your antitrust counterclaim not only lacks potency, it would, quite soon in the process, be thrown, if not laughed, out of court."

"I *know* this, you say?"

"I do," says Alec. "We're talking about heavy electrical equipment your client just bought from mine. They got an invoice from us reciting book prices. But they didn't pay book prices. They got tons of free goods under the table. Literally tons."

"It must have been a very large table," Kohn says, deadpan.

"It was your table, Harold, so you would know. And the payment terms? Were they book? You know they were far more lenient than that. So when you offered to represent all American public utilities, you did not offer a contingency deal. You offered only your customary fee arrangement. Very wise, Harold. Very knowing."

Kohn again looks out at the storm. "It's still raining," he says.

"Time for another thought?" Alec asks.

"Just one, yes. A very basic one. I'd like to know how I can know for certain that, if I were to let my claim lapse, you won't sue me?"

"That," Alec says, "is the one thing you *cannot* know for certain. Because, as we've been saying, there can be no *agreement* by us to waive that claim. On the other hand, you are perfectly free to conclude that we will act as rational businessmen."

"Rational?" Kohn muses. "How do you define that?"

"If you don't sue us, but we nonetheless later do sue you, we could expect to be on the receiving end of a rather large amount of corporate ire. For many years, PECO has been one of our largest customers. The amount of business we could expect to lose as a result of PECO ire is likely to be many times the amount we might collect on such a claim. One way for you to predict what we will do is to consider what a reasonable man... let us say, you yourself, would do in our place. Very likely that prediction would be accurate. Predictions, of course, are not certainties. The more insightful the man making them, however, the more likely they are to come true."

"So what you are saying to me—"

"I've already said. No more or less."

Harold reflects for a moment, then smiles again. "I see that Allis-Benoit has finally found themselves a lawyer." He rises and says to his group, "Shall we caucus for a moment?"

When they leave for another room, Rilesman whispers to Alec, "How the hell did you know there were free goods on our sale to PECO? You talk to our guys? Because they told me there weren't any."

"They told me the same thing."

"So? What did you do? See it in the files?"

"They haven't sent me the files, Larry. They've been dragging their feet. But you saw. Kohn just effectively confirmed it."

"Yeah, I saw that. But what did *you* do—just wing it? Our salesman says he didn't do it, and you tell Kohn he did?"

"Right," Alec says. "I didn't believe your salesman. It was the way he said it, then didn't send me the file. And there wasn't much downside, Larry, in reading it that way. If there were no price cuts on that deal—to PECO, one of our largest customers—Kohn would know he had a case and was going to sue us. What allowed this meeting is that he knew about the cuts. What he wanted to find out is whether we knew. Because, in this weird market, salesmen get fired if they don't hide the price cutting that got them the business."

Promptly Kohn returns, leading his silent group of suited executives, and, with metaphorical aplomb, the storm outside diminishes. "The way I see it," says Kohn, not bothering to sit, "you and I, Alec, are like two old-fashioned gunslingers. We're in the middle of the street, both armed, both recognizing it's too damn dangerous to draw our guns. So there we stand. And are likely to stay without moving. A standoff, one might say."

Alec says, "You understand, we have no agreement, express or implied, about anything."

"I understand," Kohn says, rolling his eyes, as if questioning his own sanity.

On the street, three cars are waiting, for Alec, Trevor, and Rilesman, who are traveling in different directions. And three drivers hold umbrellas under which the lawyers can talk. Rilesman says, "So you think that's it? A month will come and go, and no utility will sue us?"

"Yes," Alec says. "That's it."

"I haven't told you. We've settled the coal case for half what we owe. It'll be in the papers tomorrow. They took so little because they thought the utilities' litigation would wipe us out before we could pay them anything."

"Congratulations," Alec says, wanting to be off.

"So one day," says Rilesman, waxing philosophical in the rain, "an $8 billion exposure, hanging there over our heads, about to cripple us, one of the greatest companies in the economic history of America—next day, problem's gone. No one else even saw it. And no one will even know how close we came to extinction."

"Be well, Larry," Alec says. "Trevor's due in Washington, but

I'm sure he could stay for a quick drink. I've got to get back to New York."

Rilesman restrains him by the arm. "You did all this. You made it all disappear."

Alec laughs, getting into the car.

"I hate you," Rilesman says, and probably means it.

"You'll get over it," Alec says with a grin, and leaves.

In the car, heading down Market Street for the turnoff to the Pennsylvania Turnpike, Schlomo says, "You know, our car service takes messages and distributes them on our intercom."

"Yeah, I gave my secretary the number."

"Well, that explains it."

"What?" Alec says. "She call?"

"I'm told she did."

"*Now* you tell me?"

"I figured I'd let you kvell for a while."

"How thoughtful. What's the message?"

"Call the chief judge. I have the number."

"I know the number," Alec says. "Find me a goddamn pay phone." Schlomo swerves back to the curb. "Quarters!" Alec says, and gets a handful. He jumps out, grabs the phone in the booth, deposits the coinage, and dials. When the clerk announces his name, Chief Judge Kane picks up at once. "I have good news for you, young man. What's your fondest wish of the moment?"

"Eric Stapleton is gone? Kicked upstairs?"

"Fonder?"

"He's been replaced by Breck Schlumberger."

"Wish granted," Kane says. "Schlumberger, dean of the Yale Law School, is now assistant attorney general of the United States, in charge of the Antitrust Division."

"You're kidding!"

"I do many things, Alec. Most of them useful. Kidding is not one of them. Now, can you turn this into something productive?"

"Yes."

"Like getting Schlumberger to agree to arbitrate the government monopolization case against your computer client?"

"Better," Alec says. "We can get him to drop the case."

"What?"

"Stipulation of voluntary dismissal."

"He'll sign that?"

"Yeah, I think so," Alec says. "After 10 million documents and thousands of depositions, it's a simple case. Market definition. If the relevant market were U.S. only, we don't monopolize it, because the Japanese are coming, as are the Chinese and Koreans. If the market is global—and anyone with a functioning brain can see that it is—the charge of monopolization is ridiculous, because the Japanese companies are already close to dominating that market. Not only will Breck see this, he will delight in ending litigation that his predecessors have been flogging for years."

"So you're saying I can now forget about the case."

"Not entirely. A stipulation of dismissal must be 'so ordered' by the trial judge."

"And what?" says Kane. "You're suggesting Ettinger might not sign it? The government wants to relieve the federal court of the largest case on its docket—the largest, most burdensome case in the history of jurisprudence—and the sitting judge tries to stop that from happening?" The chief judge's laugh roars into the phone. "I'd love to see him try that!"

"You granted my wish," Alec says. "I grant yours."

"You're not actually going to tempt him to do something that absurd?"

"I won't have to, Judge. It's in his wiring."

Hanging up, Alec places a collect call to Lee Norris, who says, "Down on your luck?"

"I'm in a phone booth in Philadelphia. Used my last coins to call Rivvy Kane."

"Ah."

"It's over," Alec says.

"Okay, I'll play. Hunger and famine? Racial intolerance? The case?"

"The latter. Stapleton is being appointed deputy attorney general. The new head of the Antitrust Division will be my old classmate, Breck Schlumberger."

"I'll be damned," says Norris. "Ol' Breck, going back to the wars."

"Did he take your class?"

"No," Norris says. "He took con law from Tommy the Commie. Emerson. But you and he were friends?"

"Still are."

"And he will throw this case out?" Norris asks. "After the government has spent $100 million on it? And while a staff of twenty government lawyers will scream bloody murder? To say nothing of a federal judge who will go absolutely berserk?"

"Sweetens the pot from Breck's standpoint."

"So… you'll call him?"

"I shouldn't be involved," Alec says, "and don't have to be. He'll love dealing with Jack and the rest of the team. The way Breck operates, he'll basically want the case argued before him. Three, four, maybe five sessions should do it, our guys arguing against the government staff. The stupidity of the government case will end up infuriating him. He'll probably prepare the stipulation of dismissal himself."

"You're sure of this?"

"Yes," Alec says. "I am."

"Is this the doing of the chief judge?" Norris says.

"I didn't ask him to appoint Breck."

"But it was Kane who gave you the news?"

"It was, yes."

"Quite a result," Norris says. "And what's going on in Philadelphia?"

"That's over too."

"Your Allis-Benoit litigation?"

"Ten minutes ago."

"And then you heard from the chief judge about Breck?"

"Just now in the phone booth," Alec says.

Norris's laugh is softer than Kane's, but there's nothing in it but warmth. "At least once in their lives," he says, "every person in this world should have such a ten minutes."

When Alec steps out of the booth, he holds his face up to the rain. *This minute,* he thinks, *should be the best of it.* Except for the new hole in his life.

THIRTY-FOUR

Sal Angiapello arrives back in New York fully refreshed. His private jet lands at Westchester Airport. His luggage is handled and transported by minions. He has word delivered to Lou DiBrazzi to meet him at his apartment on Central Park West. On the drive there, as rain streaks the windows, he leisurely checks the mail placed on the backseat of his limousine. Mail sorting is done by Joe Gura, a cousin of the man who manages his Ionian estate.

Upstairs, Sal brings DiBrazzi into his study. "So, report," Sal says, leafing through additional envelopes that have been hand delivered, apparently that morning.

"All went smoothly," DiBrazzi says. "She's in the house in Fort Lee. Arrived on time. Two men held her. I gave her the needle."

Sal nods, as if hearing of the successful delivery of a rug. "I think it's now time for the young one," he says. "I want them brought to the island and made ready."

"Very good," says DiBrazzi. "Of course the young one is still being guarded."

"So?" Sal remains standing, indicating he wishes the meeting to end.

"I'm just mentioning it, boss. The people protecting her are professionals."

"And you're not?"

"It's a question of the best time, boss. Thought I should consult you on that. When she's in school—"

"No," Sal says.

"I agree," says DiBrazzio. "But she also spends time at your nephew's apartment."

"Hmm. No. I'd rather he didn't… observe this." Sal sits at his desk. "You have an alternate plan?"

"Side street. We'll track her with a couple of vans. At the right time, swoop in. Give her the needle. Get her inside. Fend off whoever with silencers. There'll be a couple of casualties at most. Forty-five minutes later, she's in the back of a plane, in a bag, naked, and scared outta her mind."

Sal visualizes the scene, then tilts his head in approval. "Don't screw this up," he says.

"I won't."

"Who you have helping on this?"

Before DiBrazzi can answer, Nicoli's cousin, Joe Gura, opens the study door. "Sorry, Don Salvatore. There's a kid here, a teenager, claiming to be your niece."

Word reaches Ben Braddock that Alec has returned from Philadelphia. He calls Frank Macalister and says, "Meet me in Brno's office. Now." Before Alec can hang up his coat, the two senior partners are upon him. He gives them a quick report of the meeting at PECO and his conversation with Kane.

"Have you spoken to Stamper?" Ben asks.

"Lee called him," Alec says. "They've already made contact with Schlumberger. That case is history."

Mac says, "And what about yours? You think the utilities will stay in their caves?"

"They'll wait. Every one of them. For someone else to make a move. And no one will."

"Including PECO?"

"That's the thing," Alec says. "PECO is the one they're all expecting to sue and give them all another month to think about it. When Kohn lets PECO's claim lapse, everyone else's claim will swirl down the tubes right along with it."

"And you think you can trust Kohn not to file?" Mac says.

"Yeah, I do."

Braddock sits on the sofa. "Okay. Glad to hear it. I gave you an assignment: to get rid of the electrical equipment litigation before it went to trial and destroyed our oldest client, Allis-Benoit; and to get rid of the computer litigation before it went to judgment and destroyed our biggest client, U.S. Computer Corp. Now that you've finally done those things, you've got time to attend to a new matter of some importance that's just been offered."

"I thought I might take a few days."

"Take a few days?" says Braddock. "What the hell does that mean?"

"Means a vacation, Ben. With my daughter."

"Vacation?" Ben looks at Mac, as if for the definition of yet another strange word. "What the fuck's that?"

"Days in the sun?" Alec says. "Beach on an island? As I recall, you own a house in the Hamptons, so you must have some familiarity with the experience."

"My lazy kids go there. But look, you do what you want. I'll give this case to someone else."

"Good."

"How 'bout you, Mac?" Braddock asks.

"Is that the steel case?" Mac's tone is far too innocent.

"Yeah," Braddock says. "The domestic steel industry. *Our* steel industry. Getting killed by subsidized steel from abroad. British steel, for example, comes here, sells at $400 a ton; gets subsidies from the UK totaling $405 a ton. We can't compete with that."

"What's the remedy?" Alec asks.

"What do you care? You want to sit on a beach."

"Right," Alec says. "That's what I want."

"It's called a counterveiling duty," Braddock says. "You want one, you petition the International Trade Commission, from which appeals go to the Court of International Trade. You prove you're not getting a subsidy, the foreign company is, and the domestic industry is injured. The duty equals the amount of the subsidy and levels the playing field, so our companies can compete. There are literally hundreds of cases to prosecute, because steel is the macho industry. Almost every country in the world has one and gives it subsidies to exist. In effect, they're exporting unemployment."

Alec says, "Sounds great for Mac."

"No hole in my schedule, sorry," Mac says.

"One of the younger guys, then, right?" Alec says. "New partners, new clients, perfect fit."

They're both staring at him. "Actually," Braddock says, "they want you."

"You've made that up."

"No. I simply talked to them for a few minutes about which of our partners might be available, and they chose you."

Alec sits on top of his desk and stares back at them. "Then they can wait a week," he says.

Braddock flashes a rare smile. "I'll get it organized."

Sarah says to the man who is plaguing her life, "This is between you and me."

"Mr. DiBrazzi is my close associate," Sal says.

"I don't want him here," Sarah says, her eyes fixed on her tormentor.

Sal, smiling, nods at DiBrazzi, who gives a shrug and leaves the room. As the door closes, Sal says, "I'm actually very pleased to see you."

"You've been following me. People working for you have."

"True," Sal says.

"You admit it?"

"Yes. I am interested in you."

"In me or my money?"

"You say 'your money,' and under civil law, you are correct. But the family, whose rules apply to you, operates under a different law."

"Which you," Sarah says, "as head of family, lay down and interpret."

"Bright girl."

"Nice gig," Sarah says.

"Believe me, I've earned it."

"Your rules mean nothing to me."

"Which doesn't surprise me," Sal says. "It's the way you've been brought up."

"Y'know, I don't really remember Phil very well—"

"You call him Phil?"

"I have a real dad. And from what I do remember, Phil was a lot like you."

"Oh, yes?"

"He also made the rules. And he couldn't understand why anyone would question them."

"Did you?" Sal asks.

"I was five years old."

Sal laughs, and Sarah talks over it. "So why I came here today, the way I see it, we're at an impasse, you and me, because you're being very foolish, if you don't mind my saying so." At his expression, Sarah says, "I can see you do mind, but that's just too bad. The point is, I'm not going to hand over my money, least of all to you. You obviously know that, so you sent Tino to get it. And if you'd just leave things alone, let them develop naturally, your plan, if that's really your plan—to have my money in the family—might actually succeed. I really like Tino. But if you insist on interfering, trying to control everything, you'll screw it up. That's called irony, in case you didn't know."

Sal laughs again, this time more heartily.

Sarah says, "I'm so glad I amuse you."

"You are a delightful young woman."

"I'm sixteen."

"I know how old you are. But you are very naive, even for sixteen."

"Okay, what am I missing?"

"Well, for starters," Sal says, "you come here out of the blue, intrude yourself on my meeting as if I were someone you could do that to, announce yourself as my niece, and expect to charm me into submission—twist me around one of your charming little fingers. I am charmed, my dear, but there has never been a possibility that I would be submissive. And I am not your uncle. I am your second cousin. What is more, your father—your blood father—was not my friend."

"Is that it?"

"Of your naïveté? As I said, barely the beginning. We now turn to the serious part."

"Which is what? That I should know that if I come to your home, you're going to kidnap me? What do you think it feels like every time I go outside having a bunch of your goons following me? You think I don't know they can jump me at any time you blow your tin horn? And get away with it? With people trying to protect me—people I like—getting murdered in the street?"

Sal sits back in an attitude of reappraisal. "No, I thought you probably understood such a risk. What I doubt you appreciate is what it feels like to be in captivity." He gives her a thin smile. "But you will." He presses a button on his desk. "Let me reintroduce you to Mr. DiBrazzi. For a time, he will own you. And he will want to do things to you that you probably cannot even imagine. But you will want to do what he says. Because the alternative would cause you more pain than you will be able to endure."

Alec leaves the office early. Schlomo suggests taking the streets. Alec says gamble on the FDR Drive. Traffic is hellacious. When they finally get to Alec's building uptown, Harvey Grand stands waiting outside. "They told me you'd left. I came straight here. I have bad news."

"We need the car?" Alec asks.

"Just a phone. ASAP."

Alec thanks Schlomo and leads Harvey into the building. They ride silently upstairs,\ while a jovial elevator operator natters on about the rain. Harvey begins as soon as they get inside. "We trailed Sarah's walk through the Ninety-Sixth Street Transverse and south on Central Park West. Usual route when she visits Tino. Only this time she didn't. She took us totally by surprise by ducking into Sal's building. We covered the front; we covered the back. We know Sal maintains a heliport on the roof. Getting up there required manhandling three building employees, which may have alerted Sal. Two of our guys broke into his apartment, which was empty. I made the roof in time to see the chopper pull out. Shooting it down was obviously not a feasible option. We stood there helplessly, watching it leave."

In the front hall, Alec, face grim, works out in his mind any other options that might now be available.

Harvey says, "I did not—and this is my fuckup—have anyone at the Westchester Airport, even though I know that's where Sal keeps his Learjet."

"We can stop his takeoff," Alec says, trying to stay calm, trying to think straight.

"Too late. They took off three minutes ago."

"We have the flight plan?" They both head into the living room.

"They're refueling in Shannon," Harvey says, "then off to Sal's island."

"Maybe we can stop them in Shannon."

"That's out of my league," Harvey says.

"I know the ambassador to Ireland," Alec says. "The father-in-law of a friend of mine. But whether he'd stop, or even could stop, a plane from taking off from an Irish airport… on my say-so… I'm not sure."

"Let's get him on the phone," Harvey says. "At least he'll take your call."

"Look, there's a separate phone in my study. Why don't you track down the embassy number in Dublin. I'm going to try Lee."

"Lee Norris?" Harvey says.

"Yeah."

"Harvey pushes his lip up in an appreciative expression, then bites it. "There's more bad news. Sal's organization has a safe house in Fort Lee. It's included in our surveillance. Before Sarah went into Sal's place on Central Park West, Jesse was seen entering the house in Fort Lee."

"Jesse?" Alec says, not fully comprehending it.

"Weirdly, she seemed okay with it, no pressure. She was even carrying a suitcase. But the guy she went in with was Lou DiBrazzi, who is one of Sal's lieutenants."

"Oh, Jesus!" Alec says.

"You knew something about this?"

"That she was being conned, yes. And I told her. But I didn't predict this."

"This is a fucking mess," Harvey mutters, and heads to the study.

Using the living room phone, Alec gets Lee Norris on the first ring. "You just caught me," he says. "I've already let everyone else go home and was about to do the same myself."

"My daughter and sister-in-law have been kidnapped."

"What did you say?"

"They were taken by Sal Angiapello, who is a mob boss you may have heard of."

"Alec, what the hell have you been doing with a mob boss?"

"Well, there's a history. I thought you knew."

"Oh shit, right," Norris says. "You once killed one. I keep not placing you in that context. And what is this? Retribution?"

"It's complicated."

"I'll bet," Norris says.

"Do you know our ambassador in Dublin?"

"What do you want him for?"

"Angiapello will be refueling his jet in Shannon in about four hours."

"And you want what?" Norris says. "Our embassy to get the Irish police to seize the plane? On your say-so or mine? In four hours from now, which is in the middle of the night for them?"

"Our ambassador can't do this?"

"By the time I track him down—maybe wake him up—all the red tape he faces? The people he'd have to find and call? I doubt he'd even try."

"Will you try?" Alec says. "I'll also call; I know him, but it would come better from you."

"Yes, I'll try. But as I said—"

"I know," Alec says.

"Do you know where Angiapello's going after Shannon?"

"Yeah," Alec says. "His island."

"Oh, yes," Norris says. "I know about that island. All right, I'll tell you what I think I can do, which might have a better chance of succeeding."

THIRTY-FIVE

Sarah awakes in a bag. It has air holes through which she can see light, but it's a definite bag. Her head thumps with pain; her clothes stick with sweat; she inhales grit, and it chokes her. Confusion. Terror. She screams. The voice responding stifles her own. It's Jesse's. They both start screaming each other's name. As an outlet for hysteria, it almost, temporarily, calms them.

"You? Jesse, is it really you?"

"Sarah?"

"Where the fuck are we?" Sarah shouts.

"This must be a plane."

"Did they drug you?"

"I think so," Jesse says. "Never saw it. Blacked out."

"Are we alone? Some compartment or something?"

"I have no idea."

"Any idea where they're taking us?" Sarah says.

"No."

"I'm in a sort of bag," Sarah says.

"Same for me. I think it's a body bag."

"Have you tried to get out?"

After a longish pause, Jesse says, "No," which frightens Sarah even more.

"Why not?" Sarah says.

"Because those bastards took my clothes."

"Oh, God," Sarah says.

They both hear some men laughing. Then a rough voice. "Shut the fuck up."

"Where are you taking us?" Sarah shouts from the bag.

Another laugh. It's Lou DiBrazzi. "To hell," he says. "Now do what you're told. After we land, we'll clean you up and get you ready."

"For what?" Sarah, now screaming again.

"Hey! I said shut the fuck up. Or we'll start working you over on the plane."

Norris streams by in a limo. Alec and Harvey are waiting downstairs. "So what's the drill?" Alec asks, getting in.

"I couldn't reach the ambassador," Norris says. "He's on a plane somewhere. But I've managed to line up something else. A chopper to a naval station in Maryland, NAS Pax River. Where I'm hoping we can get on a plane that can land on a carrier."

"Hoping?" Alec says.

"Yeah. I'm afraid the president will have to approve this. I'm not a fan of Nixon's, and he doubtless knows that, but I treated him with respect during the transition, and our dealings have always been cordial. And who knows—maybe he'll think I might be reappointed secretary of state in the next Democratic administration, and he'll need something from me. But the people he'll listen to on this are his counsel, Len Garment, and his own secretary of state, Bill Rogers, who I do know reasonably well. I haven't gotten through yet to Nixon or Rogers, but I did talk to Garment, who, incidentally, speaks highly of you, Alec."

"Len Garment, Christ yes. I'd forgotten he followed Nixon to Washington."

"How do you know him? He didn't say."

"He's a great trial lawyer. He won a huge jury award against Telemarch News, and I worked on the appeal. Opposite sides, but we got along fine."

"Where is the carrier we're trying to get on?" Harvey asks.

"Near Naples," Norris says. "Part of the Sixth Fleet. And in that, we're lucky in several respects. The carrier is already heading toward the Malta Channel with a destroyer escort. It's the destroyer I want to take us to Angiapello. Aboard that carrier is the best friend I made in the military while I was in Washington, Gerry Starnes, more formally addressed as Vice Admiral Gerald X. Starnes, commander of the Sixth Fleet. And Gerry is the kind of guy who might actually welcome the opportunity for a maneuver of this sort. *If* it is blessed by the secretary. And, oh yes, the president."

"Garment will push this?" Alec asks.

"He's the one who's getting us on the chopper," Norris says.

Harvey says, "Nixon should jump at it. Rescuing two young lovelies from the clutches of the evil Mafia! It's tailor-made for him. Exactly the kind of publicity he needs."

"One might think," Norris says.

"So what're you not telling us?" Alec says, picking up the somber note in Lee's voice.

"Well, in truth, Garment was not optimistic. He said the obvious, that Nixon has other things on his plate. But also—and this actually worries me more—Nixon is, as Garment put it, 'in one of his moods.' I know the man suffers from depression. And he can get into a state in which he's unreachable."

Alec looks as if he's entering a similar state.

Norris says, "It's what we've got going, Alec."

"I know. Thank you. I'm grateful. And I know few people in this world could even get us on that chopper."

"What worries me," Harvey says. "Even if we get on the plane—the blunt fact is, Sal Angiapello will be holding Sarah and Jesse on an island he controls. So we're vulnerable as hell, and he's got time on his side. No matter how many destroyers we have."

"It's a nasty hostage situation," Norris acknowledges. "But his island has a cannabis plantation and factory, plus two huge munitions warehouses. The stuff is worth billions. It's all hostage to a destroyer's guns. Also, he's got to know that if he harms either woman, we'd cart him back to New York, throw him in prison, and lose the key."

Harvey says, "I'm not sure we can count on his acting rationally. At least by our standards."

"We need to talk to him," Alec says. "Before we simply storm the island."

"By radio," Norris says. "On the ship. If we get there. And if he'll take the call."

"By the way," Alec asks with sudden awareness. "You two know each other?"

Harvey smiles from the jump seat. "I've done a few things for Lee. Nothing, however, near the scale of commandeering the Sixth Fleet."

Lou DiBrazzi is awakened by one of the two island men he's traveling with. With their straggly hair and beards, they both look like they were brought up in caves. For DiBrazzi, it's like waking into a nightmare rather than coming out of one. The older of the two, Arturo, the henchman who jostled him out of sleep, says, "It's a long flight, Lou."

"Getting longer," says Di Brazzi sardonically.

"Franco and I thought we'd break it up. The traveling time. Have a little fun." He nods in the direction of the body bags, in which the young women, silent for some time, are presumably sleeping.

The plane is the smaller of Sal Angiapello's two jets, but still has four seats and an area of several feet behind where the body bags lie quietly. DiBrazzi says, "Fun? What do you mean, fun?"

"Take them out of the bags, you know." Arturo shrugs.

"No," DiBrazzi says, and shuts his eyes again.

"No, you don't know, or no, you don't want it to happen?"

Eyes open at this, DiBrazzi glares at him.

"Shit, Lou, what's the big deal? The younger one, we haven't even taken her clothes off yet. We could watch her squirm. It'd be fun."

"I said no, dammit!" DiBrazzi sits up in his single seat and gives the bearded man a threatening look across the aisle.

"You think Don Salvatore will mind?" Arturo persists. "He won't care. He's gonna put them in trade anyhow. We won't leave any marks. We'll just let them out of the bags, make them crawl around for a while, do things."

DiBrazzi snaps off his seat belt and stands over both of them. "I'm gonna say this once. These women are mine to be trained. On orders from Don Salvatore. You do anything to them I haven't directed, you'll be dead when you step off this plane."

Alec stands outside a hangar at Naval Air Station PAX River. Viewed from the helicopter, the peninsula on which the station is built laps into the Chesapeake Bay like a giant tongue dotted with lights. Now Alec sees the flat surface of the runway and the peninsula beyond as a cruel joke of frustrated opportunity.

They had landed more than an hour ago and been given a tiny room—more like a compartment jerry-rigged on an inside wall of the hangar. Its furnishings consist of three steel chairs and a steel desk with a phone on it. Norris has tried to reach Len Garment twice. Each time Garment's secretary has said, "I'm sorry, he's still in with the president."

When Norris relayed this, Alec said, "Then they must be talking about something else. This is not that complicated."

"Redirecting a mission of the Sixth Fleet?" Norris said with a grim laugh. "A bit more complicated than you might think."

Alec's mind is filled with images he cannot erase. He knows Sal Angiapello transacts a business in flesh. And it's not difficult to imagine how Sal's human commodities must be broken to allow that business to flourish. Every minute in which Sarah and Jesse are in bondage to this man is torture to Alec. There are Navy jets lined up all over this tarmac. If he could get one off the ground, he'd already be on his way to the Ionian Sea.

So what may well have been the finest hours of Alec's legal career have turned themselves into the worst hours of his life. And the sickening images are warping his judgment. Lee Norris has enjoyed one of the most distinguished careers in American history. He's now putting it on the line. *For me,* Alec thinks, *and those I love, whom he doesn't even know. I can at least keep my head clear and lend some assistance.*

Lack of sleep had caught up with him in the helicopter, and it's now adding to his malaise. He rubs his face and goes back to the room inside the hangar, where Harvey and Lee are tilted back in chairs with their eyes half closed.

"No word yet, I assume," Alec says.

"Can't be much longer," Norris says.

Alec stretches out on the industrial-grade carpet and is asleep in five minutes. Five minutes later the phone rings.

Norris snatches it. "Len?" Then listens for thirty seconds before saying, "Can you hold for a moment?" He turns to Alec. "Regrets, but the answer is no."

"Let me talk to him."

Norris hands Alec the phone.

"Len, this is Alec."

"Alec," Garment says. "I'm so sorry. Believe me, I tried. Bill Rogers called while I was in with the president, and he tried. As I just told Lee, the president wants to leave this with the Italian authorities. Rogers will try that, although we both told the president the situation is diplomatically tricky. That island is literally a sovereign state. If anyone has a right to go in there, it's us, not Italy, since Angiapello has kidnapped American citizens."

Nixon's decision is a death knell, and Alec tries to hold his rage. "I'd like you to tell him something else," Alec says. "You remember his Supreme Court argument in our Telemarch case?"

"Of course. I wrote it for him."

"Well, he probably never knew my name, but tell him—or get word to him somehow—that I'm the guy he had that conversation with after the argument on the courthouse steps."

"He'll know what that means?"

"I think so." Alec reconsiders. "Well, I hope so."

"Okay. It's probably going to have to be a note, at this stage."

"As long as you can get it to him right now," Alec says.

"Yeah, I can do that. Let me get off." And Garment hangs up.

Alec finds both men waiting for an explanation. He says, "It's a stupid story, but who the hell knows." He fills a cup from the NAS-issued jug of coffee left for them in this room. "When Nixon lost in California, he came to New York as a partner in Len Garment's firm. My firm had just gotten the Supreme Court to take on what turned out to be a landmark right-of-privacy case. Garment had won the case at trial and in the New York appellate courts, but he thought an argument in the Supreme Court would be a good showcase for Nixon. It wasn't. And I think that stunned our present leader. After the argument, the place was a madhouse of reporters wanting quotes. Nixon was obviously pissed off and wasn't handling it well. Somehow, on the steps, the press mob separated Nixon from his group, but pushed him up against me, and I ushered him downstairs. I said, 'I work for the man you just argued against, but I respect what you did. That court does not agree with your position—it's not fashionable or popular right now—but you stood up to them as bravely as any lawyer could.'

"He said to me—and you've got to realize, we had a gang of reporters screaming behind us—we were like this little island of calm—he said, 'How old are you?' Which kind of surprised me. But I said, 'Twenty-eight.' And he said, 'Well, you're a whippersnapper, but I appreciate what you've said.' And then he turned back to the hungry horde and dealt with them pretty calmly."

"Whippersnapper?" Harvey says.

"Yeah, that's the way he talks."

"And you think remembering that will now turn him around?"

"Don't know, Harvey. But it may put a face on the victim. One of them, anyway. The guy whose life he's turning to shit."

They drink coffee for another half hour. Alec finally says, to break the silence, "There's this so-called leader in Washington—a man of limited stability and dubious character—who may or may not deign to glance at a note. Or change his mind, even if he does. Or do anything whatever to save two young women from a miserable death. And we have no choice but to sit here and wait for this son of a bitch to react." Lee Norris looks down, and Harvey Grand shuts his eyes. There's nothing they can say to improve the situation.

In another ten minutes, the phone rings again. Norris says to Alec, "You take it."

Alec picks up. "Len?"

Garment says, "I don't know what worked, Alec, or whether he even saw the note. But you have your destroyer."

They bump down on the carrier soon after dawn, slammed back and forth, as they were warned, by the clutch of the cable. The miracle is that a swaying plane can touch down at all on a moving flight deck in the middle of the sea. Alec got a little sleep on the flight to give him the energy to climb out of the plane on his own. Harvey pops out and onto the deck, as if warming up for an Olympic triathlon. A large man, not young, he still moves like an athlete. Norris needs two midshipmen to hoist him down. Alec asks one of them, "Pilot said we were over Malta. Where is it?"

"Turn around," says the young man.

And there's the island, a purple hilly haze, already in the distance, off the stern of the ship.

Vice Admiral Gerald Starnes meets with them on the flag bridge. He's a human blade, probably six feet, five inches tall, high narrow forehead, swooping nose, thick straight, grayish hair, and thin lips pressed with the seriousness of the business. "You guys probably need some sleep. You have a choice—I suggest you crash on the destroyer. Sooner you get there, the better. Given the distance to your destination, you should have until midafternoon."

Norris says, "We're damn grateful for this, Gerry."

"Look, I hope it works. Those are savage people. A true fact? With Nam winding down, and even before, I've had my eye on that island. It's one of the area's major munitions suppliers. I don't know what's been protecting them, but I was damn glad to get that order from the White House last night."

"I think," Norris says, "we'd just as soon go right to the destroyer."

"Copter's the fastest way."

Norris looks at Alec and Harvey, who both nod.

"Look," the vice admiral says directly to Alec. "I have a daughter too. I know what you're going through. But I'm putting you in excellent hands. If anyone can pull this off, it's Ned Townsend, the commander of that vessel. He's the most resourceful officer in this fleet."

After conveying more thanks, the three lawyers are escorted down the staircases to the flight deck. Alec takes with him an impression of the vice admiral's craggy face, which reads—despite the man's words—deep pessimism about the outcome of this mission.

THIRTY-SIX

Jesse showers in a stall surfaced in Portuguese tiles, which, under the circumstances, appear incongruously florid. It is not only grime she washes from her body. It's also the leer of the men who had hauled her upstairs. They had taken her from the plane in that bag and tossed it, with her in it, onto a bed. From inside, she watched it being unzipped, suffered their eyes exploring her body, their filthy laughs, and then heard the door to the room being locked. She waited before peeking out. They were gone. She blinked at the sunlight. She did not expect to emerge from this kidnapping without some violent assault, but those men presumably were under orders, for now, not to touch her. Another bag with Sarah in it was open on the same bed. Apparently drugged again, she was asleep. They had not taken her clothes off. *Dispensation for a blood relative?* Yet seeing Sarah lying there, a kid in a school uniform, made this episode even more intolerable.

Jesse steps out of the shower, carries a towel with her into the bedroom, glances at the view from the front window. The house is on a knob of a hill that slants down to the water. She sees manicured lawns, palm trees, and a wide beach on a cove partially protected by small jetties that jut into the sea. The bedroom's one closet racks an array of women's clothes, none new, but all designer quality and clean. A dresser literally bulges with lingerie. She covers herself quickly with what first comes to hand. A plate of cut fruit sits on a side table with a bottle of water. She devours two slices of pineapple and takes a long drink, too hungry and thirsty to worry about being drugged again. Then she thinks about trying to wake Sarah.

Instead she sits on the small bed in the room, feeling anger overcoming her terror. For the first time in her life, she wishes she had a loaded gun in her hands. Whoever stripped her and put her in that bag, whoever carted her to that plane and this island, deserves to be shot.

Sarah stirs, begins to murmur something, then lets out a cry. Jesse rushes to quiet her. With a hand over Sarah's mouth, she says, "Easy, easy. We're alone, we have to talk." She helps Sarah from the bag, helps her to stand. "There's food, a shower, we seem to have some time."

Sarah nods. "Where are we?"

"My guess, Sal's house, on his island. They dumped us in this room and haven't been back since. It's been not quite an hour. Take some food and water. The fruit is actually quite good. We should try to develop some sort of plan."

"Alec will come for us," Sarah says.

"That's the plan?"

"He will. I know him. He'll come here with men. He'll come after that bastard, that despicable Angiapello. He'll probably kill him."

"Sarah," Jesse says, "even if he can figure out where we are, and round up a small army, how the hell could he even land on this island without…?" She waves her hands in frustration. "How could he land safely? We have to think what we can do for ourselves."

The door opens. An older man with an impressively jutting nose and well-cut blue blazer stands in the doorway. "Don Salvatore wishes you downstairs."

"We need a moment," Jesse says.

"Oh, yes." The man smiles. "You think Don Salvatore's wishes are small things that can be delayed?" He advances into the room.

"We're coming," Jesse says.

"Yes. Much better for you. Follow me."

After some sleep, which wasn't totally restful, Alec and his compatriots sit around a table with naval officers in what is probably a mess room, but they aren't eating. Commander Addison (Ned) Townsend chairs the meeting. A former halfback for a Naval Academy team in the days it had national ranking, Townsend had served with distinction in World War II and now nears retirement. His white hair, though thick, might imply readiness for the golden years. His smooth, sharp features, jutting chin, and manner suggest a man who would always be more at home captaining a destroyer. He says, "Hostages… always a nasty situation. But this one…." He shakes his head like a doctor with a diagnosis he'd rather not give. "There's no great way to sneak onto this island. A destroyer coming toward them is hardly inconspicuous. We're looking at a small, mainly flat oval, rocky at the shores, loaded with security cameras scanning the coast, and studded with machine guns. Even if our men could get there underwater, they'd be vulnerable to a barrage of gunfire before they reached the house, or wherever the women are being held. Parachuting men in from the carrier would likely get most of them killed and the women along with them. One approach that might work is destroying one of Angiapello's warehouses with our guns, and trading the other for the women."

Norris asks, "Have we gotten Angiapello on the phone yet?"

"No luck," says Townsend.

A midshipman arrives to serve them all coffee. It gives them a minute more to think. Townsend then continues, "As I said, every option here is risky. What I'd recommend is, we go in blazing. Turn all our guns on everything. Bring planes in from the carrier to bomb and strafe. Throw everyone into confusion, eliminate as many of them as we can. And start invading the island as we shell it. Most likely, Angiapello's got one place he regards as safe, and he'll go for it, taking the women with him. He has every incentive to keep them alive. They're his bargaining chip."

"And what would you see as the outcome?" Norris asks.

"Angiapello squirreled up. With guns on the women. Surrounded by fifty, sixty of us. Most of his army killed in the battle. His munitions destroyed. At that stage, if we get there, the risk is way down."

"*If* we get there," Harvey says.

"You don't like it?" Norris says.

"What's not to like?" Harvey says wryly. "We have no idea where Sarah and Jesse are being held. We start shelling the island, there's a not-insignificant chance that one of those blasts will find them. Especially if we blow up two warehouses full of munitions. And once our men land and the shooting starts, there'll be lots of stray bullets to catch anyone. What's more, your best-case scenario—Sal with a couple of gunmen surrounded by fifty of us— what I see is Sal, with at least ten of his own, armed to the teeth, willing to shoot it out. With the women out in front of them as human shields. Or even, telling you before you start bombing, that he's tying the women up someplace as a target."

"As I said—"

"Right, Ned, risky" says Norris.

And everyone looks at Alec. He takes a swig of coffee and says, "I think the chances are better if I go in alone."

Which stuns them into silence.

Townsend says, "Forgive my saying so, son, but that's nuts. It achieves nothing but your certain death. They'll either shoot you on the beach or bring you back to be tortured. These are very primitive people."

"Maybe," Alec says. "Eventually. But there are facts you don't know, Commander. Jesse Madigan is there because of me. My daughter is there because of her inheritance, which I control. Sal's not likely to kill me until we've had a chance to talk. Which is to say, a chance to negotiate."

Townsend studies him for a moment. "What was your sport?"

"My what?"

"In college, what sport did you play? You look like you might have been an athlete."

"I was on the track-and-field team."

"Event?"

"High jump," Alec says, wondering where this was going.

"I was hoping you'd say the hundred-yard dash. Because when you're on that beach and feel the gunfire wing by and spit up at you, you're gonna wanna run as fast as you can back to the boat you came in."

"I don't think I'd do that," Alec says.

"You ever been in combat?"

"No."

"Then you can't know." Townsend pours some more coffee for himself. "Sorry. Just trying to get this job done." He drinks it black and sips it. "I understand, it's your daughter, it's your sister-in-law, you're a lawyer, you want to negotiate. And suppose you get up to the house, what do you have to give him? Your daughter's inheritance and your life?"

"Neither, if I can help it," Alec says.

"Oh, really?" Harvey says, now joining in opposition with Townsend. "You'll just think of something on the spot? Just wing it when you get there?"

"I'll know a lot more than I do now."

The phone rings, Townsend picks up. He listens, then addresses the group, his expression never moving off grave. "Angiapello has made contact through one of his lieutenants. He'll permit you, Alec, to come onto the island alone."

As Nicoli escorts Jesse and Sarah from the room upstairs, two dark young men with serious weapons fall in behind them. Jesse lags a bit on the landing to scan the house and receives a gun butt in the spine. They descend a curved, open staircase and walk on gleaming wood floors past whitewashed walls, passing furnishings decked out in bright colors. The main room is ringed in French doors, framing island views in three directions. A corner door opens onto Sal's study. From behind his desk, Sal waves the men to leave him alone with the two women. He invites neither to sit, though there are chairs in front of his desk, and Sarah and Jesse remain standing.

Sal points to Sarah. "Your adoptive father—"

"He will punish you!" Sarah blurts out. "For this! For doing this to us!"

"At the moment," Sal says calmly, "he's on a ship."

"That's what I said! I knew he'd come! With men, right? And you're scared!"

Sal gives her a curious look, like a wolf touching a window with his tongue. "He's coming at my invitation. The ship is about a mile offshore, and he'll be here very shortly. Alone. My condition for allowing him to see you. And when he steps on this island, he'll be subject to my wish, to do with what I want. As are you."

Jesse's anger is too hot to be hidden. "What the hell do you want?" she says loudly.

"Now? To give you a chance to save his life. And your own." Sal says this as if genuinely believing he's offering kindness. He gestures to the chairs, which they take reluctantly. "I thought it best to explain to you *now* how you might do that. So listen. Carefully. It will be good for everyone. When he arrives, I will tell him what he must do, which is to go back to his ship, sail it away, and never return. I will state this demand flatly. You—both of you—will urge it most passionately. In terms he cannot fail to comply with. You understand?"

Jesse says, "So there are men on that ship. Men with guns."

"No doubt."

"And they're what? Police? Coast Guard?" asks Jesse. "Where

are we? Your island, presumably. Near Sicily, right? So I suppose it's the Italian police. And if you kill him, they'll execute you!"

"We'd be well out of here, as would be his corpse."

"They'll intercept your flight," Jesse says.

Sal shakes his head with impatience. "You may have such hopes, if you like."

"And what are your... plans for us?"

"As I'm trying to tell you, my dear young woman, that rather depends on his cooperation and yours. If he does what he's told, and you help persuade him to do it, he will be unharmed and you will live out your years in ease."

Sarah says, "We'll be free to leave? You will give us transportation off this island?"

"No," Sal says abruptly. "You are no longer free. Either of you. But the conditions of your captivity can vary. In fact, over a wide range. All my clients expect their women to provide pleasure, to be sure. Many, however, can enjoy them only by methods you would find extremely... unpleasant."

Jesse tries to show nothing. "It's true, then," she says. "You're a sex slaver."

Sal nods, as if tiring of this conversation. "There are less pejorative terms, but, yes, I deal in... young women. An adjunct to my other businesses. Customers of the one—drugs or arms—tend to buy more extravagantly when supplied with the other. Although the inclinations of some of these people, well...."

"They're sadists," Jesse says with disgust.

"Yes. You would regard them as sadists."

"You don't?"

"No," Sal says, "I would agree. They like giving pain. And the death rate in their households is not inconsiderable. They need fresh supplies at least monthly. So you see what your decision amounts to? Choose wrong, it's your death sentence. And Mr. Brno's. To deliver you to such people, or him to the sport of my men, are not things *I* would do for amusement. I'm a businessman." His manner is cordial. "Now we've talked enough."

Sal presses a button on his desk, and Nicoli Gura enters at once. Sal says, "These two have matters to mull over. Bring them to the basement and let me know when you have Brno."

Alec is changing into Navy fatigues when Ned Townsend enters his cabin. The commander of the ship carries shoe boxes under both arms. "The high jump, right? That was your event?"

"A very long time ago."

"Well, these might be useful," Townsend says. "What's your size?" He drops the boxes on the bed, and Alec chooses one.

"These are tennis shoes," Alec says, "but thanks."

"Just be careful how you handle them."

"Why's that?" Alec says. Then, as if cracking a joke, "They have knives springing out of them?"

"That's right," Townsend says.

"What?"

"They are equipped with retractable blades."

Alec puts the shoes down carefully. "What the fuck?"

"Stand easy, fella. Lock's on. You're thinking this is a bit James Bondish. Actually OSS, then CIA, had been working on these way before Fleming even started writing the series. We, the Navy, picked it up toward the end of the war. World War II. It's now standard Seals equipment. So let's make sure these fit and you know how to use them." Townsend pulls the size-eleven shoes from the box Alec selected, holds one up, and points. "You bang the heel on the ground, it releases the lock, and a lever pops out. You scrape the heel to your left, moves the lever to the right, and the blade springs out of the toe. Like so." He demonstrates. "It's very sharp. So be careful who you're aiming it at. To get the knife back into the shoe, flip the lever to center, and bang it closed." Again, a demonstration. "Got it?"

"Let me try," Alec says, and starts putting the shoe on.

"Actually, we usually give a bit of training with these things."

"You have a boat ready for me to get into?"

"Pulling into starboard now."

"Then I'd better get on it. I'll practice while going in."

Townsend nods, and Alec laces the shoes. Townsend leads him down a narrow corridor to a ladder that they climb to the deck. It's not quite nightfall, but there's no sun, and the wind is like a beast smacking out of hiding. Townsend shouts over it, "We're getting a storm."

Alec gazes down the side of the ship to what looks like a lifeboat equipped with an outboard motor. Though roped to the ladder, the boat bobs like the proverbial cork in the sea. Townsend shouts again into the wind, "It's a relic—an inflatable seven-man landing craft. Best we can do for this job. You know how to work one of those motors?"

"Yeah, I do," Alec says.

"This is a deep channel, and we're in fairly close. With that motor, which is souped, you'll be landing pretty fast."

"Faster the better."

"You know what you're doing is suicidal?"

"I know the risks," Alec says.

"With the shoes, maybe you can take out a couple of those bastards. Then… I doubt they'll just kill you. And I have nothing on board, no magic capsule to put an end to it. What they do to you, you will feel."

Alec's breath feels raw in his throat. "I know the likely result of this for myself."

"And what? You think Angiapello will take you in trade and release the women? Is that what you're planning to offer him?" Townsend's tone, even at the top of his voice, properly demarks such a plan as preposterous.

"No," Alec says loudly, trying to be heard over the sound of the ship's motor, the wind, and the sea. "I've no idea right now

how, if at all, this can be done. I've got to get there to find out."
At Townsend's sad shake of the head, Alec adds, "Look, I don't
like this any more than you think I should. If there were any alternative less awful, I'd take it."

"I've given you one," Townsend says.

Climbing onto the ladder, Alec says. "By all means, get your
men ready for a landing. If I can't get Sarah and Jesse safe on this
ship, then you can start blasting away. What I need to stop before
you can mobilize and get there is what they might be doing to
them now."

A cramped room, mostly underground, with stone walls and
floors, and one small window near the ceiling. The room is furnished with a wide bed, a tall wooden cabinet, and one large lad-
der-back chair. On it, Lou DiBrazzi sits waiting. Gura, releasing
the women to this man, gives him a warning look before leaving.

DiBrazzi says sharply to the women, "Stand away from
the door." With belligerent stares at the man, they stand firm.
DiBrazzi thrusts himself up, and they scatter. He removes a key
from his pocket and locks them all in. "I have the impression,"
he says, walking back to the chair, "that you two don't understand your situation." He looks at them as if he might expect a
response, but, receiving none, continues. "Well, you will. Eventually. What's required is training. Obedience training. That's my
job. Which I do well, as you will see."

He goes to the cabinet, opens it, gestures for them to look
inside. It is filled with stock, almost comical, objects of sadomas-
ochistic play. At their reaction, he smiles. "The object is to teach
you not simply obedience, but how to deliver obedience with
charm." His eyes light up with the prospect. "There's nothing
complicated to the process. It entails pain. Fear of pain. Fear of
many things far worse than compliance. So… we have some time

before your hero arrives. I think we should use it. Get started, what do you say? First lesson? Maybe you'll learn quickly. And maybe we'll bring Brno in later to watch, hmm?"

He pulls a riding crop from the cabinet. "We are in what is known as the whip room. There are other whips in this cabinet that cut. There are other rooms in this basement that offer harsher—" a thought comes to him, at which he smiles—"and you might say, more pointed, even more heated… learning experiences." He laughs in appreciation of his own double meaning. "But we're still at an early stage. So, to start, I'll use this comparatively"—he whacks it in his palm—"gentle device, for which I will need both of you to lie face down on the bed."

"Fuck you," says Sarah.

DiBrazzi laughs again. "Yes, of course, you would resist. Because you don't yet know the alternative. You will soon lie facedown on the bed. The only question is, will you do so voluntarily, or because the several men I will call in here—and who would like nothing better than to witness your humiliation—will lift you up and toss you there. They will then need to stay, to hold you down, to remove your clothes, etcetera. I personally would prefer we do this without the fuss and the audience, but it's up to you. So tell me. What's your choice?"

Most of the trip in, Alec practices opening the shoe blades as directed. It's amazingly simple, and they work perfectly. Close to the shore, Alec realizes he's drifting away from it and west of it. His brain flashes, *riptide!* Doubly frustrating, because there are jetties that might protect him if he could motor inside. Somewhere from the recesses of memory comes the thought: *Do not fight a rip current! Go with it!* And that's what he does, allowing the inflated craft to race parallel to the beach, but farther and farther away from it. Breakers crash over him, and the storm beats down, stinging his eyes, clasping his shirt to his body. He knows he must try turning into the shore, though he's now well past it. *But turning in might find a break in this current!* he thinks. It doesn't on his first attempt, and the boat is thrown even farther off course.

But now, past the breakers again, he can make out, if just barely, a blue patch in the green water, and he swings the boat to it. *No riptide!* He races the motor toward shore, then skims back toward the beach. As fast as it came, the storm stops. And in five minutes, Alec cruises in safely.

Nicoli Gura waits onshore as Alec struggles to beach the landing craft. Gura pulls a radiophone from his pocket, reports on Alec's arrival, then wades into the surf to help. No words of greeting or introduction, Gura simply takes the opposite side of the boat and assists in the motions necessary to bring the small craft from the water against the current and the wind. With the job done, and the two of them, both soaked, gathering breath on the beach, Gura says, "Raise your arms."

"You want to search me?"

"Of course."

"If I had a gun," Alec says, "I'd already have shot you."

"If you were stupid enough to use it now, then you would be shot by the guns trained on you from the house."

"You're suggesting I use it later," Alec says.

"Raise your arms," Gura says with asperity, and conducts the search.

Alec says, "You've done this before."

"You will want to follow me," Gura says, registering no sign of humor.

In the wind and dark they trudge on the sand toward the house. Alec says, "You of course work for Sal Angiapello."

"Don Salvatore. I am the manager of this island."

"Would you tell me your name?" Alec asks.

"I am Nicoli Gura."

"You've seen my daughter and sister-in-law?"

"I just left them. They had not been harmed."

"Had not been?" Alec repeats. "Is there a 'yet' in that sentence?"

"What do you think?" Nicoli says. "They've been brought here for a vacation?"

"No," Alec says. "I do not think that. And would you mind if we increased our pace?"

Gura stops. "I've given notice of your arrival. The two young women have been brought to Don Salvatore. What happens to them now depends entirely on what you say and do. If it's bad, increasing our pace will only make it happen sooner."

THIRTY-SEVEN

Sarah and Jesse are herded into the study by three *soldati*, Lou DiBrazzi leading the way. Sal Angiapello is still working at his desk. The chairs that once stood in front of it have been moved against the interior wall. Sal briefly nods toward the chairs before resuming his work, and the women are shoved there by the guards, who step to the back of the room. Jesse says, "Why are you mistreating us like this?"

Sal looks up. "Mistreating? How have you been mistreated?"

"You're unaware of what's happening?" she says, flamed with indignation. "We were not offered these chairs. We were manhandled into them. Thrown here like sacks of dirt. Perhaps you think we are sacks of dirt."

"I have no such thought," Sal says.

"And in your basement. That man"—she points to DiBrazzi—"was threatening to thrash us with riding crops."

"Yes."

"Yes? Women are beaten in your home, and ho hum? How ordinary? What kind of monster are you?"

"A busy one," Sal says and returns to his papers.

"This is bullshit," Jesse says. "A billionaire gangster does paperwork? You have the nerve to let sadists torture us, but not to look us in the face?"

"It's my understanding that you were not whipped."

"And it's mine that it was a temporary reprieve."

Sal turns to Sarah. "And what do you think?"

Sarah closes her eyes, then blinks, as if coming out of a coma. "What do I think? After being kidnapped, brutalized, threatened

with God knows what else? You want to know what I *think?*"
She gives a laugh one would not associate with a sixteen-year-old.
"I want to go home," she says, suddenly overcome by fatigue.
"What do *you* think?"

"Maybe it will happen. Eventually. Let's see how persuasive
you are. When Mr. Brno arrives."

Nicoli Gura leads Alec to a side door of the house. "Why not the
front?" Alec asks.

"This is closer to Don Salvatore's study."

"Where the women are now?"

"Yes."

"And so it's also the closest exit."

"That would be a logical conclusion," Gura says.

"Are you trying to tell me something?"

"Only the facts."

"The women will be guarded by soldiers?" Alec asks.

"You'll see soon enough."

"How many?"

"As I said."

"All armed?"

"Just go inside."

Alec puts his hand on the door handle. "And you, Nicoli," he
says, "do you approve of what's happening here?"

Gura says, "I think you had better go in."

The door opens to a small mudroom, which leads to a living
room lit dimly by several lamps. Across the room, light blazes
from the open door to the study. Alec enters that room with the
demeanor of a houseguest joining the party. There's Sal smiling at
the desk, DiBrazzi smirking, their armed men coming alert. "Tell
me what you can," Alec says quickly to Jesse, who, like Sarah, is
startled by his casual entry.

"It's bad," Jesse says, "and will get worse. A lot worse."

"Sarah?"

"Get us out of here, Alec!" she pleads, her voice careening off the walls.

He turns to Sal. "You've seen the destroyer in your channel?"

"Oh, yes."

"There's an aircraft carrier two knots away."

Sal spreads his hands, as if to say he would be surprised by anything less.

"They expect me back with my daughter and Miss Madigan well within the hour. If not, they will assume we're dead, or as good as, and will blast this island out of the water. Your accounts will be seized in every country of the world. Your other assets will be confiscated. There will be nothing left to you, or of you. Do you understand?"

"The threat?" Sal says, as if it were trivial. "Yes, of course. So I will give you another to think about. I want you to return to your boat on the beach, putter it as fast as you can to the big boat in the channel, have them turn that around, and sail away. You have forty minutes from now to accomplish that." He looks at the grandfather clock behind him. "Because, in that time, if not done, we will remove one limb of one of these young women and place it on a board on the beach—so that your telescopes can confirm we do what we say. Every five minutes, if your vessels are still in my harbor, another amputation. No anesthesia. Until both of them are quadriplegics. You understand *that?*"

In high-jumping parlance, it's called the Western roll, where the lead leg is kicked up vigorously to lift the body into a layout over the bar. Not normally done from a standing position, but it can be, especially if there's no bar. It's much better, though, with a two-step stride. So in the middle of Sal's speech, Alec takes two unsuspicious steps backward, then strides and leaps, feet first, blade extended, over Sal's desk and into his neck, the thrust kicking over Sal's chair. The *capo famiglia* falls flat on the floor, blood spurting from his jugular vein. In seconds, he is dead, and Alec is back up on his feet. Lou DiBrazzi, who had foreseen no need to arm himself in a room filled with *soldati*, hurls himself at the intruder, only to receive a kick in the groin that leaves him castrated and, in seconds, unconscious and dying.

Extraordinarily, none of the soldiers fires his gun, Alec's leap, perhaps, being too fast and unexpected. Or in the small space, they feared shooting the capo himself. There is now the silence of shocked troops. *And three lives,* Alec's brain screams at him, *depend on it!* He addresses himself to the man who, he guesses, would be the ranking officer in the room. "You have a decision to make, Nicoli. It will be the most important you have ever made, and it must be made now. Immediately. You can carry out this dead man's threat, and kill everyone else here, including yourself. Or you can allow these two young women to leave with me, which will allow you to live and take charge of the family business."

"Whatever's left of it," Gura says with an ironical twist to his mouth.

"That too, I think, would depend on your actions."

"And how do I know that, once you go, your navy won't start bombing and strafing?"

"You don't. I can't guarantee it. I will argue for it, I promise you that. And once you've shown your good faith by releasing us, what incentive does the United States Navy have to risk lives or pump costly missiles into your people and their sheds?"

Nicoli surveys the three soldiers, who look back to him for instructions. He shows only indecision. "I've known you for five minutes. I just watched you kill two people. How can I trust anything you say?"

"You don't have to, Nicoli. Rely on what you know, because it's obvious. Those ships out there—why did they come and who did they come for? Obvious. They came here at my request and for these young women. They're not going to leave until they have us on board. Your chance to survive—and your only chance—is to permit that to happen. Right now! Any other decision—they will commence bombing, and they will invade. And you will not like that, even if you survive the bombing. They will not deal well with you when they arrive."

"I could send you back with the message that Don Salvatore suggested."

"Two things about that," Alec notes, as if providing legal counsel. "Though it's been only five minutes for us, I don't see you as the kind of man who would amputate body parts from women. Just my read. But even if I believed the threat, there are hundreds of men on that destroyer who will be racing toward this island if they don't see the three of us on a boat within minutes. And the bombing will start as soon as they embark. So do we all live, Nicoli, or are you—for absolutely no good reason of your own—about to bring the fires of hell down on us all?"

Gura hesitates only briefly. "Go. And take the women. Though it's been only five minutes, I will trust your word."

Time is most assuredly of the essence. Everyone involved knows it. Gura even helps get them aboard and brings two of the men to assist them. He also points east of the shore. "That way," he says, "to avoid the riptide." On the landing craft, Alec runs the motor and navigates; Sarah and Jesse sit grimly; no one speaks. The wind is up and whipping into their faces; the boat rocks, water spatters in everyone's eyes, but as the destroyer gets nearer, the prospect of safety—a miracle ten minutes before—now seems palpably real.

Alec approaches the bow of the larger ship, slides along its starboard side, and cuts the motor as two seamen rope them in. The entire craft is pulleyed up the hull. Arms on deck lift Sarah and Jesse to waiting medical attendants, while Alec is escorted to the quarterdeck. A young ensign brings him to Ned Townsend, who looks up from a map of Angiapello Island. "Is your return the result of negotiation or heroics?"

"The shoes were useful," Alec says. "Thanks."

"So you killed him? Angiapello?"

"He looked dead to me. As did some guy who looked like the chief lieutenant. The departure was negotiated from there."

"What did you agree to give up?"

"Nothing. No promises. But I did agree to argue leniency. For their lives and their business."

"Their illegal business."

"Yes."

"I can't do that," Townsend says.

"You could give them something."

"Their lives would be plenty."

"You don't really have to bomb their farm," Alec says.

"You mean the hemp fields?"

"Yes."

Townsend laughs. "All right. I suppose they're a very small part of that market. But I've got two missiles that will sink their munitions into the sea. That's on orders from the vice admiral."

"Fair deal."

"You're probably a pretty good lawyer."

"Yeah, well, right now I could use a bed."

THIRTY-EIGHT

Alec is awakened by the glare of the sea beamed like a spotlight through the porthole of his cabin. He struggles out into the passageway. A passing seaman puts him in course for the officers' wardroom, where Ned Townsend is finishing breakfast with Lee Norris and Harvey Grant. "Help yourself," Townsend says, gesturing toward a side-table buffet. "Should still be warm." Wasn't, but Alec eats eggs and toast anyway after downing a glass of OJ.

Townsend says, "We're letting your daughter use our radio-phone. It's contrary to the book, but—after her ordeal—it's the least we could do. And speaking of bending regulations, she went jogging this morning on the deck."

Harvey laughs, familiar with Sarah's habits. Norris says, "And she breezed by here for a roll and jam. With a few words about last night. I'd say, *you're* on a roll. A Western roll into an evil gang lord? Christ, man! Are you now going to be impossible to live with?"

"She regaled you?"

"She told us what happened, Alec."

"Not an objective observer." Alec, going for coffee, says, "Anyone seen Jesse?"

"She's still in her cabin, I think," Townsend says.

"Which is where?"

"Go back to yours and turn right."

"And?" Alec says. "Go how far?"

"A foot or two. She's in the next cabin."

Everyone but Alec seems to find that hilarious.

❖

Sarah's in the control room on the phone with Tino, who had been waiting for her call for two days. "You're *where?*" he says.

"On a Navy destroyer. They're allowing me to use their phone, but only for a minute, and I'm not alone."

"Give me a hint. What the hell are you doing on a Navy destroyer?"

"Escaping from your uncle's island. He's dead, by the way. He kidnapped me, and Alec killed him."

"Oh my God!"

"It's a long story."

"I want to hear it!"

"I know, I know, but now I have to go."

"But you're okay?" Tino says.

"Absolutely."

"I was going out of my mind."

"Yeah" she says. "Figured. That's why I called. I'll be back soon and tell you all about it."

"This is really crazy."

"What? My calling you from a destroyer?"

"Everything about this is crazy."

"You weren't thinking of 'everything.' "

"Yes, everything," he says. "Including the fact that I think I'm my uncle's heir."

"Oh for Christ's sake."

"You and I together may have more dirty money than almost anyone alive."

"Then it's not really ours," she says, "and we should put it to good use."

"Together?"

"We'll see, Tino. We'll decide that when we grow up."

Alec knocks. Hearing no answer, he tries the door. It swings open, and he steps into the room. Jesse sits on the bed. She wears the uniform skirt and blouse of a female naval officer, which were, presumably, the only fresh clothes they had to give her.

"How you feeling?" Alec asks.

"Stupid," she says. "That's how I feel."

"Because of the uniform?"

"No, Alec. Because of my bad judgment."

"Anyone can be conned."

"That's not what I meant."

"Okay," he says carefully, inviting more.

She says, putting her hands flat down at her sides, "At the worst, after being drugged and assaulted by those subhuman creatures—when everything looked absolutely hopeless—Sarah never lost faith. She knew. She knew you would come, she was certain of it. And that you would rescue us."

"You were less sure."

"Less sure?" Jesse laughs. "I only hoped you wouldn't try anything that reckless. That crazy reckless. And then you show up with the goddamn United States Navy in your pocket! I mean, Jesus, Alec! How the fuck did you do that?"

"I thought the interesting accessory was the shoe blade."

"Ha! That was amazing, yes."

"So what do you think now?" he asks.

"About what?" she says.

"The going through hell part?"

"Whether you'd do it?"

"For you, yes," Alec says. "You had a question about that."

"Well, Sarah was there too."

"So your 50 percent share of my going through hell isn't good enough?"

"No, it's good enough," she says. "Thank God you did, for my life, but you didn't have to for my state of mind. I'd already recognized how stupid I'd been."

"I won't ask you when."

"About five minutes after walking out of our apartment."

"*Our* apartment?" he says.

"Yes," she says. "That's how it felt. When I left it."

Alec sits next to her on the bed. "So I don't want this to get any sappier than it's now becoming, but I feel I must say this. The commander of our ship—one Addison J. Townsend—has the power to—"

"Yes," Jesse says, interrupting. "I will."

"Will what?"

"He can do marriages at sea," she says, "and we should ask him for one."

"How's your schedule for this afternoon?" he asks.

"What's wrong with now?"

"Now?" he says as casually as he can make it sound. "Works for me."

THIRTY-NINE

Thirty days come and go. Not a single public utility in the United States files suit against Allis-Benoit or Edison Electric. So that crisis passes, with only a very few people ever having known it had occurred.

Breck Schlumberger, assistant attorney general for the Antitrust Division, files a stipulation of voluntary dismissal, agreeing to put an end to the largest and most notorious civil lawsuit in the history of mankind. Judge Ettinger refuses to sign it. He gets mandamused for a fourth time, and again excoriated by the Court of Appeals, which extinguishes the case with finality. In short order, the rest of the world forgets all about that.

Alec Brno and Jesse Madigan, having been married aboard ship, take up residence once more in Grantland Rice's old apartment on Ninety-Seventh Street. Jesse now makes movies—indie films she writes and directs—which she enjoys doing immensely, with some critical, though not yet any commercial, success. Alec continues to deal, in court and out, with the misadventures of other people. Some of these professional exploits attract public attention, which quickly fades. No one forgets, however, that it was the freakish fortune of the lawyer with the odd name to have executed two crowned heads of the Mafia.

Years after the incident on Angiapello Island, Sarah and Tino, having both graduated from college and law school, establish their own charitable foundation. They live together happily but aren't married. "Why not?" Jesse asks from time to time. Sarah answers with another question, "If it ain't broke, why fix it?" To which Jesse responds, "Not broke, my dear girl, is one thing.

There's another that's infinitely better. Just ask your dad."

"Oh, him," Sarah says. "He's as besotted as you are."

ABOUT THE AUTHOR

Alan Hruska is the author of the novels *It Happened at Two in the Morning*, *Pardon the Ravens*, and *Wrong Man Running*; the writer of several plays produced in New York and London; and the writer and director of the films *Reunion*, *The Warrior Class*, and *The Man on Her Mind*. A New York native and a graduate of Yale University and Yale Law School, he is a former trial lawyer who was involved in some of the most significant litigation of the last half of the twentieth century. *The Inglorious Arts* is his fourth novel. Hruska resides in New York City.